D0448745

THEIRS NOT TO REASON WHY

DAMNATION

JEAN JOHNSON

ACE BOOKS, NEW YORK

THE BERKLEY PUBLISHING GROUP
Published by the Penguin Group
Penguin Group (USA) LLC
375 Hudson Street, New York, New York 10014

USA • Canada • UK • Ireland • Australia • New Zealand • India • South Africa • China

penguin.com

A Penguin Random House Company

DAMNATION

An Ace Book / published by arrangement with the author

Ace Books are published by The Berkley Publishing Group.
ACE and the "A" design are trademarks of Penguin Group (USA) LLC.

For information, address: The Berkley Publishing Group,
a division of Penguin Group (USA) LLC,
375 Hudson Street, New York, New York 10014.

ISBN: 978-0-425-27787-4

PUBLISHING HISTORY
Ace mass-market edition / December 2014

PRINTED IN THE UNITED STATES OF AMERICA

10 9 8 7 6 5 4 3 2 1

Cover art by Gene Mollica.
Interior text design by Laura K. Corless.

AUTHOR'S NOTE

The original story for part four of the series Theirs Not to Reason Why ended up being too large and too cohesively written to edit down or contain in just one book yet still be manageable. (My fault totally!) The first portion has been made available in the novel *Hardship*. That story now resumes in *Damnation*.

Each book can be read without too much difficulty on its own, as the break chosen between the two was a natural pause between two major story arcs. However, this is a five-part (five-book, no longer four-book) story, so it may be best to read all of them in order. With that in mind, I have elected to include a recap of what happened in the previous novel (book four, *Hardship*), so that readers of this book can be brought back up to speed quickly and smoothly, whether it's been a few months since you read the last one or if you're picking this book up for the first time and are wondering what's going on.

. . . Naturally, this section will contain spoilers for the previous book. Feel free to skip straight to the start of the current story, if you'd prefer.

On June 3, 2498 Terran Standard, Ship's Captain Ia of the Terran United Planets Space Force, Branch Special Forces, was dropped off by Feyori companions on the jointly held Terran-V'Dan colonyworld of Dabin, home planet of her first officer, Commander Meyun Harper. Her crew had been transported to the colonyworld days earlier, while Ia oversaw the destruction of her previous ship, the TUPSF *Hellfire*, to keep it out of enemy hands. Her intent upon arriving on Dabin was to advise not only Captain Roghetti of the TUPSF Army, who had been sharing an encampment with her displaced crew, but the head of his Army Division, Brigadier General José Mattox, on how to push their enemy, the amphibious Salik, off the blockaded and embattled planet.

However, the brigadier general and his staff at Army HQ turned out to be under the psychic influence of a Feyori named Ginger, who, in the guise of a heavyworld-adapted dog, had been adopted as a sort of mascot by the Headquarters staff. The energy-being constantly influenced Mattox and his staff to ignore Ia's precognitive-based battle plans, while her cofaction partner, another local Feyori named Teshwun, hid all the changes on the nearest stretches of the timeplains from Ia's precognitive view, making everything look as if it were proceeding according to plan, up until the actual moment when observed incidents did not match at all with what was being seen on the timeplains.

This disparity led to Roghetti's encampment being ambushed and both Companies being routed, forced to flee under heavy fire by Salik forces. Ia, injured and frustrated by her inability to predict the immediate future, divided the Company, placing most of it under Commander Harper's command. She then took herself off to disrupt the enemy's attacks, reasoning that the Feyori would focus on getting the Salik to follow and attempt to destroy her as the bigger threat to their plans, rather than her Company.

Joined by Private Mara Sunrise, a covert-ops soldier demoted and disgraced for a politically awkward incident before becoming a member of Ia's crew, Ia eventually made her way to Army HQ. Shortly after arriving, she discerned and revealed Ginger to be an actual Meddler and not a mere dog. Ia then directed Mattox and his officers to revise all their current battle plans. Unfortunately, Mattox was still under the Meddler's influence and resisted.

Taking a break from the frustrations of Army HQ, Ia experienced an epiphany of how to counteract the Feyori influence on the timeplains. Once their control was flung off, she zeroed in on their location and demanded to face her ultimate Feyori enemy, Miklinn, in a leadership challenge. When he finally appeared, the Meddler refused at first to duel her; only when he started losing followers did he agree. Ia boldly faced him as a matter-based Human, and abraded away the years of his life via her psychic abilities, killing him.

She then took vengeance on Teshwun as well for daring to Meddle in her area of control, Time itself, as well as for the loss of several of her crew members, deaths caused by his temporal interference. The rest of the Feyori were warned that there was no more neutral with her, only faction and immediate cooperation . . . and that any further attempts to counterfaction her would end in that Feyori's death, as she now had the ability to reach through Time itself to grab and destroy any Meddler who dared to interfere. Chaining Ginger to the timestreams to force the Feyori into fixing and bridging all the problems her interference had created on Dabin, Ia returned to Army HQ.

Mattox continued to thwart and ignore Ia's efforts at correcting the battle plans, to the point where he gave her, an officer in an entirely different Branch, a direct order to depart Army HQ. Seizing on this illegal move, Ia filed a formal charge against the brigadier general, accusing him of being unfit for combat duty despite knowing this would cause her own actions to undergo strict scrutiny as the accusing officer. After heavy interrogation into her motives and actions by the Space Force Command Staff, Admiral-General Christine Myang removed Mattox from command of the Army Division on Dabin, promoted Ia to the rank of four-star General and peer of the Command Staff, and placed her in charge of the mess on that colonyworld.

Stunned but willing to run with it, Ia implemented several battle plans to make up for the damage done by Ginger and Teshwun, including the widespread use of Dabinian passion-moss spores not only on Dabin, but on other colonyworlds as well, as the inhaled moss spores affected Salik physiology much in the same way that onions would affect Terran dogs and cats. At the end of the book, the V'Dan Fleet arrived in force to break the Salik blockade isolating Dabin from the rest of the Alliance. A local reporter, Denora de Marco, requested a brief moment to interview General Ia. Afterward, Ia and her crew boarded the lead V'Dan vessel to be transported by their allies to their newly commissioned ship, the TUPSF *Damnation*.

On July 27, 2498 T.S., while still aboard that same ship, Ia conferred via comm link with the Emperor of V'Dan regarding past and future plans, then agreed to give one of the V'Dan crew members precognitive advice on his son's future life.

I selected *Hardship* to end at this point as it brought the Dabin half of the story arc to a natural, reasonable conclusion. *Damnation* begins a few weeks later, after Ia's new ship has been crewed. I wanted to keep the original name for the novel attached to the second half, as that is technically when Ia and her crew take control of the TUPSF *Damnation* and begin the second half of the story. *Hardship*'s title was therefore selected as a nod to the difficulties Ia and company experienced while stuck planetside between ships.

On a side note, there was a brief moment of merriment when my editor asked me during our phone conversation to clarify whether it was one word, as in "difficulties," or two words, literally "*Hard Ship*." Since there was no actual, physical vessel involved during this first half of the divided book, I reassured her that no, I meant the one-word version, meaning "difficulties."

. . . I was concerned that readers might not want to pay for two books, but I really could not find any way to cut out any scenes beyond the few I already had removed in the initial editing process. I was also concerned that they wouldn't want to pay the high cost of an extra-thick, awkward-to-hold, and potentially-falls-apart-under-its-own-weight single-novel version. But within minutes of posting the news of the split to my Facebook page (Fans of Author Jean Johnson; links can be found at my website, JeanJohnson.net), I received several joyful responses from readers who told me they would be more than happy to buy both books rather than just one big unwieldy volume.

Of course, I know there will still be some grumbling from others, despite this immediate and gratifying reaction. My only defense is that my publisher Ace, my editor Cindy, and I as the author all want to bring you the best story I could pull together without butchering it to pieces on the editing table. Instead of a manuscript massacre, it's been rendered into two parts neatly cut in half. So, presto chango, here's my cape and magician's box and saw. Now, let's put the final pieces of this story together.

For my usual acknowledgments, I would like to thank yet again Cindy and the staff over at Ace for being so kind about my health-problem-related delays, for being willing to split rather than reduce this story, and for supporting me throughout my military science fiction debut after having first launched me through Berkley into a successful paranormal romance career. My thanks to Buzzy, NotSoSaintly, Stormi, and Briemh for their help in pre-editing; to Mai, Syraethial, and Squiglemouse for their last-minute advice on a very important if seemingly very minor detail; and to everyone in between. My biggest thanks go to the managing editor and the staff at The Berkley Publishing Group and Ace for turning around the edits on this last story so that I could go off to the UK and Worldcon without dropping my responsibilities due to the timing of everything. They are awesome, hands down. You readers never see any of this stuff because you always get the final, polished product, but they're there and they're working their hardest for your entertainment, the same as I am.

And, of course, as always, this entire series is dedicated to those who have been, are, and shall be willing to place their lives on the line to protect those around them, most especially every person who has served in a military. Thank you.

Thank you.

Ladies and gentlemen, in conclusion of the tale of Theirs Not to Reason Why, Ia's long, hard fight to save her galaxy from the destruction three hundred years into the future, well past the point where most everyone in this story will be long dead and gone . . . I give you *Damnation*.

Enjoy,
Jean

CHAPTER 1

What did it feel like to step for the first time onto the Damnation, *back in August of '98? That's an unfair question—unfair to you, I mean. I "first stepped" onto the* Damnation *when I was fifteen. I knew every pipeline, every cabin, every cannon, and every corridor on her before I was old enough to legally drive. And I knew the Hellfire just as well, and just as early on, long before my military career began. I have known every single ship I ever boarded long before I touched foot to deckplate, just as I have known nearly every single person I have ever worked with in advance of that first day, Harper excepted.*

But I will admit I did enjoy that new-ship smell. You don't get that many smells in the timestreams, oddly enough, unless it's temporally important somehow. It almost never is, though. As for the Damnation *itself . . . it was longer, better laid out, and equipped with certain amenities that some would call luxuries but which have kept my crew sane. It's hard to relax when you fly from one battle to the next with rarely a pause for anything else.*

> *Beyond that . . . it's just like being back on board the*
> Hellfire. *This ship is our home. In a way, it always has*
> *been. In a way, it always will be.*
>
> ~Ia

AUGUST 14, 2498 TERRAN STANDARD
TUPSF *LEO MAJOR*
SCADIA, AQAT-15 SYSTEM

The *Leo Major* did not smell like the *Damnation*. Where Ia's
ship still smelled of fresh paint, carpeting, newly installed
aquaponics, and various kinds of plexi, this larger but heavily
battered starship smelled of internal fires, sweat, and dried
blood. It also bore the odd odor of hard vacuum, not quite metallic and not quite like dust, the smell of cold frost mingled
with the scents of chilled solder and other sealants.

From the swirled bits of debris on the deckplates, they
may have gotten the hangar bay functionally airtight, but it
was clear there had been far more important repairs on their
mind than merely sweeping up. The *Leo Major* wasn't ready
even for insystem maneuvers, or those bits of metal and plexi
would have been vacuumed up by now for fear of them being
turned into lethal projectiles during a sudden vector change.
The civilian spacedock orbiting the third planet from the
local sun wasn't quite prepared to service a ship of the *Leo*'s
size, but they were doing their best. With the bay sealed and
capable of accepting larger deliveries, the work could go a lot
faster now.

Saluting the bandaged ensign who had granted her permission to board, Ia waved off the young man's offer to guide
her with a murmured, "No need to bother, Ensign; I already
know the way. Please fetch a three-ton hoversled for Private
Runde and prepare to board live cargo for the life-support
bays."

"Uhh . . . aye aye, sir," the ensign stammered, eyeing Ia as
she headed into the damaged ship.

She did know the way, though she had never stepped foot
aboard a battlecruiser of the Talon Class before. Three levels
up to Deck 25, five cross-corridors aft to Lima, and one side

trip toward the port brought her to the boardroom for the Marines Company stationed aboard. Here, the visible damage to the ship was considerably less, though the damage to the brown-clad men and women inside was quite evident.

One of the women, sporting a blue regen pack strapped over one ear, caught the movement of Ia's approach out of the corner of her eye. She turned to see who had entered, caught sight of Ia's Dress Blacks with its two-tone stripes of green and gray, the four stars pinned to her collar points and shoulder boards, and stiffened. "—General on Deck!"

"At Ease, meioas," Ia quickly ordered, since there was more than one soldier with an injured arm in the room. "I'm not here for your salutes. You earned my respect when you donned the Brown of the Marines, and earned it again with how well you fought today."

Some of them relaxed at her praise. Others stood a little taller with the pride her words invoked. Most of them parted to either side a little, opening up an aisle between her and their current commander. Standing in front of the officer's desk, on the dais in front of the sloped tiers of seats, was a man she had not seen in over eight years. He stared at her, squinted . . . and then sagged back against the table, resting his hips against the edge.

"Well, double-dip me," Brad Arstoll muttered slowly, staring at Ia as she closed the distance between them. "It *is* you! I'd heard some wild-asteroid tales about someone with your name pulling all sorts of *shova* out there, but . . . it really *is* you, isn't it? And a *shakking* general—look at you!"

Ia gave him a half smile and spread her hands slightly. "In the four-star flesh. I'm here on the *Leo* for two reasons. Three, if you count the shakedown flight out here to help you and the Scadian Army fight off the Salik invaders earlier today."

"Well, we appreciated that," he agreed.

"No thanks are needed. First off," she stated, digging a hand into her Dress Black jacket, pulling out a small black box. "I am authorized by the DoI to confirm your field promotion, *Captain* Brad Arstoll. Effective immediately, you are now officially in charge of D Company, 3rd Legion, and not just the Acting Captain for D Company, 3rd Legion, 3rd Battalion, 4th Brigade, 4th Division, 2nd Cordon Marine Corps.

This box holds a data file with the pertinent DoI paperwork . . . plus your silver tracks, of course. You've earned them."

"Thank you, sir," Arstoll murmured, accepting the package. "I wish I hadn't."

"I know," Ia murmured back, knowing he meant he wished he hadn't earned it at the expense of the loss of his CO. "Captain Ling-Bradley was a good leader. But so are you." She tapped the box now in his hand. "There's a second datachip in here with a few precognitive directives you might find useful. Beyond that, I know the Corps trained you well. You have my confidence, and that of the Command Staff."

"Huh," he grunted, a humorless laugh. "Of *course* they'd be confident. The Prophet of a Thousand Years told them so. If this is just a favor to an old Basic Squadmate . . ."

"You've *earned* it, so step up to the job and suffer, soldier," Ia corrected him firmly, pushing the box against his chest. He winced a little; his ribs were taped, waiting for the bone-set serum to finish healing the fractures earned in combat. She didn't push hard, though, and removed her hand once he got the point. "Second . . . I lost five good men and women on Dabin. Lives I shouldn't have had to lose," Ia admitted, jaw tightening for a moment. "I may be a massive precog, but I can't control everything. Because of it, I need replacements. I have two already in transit to meet up with my ship in the Tilfa System, but I'm here for the other three.

"If you don't mind, I'd like to take one of your Marines," she added, glancing over her shoulder at the men and women listening with various levels of boredom as the two of them had caught up with old news. Her words piqued interest even in the most bored of the soldiers. "The last two I need are serving in the Scadian Army in the Orbital Fleet. I convinced the Admiral-General to help with some pre-maneuverings on getting them transferred, so I have a writ from the Scadian military leadership allowing me to recruit whoever I like. I'll still have to do a little diplomatic dancing once I get down to the surface, but it'll be worth it."

"*Shakk* . . . I wonder what strings you had to pull to get *that* done," Arstoll muttered, eyeing her. "These colonists are proud as hell about serving their planet. They wouldn't even have accepted *our* help if they'd had enough ships to cover all vectors. They don't lack the fighting skill or the tactical smarts, and they don't lack any bravery; they just lack the equipment to get the job done."

"I know. That's why I need two of them. They're the best shot I have at filling the gaping holes the Salik blew in the best crew of the Space Force. As for the Marine . . . I'll need your Private Second Class Julia Garcia."

"Garcia?" Arstoll exclaimed, eyes wide with disbelief. Other voices joined him in their confusion.

"Wrong-Way Garcia?"

"That piece of *skut*?"

"Sir, if you think *Garcia* is going to . . . er . . ." The speaker, the woman with the missing ear, trailed off as Ia turned to face Arstoll's soldiers. Her hard stare silenced all of them.

"Private Garcia," Ia enunciated carefully, with just enough volume to fill the boardroom as she shifted her gaze from face to face, "is a far better soldier, and a far better Marine, than all of you combined. In my hands, within one year, she will be the hero of a hundred fights and the savior of more than a million lives . . . and that is *not* hyperbole, meioas. I have foreseen it—speaking of which," she added, lightening her tone as she shifted her gaze to one of the taller, redheaded men. "Private McCraery, remember to hit the deck flat out instead of just duck on the sixteenth of September, at about two o'clock local. You'll know when. I'd rather you didn't get your head blown off because you overestimated the height of the incoming attack. Captain Arstoll will still need you afterward, so keep yourself alive."

"Uh . . . yes, sir," he agreed hesitantly.

"Private Sangwan, since you were trying to be so *generous* with praise for Private Garcia," Ia added, turning back to the woman with the regenerating ear, "you can go help her pack her things. We leave in thirty-three minutes from Docking Bay B. Dismissed. Corporal Vance, you were about to ask your CO for a priority list of mechsuit repairs, on behalf of the *Leo Major*'s manufactory bays. You will need A through C Squad functional in the 1st Platoon, followed by B through E in the 2nd. The rest in those two Platoons have minor repairs they can manage on their own. The 3rd and the 4th

Platoons will just have to wait their turn on the things they cannot fix themselves—Private Sangwan, you have been *dismissed*."

"Beg pardon, sir?" she asked, glancing between Ia and Arstoll, then at Ia's green-and-gray stripes . . . which were on the sleeves and pant legs of an otherwise all-black uniform. Though her last name was the same as one of Ia's yeoman pilots, they weren't related. If they had been, she would have heard of Ia by now. "Aren't you like Special Forces, or Army, or something?"

Ia pointed at the stars on her shoulder board, speaking slowly and clearly. "I am Command Staff, soldier. *Everybody* in the Space Force is under my chain of command, save only for my peers on the Staff, the Admiral-General, Secondaire, and Premiere of the Council. You have your orders. Dismissed."

"Sir, yes, sir," she muttered, face flushed with embarrassment. Turning crisply, Sangwan headed for the doors out of the Company boardroom.

"Captain Arstoll, when you have a few minutes later on today, please remind your troops how the Space Force chain of command works," Ia stated dryly, watching the other woman retreat.

"Sir, yes, sir," he agreed, giving the departing, flinching Sangwan a hard look. "I'll have her checked for a lingering concussion, too. I *thought* my Marines could count four stars on their own."

A few of the others carefully looked anywhere but at their CO and the visiting, white-haired brass in front of him.

Nodding, Ia closed her eyes for a moment, focusing, then opened them. "Sergeant Yangley, the Navy order forms for what you need to requisition materials for the life-support bays are now appearing on your workstation screens back in the clerk's office. I've already filled in the authorization codes for everything but the fish stock. Scadia doesn't have enough of the right kind of fish just yet for your shipboard aquaculture needs.

"Being aware of that, I have brought over a tank of tilapia from the *Damnation*, along with enough feed to last them until you get the cycle balanced in the second bay and it becomes self-sufficient. Private Runde will already be loading them onto the hoversled fetched for her from the ensign on duty. Make sure to sign for them. Get to it."

"General, yes, sir," the sergeant replied crisply, turning to leave on his appointed task.

"Good meioa. The rest of you already know what you need to do. Since I am aware of those needs, and that when you put your minds to it, you are a competent crew, you don't have to ask your Captain anything right now; you have *my* permission for the tasks at hand. Go do them," Ia directed the men and women before her. "That means *dismissed*."

They scattered. When the last of them had left the room, Ia moved over to lean back against the table next to her old Basic Training Squadmate. It felt good to slouch a little, good to rest for a moment.

"Rank hath its privileges," she murmured, glancing at him. "I hope you don't mind my sending them off like that, but they honestly can handle everything, and this is literally the only time off I'll have from my duties for months to come, waiting for Garcia to pack. It's not much of a Leave, but I'll take whatever I can get. So . . . How are you doing, Brad? I mean, *really* doing?"

Brad shook his head. "Between you, me, and the bulkheads?" he asked in a bare murmur, not nearly as sure as she was that there weren't any listeners still nearby. "Like fresh, steaming shit. I had the Captain on the commscreen when the hull breach hit our docking bay. I *saw* him get sucked outside. He was not in a pressure-suit. This is *not* how I wanted my next command."

Ia clasped his shoulder, giving him a brief moment of comfort. "I know. I wish I could've helped prevent it . . . and I know you'll hate me for saying this, but . . . you're going to be the right person in the right place at the right time because of this. Not just today, but multiple times in the next few years. The universe needs Captain Brad Arstoll to take full command of D Company. Do good things with it. Save lots of lives. Make as good a career for yourself and the meioas under you as you can."

"How do you live with yourself?" Arstoll asked her, frowning at his former Squadmate. "Seeing what you do. Knowing what you do. *Doing* what you do, and *not* doing. If even half the rumors running around the Space Force in the last few weeks are true . . . how is it that you've stayed *sane*?"

"I have too much work to do to go mad and not enough time to dwell on my mistakes. Or to keep track of old comrades, other than snatches here and there. You ever heard what happened to Sung, and Crosp, and the others from Basic?" Ia asked. "Spyder's with me, and Sergeant Tae's the uncle of my first officer, of all things, but I've been too busy with other concerns to check on the rest."

"Uhh . . . Crosp got called back home to take up the reins of the family business. That was before the war started," Brad dredged up out of his memory. "Sung . . . hell if I know. The one thing I knew, she was being shipped off from Basic to stand guard at some embassy among the Gatsugi. She's probably still doing that. Sergeant Linley always praised her hand-to-hand and her observational skills, said she'd be great for guard work. Oh, and ZeeZee made it to Sergeant First Class last year. Wait, you said Spyder's with you?"

Ia nodded. "Lieutenant Second Class—Field Honor, like you and me—and he's in charge of my 2nd Platoon, plus serves as the tactical coordinator for all mass troop movements. That got put to the test on Dabin just recently, which is why I need replacements. He does say 'hi,' by the way. Sorry, I almost forgot to mention that. I've had a lot on my mind lately."

"I can only imagine what you have to keep track of. Can you, ah . . . you know, see them right now?" Brad asked her. "I mean, see the others in our old Squad since you say you've got a few minutes?"

Ia lifted her brows at the suggestion, then shrugged. "I suppose I can check."

Closing her eyes, she flipped herself onto the timeplains and searched. It didn't take long to find the old threads from her Basic days, nor to follow them down through to the current day. Sobered, she opened her eyes again.

"I'm sorry to report that Sung died during the initial invasion of the Gatsugi homeworld. She was taken out while defending the Terran Embassy from a clutch of Salik robots," Ia stated quietly. "She took more than a few with her, but they still took her out."

"Damn," Arstoll whispered, hanging his head. "I liked her."

Another brief glimpse—since she had the time to spare for it—gave Ia another view on their old Squadmates. "I can see ZeeZee's still a Sergeant First Class. He'll live for at least three more years, but I cannot guarantee beyond that point. The second war front will evoke too many shifting possibilities for his sector of space. Crosp . . . has two kids, twins, and looks like he acquired a thriving munitions business with military contracts, so he's still supporting the war effort in his own way.

"The rest are . . . still enlisted in the Corps in various duty posts around the war front, except for Kumanei. She opted for pilot training in the Navy, and is flying drop ships as a Chief Yeoman out of . . . Battle Platform *Anna Yesarova*," Ia concluded, double-checking the name. "I can't tell you where, though; that's Classified above your pay grade."

"What's this second war front you mentioned?" Arstoll asked, distracting himself from the grim news of Sung's death.

"The Greys are coming back. Don't share it with your troops just yet," Ia added, ignoring his sharp, worried look. "They don't need to fret themselves to death over it."

"*Shakk* . . . Ia, *can* anything be done against them?" he asked. "I don't think our tech's progressed nearly enough to even sneeze on them, but . . . well, we beat them back with psis last time, so we do have enough of 'em this time, right?"

She shook her head. "They're a dying race, and they're growing more and more desperate. It's even odds they'll get their hands on the Salik anti-psi machinery, and if they do, it'll be a very hard-fought war. But we *will* stop them. I have foreseen it," she murmured, staring across the boardroom without actually seeing its rows of padded seats.

He gave her a wary look. Ia patted him lightly on the shoulder.

"Relax, and don't worry about it. It's all well above your pay grade, either way. Concentrate on your *own* troops," she advised him, nodding at the half-wrecked boardroom around them. "This corner of the galaxy is just as important as any other out there. Tell me what you think of these Scadians. I may be able to *see* them in the waters of time, and I know what I'll need to do with them, but that doesn't mean I've ever dealt with them before. Knowing and doing are two different things. We learned that in Basic."

"We did. As for the Scadians . . . They're . . . insane. In the most *benign* ways imaginable," Arstoll explained, or at least tried, gesturing vaguely as he spoke. "The most honorable people I have ever met. And the most stubborn in many ways. Peculiar, too. Friendly, polite, and cheerful, but odd beyond measure. Some of the *best* close-quarters fighting I have ever seen. Do not let them goad you into a swordfight. I thought *we* learned swordfighting back in Basic, but these meioas—both genders—will make minced garlic out of you."

"Minced garlic?" Ia asked, skeptical at his word choice.

"Minced garlic, minced onions, minced whatever. They'll slice you to shreds that thoroughly and leave you crying while they do so. The Marines have nothing on 'em with a blade in their hands," he added, tucking his arms across his chest once more. "In fact, they could probably give the Afaso a run for their money, too. But only with a blade, or some other melee weapon. They don't do nearly as much of the weaponless stuff."

"I'll take that under advisement, but it's a fifty-fifty chance I'll be challenged anyway," Ia admitted. At his sharp look, she explained. "I told you, have to go down to the capital city of Regnum to appropriate two of their soldiers. To do so, I have to get permission from the colonial leader, their 'Emperor' . . . who just might demand that *I* show myself 'worthy of being their warleader,' to put it in Scadian terms."

"Which means a swordfight," Arstoll muttered, not without sympathy. "You're *shakked*. I remember your being good with a blade back in Basic, thanks to all that fancy Afaso training you'd had, but these meioas are beyond good, like a General is beyond a mere Captain . . . begging pardon, sir."

"Don't worry about me, Arstoll. Worry about continuing to help Commander Eosod get the *Leo Major* back into fighting form. Put all of C and D under the engineering department, so they have the extra hands they'll need," she told him, meaning the latter two of his four Platoon groups. "You won't need them in fighting trim for the next week, when A and B will do. Hold the fort around here until late November. By that point, the Salik will have a lot more to worry about than a backwater colonyworld of historical re-creationists.

"If the locals give you or the commander trouble, remind them that every single person on this ship has given their word of honor—that phrasing exactly—to defend the lives of every single person on or around Scadia. Tell them that each one of you will die before you break your vows. That'll impress them. Just make sure to follow through on it," Ia warned him. "You're representing the entire honor of the Space Force in this command, between you and Captain Eosod. Your ability to hold true to your word of honor will have repercussions on Terran-Scadian military relations for the next four hundred years, and that's not hyperbole. That's another reason why I wanted to keep you here. I know you can do it."

"Then I'll try to remember all that," he promised. They sat in silence for a few moments, then Arstoll cursed under his breath. "Dammit . . . you can't give me any winning lottery numbers, can you? Fatality Forty-Nine gets in the way, doesn't it?"

Ia gave him a wry smile. "Yes, it does. I would if I could, but I can't. Even if the regs weren't in the way, your winning a lot of money at this point in your life would change that life for the worse." At her words, he only chuckled. She eyed him warily. "Why does *that* thought amuse you?"

Leaning back on his palms, her former training mate shrugged. "I was just thinking for a moment you must have the most wonderful powers in the universe, to be able to see anything, *know* anything . . . but it's not really all that wonderful because you can't *do* anything you want, can you?" At the shake of her head, he tipped his own. "That thought amuses me. I don't know why."

Ia thought about it and decided she wasn't offended by his laugh. "Maybe because it makes me Human?"

"Maybe," he agreed. "I don't think I'd laugh at a God, but then I've never met one. Stay Human, Ia. Remember that you're fallible. That your power comes with a price, and—"

"—And a responsibility. Yes, I know," she admitted, completing the sentence with him. "I won't ever be able to forget my failures. The best I can do is strive to make sure they don't happen again."

Again, they let a companionable silence fall between them. Or rather, quiet. Sounds of repairs could be heard reverberating through the decking from somewhere in the distance. It reminded Ia of when she had first claimed command of the *Hellfire*. Finally, she drew in a deep breath and straightened, though she didn't yet stand.

"So. While you have a member of the Command Staff a captive listener, so to speak—since I have another fourteen minutes before I'm due to meet Garcia in the docking bay—is there anything you'd like to discuss, or request?"

Folding his arms, he gave it some thought, then spoke decisively. "Space mines. Insystem, not orbital. If you cannot get us another ship, get us some repositionable mines. I'd also take a couple squadrons of fighter craft if I could, make 'em a gift to the Emperor. The Scadian Army lost too many in the last few fights."

Ia thought about his requests for a moment—checking them in the timestreams—then nodded. "You'll have the fighters in three days, but while I can get you the mines, it'll take a little longer. I already foresaw the need for the fighters, so they're on their way. Older craft, which would've been decommissioned and recycled for the private sector, but they're still good enough in a fight. The Scadians will make good use of 'em. Didn't think about the mines, though. It'll work, but it'll take at least seven, eight days."

"It'll do. Anything I can do for you?" Arstoll asked her.

Reaching behind him, she tapped the box containing his new rank insignia and the datachip she had promised, which he had set down on the tabletop at some point. "Pay attention to my suggestions. Live as long and happily as you care to. Stay Human yourself, admit when you're wrong, and keep going. Be honest when talking to others about me; let 'em know what you thought of me in Basic, however flattering and unflattering those thoughts may be, as well as what you think of me now. I need to be a legend in order to lead everyone on the right paths to win all these wars, but I need to be a *Human* legend, with failings as well as successes, foes as well as friends. Otherwise, people won't always believe *in* me, even if they might believe me. Anything else?"

". . . Got any medals for my people?" he asked her next. "Or the crew of this ship?"

Ia shook her head. "Those have to be reviewed by the right departments, based on all your post-battle reports. I can't hand them out arbitrarily. Not without risking my own hide. But there *will* be medals awarded. You really did fight hard and well here," she promised him. "I'll be putting down everything in my post-battle report."

"How much damage did your own ship take?" Arstoll asked, curious.

She grinned. "We scratched the hull in a few places, enough to need swapping out the ceristeel panels so the repair teams can buff them smooth, plus three FTL panels and a shield array. But it's nothing they can't fix by the time I'm back on board. Of course, it's a brand-new ship," she added in explanation. "Commander Harper—he's my first officer, my logistics officer, and my chief engineer all in one, as well as Sergeant Tae's nephew—he was swearing up a storm at me for having to organize fifteen different replacement parts for the hull. You should hear him when I've *really* dinged our hide. If I took any of his insults and threats seriously, he'd be court-martialed three ways from Sunday on a monthly basis, if not weekly."

Arstoll smiled at that, then frowned. "He's covering all three of those jobs?" he asked her. "I didn't see much of it, but isn't that odd-looking ship of yours big enough to have all the officers you need?"

"It's a new class, sized to crew at least 500, but I'm running it with less than 160 at the moment—161 once I get all my replacements. I keep forgetting to count myself," she confessed. "Everyone runs at least three, four positions on board. Even the chaplain and me—the chaplain, the doctor, even our Company clerks are all combat-ready, *and* combat-proved, from tactical training to hand-to-hand combat skills. There's a reason why my crew is now the best of the best."

"And you want *Garcia*?" he muttered dubiously, thinking about it. "Ia . . . she's no good here. She's easily confused. She lags behind in a lot of things . . . I don't know how she made it through Basic, to be honest. Are you sure you want *her* on your ship?"

"The thing most people don't realize, Brad, is that I don't dare pull anyone away from any other position in the known galaxy who is *needed* in that position," Ia told him. "I can only take the throwaways, those whose lives *or* deaths wouldn't make a damned bit of difference spent anywhere else. But on *my* ship, as one of all the men and women I've selected? Those lives spent *there* will finally count for something. Garcia passed Basic in the Marine Corps because she was in the right environment, with the right people around her, supporting and encouraging her. She's failing here because she doesn't fit in here. It's not right for her. She will fit in again on my ship, and do great things under my care."

"Then I'll be glad you're caring for her," Arstoll said. He offered her his hand. When she lifted hers, he clasped it wrist to wrist, meeting her gaze steadily. "Make sure you take care of her. You *promise* me that, one officer to another, as well as one Squadmate to another. I've lost too many lives today as it is."

"I promise I'll take care of Garcia, Brad, to the best of my ability, and to the best of hers once I get her to believe in herself again. I've lost too many as well," Ia agreed. Releasing his forearm, she clapped him on the back, then straightened, pushing away from the table. "Time for me to head to the docking bay. We still have to make planetfall, get the other two on board, and get back to the ship by the time Harper finishes our repairs."

"And then what?" Arstoll asked her, following her toward the doors. "Or is that Classified?"

"Most of it is, and well beyond your pay grade . . . but once I have these three on board, we race for the Gatsugi homeworld. The various heads of state will be holding a meeting, where I'll be begging for certain cross-government military powers. I'm still not entirely sure why the Admiral-General made me a four-star," she confessed, "but she did, and it's made my job unbelievably easier, so I'm going to run with it as far and fast as I can."

"Hauling bus all the way?" Arstoll offered. "Like you did at the end of Hell Week?"

"Farther and faster, if I can," Ia quipped back. "Tae says they've now made it an end-of-Hell-Week challenge for teams of recruits to pull a ground bus a hundred meters. And yes, they have to remember to release the parking brake, first." She flashed him a brief, wry smile, then offered her hand. "Time to go. Good luck, Arstoll."

"Good luck, Ia. *Eyah?*" he asked her as he clasped it one last time, using the sign and countersign of the Marines and their V'Dan counterparts.

"Hoo-rah," she agreed.

AUGUST 20, 2498 T.S.
SIC TRANSIT

August Ia finished the last of her battle-guiding tasks and pulled out of the timestreams. What she wanted was a hot bath and a long nap. What she had to do was leave the comfort of her easy chair—salvaged from her old quarters on the *Hellfire* and installed in the nearly identical version on the *Damnation*—and head for the practice salles. Her mind might be tired, but her body was full of energy. A nap was therefore out of the question, at least until she exhausted herself physically.

Once again, they were working and living in twice Standard gravity, and that meant working out every day to ensure everyone on board remained combat-ready. That required daily exercise. More than that, it required daily exercise in her old weight suit. At some point down the road, she *would* be back on Sanctuary, fighting on its surface for the survival of the key element that would make everything she had planned actually work:

A home, a sense of culture and family for the Savior, who would otherwise have none, and who would slowly lose her humanity without one.

Ia's new quarters—her own version of home, or at least a place to rest—were still located amidships, just behind the new, larger bridge, and were still comparatively small. Still located on Deck 6, the journey to the exercise cabins required her to find the nearest lift to travel down to Deck 12, below the cylindrical core of the new, improved Godstrike cannon, Mark II. Of course, she hadn't fired it yet, but that was for a very good reason. The old one had required seven or eight ships in alignment, with its caloric rating of 90.3 percent. The new one reached 94.5 percent, and being palpably larger, would require considerably more care in firing it.

The needle-shaped ship hadn't really grown much in girth compared to the old version, maybe a dozen meters in extra armor plating and a slightly larger focal core. Instead, it had grown mostly in length by a couple hundred meters. Despite that, the ship still held twenty-four functional decks spanning five section seals. That extra distance deepened the wavelength, allowing not one but two "wolf" infrared resonances to be buried in the beam it cast. Some of the extra space right outside the core had been filled with yet more Sterling engines to capture and reuse the relatively little heat that would spill free from the main cannon and that 5.5 percent loss rate. The rest had been filled with a few useful facilities for the crew and extra water tanks.

Still, since the rest of the *Damnation* had been built to Ia's specifications from scratch, its cabins hadn't suffered the forced-conversion requirements the *Hellfire* had undergone. The Company boardroom had been relocated amidships instead of being consigned to the far end of the bow segment just to make room for a proper Wake Zone next to a decent-sized galley. Bow and stern now contained more in the way of manufactory and storage bays as well as the shuttle bays. The new, improved Wake Zone included two different lounge areas; between them rested a dedicated galley space fancy enough to be called a dining hall, almost a restaurant.

Most of the exercise areas were located either in the fore or aft sections. One of the weight rooms had a sauna, a wood-paneled steam room—an extravagance, admittedly, but almost as good as Leave away from the ship. The other had a trio of soaking tubs. The one with the locker room where her weight suit was stored, tucked into its own storage cupboard next to the one with her exercise gear, had the sauna. It was a good place to sit and think for a few minutes, letting her body relax in the sultry heat while her mind raced.

The ventilation system was doing its best to keep up with its use, but the air was still humid and ripe with sweat when she entered the locker room. Most of the latter was coming from the aft weight room. The *hiss* and *whoosh* of hydraulic fluids met her ears as she strapped on the tile-weighted web-work she had gained all the way back in Basic Training, when she had first met people like Arstoll, Mendez, Sung, and Spyder. Some of her old training mates were still alive. Some were not. Some would still die in this war, and some would live well beyond it.

Some would only live on in legend.

Philadelphia Benjamin, Cald Feldman . . . Tugging on her weighted gloves, Ia grimly contemplated how she could use their names to inspire future generations of soldiers and civilians alike. *Benjamin's family history could inspire the working classes. Feldman* . . . *well, I suppose he could inspire military and civilian prisoners trying to turn their lives around like he did his. Franke's death will be harder to make heroic* . . . *being eaten alive is a bad way to go, hard to put a positive spin on that* . . . *But Nabouleh, she was one hell of a pilot. Not a fancy flier like Shikoku Yama, but courageous under fire.*

Franke and Svarson, I'll make them both known for heroism in how they lived, not in how they died, Ia decided. *I'll have to compose some messages for the Afaso to distribute across the Alliance, so they can start spreading rumors and tales of the Fallen of the Damned. And, of course, the living among the Damned. I wonder if Clairmont and York have started composing together in earnest, yet. They'll make a helluva good entertainment team once they do.*

Tired as she was, she didn't want to take a peek into the timestreams to find out, yet. Not when she could just ask them outright after she was done exercising. They were all in transit. She had a little bit of free time.

"General, sir."

Ia looked up at the short, stocky, muscular figure of Alexus Kardos. His deeply tanned skin looked like it might have been due to some aboriginal blood, something either from Australian Province or Oceania, maybe southeast Asia, but his large brown curls and his aquiline nose looked more European. He looked grim, as if he had something on his mind. Ia knew what it most likely was, of course. This particular confrontation had only been a sixteen percent chance for happening here and now, but it was just as well, since it would have happened at some point anyway.

So much for "free time." Better to get it out of the way now, before it's had a chance to fester. Lifting her chin, Ia nodded politely. "Sergeant. I know what you're going to say because I already know what you're concerned about."

"You do?" he asked, derailed by her admission. "How could you . . . ?"

She tapped the side of her head briefly. "Precog, remember? I've already foreseen several variations on this conversation. You're upset by the discrepancies stirred up by the rules written into the Damned handbook, versus actual Terran Space Force regulations," Ia stated, glad she was no longer under Restricted Leave, having to be recorded every second of every day. "You find it difficult to reconcile your duty to the Space Force, versus my standing orders to lie to our superiors about certain things taking place on board this ship."

"Well, yes. I was raised to be honest, to act with honor. Lying isn't honorable," the naturalized Scadian protested.

Rising from the bench—surpassing him in height by several centimeters despite the fact they had both been born and raised on the same homeworld—Ia sighed and worked on strapping on her weight gloves. "I myself would rather tell the truth, Sergeant. But however honorable a knight may be in a duel . . . well, there comes a point where deception must be employed against an opponent in order to secure an objective. It doesn't even have to be a melee feint or an ambush in a war. It can be as simple as refraining from mentioning something to an ally, so that the ally in question does not act precipitously or react wrongfully.

"A lot of those standing orders in the Company bible are there because of the lattermost reasons. It would simply be too *dangerous* for others outside this ship to know certain of our secrets." Ia sought for a way to get him to understand why such things were necessary. "They would interfere, like a . . . like a bystander with absolutely no understanding of either architecture or stained-glass construction trying to push aside a master craftsman in the middle of assembling a rose window in a cathedral."

"A rose window," he repeated skeptically.

"A stained-glass window of great depth and complexity,"

Ia told him. "This window I am building exists not just in three dimensions, but in four. Some things, I am free to admit to here and now. Some things, I have revealed slowly, over many months and years. And some things cannot be revealed at all. Not for a very long time, if ever. But these things, managing these secrets, is *my* task. *Your* task is simply to keep your mouth shut, serve as a Squad leader and a sergeant, and prepare yourself to serve a very worthy group of people on Sanctuary with every scrap of fighting skill, innate honor, and security-trained cunning you possess."

"For how long?" Kardos challenged her. "How long do I have to serve on your homeworld before I get to return to Scadia?"

Oh, lovely. This *percentage. Let's see how I can make this end well.* Dipping her fingers into the timestreams, Ia sought for a way to get out of this without either his resentment or a very unfair verbal fight. She rubbed at her forehead with a weight-suited hand, then sighed, stared at it, and peeled off her glove. Once it was bare, she offered it to him, palm up. "Take my hand, and come see what great deeds *you* would do on Sanctuary if you gave yourself wholeheartedly to the task I need to assign to you."

Kardos knew what she was and what she could do. There had been plenty of time for him to hear about her abilities from the other members of the crew. Ia also knew that psychic abilities were not exactly a point of open discussion on Scadia. Such things might have been scientifically proved for the last several centuries, but they did not belong in a medieval setting like the kind the Societatis tried to emulate.

To his credit, he hesitated only a moment before clasping her hand. She flipped them both onto the timeplains, pulling him quickly out of his own life-waters before the overlapping images could confuse him.

"You already know that I need you to go to Sanctuary to protect the lives of the Director and other key government members of the Free World Colony," Ia stated, guiding him along the grassy banks, heading downstream into the future. *"I do not doubt your willingness to teach others how to fight, how to defend themselves, and how to treat the people around them, and placed under them, with respect and courtesy.*

"*I could remind you of how I bartered alliance in perpetuity between the people of Scadia and the eventual Third Human Empire, in exchange for your presence on our mutual birthworld. I could speak for hours on how the leaders of the Church of the One True God intend to use treachery and deception, sabotage and even assassination to clear out all rivals against their power, the foremost of which will be the FWC.*

"*But you know all of this, or you will as soon as you see the situation on Sanctuary for yourself,*" Ia dismissed. She strolled along the stream banks, shrinking them down to rivulets they could easily step over as she searched for just the right one to make him understand. "*What you haven't seen is what the pressures of two hundred years of vicious, cold, implacable, carefully paced civil war will do to the people of the Free World Colony.*"

"*Two hundred years of war? Another blockade?*" Alexus asked her.

"*Sort of. Sanctuary must remain isolated for two hundred years, and that means not only enduring being lost behind the shifting of the Grey border in the next few years, they must endure an ongoing civil war for roughly two hundred years before it can be allowed to end. Generations of maintaining their independence and uniqueness in the face of harsh adversity.*

"*Because of this, they must not only learn the patience of a shield wall as each generation takes on the burden of holding their ground for the day their descendants can break free, they must also have an* outlet *for their frustrations. Exiled underground, with each community under constant threat of attack, they must one and all learn to fight . . . but they must learn to fight with* honor *amongst themselves, or they will rip each other apart while they wait.*

"*An armed society is a polite society . . . but only once they have established their rules of conduct.*"

Stopping in front of one particular stream, Ia stepped down into the waters. When Kardos hesitated, she tugged him down even as she shifted the bank out from under him, landing him in the life-waters of a certain male 137 years into the future. Immersing him in a solution to that problem.

They were a youngish man with two names. A private name which only his immediate family knew, *Nicolo Kardos*—one of several great-plus descendants of the first Duello Prime, *Alexus Kardos*—and a world-name, *Bladespire*, by which he plied his trade. Today, that trade involved listening to the frustrated tears of an older man. Fingers gnarled by old age and limbs weakened by a touch of gravity sickness, he was unable to lift a blade long enough to fight. Yet he wanted to, needed to, in order to answer the insults flung at him by a much younger business rival. Insults that were disparaging his goods as well as his honor, and which were beginning to drive away trade from his shop.

The elderly man's only daughter was pregnant, or she'd have done something about it herself. She had no siblings, and her husband had died during an attack, so there were no siblings or son-in-law to fight for him, either. So he had come to Bladespire, one of the Duelle, to hire the man to fight for him. The younger man insulted the elder because he thought he could get away with it; old age had rendered his target personally unable to fight, and the younger was becoming a bully because of it.

Impassive though he seemed on the outside, Duello Bladespire had heard of this feud and was pleased the merchant had come to him to knock out some of the younger shop owner's arrogance.

Ia skipped them forward in the man's life-stream, once Alexus had learned the reasons for what came next. She made sure they immersed only lightly in this life-stream; they didn't need to live every second of it personally. Just viewing it and knowing the passing of surface thoughts would be enough.

The fight, arranged the following day, proved the elder merchant had chosen well. It took place in a challenge ring, as all such duels were required, and it took place with what the Societatis people would call "live steel," real swords with real edges and real points. While the elder shop owner watched off to one side, muttering encouragements and clenching his muscles in sympathy for each slash and parry, Bladespire slowly and thoroughly humiliated the younger shopkeeper.

The Duello did so verbally as well as physically. Blade-spire delivered admonishments about respecting one's elders, speaking the truth instead of false claims about his rival's goods, and eventually bringing it to an end with a single, simple cut, drawing blood from the younger merchant's hand. At the periphery of the life-stream's awareness, others watched as well, members of the local community. Some cat-called on the side of the younger man, but only a few. Most chided on the side of the elder, lending social pressure to the younger man's shaming.

When it ended with that cut and the few drops of blood that welled up, at that moment, all conversations around the challenge ring ceased. Bladespire stepped back, disengaging from the schlager duel. "By the terms of the Codex Duelle, I have won. You will cease your harassment, or face my blade again on his behalf, where I will by law have the right to beat you senseless. You will be a good neighbor and support his endeavors rather than seek to destroy them. Is that clear?"

His expression more subdued than sullen, the young mer-chant reluctantly agreed. Bladespire had worked him into a sweat, and had done so without himself growing more than mildly warm. But then he was trained to fight all day long if need be.

. . . A brief glimpse of the future through Bladespire's watchful eyes showed the younger merchant ignoring his neighbor. It was close enough for the elder man's tastes and needs, who cordially ignored him in return. Honor was satis-fied, and the quarrel had more or less ended. The old man's honor seemed to be satisfied with that . . . and their neigh-bors were happy with the lack of hostilities.

Ia drew them out of Bladespire's waters. Regaining the bank, she looked at the stout, muscled soldier. *"The Codex Duelle is a system of ritualized combat. If a Free World Col-onist has a grievance with a neighbor, and they cannot settle it with a peaceful discussion, they take it to the challenge rings. Most such things are fought to the yield. Some are fought to the first drop of blood, or to unconsciousness. A rare few will be fought to the death, but very, very few. It will have been designed and implemented by* you," she informed him. *"This, and protecting the head of the FWC government, are your greatest tasks. Because everyone in the FWC must learn to fight, and must carry a weapon in case of a Church invasion, combat must therefore be ritualized. Formalized. As the Scadians themselves say, 'An armed society is . . .'?"*

"'A polite society,'" Kardos finished for her when she let the old saying trail out expectantly. *"But . . . only when the rules are codified and implemented. Right."*

"Everyone must learn to fight, because the Church will label everyone as a heretic and an enemy of the state, from the eldest of the elderly down through to the newest of the newborn infants," Ia asserted, looking at the life-waters around them. *"And as they learn to fight, while they learn to fight, they must learn when to fight. When it is appropriate, when it is inappropriate, how far they may take it, how far they may not . . .*

"It is one thing to fight an enemy for your life," Ia stated, strolling farther downstream. Kardos moved with her since she still held his hand in hers, tugging him along. *"It is another thing to fight a friend in jest. The people of Sanctuary need to know where the various lines are drawn, and it must become so deeply ingrained in their culture that it will enforce the ideals of personal honor and personal responsibility.*

"Such a task requires the very best of meioas to design it, implement it, and instruct others in it." She paused, wrinkled her nose, then added, *"Simultaneously, the same position must be filled by someone who understands the need for deception, secrecy, and counter-assassination measures, because the Church will not always fight openly. They certainly won't fight honorably.*

"In fact, through much of the ongoing war, they will fight with great dishonor. You must be prepared to catch and counter every one of their tricks and teach others to know how to turn those tricks back on the Church's spies and infiltrators, without descending fully into such practices yourselves. Occasionally, yes, you will use such practices when the need is great, but not each and every instance. Such restraint requires a code of honor that is deeply ingrained and enmeshed in a culture, even as its adherents acknowledge the practical need to know and utilize the enemy's tricks.

"It is not," Ia acknowledged dryly, *"an easy balance to*

maintain." She looked at Kardos. "*What I ask of you will never be easy. But it is worthwhile. When the Fire Girl Prophecies come true on my homeworld and the Zenobian Empire is born, they must be strong yet compassionate, self-sufficient yet generous, fierce yet honorable. They must be all of these things and more, because if they are not, then the Savior will not have a home. She will not have a refuge where idealism is pattern-welded to pragmatism and tempered with honor.*

"*She will not have a refuge in which to nurture her own sense of honor, not without the people of Sanctuary having a sense of honor themselves. Without that tempering, she will not be forged into the strong weapon we all need her to be. When the moment comes for her to bend and spring back into place, surviving under great pressure . . . she will instead break. And when she breaks, this is all that will be left of our galaxy's future.*"

She stopped at the edge of the desert that had plagued her since her precognition had blossomed back when she was fifteen. He squinted, stared into the desolate distance ahead of them, with barely a desiccated weed here and there breaking the cracked, dusty, dried-up streambeds, and glanced behind him to double-check the healthy green of the grass and the darker leaves of the occasional bush still existed. That the waters of all those lives still flowed, in the past. They certainly didn't in the future.

"*I can instruct my fellow colonists right and left via the written word, even leave them a few recorded images . . . but I cannot* live *among them as the example they need. I will never* be able to live among them. There are still too many tasks awaiting me elsewhere, things which only I can do,*" Ia told him, facing Kardos. "*This, however, is something that* you *can do. As a Scadian at heart, if not by birth, you are the best man for this task, and the* only *Scadian who can survive living in the high gravity of my homeworld, the world where you were born and raised before emigrating. This is what I* must *ask of you because my own sense of honor, my sense of duty, and my conscience, demand that I ask it of you.*"

"*And how long will this precious task take?*" Alexus asked her, giving her a shuttered look.

Ia didn't blink. *"The rest of your life."*

He drew in a breath to protest. She shook her head.

"I ask you nothing which I would not do myself if I could, Alexus. But while I could lead my people into a way of life that includes such deep-rooted honor and watchful pragmatism as they will need, they cannot fight the Salik with the skill and the knowledge that will end this war, never mind the Greys. You cannot fight the Salik or the Greys with that level of precision. I am too badly needed away from my homeworld to stay behind.

"But this, you can do. You are uniquely suited for it. Will you give what I have shown you careful consideration?" she asked. *"We still have several months to go before we reach Sanctuary and the point of no return. I cannot wait forever for an answer, but I can give you a few of those months in which to think, before you either agree to take up this task, or I must take the time and effort to find someone less qualified to fill your shoes."*

Kardos frowned at the grass behind them, the half-dried streams by their feet, and the ceaseless, bleak desert ahead. *"You said these people of Sanctuary, your people, would have to learn dishonorable ways of fighting as well as honorable. I only know what is honorable. I am not the right person to teach them such things."*

Ia smiled slightly, watching him as he studied the timeplains instead of looking at her. He didn't notice, but she could see his life's waters thickening and deepening a short distance downstream.

"That has already been considered. Commander Helstead is a former member of the Knifeman Corps," she stated, pronouncing the word as *corpse* instead of *core*. Even here, on the timeplains, that distinction was still important. *"So is Private Sunrise. Both are also trained in Troubleshooter protocols and methods. Helstead has already given similar lessons to a number of my crew and is willing to give you the appropriate training, too.*

"Since it will take months for you to learn everything, I have arranged for your lessons to begin in two days. You needn't make up your mind for a few months yet, as I have said—but even if you decline, it will be good for you to learn

these things so that you know the proper counters to them, so learning them is an order, not an option.

"Do make up your mind by no later than the start of December," she warned him, drawing them back toward their starting point on the sunlit prairie. *"If you choose to refuse, I must hurry to train a less suitable heavyworlder as your successor and write out a rather large list of precognitive guides and directives for the other man to study and implement over the next sixty or so years. For you . . . it would be part of your nature to do such things. For him, it would only come with great care and practice. I'd prefer to take the easier way."*

"Why would my training start in two days?" Kardos asked her. *"Why not start it as soon as we leave this . . . place?"* he asked, gesturing with his free hand at the timeplains while they walked.

"Because Lieutenant Spyder has finally found your mech-suit and is busy getting it unpacked, charged up, and ready for you to practice in, once you're done working out," Ia told him. She stopped beside their entry point, the moment of Now in both of their lives. *"You'll be very busy learning how to move safely in it for the next two days. You'll need to know how to fight in it when we reach Sanctuary next May. Whether or not you choose to stay and help my people by spending the rest of your life on Sanctuary, you* will *help fight for their survival while we are all scheduled to be there. You and I are the only two people who can manage the rigors of combat in Sanctuarian gravity without needing a weave or using tele-kinesis to combat the planet's pull, and that means you'll be stuck as my teammate while I'm down there."*

A tug flipped them back into their own bodies. Kardos swayed on his feet, blinking owlishly. Reaching up with her other hand, Ia steadied him.

". . . Easy," she murmured out loud. "Your brain's been racing at half the speed of light while the rest of your body was still plodding along at an orbital rate."

"Half Cee?" he repeated, trying to grasp that fact.

"Well, bare seconds out here, minutes in there," Ia told him. "Just sit down for a bit and catch your mental balance," she added, guiding him to rest on the locker-room bench.

"You'll feel better in a minute or so. It's a great way to share a great deal of information in a fraction of the time it would normally take, but it does exact a toll on both body and mind if you're not used to it.

"Now, if you'll kindly excuse me, *I* have to get myself in good enough shape to fight on the surface of my homeworld, and I have barely nine months in which to do so. Don't forget to have engineering increase the gravitic pull under your machines when you're working out. If nothing else, you'll still need to reacclimate to Sanctuarian gravity when you accompany me to the surface. I've put in a writ for the field strength in your quarters to slowly increase while you're awake, same as my own."

Nodding, he stayed behind while she headed for the weight room. Ia hoped she had given him a lot to think about. At the very least, she had managed to avoid getting into a swordfight with him. He was good with a blade, better even than Helstead, who was Afaso-trained. But he didn't have Ia's battle-honed precognition on his side, and he didn't have a monocrystalline, monofractally sharp sword to wield like she did.

Yet.

It was on her list of things to make, next time she went home, along with certain protections unique to Sanctuary that would keep the Greys off-world. The top one hundred Duella and Duello, the best of the Duelle, professional swordfighters, would eventually become the honor guard, the visible bodyguards for the rulers of the Fire Bird Throne. They would need armor and weapons appropriate to both their culture and the practical needs of close-quarters combat. It wouldn't be quite like what the Societatis had, but it would be needed. Panoply and pageantry were just two more tools in the toolbox she had to give to her people, if augmented by the unique resources of her homeworld.

She hoped he would choose to serve the nascent Third Human Empire. It would make things easier for her. Or at least less tedious. Settling onto one of the machine benches, Ia rested for a moment, her expression carefully blank rather than tired. There were nine others using the facilities at the moment, and she didn't want her crew to know how weary she was getting of all of this.

Fighting for survival and the success of a battle was in many ways easier than the grind of fighting for understanding and cooperation. *One of these days, it'd be nice to encounter a group of people who jump when I say jump and don't stop to argue about how high.*

CHAPTER 2

Which part of that visit to Beautiful-Blue did you want to discuss? The part where my crew received their hard-won medals for surviving the disasters on Dabin, which they shouldn't have had to do? The part where I had to accept and forward the Black Hearts for the five soldiers who died under my and Harper's command? Or the part where I finally convinced half a dozen sentient races to . . .

Oh. That part. Truthfully, I would have gladly traded all of that to have had Svarson, Benjamin, Feldman, Franke, and Nabouleh still alive, and the whole mess on Dabin undone—and yes, meeting you was one of the better moments from our time on Dabin. You yourself have come far from our very first interview . . .

Yes, all of the other awards were gratifying in their own way. Yes, it was humbling to receive the Terran Medal of Honor, and I won't ever forget it. But what happened after *that awards ceremony on Beautiful-Blue is far more memorable for me. I've always been far more interested in the results of my efforts, in the good I can do, and not in anything glittery, meioa-e.*

~Ia

AUGUST 22, 2498 T.S.
BEAUTIFUL-BLUE, SUGAI SYSTEM

Her ear still hurt. Despite her self-healing abilities, Ia felt the curve of her right ear throbbing as the tissues slowly knitted themselves whole around the newest hole on that side of her head. Not nearly as badly as losing her eye had hurt, but it was an annoyance all the same.

Of course, gaining the hole had been a singular honor. After gargling an antiseptic mouthwash, the Queen of the Solaricans herself had bitten the curve of Ia's equally swabbed ear. She had needed to do so by Solarican custom, for only their queen could make the hole for the extra piercing that, linked by a special chain and post to the previous two, marked Ia as an official Royal Seer War Princess, and not merely a War Princess. It was a mouthful of a title, but it made Ia an equal in rank and command with Royal Sector War Prince K'sennshin. That was the meioa-o in charge of all the military forces for the Solarican colonies that were a part of the Alliance, and he had greeted her as an equal without equivocation the moment the chain-linked rings were in place.

Knowing in advance it was coming and not wanting to be outdone, Myang had ordered a new uniform for Ia, issued by hyperrelayed order to the *Damnation* as soon as the ship came into the Sugai System. That decision had no doubt been spurred by the realization through diplomatic channels that the Solarican Queen was "appropriating" the Prophet of a Thousand Years to be part of her people's military structure . . . whether or not the Terrans approved of it. That meant Ia wore formal Dress Blacks; she couldn't escape them now that she was a four-star member of the Command Staff. But the cuff-buttoned sleeves and boot-length slacks now bore four stripes down each side, dull green, muddy brown, misty blue, and pewter gray, by the Admiral-General's orders.

The presence of all four colors implied that she was now firmly a part of all four Branches of the Space Force, and not just her own Cordon in the Space Force or her temporary placement over a single Division of the SF Army on Dabin. Even Admiral Genibes, her former superior, had only the blue stripe of the Navy and the gray stripe of the Special Forces decorating his Dress Blacks. But Myang had ordered Ia to consider the whole of the Space Force as under her purview, precognitively . . . though the canny woman had not yet given her the actual authority to *make* orders. Everything still had to be constructed as suggestions and sent to the appropriate Admirals and Generals for review.

All things considered, though, it was an encouraging sign. At this rate, Ia would get the authority to make those suggestions as outright commands. Eventually, with a high probability . . . but not as a certainty. Nothing was certain. Her shoulder, her briefly lost eye, Hollick-turned-N'keth, Ginger-Meddled-Mattox, herself nearly ruining everything through an urge to give a flippant reply . . . nothing was one hundred percent pure, surefire certain in her life.

Except maybe the boredom of speeches . . .

They were still going through the florid introductory speeches and political-posturing stages, things which Ia considered a waste of precious time. But she had to be here for this meeting, so the slowly fading pain in her ear was a semi-welcome distraction. Almost every single ruler or leader of the current Alliance nations, both secular and military, had been gathered into this room. Or set of rooms, technically. Not the Salik nor the Choya, of course, since they were the enemy, but the Terran Humans, the V'Dan Humans, the Gatsugi, K'Katta, Tlassians, Solaricans—overall Queen and local War Prince—and the two species that required their own chambers to exist.

The Chinsoiy leaders rested on tall, slanting, stool-like furnishings behind a thick-shielded window in a chamber designed to pulse the low-level radiations necessary for their silicon-based life without irradiating the others. They were strange, somewhat translucent beings, shaped something like a cross between a hominid and a pteranodon, with wings that bore hand-like fingers placed at the upper mid joint, ridged crests on their heads, and their opalescent bodies draped in tool belts but not clothing.

Jeweled rings decorated the trailing edges of their wing-flaps, and their hides were painted in ultraviolet markings that denoted rank and power. Little flashes of colored stripes could be seen when they moved into or out of the black-light lamps at the edge of the window, a courtesy to the non-Chinsoiy so that the other races could tell their Glorious—secular and legal—Leader from their Fearsome—a combination of religious and military—Leader. Comm-link devices, assisted by living interpreters watching and translating on both sides, ensured that they understood and had a chance to contribute if they could not manage to understand the discussions being held in Terranglo.

The Dlmvla did not have their highest-ranked Queen Nestor present, nor any of the other queens; they merely had their local ambassador and his attachés, the ones normally assigned to the Gatsugi Collective. Along with the Chinsoiy, the Dlmvla were not being openly or even covertly attacked by the Salik and Choya, but the leaders of the two races had been invited to attend. The Chinsoiy co-Leaders had come. The Dlmvlan had not.

Like the Chinsoiy, they were not located with the others in the main chamber. Instead, the members of that embassy were safely tucked into their own windowed chamber on the other side from the Chinsoiy because they were carbon-based methane breathers. Oxygen was as pleasant-smelling to them as methane was to the rest of the Alliance members, and just as dangerous in large quantities.

The Gatsugi had thoughtfully provided an entire suite of chambers for necessary resting, feeding, waste management, leisure, and the conducting of business for both their Chinsoiy and Dlmvlan guests. Where the Chinsoiy were pale and opalescent in a dim, bluish-lit room, the Dlmvla were scaled, dark, and iridescent in a reddish-lit room. With their huge, multifaceted eyes and partly chitinous bodies almost twice as big as any of the other races present, they lurked in their bowl-like chairs like rainbow-dusted, reddish lumps. The ambassador was the largest and highest-seated in the group, sipping from time to time on steamed essences from a hookah-like contraption at his side, his paler-hued assistants curled up in lower bowl chairs around him.

". . . And bright/blue/firm greetings/introduction/welcome we/we now/finally give/state unto/for the esteemed/valorous/brilliant Terran General/Royal Seer War Princess Ia, who/she graces/joins/honors us/us/us . . ."

Ia carefully controlled the urge to roll her eyes. President Guw-shan Many-Arms-Many-Strengths was finally coming to the end of his florid, alien-style introductions, with the Terran Premiere, Admiral-General, and Ia herself as the very last in the room to be introduced. *Pity I can't bet anyone on how many minutes it'll take him to finish telling everyone I am here. They all know I'm a precog.*

Two minutes, seventeen seconds, and one still-rather-itchy earlobe later, Ia stopped surreptitiously rubbing at the scabs flaking from her newest earring holes. She lowered her hand, shifting forward to rest her arms on the table which she, Admiral-General Myang, and Premiere Justinn Mandella occupied. She hadn't seen the Premiere since he was still the Secondaire in his prior term, but there hadn't been time for more than the exchange of Terran medals at the ceremony earlier and a brief murmured greeting at the start of this gathering.

There never is quite enough time for anything, anymore. Which means I'd better not waste what little I do have. In the brief silence following President Guw-shan's introductions, she seized the moment to speak.

"I thank you for such eloquent introductions, Meioa President, on all our behalf," Ia stated without preamble. "But as much as protocol would have each faction taking turns to make opening statements of their own, I must beg your indulgence, all of you, to allow me to lead the first part of this meeting so that it is both quick and efficient.

"Time is a very precious commodity for me. I would rather spend as much of it on the needs of the war as wisely as I can right up front, and get things settled before it is time for me to bow out and leave the rest of you to handle those many other matters which only you can address, and of which I have no part." She looked around the room at the assembled leaders, both political and military, including the two ambassadorial environment suites. "Are there any objections, or may I have your permissions to proceed?"

More than one brow lifted: Myang's, as well as the Emperor of V'Dan. The military leader of the K'Katta—whose name nobody outside his own species could pronounce, so he had been introduced as "Chiswick" for short—curled up and in one of his forelegs, almost as if he were going to raise a hand had he been a Human. He relaxed it without speaking, however.

Ia looked over at her two leaders, seated to her left. Premiere Mandella gestured at her to take command. The Admiral-General sighed and sat back, her own hand twisting in a brief gesture that was half shrug, half permission as well.

". . . Thank you. With the spread of Dabinian passion-moss spores across several oxygen-based planets, the Salik are effectively and efficiently being driven off-world and back into the stars, back to areas where they can control their atmospheric content. They are trying to rely more heavily upon their mechanical forces, but those are being contained by the efforts of the counter-programmers, particularly the code dancers of the Gatsugi forces," Ia acknowledged, bowing slightly to the President of the Collective.

President Guw-shan preened a little, flexing both sets of shoulders back while his creamy not-hair strands fluffed up a little. He drew in a breath to speak but stopped himself when Ia held up her hand, middle and ring fingers folded down. The hand sign was Gatsugi, not Human, and mostly an approximation, as his species had three fingers and a thumb per hand, not four and a thumb. It acknowledged his urge to speak, conceded the contributions he would have made, and requested his silent patience.

For a species that had evolved with the need to be super-quiet at times in the face of aurally superior foes, the only way she could have been more eloquent without audible words was if she could have changed the golden tan hue of her skin. From the flush of brown-tinged blue that briefly mottled his skin, her gesture mollified him despite the way it irritated him to be cut off before he could speak.

"But we still have a long ways to go, meioas," she cautioned. "There are still numerous Salik installations hidden in interstitial space. With the Salik forces being forced back into space, our own fleets are being worn down by the constant fighting. Ambassador Juljvm, Nestor-Adjunct," she stated, addressing the Dlmvlan ambassador behind his comm-augmented window. "Your people have long remained neutral in this war. Your starships are numerous, intact, and whole—you have just as many vessels available for combat as the entire Alliance

combined, and probably more, since you have no attrition
from war. Is your government willing to break their neutrality
at this point in time to join with the rest of us in destroying
the Salik War Fleet?"

The Dlmvlan ambassador hesitated a long moment. His aides
could be seen muttering words, even gesturing; the movements
were alien, but it was obviously an argument, for the Nestor-
Adjunct slashed one clawed limb outward, and the others subsided, sinking back into their nest-chairs. On the oxygen side of
the glass, the others waited tensely for the outcome.

Finally, Ambassador Juljvm touched the comm controls
attached to his bowl chair and spoke in Terranglo. "This the
Queen Nestors refuse to do. Neutral at this time we remain,
and will defend our sovereign selves alone."

Subtle movements and soft sounds around the room spoke
of several species' versions of disappointment. Even of disgust, for Ia could hear a very faint, "*Shakk*," from the woman
to her immediate left. She, however, nodded, acknowledging
the news without any signs of dismay. "That is the sovereign
right of your leadership. One more question, Ambassador.
How do *you* feel about our request, and your leaders' orders?"

The Dlmvlan ambassador hissed and snapped his claw-
tipped fingers against each other before speaking. "It would
be . . . illogical politically to state my reactions exact, General Ee Ah," he said. "I gift but with you my disgust."

"I acknowledge your gift, and gift you in turn with my de-
lighted acceptance for your government's answer," Ia returned
calmly. The Nestor-Adjunct shifted in bemusement, but Ia
continued smoothly. "Since the Dlmvlan forces at this time
are choosing to obey their Queen Nestor Council, and thus
shall continue to remain neutral in this conflict, you are dismissed for a short while, Ambassador. The others will contact you when I and my business are gone—I shall trust that
the other races of the Alliance will continue to treat you and
your people with respect, courtesy, and fair trade despite our
deep disappointment that you could not join us openly in
quelling the Salik menace. Thank you for attending. Please
remain ready to return in a little while, when your counsel
will be needed for various trade agreements."

He tilted his head, with its leathery brown hide and

multifaceted eyes. "We gift you with our thanks for accepting our sovereign needs, General."

Touching the comm control, then another button, he closed the shutter on the observation window. As it slid down, the ambassador and his aides could be seen rising from their bowl chairs, their rust and brown hides gleaming with faint metallic hues to match the metallic threads woven through what passed for their clothes.

The Chinsoiy Glorious Leader activated her own comm . . . though the gender "female" didn't have an exact analog in her species to what was more common among the carbon-based members. "Seem surprised you do not, General. His answer was this so well anticipated in you?"

"I have made allowances in my plans for the Dlmvla, Glorious Leader Zyx. Just as I have made allowances for all of you and your own possible responses up to a point. But only up to a point." Rising from her chair at the table, she clasped her hands behind her back in a stance somewhere between Parade Rest and at Attention. "I have already gambled the lives of 4,179 Humans and fifteen Tlassians on what the Dlmvla will and will not do. They, however, are not your concern. They are mine, and mine alone, for the burdens you already bear in this war are more than enough for the rest of you to handle.

"I will deal with the Dlmvla later, when it is appropriate at the right point in time. *Your* concerns, I must deal with right now." She glanced over at Myang and Mandella, and let the corner of her mouth twist up wryly on one side for a brief moment. "I would have asked to be here, and would have asked for these things even had I still been a mere Ship's Captain . . . but with the faith of my superiors behind me, it is slightly easier to ask these things now. Easier, but not guaranteed, save by your choice.

"Premiere Mandella and Admiral-General Myang have made me a General of the Command Staff of the Terran Space Force. Queen Surshan has given me the rank of Royal War Seer Princess, and with it joint command of all Solarican forces within Alliance territory. His Eternity, Emperor Ki'en-qua of V'Dan, would grant me the same level of authority as a Grand General.

"I would like to ask the rest of you to give me equal authority over your own military forces at this time. Tlassian, Gatsugi, K'Katta, Chinsoiy . . . and to ask my fellow Terrans, the V'Dan, and the Solaricans to join with you to grant me the position of General of the Alliance Forces. As I said at the start of this meeting," Ia said, filling the stunned silence with the calm reminder, "I don't have a lot of time available, and I would far rather spend what little time I do have in useful action rather than in wasteful discussion."

Chiswick chittered. His translator box spoke a moment later, converting his words into Terranglo. "What sort of useful actions would require such high authority to be given to a foreign Guardian? What are your end-goals for this level of power?"

"As it has always been, my end-goal is to save the greatest number of lives so that they may lead the best lives possible, long into the future. To do that, however, we must deal with the Salik in a very specific way—the Blockade, as you may have noticed," Ia stated dryly, "did not work very well. It will not succeed a second time. Not even in the short term. I have spent the last eleven-plus years trying to find not just the best solution that will deal with them . . . but a better solution than the one I found when I was fifteen."

She looked down at the table for a long moment, then looked up and around the room, meeting each set of eyes, or their equivalent in the case of the Chinsoiy.

"I have *not* found a better solution.

"There is only one path that leaves this Alliance—this whole galaxy—still alive, still functional, and prepared to face the ancient enemy of the Grey Ones. I'll remind you that this is the enemy they *fled* because *they* could not fight that foe, with all their advanced technology. It is an enemy our descendants must be able to face and fight three hundred years from now. In order to ensure that the greatest number of people will still be around, and the *right* people are alive to face that implacable, unstoppable foe . . . the Salik must be dealt with in a very specific way.

"It will be a very unpleasant way, but I have found no other path that delivers the long-term objectives we must all keep in mind, for our great-grandchildren's sake," Ia stated grimly.

She couldn't give details—didn't dare give details—but she could try to warn them. She had to try, at any rate.

"How great is thisss 'unnpleasssant'?" the Tlassian Warchief asked her.

"I was given the military nickname of 'Bloody Mary' after my very first tour of combat eight years ago," Ia stated. "I was given it because I ended that fight painted from helm to boot in both Salik and Choya blood. I have kept that name fresh and dripping in every encounter with our foes since that day." She looked around the room again, meeting the mouse black eyes of the Gatsugi President, the crystalline orbs of the Chinsoiy, even the brown stare of the Admiral-General at her side. It was to Christine Myang that Ia spoke. "But . . . I have not *earned* that nickname, sir. Not yet.

"I have spent eleven years of my life looking for a better solution than what lies ahead. I have not found one that would avoid the coming bloodshed yet still saves all the rest of our lives. As a soldier and an officer, I *must* accept that there will be casualties in a war. That there will be deaths. My job is to minimize the number of lives lost where I can . . . but the Salik won't stop trying to enslave and devour the rest of us. It is their nature, one which they fully embrace." She lifted her gaze to the Tlassian Warchief, his brown-and-gold uniform blending with his green-and-gold skin. "If I am in charge, then I can maximize the number of lives saved for our side . . . and if *I* am in charge, then I alone will bear the blame for the lives lost on *both* sides, when I do earn my nickname in full.

"The Salik must die. In the right time. At the right place. In the right way . . . as a race."

"You/You would/will lead/direct our peoples/troops/Alliance into full/full/massive combat/attacks against/on the Salik?" President Guw-shan asked her. "Without/Lacking the Dlmvla vessels/ships . . ."

Ia shook her head quickly, glad Myang had ordered her to leave her Dress cap behind. It would have been shaken free had it still been perched on her short-trimmed locks. "No. The actions of the Dlmvla are going to be what they *must* be, for all of us to survive. I have already calculated and even manipulated their efforts in this war, so we shall leave them to it. As for the Salik . . . we will have standard engagements up until the crisis point . . . and then we will engage in strictly defensive actions only. The Salik will be the authors of their own downfall. *If* everything goes right."

"Hy do not underrrstand," Queen Surshan stated, her Terranglo heavily accented. "How woullld dis earrn you de warr nnickname, if all we do is defennd?"

"I cannot tell you what is coming—*do not ask me to tell you*," Ia added firmly, hearing the woman to her left inhale on an impending question. "Do not order me, for I will *not* say. There are only two people in this galaxy who know exactly what is coming. Myself, and one Feyori. I only told him because I needed *his* cooperation in order to set up a line of circumstances that have finally brought the Feyori to follow at my side.

"I knew precognitively I could trust him to keep his mouth shut, which he has. And I knew we would need the help of the Feyori to deal with what must be, where the Salik are concerned. For the rest of it . . . I cannot take the risk of even one-hundred-thousandth of one percent of a chance of the Salik finding out what will happen before it is too late for them."

"But what is dis thinng we will defennd against?" the Solarican ruler asked.

"I cannot tell you, Your Majesty. I even went to the Salik homeworld to warn them against undertaking this war, that in doing so it would end with the death of their entire race . . . but I did not, could not, and will not tell them what is coming," she added, pointing off to the side. "None of us can risk their even getting a *hint* of what will happen before it is too late. Because they will turn the tide of it against *us*, and drown us in the incoming waves."

Even the Chinsoiy knew what a tide was, for all that their seas weren't entirely made of water. But that didn't stop their Fearsome Leader from asking over the comm, ". . . It is of a superweapon you speak? To have turned it against us? Your ship?"

She shook her head. "Not exactly, meioa; my ship will be part of the cleanup, but not the cause of the coming mess. And it is a type of superweapon, one which they themselves created at the end of the First Salik War, and which they lost track of in the intervening centuries. But it is not a weapon that *we* can wield. It is not *my* wielding of this weapon that will earn me my nickname. It is because I cannot and *will not* do anything to *stop* it from being wielded," she warned them. "Not and still be able to save the rest of us.

"I have tried for eleven years to find some other way, juggled the possibilities and massaged the probabilities, trying to find *any* other way. But the only way for the rest of us to survive is to get the Salik out of the equation," she amended quietly. Almost speaking the full truth. All she could do was hint . . . and see the dawning of understanding in the Human and alien faces around her for the things she could not openly say. "Out of compassion, I have looked. Out of frugality, I have looked. Out of *honor*, I have looked. I am sorry—more than any of you know—but there is no other way.

"Let *me* take the burden of this decision from you. Let *my* name be the one blackened and bloodied by what will have to happen," she persuaded. "I accepted long ago what must be done and have continued to accept it even as I searched for better ways, only to find none. I have the will to carry it through with the least loss of lives for our own side . . . which is the only side I can save." She met the multiple black orbs of the K'Katta Chief Guardian, the golden gaze of the local War Prince, K'sennshin, even the hazel gray eyes of Ki'en-qua.

He looked back at her steadily. Ki'en-qua's question was not unexpected, given V'Dan culture. "Will you show at least *one* of us what you have foreseen? You cannot expect even me to believe you without some proof that this task is necessary—and I say that even with you already having proved beyond all doubt your powers and your identity to my people."

"Yes. But not you, Eternity," Ia told him. "No one would believe you if you said you trusted me because my existence is tied up too much in the Sh'nai faith of your people." She glanced to her right, where the Solarican Queen sat, watching her. "Nor you, Queen Surshan. Your people have a . . . unique relationship with another interest group in this whole matter that would also compromise your neutrality."

Surshan flicked her ears back but did not counter Ia's veiled argument. The fact that the Solaricans had an understanding with the Feyori was not something openly known. Ia knew Surshan appreciated her tact in not mentioning it.

"Who, then?" Myang asked her. "Certainly not me, or *I'd* come under accusations of 'undue influence.'"

"Your choice to elevate me to the rank of General was more than enough aid, sir. Actually . . . I would prefer to choose one of the Chinsoiy Leaders. Your minds are not at all like a Human's," Ia said, turning to look at the quasi female on the other side of the thick, protectively darkened glass. "If I can show you, and you can understand it well enough, then that will have the highest probability of satisfying most everyone else in the Alliance."

"Enter you cannot my chambers," the ambassador stated bluntly, "or die will you. This cannot be allowed."

"Yes, and that is another reason why the rest *must* remain ignorant," Ia countered calmly. "My abilities have grown strong enough that I don't *have* to physically touch anyone anymore to show them what lies ahead in the fields of Time. If most of you remain clueless about what will happen next year, then there can be no accusations of undue influence from me and my abilities.

"I will have *no* accusations that I manipulated the leaders of the Alliance," she added with some heat behind the words. That question would come up in the future, and she wanted it made clear to these same leaders that she would do nothing of the sort. "My task is merely to show you what no one else can yet see, to tell you the things you need to know, and to advise you on the exact steps needed to salvage a victory from the coming mess.

"But I cannot take those steps *for* you. Not without your permission. And I certainly cannot fight this whole war by myself," she added in a dry aside. "You must act upon what your own common sense and your compassion for your fellow sentients insist that you do."

"You spake of thrrree warrrs," Queen Surshan said. "De Salik, annnd one I prrresume thrrree Terrannn hunndred yearrs into de future. What is dis seconnd warrr?"

"Four, if you count the coming war on my homeworld, but that one doesn't concern the Alliance since it will happen beyond your reach. The one you speak of involves the Greys. They are coming back, and they will invade Terran space. And yes, I have strategies lined up for dealing with them, even in the face of our extremely inferior, inadequate technology. We *will* stop them if we do things in the right time, in the right way; you have my Prophetic Stamp on that," Ia told them, forestalling any burgeoning sense of panic. "But first, we must continue to push the Salik forces off our many colonyworlds and push them back to their original territories. Then, a few of us—myself and my ship included—will face the Greys, show them certain things, and by doing so will give ourselves some breathing room by making them pause for a little while. Then we will finish the Second Salik War and return our attention to the Grey problem.

"Eventually, they will be constrained, shamed, and contained—don't ask me to explain the shamed part. It's too far into the future right now for you to need to know. What you should know right now is that a few borders will be redrawn along the back side of Terran space . . . but by doing so, we will have three hundred years of stability and prosperity in the Alliance zone after the Second Grey War ends, if everything goes right.

"Or rather, your descendants will have peace, since we are talking three hundred years, here," she amended, tipping her head slightly. "At the end of approximately three Terran centuries, those descendants will have to face an enemy that still scares the biological waste out of the Greys. I have plans for dealing with that far-flung war as well . . . but some of the details of that far-distant war are very much dependent on what we all choose to do here and now."

"I choose seeing these future sights," the Chinsoiy Fearsome Leader stated in the silence following her words. "*If* safely you can. It is good for one of us to see what you see, viewing sound reasons."

Ia nodded and stepped away from Myang. Her experiences in facing down Miklinn had given her insight into the true extent of her own abilities, and she had practiced while on board the *Damnation*, mostly with help from Helstead, Harper, and Rico. Spyder had declined, and she hadn't bothered to ask the rest. But this was not a fellow Human. "If you will rest your body, Fearsome Leader Kzul, I will begin."

The Glorious Leader moved aside, allowing her counterpart access to a lounger in the dimly seen observation room.

The Human analog to the position the Chinsoiy took was akin to a surfer lying on a slanted surfboard. The silicon-based species did not sit quite like anyone else. He shifted twice, then stilled. ". . . I am resting."

Going slowly, Ia lifted her hand and flipped her mind in, then out. She didn't need to move but did want to warn the others visually that she was beginning the process. She didn't want anyone to interfere at the wrong moment.

Chinsoiy brains weren't like carbon-based ones. She couldn't accelerate the alien's thoughts to match her own mental speeds. Her xenotelepathy still wasn't very strong—not really strong enough for this task, in a way—but she could reach out to Kzul with enough strength *from* the timeplains. In specific, from an alternate life-stream where *she* was a fellow Chinsoiy, as well as the Prophet of a Thousand Years.

Fearsome Leader gasped, plunging into the timeplains without much warning. Glorious Leader flinched, leaning over his slanted perch with the species equivalent of a worried look, but carefully did not touch her counterpart. Neither did the two painted guards, though they stared at the white-haired Human on the other side of the observation glass.

Ignoring them, Ia focused on drawing the reclining alien into that alternate timeline. *She* wasn't a Chinsoiy, couldn't think like them with all the nuances required to impart true understanding . . . but one of her alternate selves was. With her Feyori blood awakened, she could and did draw that alternate self out of the other waters so that silicon-based-Ia could accelerate and explain, while carbon-based-Ia trailed behind them for a moment like a third wheel on an awkward, grim date. But only for a moment; without a word, Chinsoiy-Ia passed over the Human counterpart to Fearsome Leader Kzul in the other universe. Together, they guided their respective guests through the minefields of the future.

This brain, she could speed up through the process, though it cost her effort and energy. Not for splitting her attention and her abilities in half but for splitting them into three parts: one part cushioned the silicon-based Kzul; one part enlightened the carbon-based Human version; and one part consulted with her other self, the Chinsoiy version of the Prophet. Events in the other universe were not happening quite like in this one, but enough alike for this exchange to help. Together, they targeted and tapped, guided and adjusted, double-checking each other's timelines as well as their own.

Ships and worlds burned. Bombs exploded; a planet boiled its seas into the searing sky. A gaping hole in the night slid by as they raced from system to disintegrating system, disturbingly bleak and black even in the depths of space. A *wrongness* that had to be stopped. She would have to stop that hole from happening in her own universe, but she had to show it so that at least one other in each universe would know what was coming, and confirm that the extra steps she had to take were necessary. That certain under-the-table deals had to be made, to stop it from existing, and to stop a war under way.

A great gray wall approached, lit by the glow of a young sun. Drones robbed planets of their stone and stole stars of their flame . . . and that single, mind-filling wall slowly became two: equally as terrible, and twice as frightening as before. The drones of both avoided that slowly growing void-spot with unseemly haste, even for their great, devouring speed. Avoided it and moved on, stripping system after system with terrifying efficiency.

Darkness stayed when the machine-wielding locusts left. Not the frightening void-within-a-void of that one little glimpse, but an emptiness nonetheless. Bereft of planets, of stars, of even the tiniest wisps of nebulae beyond the faint, far-flung light of distant galaxies, the utter lack of what had once been a thriving galaxy made the military leader keen and flex his membranes. Made his carbon-based counterpart suck in a discomforted breath through a very Human grimace.

Not every alternate-reality version of Ia could do this, or would do it, or even needed to do it. Right now, it helped both of their universes, and that was reason enough to cooperate. Dispassionately, third-corner-Ia watched as the other two parts of her mind worked, keeping focus on the two disparate activities. The silicon-based version took a lot longer to wade through everything, leaving her and her fellow Human to stand there on the timeplains. The Human version of Fearsome Leader glanced at her.

"So . . . you are the Human equivalent of her? A Prophet from another dimension? Why couldn't you be in ours, rather

than settling us with this alien one?" he asked her, lifting his chin at her counterpart. *"Do you know what we Terrans could do if we had you on our side?"*

Silicon-Ia was murmuring in the liquid language of her kind, explaining what Kzul was seeing as the void shifted into the one timeline, and the bleak emptiness re-blossomed with untouched stars. A desert analogy would have been useless to the Chinsoiy's point of view, so the Chinsoiy version was using other analogies while explaining the desert's significance versus the garden's.

Carbon-Ia shook her head. *"You were born in that other universe. I was born in this one. This is the only place where these two realities touch, outside the grasp of Death itself."* She turned to face the male Admiral-General, her brow quirked and her mouth twisted in irony. *"Besides, you do have me on your side: the Chinsoiy-me. That meioa cares every bit as much for carbon-kind as she does her own silicon-based species—I'll remind you that in your universe, just as in mine, the Chinsoiy are not being threatened by the very literal Salik appetite for warfare and destruction, yet she is still bending her abilities and guiding her people to act for your benefit, above and beyond the call of any normal duty.*

"Be content with the fact that we both care enough to help you understand, in the hopes that you will help the rest of your universe's Alliance to understand and act as well. This is why my silicon counterpart is informing your counterpart, so that my universe will survive, too."

He studied her, this Admiral-General Thad Puyen, and dipped his head. *"I see why your counterpart's Fearsome Leader has made you—her—a Highest Flight Leader."*

Before he could ask another question, the other two ended their conversation. Carbon-Ia handed back control of the Admiral-General to her counterpart and took back her Chinsoiy guest. As the other two faded from view, Fearsome Leader Kzul stared at her, opalescent skin gleaming in the golden light of the timeplains. Silicon-Ia had left them in a section where the purple sky was streaked with greenish peach clouds, echoing the patchy, uncertain future that lay ahead of both universes.

". . . This a strange place is," he stated as the other two left. He lifted an arm, membrane stretching, in order to gesture at

the sky. *"Sun-sear feels good on my wings, yet unharmed you stand, unblistered, undamaged. And the blackness-within-black, tasted of the Door for the Dead, as the Dlmvla do say it."*

"The things you saw in the images are true possibilities," Ia replied. *"If I don't set things up just right to stop the coming enemy, with your help, with the others' help, and by sacrificing a lot to stop what you saw . . . The blackness, the wrongness . . . is the destruction of the fabric of the universe, spreading in accelerated, destructive entropy. Stopping it will not be pleasant, but it will be done, and in doing so, it will put an end to the Grey Wars,"* Ia said. *"The Greys will be ashamed that their technology, clashing with ours, almost destroyed everything, an event that I have predicted, and which will convince them to do what I say."*

The Chinsoiy tilted his head, considering her words, then gestured vaguely at the timeplains around them. *"And this? Visions of future possibles?"*

"The things you see right now are only analogs, meioa. Metaphors," Ia explained patiently. *"What you see within the rivers are true possibilities, but up here, where it is dry, I have given both of us the ability to see these temporal energies in a way that each of us can understand."*

Kzul tilted his head. *"What energies are seen when not in use of metaphor-analogy? What true-sight is of this?"*

The question was a little unexpected. Ia would have thought the alien would want to know more about what he had been shown rather than the very nature of the timeplains. Tipping her own head back, she stared up at the non-hydrous clouds of his homeworld and pondered the question. Slowly, she morphed it to the golden grass and blue skies of a more Human-style world. Morphed it back to her vision of Time in all its infinite varieties.

"I have always seen this *planetary surface, meioa. It is my starting point for understanding. But for all we see it as a three-dimensional world . . . it is barely two-dimensional, and the underlying reality is very much beyond that."*

Extending a wing-arm, he offered her his fingers, long and oddly jointed. *"Show me."*

The corner of her mind that had been consulting with her counterpart now quickly skimmed the timelines behind the alien's back. It . . . would not hurt, she realized. It might even help. Nodding slowly, she licked her lips, focused, and stopped the analogy. Stopped the wind, stopped the clouds, stopped even the rippling waters of multiple, multiple lives. In the stillness and the silence, she breathed a single word.

". . . Time."

Their view of unending, rolling fields of golden grass and thousands of rivulets shattered into a million overlapping images. Everywhere the pair looked, existence itself vibrated and jostled like waves of sound rolling off a plucked wallharp string. The sunlight vanished, dropping them into an intense, rich blackness that held as much of everything as that blighted crack in reality had held absolute nothing.

The difference pressed in on them from all sides, cradling and supporting Human and Chinsoiy alike. Little sparks triggering huge, rolling, concentric rings, concentric spheres, concentric hyperspheres . . . If the zero dimension was a point, and the first dimension a line, the second a square, and the third a cube, each one building upon the previous at a right angle to itself . . . then Time was a hypercube, a cube within a cube, each the exact equal in size, but still tucked one within another at a perfect, impossible right angle.

Physics demanded that no one body could occupy the exact same spot as any other, so the hypercubes, the hyperspheres, constantly jostled for dominance in their selected spot, pushing each other back and forth. Each expenditure of fourth-dimensional energy induced a slight change from entropy, a change of willpower. This . . . *this* . . . was the movement that sentient beings called Time . . . and yet it was so little a thing, such a tiny thing. Little, because there was yet another layer to everything. Because at a right angle to *that*, to the hypercubes and hyperspheres, lay the realm of the multiverse.

Choice after choice lay beyond the hypersphere of Time, overlapping and jostling for place as well, for the nested cubespheres could move right *or* left, up *or* down, back *or* forth, in *or* out, plus the dimensional choices of yes *or* no . . . and they wanted to move in *all* directions at once.

Like fireworks bursting outward, only to have each spark burst again into new blossoming spheres, and new ones still,

Time pulsed in an interdimensional heartbeat of dizzying, overlapping magnitude, stretching on into an infinity which neither mind could comprehend, but which wasn't threatening or maddening at this level of intensity. It simply *was*.

But they weren't sparks. They were *things*, and they were *actions*. They were *choices*. Some of what they were and some of what they did moved because they were guided by the rules of existence, and some were guided by these tiny scraps of universe made self-aware.

Ia gently extracted them both from the multidimensional view, carefully rebuilding first the faintest glow of dawn, then the sensation of grass underfoot as the tufts came back into view, then the trickling sound of water as the rising sun glimmered off the streams around them.

"It is a form of energy, and it is a state of being," she murmured, grateful the Chinsoiy were a race that understood and appreciated music. Analogy was the only way she could put into words what they had both seen. *"These moments, these jostlings for dominance and existence, are metal strings, strung on a frame and mounted on a wall. I am merely a pick sent to pluck them . . . but I am a pick that can peer into the composer's mind and strive to change the melody before each note is written down and played in the great concert we call existence, in the hopes of bringing forth a greater song with a far better harmony. This is what I strive to do. This is what I have always tried to do."*

Fearsome Leader bowed slightly to her. *"I have seen. I as well strive for harmony. The Salik are discord, of too much strength, not enough give. Breaking of glass leads to shattering of vital fluids. Silence, if unfortunate, is better the choice . . . even if must be the whole section of instruments removed."*

"It is *a most unfortunate necessity, since even they have produced some beautiful notes from time to time,"* Ia murmured wryly. *"But they refuse to play in concordance with the rest of us."*

Kzul flexed an arm, rippling his membrane-wing. *"Without losing its pleasure, one cannot play forever the same song. They will not change their notes. We must change our notes and song. It is . . . regretted their instrument must be gone."*

"Yes. But necessary," Ia agreed. *"I return you now to your body, Fearsome Kzul. Breathe steadily when you return, and do not rise quickly. Let the energy of the radiations revive you."*

He bowed again, his skin gleaming opalescent in the light of the rising temporal sun. Ia lowered her aching arm and opened her eyes in reality, and found she had to squint to see past the darkened, protective glass. Stretching his limbs, the alien slowly shifted. It took him half a minute, but he rose from his lounger. Stepping up to the observation window, he braced his long-fingered hands against the pane, pressing against it even as his wing tips stretched out a little, the flaps falling in graceful folds to either side. His voice came through the speaker, flavored with a metallic hint of the greater echoing of the timeplains.

"I have *seen*. This is something must we do, not should we do, to regain the harmony of peace. Name I now as Highest Flight Leader Ia, second to me. I have seen how she directs only where must things be. No wasted radiance. No abuses. All is honorable. Her words are now as commands to our forces. So I say, Fearsome Leader Kzul sh'Kul Vzang' *snEE'EE*," he half clicked, half whistled at the end.

His co-Leader, Glorious Leader Zyx, tilted her head. "What was seen, Fearsome Kzul?"

Stepping closer, he pressed both of his limbs against the thick safety pane, flattening the somewhat rubbery flesh of his keel. He stared at the others though, and not at his fellow Chinsoiy. "Battle. Destruction. Death. Word you Humans use. *Hope*. It is worth diving for, this *hope*."

"When you have time to order your thoughts on your experience, Fearsome," Ia suggested in the thoughtful quiet following his words, "I suggest you write them down, parse them into the trade tongue, and share them with the others. But keep silent on what will happen to the Salik for now." She glanced to her side at Myang and Mandella. "You will *all* get whatever prophetic orders I can pass along, regardless of my rank among you, but if I have an *official* rank, then my directives will be passed along much more swiftly and will be heeded without bureaucratic hassle."

"Rrrrank you have, powerrr you have, Rrroyal War Seerrr

Prrrinncess," Queen Surshan dismissed, flicking one velvet gray ear as a Human version would have flipped her hand. "Do nnnot pull in de *whole* fleet, but . . . some, you may."

Curling her fingers into claws, Ia inverted one over the other in front of her chest and bowed in the formal style of a Solarican Seer-psychic.

"I would not leave any of your worlds defenseless without solid, desperate reason, Majesty," Ia demurred. "With luck, trust, and obedience, I will not ever have to ask such a sacrifice of your people." Straightening, she looked at the others. At Emperor Ki'en-qua, at the Gatsugi President, at the K'Katta and the Tlassian leaders. "With my superiors' permission, I will accept and not abuse these levels of authority among the Solaricans, Terrans, and Chinsoiy."

"You have it among the V'Dan as well, General. You have not guided us wrong, fettered though you have been so far," Ki'en-qua stated. "I have already drawn up the orders that place you as Grand General of the War among the V'Dan— not just an equal to my High Command, but their overall leader, in anticipation of this very request."

He glanced to the gray-haired man seated at his side. Ia hadn't seen Grand General Ibeni-Zif since formally revealing her existence to him and the other representatives of the First Human Empire, over two years ago. Ibeni-Zif bowed his head, acceding to his emperor's stated wishes.

"As the High One herself once wrote, '*Iantha'nn sud-dha.*' As the Prophet wills it . . . and more importantly, as my Emperor wills it. I am no follower of the Sh'nai," he admitted dryly, "but I do concede you are the Prophet and have the knowledge to lead us safely out of this war. I thank you for sharing it, and for being willing to help all of us, not just your fellow Terrans."

Ia bowed her head to both men in thanks.

"The Granndmasssster of the Affffasso hasz never sssteered uss wronng, regardinng you," the Tlassian warlord stated. He flexed his neck muscles for a moment, partially flaring his hood. Folding his hands together over his chest, he bowed from his seat. "I will accssept Gennneral Ia asss my equal, inn the trussst she will nnnot abuse such privilegesss."

"Sschah nakh," Ia thanked him in his native tongue, fingers interlaced as she bowed in return.

"Ssthienn nakh," he returned politely. He didn't have to consult with his secular coleader; the crestless Tlassian technically was here simply to provide support—literal in terms of supplies and citizens—to the efforts of the warrior caste, which were in charge during any discussion involving a war. In this case, he even spoke for the crested priest caste, who had remained on their motherworld to ensure that at least one leader was still available to their race at all times.

"General/Warleader Ia is/is/is honorable/valiant/resourceful/ knowledged," Guw-shan stated even as Ia straightened. "We/ We do/will not/not/not object/hesitate to give/giving her/the General equal/coleadership with/alongside our military/war-leaders."

That gave her the Terrans, V'Dan, Chinsoiy, Solaricans, Tlassians, and the Gatsugi. Technically the Feyori as well, though they hadn't been invited to this event. Ia turned to face the K'Katta faction. It was not Chiswick who spoke, however, but rather the political leader, Pr'tr'k'ktrik, Pritter for the ease of Terranglo-speakers. Lighter in color than the male, and larger, she raised herself off her bench-seat, then stepped up onto it. Curling her forelegs together, claw tips interlacing in a deliberately Human-like gesture equal to clasped hands, she made her statements in a chittering-backed voice-over through her translator.

"We have studied the history, culture, and ways of the Humans, both V'Dan and Terran. We have found you to be violent, bloody, dangerous, and more than willing to slaughter your own kind over the course of your history. You have also stood ready to slaughter all other sentients . . . according to your entertainments. You even make *games*," the female translator-voice drawled, programmed to put meaning-based inflections into its efforts, "out of your deep-seated need to fight, slaughter, and compete."

"We acknowledge this," Premiere Mandella stated calmly. Not quite stiffly, but with a definite touch of wariness for the topic. Across from him, the V'Dan Emperor dipped his head in silent, wry acknowledgment as well. Mandella made a passable Gatsugi hand gesture for ironic agreement. "There are similar troubles in all sentient species to one degree or another. Life itself is a struggle to survive."

Pritter made a close approximation of the same gesture with one of her spare forelimbs, curling and splaying her finger-like claw tips. "Truth. Yet you have also shown great depths of compassion and aid for your own kind, and for those who are not your own kind. Even for non-sentientkind. You make pets out of the creatures you would otherwise eat . . . and you continue to eat their kin. You are, as a species, illogical and insane. We are the embodiment of your species-deep fears and nightmares," her translator box offered in its neutral-female voice over her quiet chitterings, "yet the vast majority of you have overcome the, ah . . . *willies*, I believe is the term?"

Mandella chuckled softly, relaxing a little. "Yes. An archaic term, but very apt. Meeting such a polite and caring race as yours has helped many of us overcome such fears—"

"—Yes, Premiere," Pritter interrupted, raising a third foreleg in another Human-based gesture, this time for quiet and patience. Ia noted with detached amusement that the alien had one of her claws pulled in, similar to the Gatsugi gesture she herself had used. Pritter continued. "We know the long-standing histories between our kinds. The Salik are not nearly so complex to understand as the Humans . . . but for all your deep-bleeding history, you are not nearly so dangerous as they.

"We have studied the efforts of General Ia. Our spies among the Terrans have uncovered interesting truths in her early days in the military." The K'Katta paused while Mandella blinked and looked at Myang, but neither the Admiral-General nor Ia were moved by that admission. *Every* race in the Alliance spied on the others, both in military and civilian matters. It was simply good sense. What Pritter had to say next was not commonly known to the leaders around them, however. "In every instance, when asked how she felt for the Salik, this Human has said she feels pity. That hers is Human-based pity . . . but it is suspected, Salik-based as well."

"Purely Human," Ia confessed, knowing the K'Katta was looking at her with at least two of those dark eyes. "But I needed the Salik to believe it came from their own perspective of the term."

"Yes, you hunt with xenopsychology in your mind," Pritter stated, rapping the underside of her abdomen with a footclaw, the cultural equivalent of a Human tapping her skull. "So I must ask this question. Given that it sounds as if you are talking not just containment of the Salik nation, but of their destruction . . . are you talking about xenocide? Of deliberately crushing them, all of them, egg to grave, and removing them completely from this galaxy?"

Ia sucked in a breath at the blunt question. She knew how the baring of her teeth would be interpreted by the Solaricans and the Tlassians, but grimaced anyway. "Technically . . . *technically*, it will be assisted suicide, meioa. As awful as they are toward others, as bloodthirsty and flesh-hungry as they are as a species . . . I would rather have given them the chance to live if they could have changed their minds about attacking and devouring the rest of us. If they *would* have changed their minds."

"*That* is why you went to Sallha," President Pritter stated. It was not a question.

Ia answered it as if it were one, anyway. "Yes. Every life is precious. Every life should be given a chance to live, to try to find happiness, fulfillment, and purpose . . . but that does *not* mean finding happiness, fulfillment, and purpose in slaughtering others, because those lives have just as much a right to live. One of our Human religions has a saying, 'So long as it harms no one, do whatever you will.' It is a wise saying and applies even to oneself. But when those actions harm others, then that overwhelming freedom must be curtailed. Mostly, we try to curtail it in wise laws . . . but sometimes we must curtail it in strong actions.

"The good of the many outweighs the good of the few, whether it is a scale of one to five, or a hundred to a million . . . or two hundred billion versus several septillion lives. *If* the Salik could fight against their instincts and successfully change their ways, then I would be working to save them," Ia pledged. "But they will not. My being elevated to the rank of General was a far higher probability than their changing their ways . . . and I can tell you freely I did *not* expect to stand here before you as anything other than a Ship's Captain, today, to ask for a temporary elevation in rank."

"I'm glad I can still surprise you," Myang muttered. "And it still *might* be temporary if you step too far out of line."

Ia ignored it, keeping her gaze on the alien politician. "As I am driven by the compassion of my conscience, meioa, I still had to try. But the Salik will not change."

"I am ssurrrprised advannncsed as fffar as thhey did," the Solarican Queen muttered, heavily ringed ears flicking briefly backwards. "Sssentient they are. Ssophffontic, dey are nnnot. De actions of artifishul intelligence machines vould be more logical, even on a rrrampage."

"Yes. That is our regretful conclusion as well," Pritter said. Unclasping her forelegs, she planted them on the padded stool serving as her perch. "Promise me, Prophet, that you will do your best to save as many lives as you can while directing this war."

"I already have." At the upward curl of the K'Katta's forelegs, Ia spread her hands. "I am here, after all . . . and I will ask nothing of your people that I am not prepared to do, or give, or be, myself. Up to and including my own death, if need be."

"Absolutely *not*," Myang protested, scowling at Ia.

"Not on your life. We *need* you," Mandella added sternly.

"No, sirs. You need my *prophecies*," Ia corrected the Terran Premiere. "All else is negotiable."

"I absolutely *forbid* you to undertake any action which will end in your death," Myang ordered, pushing to her feet.

Ia gave her an annoyed look. "With respect, sir, even the *Feyori* are not immortal. The day I was *conceived*, I undertook the very action which will end in my death. It's called 'being alive in the first place.' And I'll remind you that it is not *my* actions alone which must be considered. Everyone else has a part to play—and you cannot use the argument that I can foresee any such death at the hands of others," she added. "All of the things I can affect and change are *probabilities*, not absolute concrete certainties—I got shot in the shoulder on a less than three percent chance, and you'd think that the other ninety-seven of those chances would have negated that.

"*You* granted me the rank of General on a probability chance far, far smaller than that. I am grateful beyond words, but I *still* have the right to refuse an order, even as a non-precognitive, when I know it is impossible to carry out, sir. And that one *is* impossible. Whether I die of old age at 105, or get hit by a rogue meteorite in the next ten seconds, I *will* eventually die, sir. I am powerful, but I am *mortal*. So that is one order I *cannot* obey. Neither can you, since a rogue asteroid could hit *you*, too."

Myang started to speak, then paused and looked up, lips moving as she counted silently. From the looks of the others, the way the Gatsugi president tipped his head cautiously upward, so did they. When more than ten seconds had passed without a rogue impact, Ia turned back to the K'Katta leader.

"Does my answer, and my willingness, satisfy your concerns, Meioa President?" she asked the alien.

Pritter remained where she stood for a long moment . . . then stepped down off the stool-shaped bench. Settling her legs around her, she rested her abdomen on the padded surface and chittered. "It will do, for now. You will be granted high rank among us. For the course of this war, your orders and your prophecies will be obeyed."

"Thank you. That is all I require." Ia dipped her head. Turning to the two Humans on her left, she shifted into Attention stance, boots together, arms at her sides. "With your permission, Admiral-General, Premiere Mandella, I wish to be free to accept these ranks and responsibilities among our allies, for the betterment of our mutual war effort, sirs."

"And if I bust you back down to Ship's Captain?" Myang asked her, raising one brow.

"I would still ask your permission for these liberties for the duration of the Salik and Grey Wars," Ia told the shorter woman. "I know my limitations, sir. I know where best I can be used and where best I must not be used. I don't have the time to spare for wasting my efforts."

Myang stared at her for a long moment, then sighed heavily. "Well, you did say you'd take the bit in your teeth and run with it."

The older woman's arms started to shift, either to fold across her chest or to plant on her hips, but the Admiral-General was just as much aware of what world they were on, and refrained from making any gestures that might be misinterpreted by their hosts. A subtle shrug was near universal as a gesture. A belligerent pose was not. She merely clasped her hands together.

"Just how far do you intend to run with this 'assisted suicide' of the Salik nation, soldier? Or should I demand that you carry a portable shield generator wherever you go in order to avoid that random meteorite strike?" she asked Ia.

"It matters not how far I run, so long as I run down the *right* path . . . and lugging a shield generator, literal or metaphor, would slow me down, sir. There are others who can follow, take up the bit, and run with it if I should hit a . . . well, a three percent problem and fall down on the job, but I do have contingencies for avoiding that three percent problem," Ia told her. "We won't fix either problem today, tomorrow, next week, or anytime soon. So between now and the end of the wars, I promise you I will dodge all the meteorites I can because I still have far too much to do."

That was enough in her superior's eyes. Christine Myang nodded sharply. "Then you have *my* permission." Turning crisply, she faced Premiere Mandella, also at Attention. "Sir. I request *your* permission to place General Ia in charge of the combined Alliance war efforts, sir."

Ia remembered how, as the Secondaire, Justinn Mandella had been willing to salute her in public rather than the other way around. She remembered how he had promised to speak at her Board of Inquiry for hiding her psychic abilities. Thankfully, that probability had been avoided because she *had* been registered and tested by a duly authorized organization as part of her "religious" affiliations, which had already been listed in her military file.

But how he thought of her now that he was the Premiere, she didn't know. Facing the dark-skinned Human, she waited for him to make up his mind. With the others on her side, she knew what her greatest probability was, and the second strongest, though both were close: forty-eight percent to forty-five. But there were still other choices, up to seven percent's worth. Seven was larger than a mere three percent.

"We cannot have one of our four-star generals in charge of this war," Mandella finally stated, remaining in his seat. Myang blinked and frowned, but Ia relaxed. She knew where he was going on this probability. "Admiral-General Myang will remain in charge of you for oversight reasons, but as your Commander in Chief, I am elevating you to . . . how did our esteemed, Eternal associate put it? Ah, yes. General of the War. Five-starred, and ranked over all where the military needs of these two wars are concerned. Are my fellow leaders all agreed that she now has this authority?"

Around the room, and even in the irradiated chamber, the leaders and coleaders all nodded and gestured their agreement.

"Then you have that rank. The paperwork will be filled out shortly. Or rather, I think we will call you a twist on an old term from our own history: the General of the Alliance Armies. As far as the Second Salik War and the coming Grey War you have warned us about, you are now in charge, Ia. Lead us how you will," he told her. "Just lead us down the *right* path, as far and fast as you can run while still looking up to keep it from heading into Hell, for the preservation of the many lives at stake."

"I will do my best, sir," Ia told him. Tucking her hand into her left pocket—rather than the right-hand one, which had held the results for the forty-five percent probability—she dug out a box containing the datachips needed. "At this point in time, it is not necessary for me to exercise the full rights and responsibilities of my new position. I will therefore gladly defer to my coleaders and their current strategies, except for what few directives I can give you at this time.

"I will let each of you know in advance before I must take full command of all of our combined forces," she stated, facing the others. "In the meantime, please accept my apologies for the difficulties the Dabinian passion moss is causing on your various worlds as an invasive species. Trust me when I say it will be easier to spend twenty-five years in a botanical nightmare of fighting the moss incursions, versus trying to deal with the cost of allowing the Salik to remain on *any* of our worlds."

". . . Of this warning, I can confirm," Fearsome Leader Kzul stated through his comm speaker. "The moss will prevent death upon death. Nerve-aches it will cause, but death it will not."

Ia nodded in his direction, silent thanks for the Chinsoiy's support. Cracking open the case, she lifted the chips out with her mind, sorted them telekinetically, and sent them across the room, grouped in sets of five and six and nine, including a cluster sent to a slot next to the observation window for the Chinsoiy delegation. Activating the controls remotely, she slipped them inside and let the mechanism pass them through the trio of airlocks to the irradiated chambers beyond. The rest settled onto tables in front of their respective parties as she outlined their strategic objectives.

"These are our strategic objectives for the next few months: We must kick the Salik into space. The only worlds they will be allowed to inhabit will be their own . . . and by that, I mean the *Salik* worlds alone. We *must* fight to get them off the Choya colonies as well." She dipped her head toward Pritter. "The Choya are not quite so blood-hungry as their current allies, and can eventually be convinced to see reason and seek peace. We must strive to do so, so we can save them from themselves.

"For the rest, the military portions are done for now, and we all have more pressing concerns to address. For myself, I have a small problem coming up in the next half hour. I would like to attend to it personally if I may have your permission to go?" she asked, glancing to her left.

Mandella nodded. "Since you say we can handle the rest on our own, we shall do so. Go do what you need to do, General of the Armies."

"Sir, yes, sir." Ia saluted crisply, received one in return from the Premiere and the Admiral-General, and turned to head toward the nearest exit.

"One more thing, General Ia," Christine Myang interrupted, her voice dripping with payback for all the times Ia had done this to her.

"Sir?" Ia stated, turning politely to face her superior.

"Denora de Marco—that reporter you gave an interview to back on Dabin, regarding the effort to free her homeworld? Apparently, you 'gave good interview' to her," Myang told her. "A very good interview. It's been replaying on most of the major news shows, Human and otherwise, and it's proved very popular.

"She has requested a series of longer follow-ups. It would

be very good public relations for the war effort for you to continue to give interviews when requested. I'll trust you to keep your mouth shut about various military and Alliance secrets . . . but you will speak with her and continue to give 'good interviews.' The Special Forces Psychology Department believes it will help the morale of soldiers and civilians alike if the general populace knows what 'The Prophet General' is doing and thinking."

"Sir, yes, sir," Ia said. "I was aware it was a possibility when I gave the initial interview. I'll do my best to keep up the morale of the Alliance as a whole in my future talks with her."

A flick of Myang's hand dismissed her. Ia turned and strode once more for the door.

Behind her, she heard Emperor Ki'en-qua state dryly, "We would like to borrow General Ia for similar interviews and statements for our own people to hear. Her initial recording confirming the legitimacy of my reign must be updated."

"You have our permission," Premiere Mandella told him.

"Thank you. Respectfully, meioa . . . do not think this means *you* are in charge of the Alliance, Premiere Mandella. We are all still equals in this chamber," Ki'en-qua warned him, as Ia touched the controls to open the door.

"I wouldn't dream of being anything less, Eternity, and I certainly will not ask for anything more," Mandella returned calmly as Ia stepped through. His voice grew fainter as she moved away. "There are still many good reasons for our two empires to remain separate. Now, we should probably call the Dlmvlan Nes—"

The airlock-style door hissed shut behind her. Gatsugi soldiers stood on duty inside the foyer-like middle chamber, their equivalent of stunner rifles held horizontally at the ready in their lower arms, laser rifles cradled vertically in the upper. They let her pass without a word. Ia waited until she was in the corridor outside—where clusters of soldiers from the different races waited patiently while their carbon-based, oxygen-breathing leaders sat and discussed interstellar policies—before slipping her headset wires over her ear and activating it with a tap on her arm unit.

"General Ia to the Damnation. *Is everyone on board, except for Yamasuka?"* Her ear still itched. Now that she wasn't

focused on navigating her way to her political needs, she was aware of it once again. She rubbed at it absently.

"Aye, sir," she heard Teevie, one of Second Watch's comm techs, reply. *"Yeoman Yamasuka is waiting on the shuttle pad as per your orders. The rest are holding a party up here in the Wake Zone, and are busy admiring their newly acquired glittery. Speaking of which, congratulations on your Medal of Honor, sir."*

"Thank you. I hope they don't give me many more, though. I'm running out of room on a knee-length coat, not to mention running out of flesh in my ear. The yeoman and I will be joining you as soon as we can, but we . . . have a little task to undertake first. Enjoy your Wake hours in the meantime. Ia out."

With the cooperation of the Alliance leaderships ending her part of their meeting so quickly, she had an extra half hour in which to personally attend to the trouble spot in question. Somewhere out there, once it was deep in interstitial space, a merchant freighter needed to break down at a specific place and time. At the moment, the unlucky ship was in dock at the edge of the next system out from the Gatsugi motherworld.

With Yeoman First Class Ariel Yamasuka's help, she could swing out there via the fancy other-than-light capabilities of the new shuttles that had come with their new ship. They could fly close enough to the space station that merchant ship was docked at for Ia to psychically plant some sabotage to guarantee the vessel would go off course and break down at just the right place and time, and not just rely on a ninety-seven percent chance that it should and would.

Ia and her shuttle pilot would come back with enough minutes left on the ever-ticking clock to stay on schedule for everything else in the days ahead. She had agents—paid for by her brother—who were standing ready to commit those same crimes, but with this early dismissal, it was a burden she could take onto herself. A burden she needed to take up personally, given what she had just pledged to the leaders of the Alliance. The unwitting crew of that ship were going to be the bait in her biggest trap of the war. Not for many months yet . . . but eventually, yes.

One more set of murders on my conscience, she thought grimly, knowing the names and faces and lives of each sentient she was about to sacrifice on board the *Bee's Knees.* Not the most auspicious of ship names, but a necessary one. *Patient Zero, as it were—or rather, the Index Case. Could've been worse, though; the captain could have gone with his alternate name for the ship, the* God Sneezed. *That would've been painfully ironic.*

Her earlobe still itched. Striding along the corridors of the palatial Gatsugi government building, she rubbed gingerly at it. She would have to see Doctor Mishka when she got back to the ship to make sure it wasn't due to some low-key infection. Or . . .

Ia skimmed the immediate timestreams, and winced. *No, it's the damned metal alloys the Solaricans used. I think Human skin might be a little more acidic than Solarican, because it's reacting with my innate electrokinesis, acting like a slagging closed circuit. Let's see if there's a fix . . . Yeah. I'll have to go see Private Dubsnjiadeb for an enamel coating from her cloisonné art supplies to protect my skin, and do so quietly since I can't exactly ditch the thing or replace it with a different metal. Not without insulting Her Majesty and losing my rank.*

OCTOBER 3, 2498 T.S.
PROXIMA CARINAE SYSTEM

"In a way, I still can't believe you want *me* to do these interviews," Denora de Marco stated over the hyperrelay link between them. The Dabinian woman shrugged and flicked her hands as she spoke, visible from the ribs up against the background of her dark purple suit and the dusky blue wall of her office. "I mean, I *know* Mark Optermitter wanted to get an interview with you, seeing as how he covers the big stories from *Confucius* Station to Sanctuary and back, and Keileen van Sommers has been bragging how she has an 'in' with the Press Room at the Tower, so it was bound to be her plum to pick. Or you could've even picked a big name like Sergei Hasmapana. So, why me? Asking off the record, of course."

At the moment, there was only a second and a half of delay

between them on the hyperrelays, hardly enough to slow down a normal conversation. Parked at the shipyards in orbit around Jupiter, Ia had borrowed a window of time for this speech.

"Off the record? A couple of reasons," she admitted. She checked the feedback view of her own image on her third tertiary screen, centered beneath the primary one displaying Denora's image. A stray lock of white hair was arching up a little in unruly rebellion. Smoothing it down, she explained why. "First and foremost, you gave a good interview. You're not afraid to ask tough questions, but you don't ask *only* the tough questions. You're personable and sympathetic, but you don't hog the camera."

"I'm not Sergei," Denora muttered. "That's *off* the record for me, too, if you don't mind," she added.

Ia smiled briefly. "That's another of the reasons. Yes, you did a good job on the Dabin interview, but you're not focused solely on getting—no, on *wringing* the most out of any interview. I'm not a wet towel that you get to twist moisture out of in order to water your story and make it grow."

"Which would be Keileen," Denora agreed wryly.

"Exactly," Ia said. "*You* want to hear what *I* actually want to say, not whatever I have to say about a specific event you're interested in, or whatever you want to *hear* about a specific story angle, regardless of what I want to say about it. There are things I cannot tell the Alliance as a whole because they're classified so high up, only a handful of people know anything about what happened. These are things that some reporters would press too hard trying to find out, and if they start to dig, it would cause trouble. I know you *do* want to know, but you're respectful in how you go about it. You know better than most when to press and dig for what your viewers need to know, and when to back off and let go."

The brunette on the other end of the comm link gave Ia a flat look. ". . . You mean, I'm the least likely reporter to screw up your precognitive efforts. There are enough Sh'nai followers here on Dabin that even I know they believe you can actually see the entire span of the future. If that's true even in the smallest part, then you are picking me because I won't screw things up for you . . . am I right?"

Ia had the grace to dip her head. "That, too. But you really do ask the right questions, the ones that make people *think* about what they're hearing. The ones that dig for the context of the facts as well as for those facts."

Denora quirked a brow at that, her expression still skeptical. "Are you speaking precognitively, General? About things you've seen me actually doing in the near future?"

"Precognitively *and* postcognitively. I've seen some of your other interviews, too," Ia told her. "You're interested in the truth, and you'll prod and poke around for it, but you accept it for what it is. You don't feel a need to force it out of a person, or worse, force it into a specific shape."

"True. My philosophy is, the truth wouldn't *be* the truth if we tried to reshape it, now would it?" the reporter stated wryly, acknowledging Ia's point. "I think sometimes my fellow reporters forget that when trying to chase down a specific spin or twist to the truth. It comes and goes in cycles, but sometimes they don't pay attention to the actual facts as much as they pay court to that perfect story they want to present. As far as *I'm* concerned, if they want to twist a story away from the truth and the facts, then they should admit to everyone that they're really trying to create works of fiction and not engaging in actual journalism."

"How very true—ah, the caf' maker just finished. Let me get a fresh cup," Ia added, turning her chair to the right to access the drinks dispenser in her office. She extracted the mug, sipped from it, and clipped it to her desk. Facing the embedded pickups on her workstation screen, she adjusted the fit of her Dress Blacks, briefly made sure the medals and ribbons weren't tangled up from her movements, then nodded. "Shall we get started?"

Denora checked what looked like a datapad—only the corner of it was visible at the edge of the viewscreen—then set it down and nodded. Shifting forward, she tapped something into her own workstation. "Don't worry about pauses or hesitations in speaking, as those can be edited out. And if you want anything removed from the interview before it airs, I'll do my best to comply. I know the Space Force is trusting me with these interviews as well as yourself, though they have asked I work with a liaison at the Army HQ here in the capital before I broadcast anything. So. Are you ready, General?"

Ia nodded and squared her shoulders, clasping her hands lightly together in her lap. "I am ready, Meioa de Marco."

"Beginning recording in three . . . two . . . This is Denora de Marco of the Dabinian branch of the Interstellar News Network," she stated, staring straight ahead in that way all seasoned reporters employed to attempt to connect with whoever was on the other side of the viewscreen. "I am here on a hyperrelay chat with none other than the newly minted head of the joint Alliance Armies, General Ia, formerly from Independent Colonyworld Sanctuary, heaviest of the inhabited heavyworlds, and now a loyal Terran soldier.

"If all goes well, the two of us will be conducting these interviews via hyperrelay chat over the next several months. Bear in mind that, given the strenuous needs of the current war and the fact that General Ia is apparently not a soldier to sit behind a desk all day, we will not always be able to bring these interviews to our viewers on a regular schedule. Hopefully, our INN audience will forgive us for these unavoidable delays, and hopefully you will all come back and follow along with each session as we get to know the mind behind the Alliance's best efforts at ending these unwanted aggressions.

"We go now live to the Harasser-Class starship TUPSF *Damnation*. Welcome, General Ia, and thank you for accepting my request for an in-depth interview. I understand you have an opening speech prepared?" de Marco asked her politely.

"Yes, I do, Meioa de Marco. Thank you for allowing me this rare opportunity. I don't have a lot of time to spare—I've never had a lot of time, to be honest," Ia added in an aside, "—but there are certain things I've always wanted to share. Indulging your request will give me the chance to review some of the things I've done, and explain some of the reasons why I did them. Like a stage magician revealing how the trick is done, I've wanted to communicate the whys of my actions, but I haven't always had the opportunity before now. And, now that I finally have the time, I feel the need to speak. So I thank you for your offer to interview me."

"The pleasure is all mine, General." Denora demurred. "So, can you tell me where and when all of this started? Your career, your ambitions, and the prodding of your precognitive abilities? What happened in your childhood to lead you to this unique position you now fill?"

"I won't waste your time with the trivial details of my childhood," Ia dismissed. "I was happy for the most part, well loved by my family, had a reasonably good education, and usually had good food to eat and clean clothes to wear . . . the usual, and therefore boring. Instead, I'll start with the day I joined the military. That's not the moment it all began, of course," she said, "but you could say it's the best starting point I have."

Denora nodded. "Then let's begin with that, shall we? According to the file the Department of Innovations handed to me, you first joined on your eighteenth birthday . . ."

CHAPTER 3

*Everyone accuses me of manipulating my enemies through
xenopsychology. My dealings with K'Katta crime lords,
Gatsugi Blockade smugglers, and, of course, multiple
wartime confrontations with the Salik are all openly doc-
umented incidents in the unclassified portions of my military files. Even the Feyori, half enemy and half ally that
they are, have been maneuvered via my grasp of their
Meddling ways. But people forget this also works for one's
allies.*

*Of course, it's not politically astute to openly admit it,
but diplomats have been doing so since the very first
representatives of one cultural, racial, or species-based
group tried to negotiate with another group. Is it wrong to
manipulate someone via their own culture, their mental
workings? Maybe yes, and maybe no. A gun is no less dangerous if wielded wrongfully or by ignorant hands . . . yet no
less helpful in the right hands wielding it at the right time.*

*So, too, are words and gifts. Intentions, meioa, have al-
ways been the deciding factor. Am I wielding a gun to shoot
someone with no reason other than to murder them, or
am I wielding a gun to shoot the person trying to murder*

someone else? Perhaps it's a dramatic analogy, but it is an understandable one.

Of course, I can tell you over and over what I was trying to do and why I was trying to do it, but in the end, history will have to be the final judge of my intentions. The everlasting price of being a prophet lies in the truism, "Only time will tell." Which is why I've wanted to tell you what my intentions are in the here and now, so that in time you can judge whether or not my efforts were aimed at the right targets. I suppose you could say it's also a way of reminding myself to look up on a regular basis as I'm busy paving the road to the galaxy's salvation, so that I don't instead pave it all the way into Hell.

But, if I ever do have to go into Hell? I'll make damned sure it's the Devil that comes running out.

~Ia

OCTOBER 21, 2498 T.S.
SIC TRANSIT

"In order to thwart further Feyori influences, I am advising you, flat out, to pass the tactical planning on how to carry out those goals into the hands of the people in the field," July Ia stated, as her October counterpart peered into the timestreams, watching for this very moment, *"who know best how to adapt their maneuvers to the immediate needs of the terrain, their personal resources, and the enemy forces they face. A method which we already know works well, and which we have known since the twenty-first century works very well."*

Her younger self dropped her arms to her sides, staring hard with her one eye at Brigadier General José Mattox. Back then, July Ia hadn't paid much attention to what the others were doing, beyond a peripheral awareness that they weren't interfering. Kneeling on the edge of her own life-stream, braced so that her nose was mere centimeters from the rippling waters, Ia searched the faces around her counterpart. Some were hesitant, a few uneasy, trapped in the awkward, inescapable moment. But the majority of the dozen or so men and women gathered in the tactical room looked like they were going to support their immediate superior over her logical words.

Mattox himself certainly wasn't going to give way. *"Ship's Captain Ia,"* he stated blandly, his expression as implacable as granite. *"Please leave the tactical room."*

Any moment now, Ia thought, watching her other self.

"Now, Captain," he ordered.

"Then you leave me no choice," her younger self stated, about to begin a chain of events that would be too dangerous at this time.

Quick as a thought—with a thought—Ia dipped her finger into the surface, connecting with her younger mind. (*Don't even think about it. Not while the Feyori are still here.*)

She watched July Ia blink twice, and abruptly change her plans. *". . . I think I'll go take up cheese-making. I'm sure it'll be more productive than this."*

The non sequitur caused several of the other Humans in the tactical room to blink and frown in equal confusion. A slight curl to Mattox's lips caught her attention, but it was so brief, October Ia had to replay it in the timestreams twice before she could be sure. Half smirk, half sneer, it was the look of someone who was taking pleasure in a brief moment of triumph over an inferior.

I guess the changes nudged into place by Ginger were welcomed by his innermost personality flaws, she thought. *Younger me will be popping onto the timeplains soon. I should get into position.*

Pushing to her feet, she headed downstream a few paces, found her entry point, and jumped in . . . but didn't flip back into her own body. Instead, she hovered around the midpoint like a gymnast resting on a horizontal bar, waiting for the right moment to drop, spin, and emerge with athletic effort for another go-round.

Her body lay on a comfortable cot in the *Damnation*'s infirmary, hooked up to nutrient drips after conferring with Mishka. It was Private Jjones who had in a roundabout way reminded Ia of the need for such precautions. Back then, the transgendered woman had advised her in a motherly way to eat and drink while directing the battles on Dabin psychically. This attempt was different only in that it would be worse. Much worse. It was only wise to be prepared for the coming strain.

October Ia knew something her younger self hadn't. Something she hadn't realized until today. It wasn't just her precognitive actions July of this year that had to be sheltered from detection. It wasn't just from the Feyori that she had to hide. It wasn't even that first moment of self-contact in March of the previous year that had to be concealed. It was her *youngest* self, from that bland morning over eleven years ago when Ia had been a young and troubled Iantha Quentin-Jones, forced to face the horrors of Time blossoming in her young, prophetic mind.

That Ia had to be kept in the dark because if her youngest, precognitively aware version of herself could have known all of this, then far too many choices would have been made out of the naïve urge to get everything done faster and better. Everything would have broken and fallen into hopeless, unfixable ruin.

Rising out of the dizzying place between body and Time, she stepped onto the bank, mentally making sure she was clad in just a gray T-shirt and pants, with no sign of the rank she would have attained. There were several possible Ia-selves that her younger self could be visiting, after all . . . just as there had been a Chinsoiy version to deal with back in August.

(*Got it in one* go,) she praised her earlier self, (*and an excellent moment in time for it. You figured out which one to confront, yet?*)

(*Miklinn,*) the younger, one-eyed Ia confirmed. (*These two are lackeys. Loyal, but stupid. I need to catch and control the fanged head of this serpent, not waste my time wrestling with its coils. And it'll be either a case of conversion to my cause, or . . . yeah.*)

(*Yeah,*) October Ia agreed. (*Either path will end up with you here, being me. But be careful all the same. Remember, to see the true path ahead of you, you'll have to come to this point in time, and work your way back upstream.*)

(*Understood. Ready?*) younger Ia asked her older self.

(*I am.*) October Ia lifted her hands, shifting the shape of the Plains into a copy of Trondhin Lake. From there, Time expanded outward, forward and back, up and down, left and right. She settled herself on the grass in a position not too dissimilar from the younger one's back at that lakeshore on the real Dabin. She didn't watch July Ia leave, just closed her eyes, gathered her composure, and readied her mental energies. A last whisper of thought pushed toward her younger, earlier self. (*Go get 'em, meioa-e . . .*)

A faint splash told her July Ia was gone. Drawing in a deep breath, Ia did what she normally tried to avoid. What she was slowly getting better at doing. This, of all tasks, was the one thing she had to master, or not only would the Feyori win, her younger selves would lose. Here, in this place where a harpstring-plucked decision could become an entire universe of reality, she matched mind to will, mind to power, and will to power. Provoking her biggest enemy with a single, hard-projected thought.

(*TIME.*)

Energy slammed outward, snapping everything up and jostling it back down again. Particularly along the path of her own past. Like the visualization of fireworks overlaid onto the darkest, richest, free-falling space that she had shown the Chinsoiy Fearsome Leader, Ia could see the underlying explosion of events jostling for dominance, for the right to briefly but triumphantly hold their place.

She covered them all. Every single point where Ginger and particularly the precognition-manipulating Teshwun had entered the timeplains. Every single point where *she* had entered the timeplains . . . all the way back to that early June morning when, as a mere fifteen-year-old, she had fallen from dream into nightmare, from blissful ignorance into the turbulent waters of her own life-stream, when her old life had drowned and been washed away. All the way down into the future, too, including every single side possibility her younger selves had, could, would, should, might, and did seek out and explore.

Every last possible glimpse of her own actions phased itself out of sync with reality, save for those where she needed to interact with herself. Ghosts of her younger selves flickered in and out of her perception, translucent images that came and went from this one moment. From this doorway, this portal she painstakingly built into the timeplains.

Older Ias. Younger Ias. Alternate-universe Ias, too . . .

because other October Ias moved in and sat down on the
stream bank before her, beside her, behind her . . . but most of
all, *with* her, united in the need to protect all their younger
selves from this dangerous knowledge of their elder versions
and their later actions.

Together, they hid the knowledge that such interactions
were possible . . . because even for the Prophet of a Thousand
Years, knowing certain things too soon could ruin everything
as surely as knowing it too late to change their galaxy's fate . . .
which they all could see happening in the farther-out possibilities. In the many, many alternate universes where Youngest Ia learned of these things, and failed.

OCTOBER 23, 2498 T.S.
SIC TRANSIT

She still wanted to go back to sleep. Too much effort and energy spent on the timeplains had left Ia drained, to the point
where she was reviewing her backlog of paperwork with the
palm of one hand propping up her forehead, and her other
hand ghosting over the keys, since it was less exhausting to
work manually than to use any psychic abilities.

Except she kept yawning and almost falling asleep. Giving
up briefly, she toed the release lever on her chair and pushed it
sideways toward the caf' dispenser . . . which was nearly
empty. All she got out of the machine was enough for two
mouthfuls of the Terran-V'Dan hybrid brew. Grunting, Ia
pushed herself back into position and pulled up the watch
roster to see which kitchen was active.

There were galleys in the bow and stern sections, as well
as the mini-galley between her office and the bridge, but they
were more designed for grabbing a quick snack, or storing a
hot meal premade in the much larger facilities of either the
fore or aft sectors. Amidships—where the bridge and her
office were located—had its own fancy kitchen, but it was
designated for Wake parties . . . and the Wake hadn't yet officially started.

*Just my luck, I still have thirty-five minutes to go before it'll
be open . . . and my own Company bible rules insist it cannot*

be used outside of Wake hours. Fore galley it is. She thumbed the controls on the comm, connecting to it. *"Fore galley, this is General Ia. I'm out of caf'. Can you spare someone to get a fresh pack up here?"*

"We're on it, sir!" a male voice replied. It took her a few moments to realize it was Clairmont. She hadn't realized that much time had passed.

That's right, he's on galley duty right now, trading off with the secondary scanner tech, who is . . . um . . . Yeah, I'm tired. Pushing away from her desk, Ia rose and walked around her office, trying to regain some energy the old-fashioned way. Except that fresh air was an oxymoron on board a ship, unless one was actually in one of the life-support bays. They weren't going to get any shipped up in sterilized compression tanks from any M-class world in the next few days either, not while they were inbound for the Dlmvlan homeworld. Not unless she wanted her crew to die of asphyxiation since the overgrown aliens breathed a mixture of nitrogen and methane, not nitrogen and oxygen.

Since she was up, she headed back into her quarters to use the head, and when she was done, she mopped her face with a cold, wet cloth. That revived some of her flagging energy, enough that she was back in the chair behind her desk, no longer relying on her palm for support, when the outer door finally chimed.

"Enter." She glanced up as the door slid open to find the new ex-Marine, Julia Garcia, entering with a square tray balanced in one hand. On it were two caf' packs for the dispenser, a steaming-hot mug of freshly brewed caf', and . . . "A bowl of something blue?" she asked, one brow quirking upward. "And white? What is that?"

"Gelatin parfait, sir," Garcia stated, carrying the tray to the desk. Ia quickly moved some of her datapads out of the way, giving the younger woman the chance to slide the tray under two of the support clips along the outer edge in their stead. The younger woman smiled shyly, her tanned cheeks turning a little pink. "Everyone's been so nice to me. So, um, helpful and supportive? And they all say it's 'cause *you* vouched for me. That you believe in me, sir. The Drill Instructors back at Camp Whiteberg believed, but . . .

"Anyway, I was looking through some recipes in the Nets

for, um, Sanctuarian dishes, an' I ran across this one for topado-flavored gelatin desserts. It's, uh, supposed to be served with a trickle of vodka and Gatsugi Blue over the top, but I know you're a psi, and I know strong psis don't like to drink much, so it's just topado gelatin and whipped cream. But it's real cream from a real cow. I pitched in with the crew when we bought some for the last birthday bash, an' this is the last of it before it goes bad, and um, I thought . . ."

Ia held up her hand, chuckling. "You thought you'd do something nice for me in return. Breathe, Private," she added as the brown-haired young woman tugged nervously on one of her two braids. Garcia looked even younger than her twenty-one years, with her hair plaited in two short little pigtails. She didn't know where the other girl had gotten a recipe for topado-flavored gelatin, but even if it tasted nasty—which it wouldn't; her gifts weren't twinging in warning—she wouldn't hurt Garcia's feelings. "I'm flattered. And I could probably use the energy from the protein and the carbs and all."

Nodding quickly, Garcia flapped a hand at the bowl and the spoon clipped on the tray next to the mug. Then started and quickly picked up the caf' packs. "I'll just, um, refill your dispenser, General, sir, while you have your little snack. The caf' in the mug's fresh, roasted not two minutes ago. Um, I was gonna bring up the bowl with your supper, but that's not for another three hours, an' I was going to be off duty at that point. That's when the Wake party's gonna happen, you know, and I was hoping to attend, but I finally got the recipe just right this morning for the gelatin—at least, uh, I think I did, and—"

"*Breathe*, Private," Ia ordered, though she softened it with a chuckle. "I'd know in advance if it were awful. My gift protects me instinctively against stuff like that. I know it's not that bad . . . though I don't know *what* it tastes like. Yet."

"Yes, sir," Garcia mumbled, and concentrated fiercely on the super-complicated—not—task of replacing the depleted caf' packs in the dispenser.

Picking up the spoon, Ia dipped it into the confection. She bypassed the whipped cream, wanting to taste one of the cream-free cubes of gelatin. It wiggled and gleamed on the spoon in a nearly transparent shade somewhere between sky and cobalt blue, but with hints of Prussian and aquamarine wherever shadows touched the stuff. Aside from the fact it was topado blue . . . it looked like any other gelatin dessert out there.

Ia lifted it to her mouth. It tasted meaty, sweet, and smooth, almost like a Jerusalem artichoke, only with a slight tang to it, the tang of topado-flour starch. The flavor pleased her; Ia hadn't had topado-flour starch—a fine, pale blue powder unlike the richer blue of straight topado flour—in far too long. While she had patches of topadoes growing in each of the five life-support bays, those were usually not made into flour, let alone flour starch. With other kinds of starch available far more cheaply on every colonyworld out there, there hadn't been any reason to export the labor-intensive version away from Sanctuary. She literally had not had it since her last visit home.

A soft sound escaped her, and she dug in with the spoon again, taking another mouthful. This time with the whipped cream. The dairy fat added a richness that made her mouth water, and her throat grunted louder in surprise.

"Sir?" Garcia asked, moving close enough to peer over Ia's right shoulder. "Is it okay? Do you want me to take it away?"

Instinct made her scoop her arm protectively around the bowl. Instinct, and a growled, blunt, *"Mine!"*

The ex-Marine gaped at her . . . and then laughed. Giggled breathlessly even, until the brunette had to half sag against the wall and half sit on Ia's desk while she wiped at the tears on her cheeks. Blushing a little, Ia smiled sheepishly at her, waiting until the other woman could breathe normally.

". . . It really *is* that good," Ia told Garcia once she was sure the younger woman would be able to actually listen. "In fact, if it's not an imposition, could you please write up the recipe and be willing to give it to my parents?"

"To your . . . parents, sir?" Garcia asked, blinking in confusion.

"My mothers run a restaurant on Sanctuary, and they specialize in topado-based cuisine, but they've never made anything like this. It must be a new recipe or something. Either way, we'll have one last stop on my homeworld before the *shakk* hits the fan, and this stuff is good enough, they'd be willing to *pay* you to learn how to make this," Ia assured her.

Garcia's blush returned to her heart-shaped face, and

deepened. She ducked her head. "I thought about runnin' a restaurant when I got out, but, um . . . that'll have to wait until the frogtopusses are dead. Can't think about stepping down from the Space Force until we got peace again, or it won't be worth it. I mean, I'm just one little person in a military two billion strong, but, uh . . ."

Ia nodded. *This* was why she had picked Julia Garcia. "You're here for the same reasons I am. One person's efforts might not seem like much, but it's one more than we'd otherwise have, and one more might be just enough one day to make that crucial difference between failure and success when we need it to matter the most."

"Well, yeah," Garcia agreed, shrugging. "That, 'n you think I'll be the most useful here, so how could I step down when the V'Dan Prophet says I'm needed? I'm agnostic, but my granny took me to Sh'nai services whenever I visited her, so I know how important you are."

"Well, don't start worshipping me, or I'll make you scrub the toilet in my head after I've had Private van de Kamp's version of chili," Ia half joked.

Garcia blanched and shook her head quickly. "*No* thank you, sir. I just about fainted from the pepper fumes in the galley last time, and I didn't dare taste it. I don't even want to think about the other end of the digestive process." Straightening, she returned to the caf' dispenser. "I'll just get this fixed up for you while you enjoy your treat, sir. And I'll get that recipe written up for your folks, too."

"I'd appreciate it," Ia murmured. She took another bite of the parfait, then concentrated on her reports. "Thank you for the parfait, by the way. It's making the tedium of all this paperwork more palatable. Literally."

The younger woman coughed, trying to cover up a laugh, then said, "You're welcome, sir. Um . . . are you going to the party? We're all going to zombie-dance at the Wake, since it's Interstellar Zombie Day, back on Earth. Doesn't matter if you aren't any good; Private von Florres is teachin' everybody how to do the moves in the first hour."

"Unfortunately, I don't have the time," Ia said, filling out more of the forms by poking at her keyboard. The parfait was giving her a nice boost of energy; in a few more bites, she might even feel up to handling the forms electrokinetically. She continued absently, her mind more on her work, "Not even if Nuin N'Keth himself somehow showed up and offered to teach me how—actually, if he *did* show up, I would definitely make the time, but he can't, and he won't, so . . ."

"Um, who's that, sir?" Garcia asked her, frowning in confusion.

Lifting her head and her attention from her paperwork, Ia thought about the question. Or rather, the chain of events leading to its answer. That chain had been rewritten with the first "death" in her Company, that of Finnimore Hollick, who had volunteered to give up his very existence so that a dead man could live, love, and sire a whole slough of descendants . . . in particular, a very important man three hundred years from now.

"Technically, he hasn't been born yet, and won't be until after we're all long gone," she said, "But he's one hell of a good dancer. Or will be, one day in the distant future. A pity none of us will live to see him, save for myself in the timestreams."

"Nothin' personal, sir, but um, I'm not the least bit interested in seein' the future," Garcia murmured, snapping the front panel back into place. She tossed the empty caf' packs into the recycler and missed seeing Ia's raised brows. Her next words clarified her meaning. "I got too much work to do in the here an' now to fret over stuff I can't do a damn about. You're all set for fresh caf', sir. Um, lemme know if you need more packs . . . or more parfait."

"Will do, Private." Nodding in both acknowledgment and dismissal, Ia scribbled her name with a stylus and tapped the point against one of the commands on her workstation console. "Have fun lurching about at the Wake, Julia."

"Will do, sir," Garcia agreed, taking herself out of the office.

OCTOBER 26, 2498 T.S.
DULSHVWL, ZZNGH PRIME SYSTEM
DLMVLAN MOTHERWORLD

Yet another Dlmvlan guard towered over the two short-by-comparison Humans, the sixth or so in their trip so far. All the Dlmvla towered over the two Humans, and for once in her life,

Ia actually felt small. She had always been tall for her age and heavyworld gravity back home, and had been roughly normal for the Space Force, average at worst. But here, she finally felt short. It was an interesting sensation.

His iridescent, faceted eyes scrutinized the authorization slips they had picked up from the orbiting Terran embassy. His deep-rumbling voice made the faceplate of Ia's pressure-suit buzz. She didn't speak his language, but she knew the proper responses to make and had programmed them into the arm unit clasped around the outside of her pressure-suit.

Touching the right buttons gave him the correct response via the patch between her unit and her suit speakers, allowing the translation program to do her talking for her. He rumbled something else, gesturing with a claw-like hand. Consulting the timestream, she typed out another reply, then stooped and unlatched the case she was carrying. Opening it up, she pulled out two trays of neatly slotted datachips, and showed him the otherwise-empty interior.

He buzzed an order and gestured, and a smaller, junior guard came trotting up, scanner equipment in hand. He—or she, it was hard to tell at that beige-hued age—scanned the contents, saluted the Dlmvlan with an odd bend of the arm, and trotted back into place, tucked off to one side. Ia approved of the precautions being shown even if they did slow her arrival. They were taking her presence seriously and were allowing her to pass after each challenge.

From somewhere beyond them, a great roar echoed up the broad corridor, the sound of a hundred thousand alien voices, if not more. The guard didn't even glance that way. He did gesture for Ia to repack her case. Helstead, waiting for Ia to do all the work, activated her headset link, though not her suit speaker. *"I will be very glad to get back to actual combat, sir. All this political muck is just that: gross mud that I don't want to wade through. I feel like I'm slogging across Dabin again."*

"I sympathize with how you feel, Delia," Ia replied under her breath, so that their conversation didn't pass through her helmet and into the alien guard's version of ears. *"But it is necessary. Thankfully, this is the last of it for a while . . . or at least before the mountain of fertilizer explodes and hits the atmospheric scrubbers."*

Checking the latches on the case, she straightened and waited patiently while the guard consulted yet another three-meter-tall native of Dulshvwl.

"I am also getting rather warm in this suit, sir," Helstead added pointedly. *"This style of p-suit is designed to reflect stellar radiation while retaining body heat in the chilly depths of space. They're not meant for tramping around in Alliance-standard temperatures for hours on end."*

"Duly noted, Commander, but we'll be here as long as we'll be here." This time, the second guard was the one who beckoned them to follow. *"Time to move."*

The corridor was a long one, broad enough for three or four Dlmvla to have walked together, or a good six or seven Humans in p-suits. The lighting was a little strange, mushroom-like lamps glowing in alternating shades of orange and green. The noise of the crowd grew as they progressed along its length, too, until they emerged in a vast, egg-shaped chamber lined with tiers of petal-like balconies. The same orange and green lights continued in little balls and bulges here and there, but they were joined with pink and blue, yellow and lilac, with a great white ring of light shining down from far overhead.

The place looked like a pinecone in a way, or rather, more like someone had turned a rounded pinecone inside out and upside down, and painted it in pastels. Most of the scale-balconies started one-third of the way up from the bottom and were painted in shades of pink and a grayish lavender. But at regular intervals, some of the balconies had been crafted from brass so well polished, it gleamed like gold.

Ia and Helstead had been escorted to one such platform about halfway up from the bottom, a third of the way up the tiers. Racks to either side of the broad alcove tucked at the back of the balcony held what looked like harness suits. They were sized and shaped for Dlmvlan bodies and came with what looked like antigravity thrusters. Other than that, the brass-edged balcony they had been escorted to was empty of all seats, Dlmvlan-style or otherwise.

Each of the other balconies held tiered ranks of bowl chairs filled with dozens of Dlmvla of all sizes and shades: cream, beige, red, brown, lavender-gray, and even a few that were near black, the eldest of the elderly for their race. Ommatidia-like eyes glittered on all sides, and though their species were not technically anything like insects as Human knew them, they did have a few spots on their bodies where their scales were as hard as armored plates. They certainly had no dual skeletons like the K'Katta, with chiton all over the outside and bones on the inside, just those few points of toughened, scaly hide outside and the usual vertebral frames inside.

In the center of the vast hall, a mound rose with twenty-one spikes, each one terminating in a broad, cupped dais. Upon each was seated one of the huge Nestor Queens, easily four meters tall, if not more; it was hard to tell exact sizes since they were seated and being attended by beige-scaled younglings, but the queens were huge. There were Nestors aplenty, and many High Nestors, but only the twenty-and-one Nestor Queens at the very top of Dlmvlan politics. Normally five at a time were permitted to tour their various colonies, but all twenty-one had gathered here on their homeworld for this particular debate.

They were not, however, the current focus of attention. All around the chamber floated huge hoverscreens. So did roughly fifteen Dlmvlan. Only one of them was being displayed on roughly half of the screens at the moment, however; the other half displayed an image quite familiar to both Ia and her second officer though Ia had never displayed the video feed for it at the time, just the audio component. She had seen it in the timestreams and had listened to it live when it had happened.

The fifteen debaters had a leader, a Dlmvlan male wrapped in an antigravity harness. He shouted in a voice amplified by their commsystems and gestured at the screens showing not his scaled face and faceted eyes, but the smooth, color-flushed skin and huge, black, mouse-like eyes of a Gatsugi. Words in Terranglo, the trade tongue of the Alliance, echoed in the wake of his own, coming from the green not-haired Gatsugi speaking fervently in the recording. Dlmvlan script marched along the edges of the screen, providing translations for those in the hall who did not speak the interstellar trade tongue.

"... *I transmit in the light, and I am* not/not/not *afraid! The hunters* will *be hunted. Stand on the branches by your choice/will/right. Climb for the strength to survive this war. Fight for your sentient brothers, and they* will *fight for you— when the easy prey has been shaken loose, their ceaseless/ wasteful hunger will send them into the trees for those who think they are safe! Strike now! Strike/Strike/Strike* now, *and cut out the tendons of their ambitions. Shove* them *into the Room for the Dead, before they can shove* you *in and shut/ lock/seal the door!"*

The Bright Speaker flinched and ducked as something smacked into the plexi wall of the broadcasting booth surrounding her. The sounds of fighting didn't get through, but the sight of it was there at the edge of the screen. For a moment, while the white-robed, four-armed alien ducked out of the way, that fighting could be seen. Some of the bodies involved were the ceristeel-armored forms of Humans, soldiers in Ia's own Company from over a year before, with a few hastily armored Gatsugi security guards from the colony's governance hall and broadcast center. Some of those figures were Salik, with their armored tentacle arms either firing their own bulky weapons or curling and lashing to strike at the Alliance members in their way.

The Dlmvlan crowded into the chamber went into an uproar, flailing their own limbs and pounding scaled body parts on railings and bowl-seat rims. The floating leader gestured, freezing the image in place while he roared and buzzed in the local tongue—then slashed his arm out, silencing half the noise. A fling of his other arm silenced the rest. The image on the screen moved again. Straightening from her crouch with a brownish gray tinge of grim determination to her skin tone, the Gatsugi continued to speak.

"Here I stand, surrounded by foes, but defended *by friends. Gatsugi and alien. Why? Why would these Terrans come to our aid, when they themselves are hunted hard? They have a quote from a Bright Speaker of their own. It has changed words and changed hands many/many/many times, for it transcends mere words, and mere hands, and mere species."*

The text on the screen could barely keep up; half a dozen of the ones displaying either the Dlmvlan debater or the Gatsugi Bright Speaker switched to massive views of native transcripts. On those screens that still showed the Gatsugi, her four arms flicked upward in the sign language of her kind, adding emphasis and meaning to her carefully, poetically chosen, fervently spoken words. Pinkish text added itself in smaller lettering to the golden cream on the text-only screens, translating that as well for the Dlmvlan watchers.

"I say it now in my own words, sign it with my own hands! They came for the Solaricans, but I was not a Solarican, and I stayed high above as they perished. They came for the V'Dan, but I was no V'Dan, and did not look nor move. They came for the K'Kattan, but my limbs were less, and I did not raise my spine . . . and the K'Katta, too, died. But I know in my soul that they are coming for me. When will I fight for myself, and how can I fight for myself, if I will not also fight for the rest?

"I am not afraid. I am not at rest. No ruler, no leader, no Nestor can tell me what I know is right, and I will fight. I am a Bright Speaker because I speak the truth! I speak it until the universe itself listens. I send/send/send in the hyper. I send/send/send in the light. I demand an answer/response from you! Will you fight?" Fists thrust together, one set over her head and one set under, knuckle-equivalents touching in braced arcs of strength, the Gatsugi stared through the cameras at her unseen viewers.

Her posture was a very *Dlmvlan* gesture, not a Gatsugi one, for the masses around them rose up, their own arms arched over their iridescent-eyed heads, fists pressed hard together. They roared as they did so, an abrupt, polysyllabic shout that echoed around the chamber in the silence that followed. A silence Ia had known would happen, and had planned for over a year ago, for her own words fell into the vast, spherical chamber, echoing from the past.

"Make no mistake," the Ia of the past warned the assembled aliens. A flatpic of her white-haired face, surrounded by what looked like profile information in Dlmvlan text, appeared on several of the screens as her broadcasted self continued. *"They will come for you, too. My Prophetic Stamp on that."*

The Queen High Nestor, seated on the highest spire, rose and growled something, towering over the assemblage with a stance that conveyed her authority even to the two Humans in their midst. Her anger and displeasure could be seen in the way she hissed and buzzed her words, in the slashing of her claw-hands, in the way she pointed at the floating debaters. The other queens arrayed on the spiked tiers below her hissed and clacked their armor-plated arms against the railings of their bowl chairs . . . provoking a loudly growled wave of counter-response from the assembly.

Not just a growl. Within moments, the crowd was in motion. Brown bodies *moved*, climbing over each other in some cases, all of them heading for those gold-polished balconies. Or rather, they headed for the harnesses that would turn them into floating debaters rather than seated spectators. At her side, Helstead whistled softly through their headset link, warily backing up toward the balcony's edge as it was the only place left for them to go.

". . . *V'Dayamn, sir,*" she muttered. "Something *stirred up their nests.*" She turned her head inside the tough plexi bubble of her pressure-suit's helm and frowned softly. *"I remember your saying that the Bright Speaker's speech would cause an uproar in the Dlmvlan Empire. That they'd do the right thing at the right point in time. But political fights are rarely resolved so quickly. I trust this isn't going to end up with us squished—and that it isn't going to take much longer. My tanks are showing just a little over an hour of oxygen left."*

"This won't take long. They're demanding to join the Alliance in our war against the Salik, in the face of strong Queen Nestor opposition," Ia murmured back, her eyes on the bodies that were headed their way. Catching Helstead by the elbow, she moved her fellow Human farther in the direction Helstead had instinctively tried to retreat. Some of the Dlmvla around them hissed in surprise at the two Humans when Ia pressed them to one side, against the angry spectators, but it was necessary.

The local gravity was a mere 0.93Gs, and both women were used to roughly twice that, even in their silvery p-suits with extra-large oxygen tanks strapped to their backs. Still, the pair staggered as they were knocked to either side by the much larger bodies of four of the now-harnessed locals leaping off the railing—and then were pressed up against the railing edge by those in the crowd who hadn't been able to get their hands on any more suits.

"Ugh! Dammit . . ." Helstead grunted. She was a heavy-worlder by birth, and thus naturally short; that meant the

Dlmvla couldn't help but half knock her over when they bumped into her in their rush to the railing. Thankfully, the barrier was too tall for either woman to be knocked off, but the aliens . . . the natives, rather, did press close. Elbowing two of them in the thigh-equivalents, Helstead got them to back off. *"Enough! Okay, sir, I give up. If these meioas are so fired up that they're going against their own leadership in order to join the war, then what are we doing here?"*

A twist of humor tickled up through Ia's normally sober thoughts. She knew Delia Helstead's background. Knew the other woman had grown up in a farming community before making her escape to the Terran Space Force to get herself off the mud-soaked heavyworld of Eiaven. With that twist of amusement coloring her voice, she held out her case.

"Here, Helstead. Hold my datachips, and watch this."

Behind the clear curve of plexi sheltering her lungs from the methane-filled local air, Helstead's jaw dropped. Not just because rural humor had not really changed much from colony to colony in hundreds of years but because her sober, somber Commanding Officer was grinning. Teeth bared in something which the aliens around them would interpret as a grimace but which was pure humor, Ia pushed back telekinetically at a Dlmvla that was crowding too close, heaved herself up onto the broad ledge of the railing, dropped her smile, and grabbed control of the conference. Or rather, the screens.

The dozens of monitors floating through the now-body-crowded air flared with blinding flashes of white.

Instinctively, all the Dlmvla swayed back from the oversized panels, both those on the balconies and those floating in antigravity harnesses. Equally surprised, the Nestor Queens hesitated, then a few of them rose to speak. There were more than enough of the former to quadruple the number of the latter, enough to override anything the Queens decreed—as was the legal right of their populace—but Ia didn't give either side the chance.

She flared the screens again with another jolt of electrokinesis, then covered half of them with her flatpic and profile . . . and the other pic with a real-time image of herself, clad in her pressure-suit. Inside the bubble of her helm, her distinctive white hair and amber-hued eyes stared at the aliens floating and standing and seated in the debate hall. Her voice, hard and stentorian, rang out across the room via the comm-system; the translation slashed in huge Dlmvlan lettering around that view of her p-suit-encased face.

". . . I *forbid* you joining the Alliance in this war!"

The uproar that followed her words was so loud, it caused a brief feedback squeal between her p-suit commsystem and her headset. Unlike Helstead, she didn't bother to slap her hands over her suit's pickups, located just above each collar-bone. The suit and the headset argued electronically for a few moments, first cutting the noise levels too low, then wobbling them up too high again for a few tries, before finally stabiliz-ing the noise at a moderate dull roar.

Ignoring the tumult, she kept her eyes on the lower spire-thrones of the twenty Nestor Queens, and the Queen High Nestor at the top in particular. She didn't flinch as several of the enraged, floating debaters headed her way, either. No one was going to hurt her, and no one would eject her. They'd do the alien equivalent of yelling at her for a bit, but otherwise she would be fine.

The largest of the leaders, the Queen High Nestor, rose to her full height and let loose a screech somewhere between a wild roar and a buzzing keen. Banging her forelimbs together, she set a syncopated rhythm, which was quickly picked up by the other queens. With all twenty-one clacking their arm-plates together in front of their comm pickups, the sound cut through the growling and the buzzing and the yelling. Those swaying toward Ia backed off, turning to face their leaders.

Ia knew only a fraction of what the Dlmvla were saying, and that only from skimming the timeplains. She just watched and waited while the High Nestor rattled off a rapid-fire speech. The alien leader then sat down, just in time to brace her bulk against the pivoting of the entire central spire. It twisted to the left while the assembled audience muttered to themselves, waiting impatiently.

The torquing of the spires brought a new clutch of Queen Nestors to face Ia, one of whom stood and lifted her upper limbs over her head, clacking them together in the same rhythm as before. The syncopated beat ceased after silence had fallen, and her voice, thin and reedy but echoing with the might of the speakers around the chamber, addressed the intruders in heavily accented Terranglo.

"We demant you identity! We demant reason you say 'no' at our sovereign azzemblee!"

Ia relaxed some of her mental grasp on the transparent floating screens, allowing the Dlmvlan translators to hastily, if belatedly, transcribe text of what she had said in their native tongue. Giving them the time to work, Ia stepped forward, onto nothing but air and the ability of her mind to affect the world via the manipulation of energy.

All debaters had to be aloft when they made their demands, though usually it was done while actually flying, through antigravity harnesses, not through telekinesis. There was a chilling reason behind it, for any debater who wished to have their words heard had to prove they were willing to die for whatever they believed. Each Nestor Queen controlled two kill switches for the debating harnesses . . . so for a vote to pass from the people trying to overturn the will of their queens, it had to surpass the ability of the Queens—or the colonial High Nestors, who had one switch apiece in the smaller assemblies—to literally kill its most loyal supporters.

She did not have a thruster harness, and could not have worn the Dlmvlan equivalent anyway, not when her body was one-third at most the size of a native. But she did have her telekinetic abilities, and walked out onto a solid line of methane-filled air. Two hovercameras, not too different from the Terran kind, swerved up to focus on her silver-suited figure. Ia let a few more of the screens slip free of her mental grip, giving their operators a chance to project her face directly rather than electrokinetically.

"I am Ia, Prophet of a Thousand Years, and the fully appointed General of the Alliance Armies of the Terrans, V'Dan, K'Katta, Tlassians, Solaricans, Chinsoiy, *and* the Feyori. My reason is your safety. My demand is your salvation." She spoke slowly, clearly, giving the translators time to post her words onto those screens. Reaching out with her mind, she touched each of the harnesses on the debaters floating around her. "Allow me to clarify my command: I *forbid* the Dlmvla nation to join the rest of the Alliance in open warfare against the Salik incursion. If you do, they will react with too much strength at the wrong point in time, and we will, one and all, to our deaths *fall*."

For one Human heartbeat, she hit the kill-switch circuits on every harness aloft. Shrill buzzing erupted, alien screeches of fear. They cut off as each harness snapped back on a split second later, thrusters countering the drop with faint whines.

"*Listen* to my words," Ia stated, strolling forward across nothing but air, as casual and sure-footed as if she were leisurely strolling through an invisible garden. "Read the translations of what I am saying. I forbid you to *join* the Alliance against the Salik." Twisting in a slow turn, she looked around, up, and down at all the aliens gathered on the balconies, in their harnesses. "Your Queens are right to worry about being drawn into *open* conflict with the Salik. If you move to stand at the sides of the Humans, the Gatsugi, and the rest, we will *not* be able to stop our mutual enemy.

"But I agree that the Bright Speaker you just watched is *also* right . . . as you just witnessed. As I spoke for myself over a Dulshvwl year ago. If you do *not* step out and act now, fighting our common enemy, you will also *fall*."

Again, the harnesses dropped in power, though this time for only half as long. Angry noises emerged from half or more of their occupants. One of the nearest of the original debaters snarled several words, swinging up and around to face her. A nearby screen translated his words in Terranglo as a courtesy. Ia didn't have to read them to get the gist of what he said, though, and addressed the Dlmvlan debater directly, interrupting him midspeech, pointing her p-suited finger within centimeters of his faceted eyes.

"I let fall 4,194 lives to get that Bright Speaker's message to *you*, meioa. I dropped them straight into the Room for the Dead to let her words and her wisdom reach *all* of you," Ia told him. She pointed again at the larger alien's face. "You were already willing to drop your *own* lives when you put on those harnesses to demand that your nation do the right thing . . . and I am here to tell you that I respect and *support* that demand." She dipped her head briefly to the debater, then stepping around him, still standing on nothing but solidified will and methane-laced air. Strolling a few steps forward, she came to a stop at Attention and faced the Nestor spire. "But doing the right thing in the *wrong* way, or at the *wrong* time, in this case is just as bad as doing *nothing*.

"So listen carefully: I *forbid* you," she repeated again, slowly and clearly, "to *join* the Alliance in *open* assistance . . . *when* you slaughter the Salik forces."

Another rumble of protest started to rise at her high-handed alien demand. The third-tier Nestor Queen flung one limb up and smacked the forearm of the other against its plates. Projected by the speakers, the two short *clacks* were as sharp as a projectile shot. Lowering her limbs, she cocked her head, faceted eyes gleaming in the overhead ring of lights.

"Say you . . . *when* we zzlaughter dem?"

Ia held out her arm to the side, activating her headset link with a blink. *"Helstead, open the case and pull out the trays."*

"Aye aye, sir."

She didn't look back to see if her second officer was doing it; she knew Helstead was already in motion. Not because of precognition or even clairvoyance, but because she trusted Helstead to act swiftly and neatly when given an order. She couldn't hear the *clicks* as Helstead set each tray on the broad, ledge-like rim of the polished-brass balcony several meters away, but nodded slightly, as much in approval of her second officer's unseen efforts as in acknowledgment of the Queen Nestor's understanding. On the floating screens, her head in its pressure-suit helm nodded in tandem as she answered the alien's question

"Yes, meioa. *When* you slaughter them."

Reaching back with her mind, she pulled the first row of chips out in a spiraling stream, then the second, and the third. This first allotment was easily four or five times the number of broken chandelier shards she had used to pluck out the throats of Salik generals three years before. Then again, this was a far less violent use of so many tiny, potential projectiles after three more years' worth of practice with her gifts.

The Dlmvla had a policy of recording, editing, *then* rebroad-casting their grand assemblies only after the fact, to prevent nest-riots if things happening inside this hall ended up inflam-matory, and to prevent state secrets from being spread openly. Ia knew the broadcasts were edited by committees of all sides involved in the debates, and that the Dlmvla were not stupid;

they would edit out her visit from the widely broadcast versions to prevent the Salik from knowing what she was suggesting here. But not from all of them.

Just because the Salik weren't yet interested in making war on the Dlmvla didn't mean they weren't covertly surveying the methane-breathers. In time, less-edited hard copies would be physically couriered to all High Nestors, Nestors, and the leaders of the various debate factions for private viewing and distribution, but only privately. They were neutral, but they were not politically stupid. Swirling the chips around her body was a bit of showmanship on her part, but it also allowed her to verify which ones were which. Letting the little rectangles spiral thrice around, she sent them outward again.

The first twenty-one went to the Nestor Queens and the Queen High Nestor perched at the very top of their pinnacle-thrones; the rest went to the governors and military leaders gathered for this conference. More of the chips continued to peel out of the trays and the case Helstead had balanced on the railing.

"I come before you not only as the Prophet of a Thousand Years," Ia stated plainly, keeping her words slow and measured for the translators, "but also as the officially appointed General of the Alliance Armies. My authorization to speak on behalf of the Alliance's war efforts against the combined Salik-Choya incursions is both authorized by all the governments I listed . . . and is absolute. I am *forbidding* you from joining the Alliance when you move to slaughter the Salik forces. I am also here to tell you what you *will* do.

"Your task is simple: You will avoid *starting* any conflict with the Salik within a particular star system's heliosphere. You will follow these directives to the exact coordinates listed, at the exact moments in time, calculated in Dlmvlan measurements, and destroy every single Salik vessel, station, and relay you find. Every last one of them, permitting none to escape alive and permitting no facility to remain intact.

"At the same time," she continued, "you will continue to openly *deny* any request for you to join the ongoing war effort, either for or against the Salik," Ia stressed, keeping her expression sober. Some of the aliens watching her face, projected on the giant transparent screens, were reasonably good at reading Human emotions. "You will protect only your own stations within any given star system. You will ignore any enemy passing peacefully through a star system you control. You may even trade peacefully with both sides as you have always done . . . and you will give no mercy to any enemy vessel you catch in interstitial space. When you find them beyond each star system's heliopause, you will hunt them down, you will open the Door for the Dead, and you will shove them all through, down to the last egg in the last nest-pond.

"Those chips will tell you *exactly* where and when to find the Salik. You have one Dlmvlan Standard day to get those lists of targets studied, memorized, and the relevant ships under way . . . and you will fight the Salik *this* way, *my* way, as the *only* way to keep the Door to the Room from closing on you, too, when the Salik themselves *fall*."

The debaters who understood Terranglo flinched . . . but did not move. None of them dropped. Ia had left the kill switches alone this time. She turned back toward the balcony she had come from, took a few steps, then spun back to face the central spire and its bowl-chair balconies. She pointed as she moved, sweeping her finger slowly up the line of the pinnacle from the lowest seats to the highest peak.

"This way, Queen Nestors, *you* get what you want, to protect your people and manage their resources in the least wasteful way. Openly joining this war would indeed be wasteful; in that much, I agree with you." She pointed at all the floating debaters with her other arm, at all the watching natives. "This way, your *people* get what they want, to help save their fellow sentients' lives, regardless of which gas we breathe. It is *very* clear by all these many debaters, both the ones floating and the ones on the balconies who wish they also had harnesses, that so many of them *are* willing to risk death itself to help the rest of the Alliance.

"*This* way, by stealth and by guile, the Salik will not realize you are fully involved until it is too late, and the Door to the Room will have already begun to close," she stated, once more headed back to Helstead. "I trust, Debaters and Nestors, that this is a reasonable, logical, yet *poetic* compromise between both sides of your debate?"

The reply from the debaters was a rumble of different noises, too many to translate, but the Queen Nestor appointed to speak for the others spoke clearly. Or as clearly as she could with her thick accent projected over the multitude of speakers. "It izz . . . agzzeptable. But leave you will. Now."

"Of course. Have a good day, gentlebeings," Ia added, lifting a hand in farewell over her shoulder. "Have a very good day. Try a Saturday. Those usually work well for most gentlebeings. *Helstead,*" she ordered, switching to her headset alone, "*step up onto the railing and prepare to teleport us back to the embassy.*"

"*Gladly, sir.*" Emptied trays replaced and case closed, Helstead pulled herself up onto the railing, which came up to her nose on her and midthigh on the Dlmvla behind her. The Dlmvlan homeworld was a lightworld, though; maneuvering was not difficult for the athletic woman. Once on her feet, the handle of the case still in her hand, she eyed Ia warily. "*Sir . . . you do know that when I translocate us from here to there, I'll also be taking along several cubic liters of local air, and replacing it with the Human version, yes?*"

"*I am very well aware of the way teleportation most commonly works among those rare psis who possess it, Lieutenant Commander, and of the resulting drawbacks it sometimes carries,*" Ia quipped. Reaching the railing, she held out her hand, and clasped the gloved fingers Helstead offered her in return. "*Take us out of here, Delia . . .* before *these kind and gentle beings realize I have deliberately chosen to depart with a giant fart left behind in their assembly hall.*"

The dirty look Helstead shot her—broken as it was with an involuntary chuckle—was not for mentioning the residue of their departure. Rather, Ia knew it was because she had made the other woman laugh at a moment when Helstead needed all of her concentration focused on her target, a semifamiliar room on a space station several hundred kilometers away in thankfully geosynchronous orbit.

The breath of oxygen-laced air they were leaving behind was deliberate, a last courting gift as it were. The Dlmvla would at first be offended, even outraged, then alarmed by the realization that *two* powerful psychics had been present. Alarmed that the lesser known of the pair was powerful enough to have altered the very air they breathed. Once they thought about her parting "gift," however, then the aliens

would be entranced, even flattered. At least, once they recon-
ciled the atmospheric insult with the fact that Ia and her second officer had come all this way to *help* the Dlmvlan fight
against the Salik.

The Dlmvla loved illogical words, actions, gifts . . . It was
art to them, an entertaining amusement. She wasn't this particular world's best poet by any means, but Ia knew they
would give her points for trying.

"Brace yourself, sir."

Between one breath and the next, several things happened.
Outside energies seized her nerves, and the world slammed
away. The shock of searing cold and freezing heat, of not
being able to breathe for a precious second, lungs overfull,
gave way to a massive jolt and the need to gasp for air when Ia
dropped three or four centimeters to a white-enameled floor.
It felt like the very first time she had turned from a Feyori
back into a human and had forgotten how things like bones
and joints and muscles had worked, only worse because she
wasn't the one in control.

It was enough to make her stumble, then drop to one knee,
releasing Helstead's hand. The nausea hit a bare heartbeat
after, slamming into her blood and her guts without warning.
At the last moment, she swallowed down the taste of her
bile—vomiting was *never* a good idea in a sealed pressure-
suit—and struggled to hold the rest of it down, breathing fast
and shallow through her nose.

Ia wanted to rip off her helmet and breathe clean air, but
knew better. As much as Helstead had just replaced a handful
of cubic meters of methane with oxygen back down in the assembly hall, she had also just replaced a handful of cubic
meters of oxygen with methane and a pair of p-suited bodies.
*Oxygen and nitrogen and trace elementals . . . breathe, Ian-
tha . . . breathe and move forward. One step at a time, nice
and easy on your stomach . . .*

Limbs trembling with the adrenaline aftermath of her abrupt
translocation, she pushed to her feet and staggered across the
airlock. Helstead, far more accustomed to the effects, had already moved out of the fart zone, though she had yet to release her helmet. Instead, the petite soldier poked at the
buttons of the airlock she had memorized so carefully. Both

women listened to the air cyclers hissing, though they couldn't feel the breeze against their pressure-suit-wrapped bodies.

Only when the hissing stopped and the ready lights edging the boxy chamber shifted from orange to green did they move, working to unseal their helmets. The oxygen rebreather packs built into the backs of the suits would keep them alive for another half hour of use, but it was always wise to conserve such things for a further round of need.

The inner door of the airlock opened, leading into a room filled with storage lockers. Both women moved into the new chamber and waited for the doors to cycle shut before stripping and changing back into their uniforms. Ia took advantage of the towelettes provided from a dispensary on the wall, wanting to wipe off the sweat that had started to pool under her suit. Delia grabbed a few as well but sat down on one of the benches for a few moments.

"I've been thinking about something, sir. I'm told that the Meddlers can teleport, too," the redhead stated without preamble. "I know that Belini visited the *Hellfire* several times that way. And that you implied in passing that your two 'friends' among the silvery-soap-bubble set helped you get to Dabin that way."

Ia shook her head. "They used faster-than-light energies that time, counteracting and suppressing the Higgs field that gives particles their mass resistance, and doing so to the point where even energy could fly faster than the speed of light— traversing the *squared* speed of light takes a lot more effort, and a lot more energy. But they can instantly transplant themselves from one location to another if they have an 'anchor' laid at that other place. They didn't have one for Dabin."

"An anchor?" Helstead repeated.

Nodding, Ia wiped away the last of the itchy-sweaty feel p-suits always gave her skin and started pulling on her underwear. Most of it was still Special Forces-issued gray in hue; only her outer clothes had changed, really. "If I understand what I observed of Belini's comings and goings in my quarters on the *Hellfire*, she laid a memory-resonance pattern in the quantum-energy states of the exact matter-based location she wanted to be able to reach when she was charged and ready to connect."

". . . Uh-huh."

Ia smiled slightly at her second officer's flat, disbelieving tone. Or rather, not-quite-comprehending tone. "Think of it as associating a specific smell with a location—no, wait, sorry; they don't have a sense of smell. Ah . . . more like humming a specific tune in a specific location. Always that same tune for that one specific location, only the 'tune' involves harnessing quantum-energy states for entanglement on a nonmatter basis, and not actual sound waves."

"A *tune*?" the redhead asked, scrubbing under her arm with one of the wipes. "Oh. Right. The vibrational string theory of quantum entanglement." She rolled her green eyes. "Ugh, I left all that tedious FTL physics stuff behind in high school, Ia . . . Do I really have to think about it now?"

"You did ask, and yes, they literally do attune their energy bodies to a specific location. But it's easy enough to understand without university-level quantum-physics classes. When they want to return to an 'entangled' place, as you so rightly put it, they shift their energy matrices to match that specific location pattern, dump massive energy into it, and phase-transit through hyperspace," Ia stated. She shrugged into her bra. "Without more than a tiny, tiny fraction of matter to slow them down, and being roughly Human-sized in diameter, what takes a courier ship using other-than-light many seconds to travel many light-years becomes near instantaneous for them.

"What takes a pinprick hyperrelay opening two seconds to transmit one way takes them about five seconds, but otherwise it's essentially instantaneous . . . and since the matter they do carry is not necessary for their well-being, it imparts no quantum stress and thus no nausea or accelerated aging. It's costly and awkward in having to regurgitate all that energy for it, but their version is very handy. By contrast, what Humans and other psychic races can do is short-distance at best . . . but it's still pretty much the exact same process. Your teleportation is simply a very localized version of their hyperspatial quantum-singularity entanglements."

Helstead gave her CO a flat look and worked on wiping herself clean. "Tell me sir," she stated dryly, "did you understand *anything* of what you said just now? Because if I recall correctly, you went straight from high school into the Marine Corps, and your degree is in military history, not transportational astrophysics."

That made Ia smile. "Technically, I didn't even finish high school. I took my equivalency exams before I turned sixteen, and that was that. Besides, I don't have to *understand* it all in this particular lifetime, Delia. I just have to *know*. Finish getting dressed," she added, letting her humor fade back into the seriousness of their visit. "Vice Commodore Jilsen will be needing a debriefing on what to expect in the aftermath of my visit, and then we'll need to catch the mail courier back to Battle Platform *Stagecoach Mary* and see how far Harper's come along with the *Damnation*'s repairs."

The look the redhead slanted her let Ia know Delia wasn't fooled by the euphemism. *Repairs* meant *special modifications* of a nature which only Ia herself knew, and maybe Harper, too. Huge, heavy, mysterious crates had been shipped to Battle Platform *White Mouse* on their last docking session, the crystalline contents of which Ia had altered in the privacy of the bow storage bays.

Helstead didn't address that, though, but returned to the previous topic with a shove of the towelette through the recycler flap. "So. Being half-Feyori . . . can *you* teleport, too?"

"I probably could," Ia admitted, voice briefly muffled by her undershirt. "*If* I had the time to learn. Which I don't. That's why I dragged you along; you've already done all the hard work for me."

"Of course I have . . . you lazy, cheating, superior officer." Delia worked on donning her own clothes, then tipped her head thoughtfully. "You think we could arrange for a shipment of those fart-fruits while we're here? The little methane-grown berry things you traded an old teddy bear for, a few years back? . . . *Ksisk*, that was it. Everybody liked them."

"It's already on the manifest for the mail courier," Ia reassured her.

NOVEMBER 8, 2498 T.S.
SUN-VENH SYSTEM

She couldn't get the subject out of her mind. Helstead's words weren't a huge distraction, but Ia kept finding herself turning over their conversation in her thoughts. Thinking of being

Feyori, and being able to suppress the Higgs field that gave matter particles their mass, allowing them to travel faster-than-light. Being psychic, and being able to teleport through brief hyperrift wormholes in an imitation of other-than-light travel. The problem of the upcoming Grey weapon and how to stop it from destroying the universe.

Her body really needed sleep. Defending this Tlassian system and its three colonies—with three separate, simultaneous battle zones, requiring numerous short, other-than-light hops—had been taxing on both her nerves and her energy reserves. But Ia's mind would not let her sleep in anything more than snatches. Thoughts and ideas kept circling around and around, pulling in disparate images. The rift in the universe. FTL energies incompletely plugging the hole caused by entropy and OTL. The chance for that hole to come unplugged. An androgynous face masking a terrifyingly brilliant mind.

Why am I thinking of Jack? Staring up at the plain, gray-painted ceiling of her sleeping cabin, Ia couldn't think of a single reason why. Except one. *Okay, she, at least, would be brilliant enough to figure out* why *my brain won't let go of Delia's comments about psychic abilities and Feyori abilities and science and technology all accomplishing the same things . . . but I can't ask Jack for help with anything like this because even if she* would *cooperate—which there's no guarantee she would—she* thinks too fast for me to follow her thought processes. Combat, yes, but thoughts . . . Not even the accelerated speed of the timeplains could help me keep up with *her* thoughts.

If only she were a more normal *sort of genius, like Mey . . . like* Meyun! *Of course! I couldn't see* him *involved in all of this because he might* end up being the solution to the problem. Right . . . right. Pushing up onto one elbow, she fumbled for the lighting controls, then squinted against the carrot-flavored, white-hued light that blinded her for a few seconds. *Lovely. Months since I last took on Feyori form, and I'm* still *occasionally tasting energies like weird flavors of food . . .*

Oh, now that's *a thought . . . is aphasia a form of psychic ability, only it's scrambled up instead of working straight?* She knew that historically some cases of schizophrenia—not all, but some—had proved to be psychic abilities left unrecognized, untrained, and uncontrolled. *Probably not in general,* she dismissed, resisting the urge to go looking for that information. She released the bed's webbing and swung her legs off the mattress. For a moment, her head swam with exhaustion; Ia stayed put for a few seconds. *Focus, Ia. You have a mystery wherein your brain, filled as it is with near-infinite but purely instinct-level information, cannot pull together an answer on its own.*

So it's up to you to dump this headache in someone else's *lap because you need your sleep, and you don't have any other time to spare.* Pushing to her feet, she headed for the door. Then abruptly reversed course and headed for her storage drawers. *And walking out of your cabin in nothing but your underwear would be a* bad *idea. Totally the wrong sort of presentation the captain of the ship needs to make.*

Captain, not General. She didn't feel like a four-star general, let alone a five-star. The reason for that was simple enough: She didn't *want* the rank. So long as she had enough authority for what needed to be done, Ia would be satisfied. Part of her couldn't quite trust how easily she had gained it, either. *Somewhere out there, an alternate universe "me" is struggling with too little power—if everything I do goes right in this universe, that means an alternate universe me is having things go wrong . . .*

I do feel sorry for her universe, but I have to be selfish and cleave to what this *one needs.*

Pants donned and T-shirt tucked in, she padded out of her bedroom on bare feet. Passing through the front cabin, and into her office, Ia scrounged for spare datapads. Only finding two, she sighed and walked into the Company office. Sadneczek, Company Sergeant, wasn't on duty . . . but Mara Sunrise was.

Ia raised her brows. "Working when you're scheduled to be off duty?"

Mara flicked her an annoyed look. "Roommate troubles."

"What? Oh . . . right." She scrubbed her free hand over her face. "The whole you turning out to be a kick-asteroid warrior instead of a mousy, boring clerk-thing." Flicking her hand, Ia shrugged. "You know you don't *have* to be a boring little clerk on board this ship anymore. Just spread the word to be discreet about it off ship, on my orders, and the others won't say a word."

"Except I still need to do the work of my boring mousy clerk's position," Sunrise pointed out. "And that doesn't cure the problems I'm having with Floathawg. God! Even his *name* is pretentious! Arrogant little . . ."

She could have let it go and dealt with it in two days, but Ia knew it was better to stop that line of reasoning now. After all, Mara wouldn't be thinking it if Ia hadn't come out of her quarters. "Mara, it's not what you think. Harley had a very hard time making the transition from V'Dan culture to Terran when his parents moved to Earth. He'd already suffered the *jungen*-fever at an early age, and had developed all those burgundy stripes. On V'Dan . . ."

Mara nodded, following her explanation. "On V'Dan, it's a lingering mark of great honor, I know . . ." She thought about a moment, and sighed. "I suppose on Earth, it would've left him feeling ostracized."

"Exactly," Ia said. "And when he met up with some hoverbike enthusiasts, they welcomed him in and considered his *jungen*-marks to be something fantastic, a retro rebellion. It gave him a reason to be proud of what in essence was a simple random genetic throwback to the pre-Terran days, something that was otherwise alienating him from his new homeworld. Hanging out with the hoverbike crowd gave him a sense of *Terran* identity in the face of his blatant, literally in-his-face V'Dan lineage."

"So *that's* why he changed his name? That part's not in the DoI files," Mara muttered. "They just list him as being a hoverbike enthusiast."

"Well, if you hadn't noticed, he *does* love hoverbikes," Ia pointed out dryly. She didn't mind that Mara had snuck a look at her teammate's files. The other woman had the clearance for it and the access as one of the Company clerks. "As for getting along with him . . . I think if you marched in there and told him *why* you had to change your name, your identity, and even your personality, I think he'd understand *you* a lot better."

The sergeant-turned-private slanted her a skeptical look. "General, sir, I am not supposed to tell anyone what happened, as part of the conditions of my parole from my political-based imprisonment."

Ia settled her hip onto the edge of Mara's workstation desk

and clasped the two scrounged datapads in her lap. "First of all, you're not supposed to tell anyone, period, unless it becomes a need-to-know basis. Second, the only personnel with the right to need-to-know are those with extremely high Clearance ratings. Thirdly, every single person on board this ship *has* that level of Clearance. And fourth of all, you have not only a massive, military-acknowledged precog telling you it's okay to tell Harley Floathawg the truth behind your presence here, you have the General of the Alliance Armies telling you *it's okay.*

"I also say that, as your roommate is making you so uncomfortable in your own quarters that you'd rather deal with paperwork in your off-hours than deal with him, he definitely needs to know."

"That's fine for now, but your permission will last only so long as the war lasts, sir," Mara pointed out. "What happens after it's all over? After we've beat the Salik, and the Greys, and you get your high authorities yanked? That is, assuming they do get yanked. I think Myang's aiming you at *her* seat, when she's ready to retire."

Sighing, Ia shrugged. "Then start pulling up the requisite paperwork for a Full and Unconditional Pardon. What you uncovered *needed* to be uncovered, even if you went about it in a rather politically *inconvenient* and technically semi-unlawful way. But you have earned my trust since joining my Company. And that means you've earned the trust of the Admiral-General," she added, pausing for a second to check the timestreams. "Given you committed your so-called crimes while a soldier, it is *my* prerogative within the scope of my current powers to issue a pardon. I think I can sweet-talk Myang into signing off on it as well, making it permanent. Provided you don't go blabbing it all over the place."

Mara relaxed into her seat, slumping out of her stiff-backed mousy-clerk posture. ". . . That would get a huge pressure off of me, if I could indeed be myself again."

"No time like the present . . . though technically this conversation was actually going to come up in a few more days. Except I couldn't sleep. Are there any spare datapads in here, or do I have to go down to the storage holds on Deck 17?" she asked, changing the subject.

"Sure, I'll get you some. How many do you need?" Sunrise asked her. She nodded at the pair in Ia's hands even as she rose from her seat. "Beyond the two you already have, I mean?"

"Oh, six or seven. I'm going to load them up with some information and dump it all in Harper's lap," she explained lightly, pausing for a half-stifled yawn. "I can't sleep because my brain is refusing to see the solution to a problem that just might have an engineering answer . . . so I might as well make *him* suffer sleeplessness instead."

Mara chuckled. "Make sure you make it up to him, sir."

"I plan on it. When we're in transit, and he's not cursing at me for all the repairs he has to oversee." She rose as well, moving to accept the tablets the other woman pulled from the storage cabinet.

Turning to hand her the first three, Mara glanced down, then did a double take. "Sir . . . aren't you supposed to be wearing ship boots? Or at least fitted slippers with magplates in the soles, in case of sudden gravity loss?"

"I'm a telekinetic, and don't need artificial gravity or boots that can snap to a metal surface if the plates go out, re-member?" Ia countered dryly. "Besides, we're docked at what passes for a Tlassian repair facility, with no enemy incursions planned for the rest of the time we're scheduled to be here."

"Oh, sure, cloud the issue with facts," Mara retorted. She handed over another four tablets, then closed the cupboard. "That's all you'll get, sir, without filling out Form 14357-98B-OSX-4 for more. And that's only because I know where you sleep at night. If you break them, it's coming out of your pay."

Ia smiled slightly at the teasing. "Go pull up the paper-work on your pardon and prep it for Grizzle to work on when he comes on duty next watch. Then get back to your quarters, wake up your teammate, and give *him* a sleepless night—that's one of my few perks, as the CO; I get to make other people suffer, too, if I can't get any sleep."

"Thank you so much for sharing, sir," Mara quipped, returning to her desk. She smiled, though.

Pads in hand, Ia left the front office and slowly made her way toward the aft engineering section. She had to pause every few dozen meters to consider what to cull from the timestreams and gently input them electrokinetically into the pads—the pausing was to make sure she didn't bump into any-thing while searching far-out possibilities. Putting together the Feyori-enhancing guns had taught her several things about what her chief engineer wanted to glean from alternate timestreams, at least.

By the time she reached Engineering, she was pretty sure she had everything, with one datapad to spare. She barely had to look up to see where she was going; everyone on duty in the compartment's upper floor pointed at Harper's office the moment they saw her. With a couple absentminded waves, Ia headed that way.

The door slid open as she approached, disgorging her first officer, who almost ran into her. Rearing back, Harper blinked at her. ". . . Ia? Didn't you say you were going off to sleep?"

"Tell that to my brain. Address the troops and handle the problem that just cropped up," she directed him, sidestepping so he could get past her and she could get into his office, "then come back in here when you're done. I have another 'special' project I need to drop in your lap, only with less in-formation on the end product than before."

"Okay . . . I'll be back within half an hour or so," he prom-ised. Then did a double take, staring at the deck. "Your feet are bare. This is the *engineering* section. Your feet are *not* supposed to be bare, General."

"The probability of my feet being damaged within the next five days is smaller than the chance of someone on board this ship spontaneously combusting," Ia dismissed, her atten-tion more on the pads in her hands as she added and adjusted more information to them. "And since no one is scheduled to do that during the entire length this crew will be aboard, it doesn't matter."

Harper sighed heavily, and asked, "Fine. Sir. Can you at least go sit in the safety of my office? And perhaps give me a clue about what you need me to do?"

"I need you to stitch up a hole in the universe, one which has not yet happened, but will . . . and we may have to use the same special crystals as before. *If* my instincts are right. I al-ready have a solution that will work . . . but I'm getting the feeling there is a better solution out there. One I might be able to piggyback off the Grey solution you've been prepping the ship for." She looked up at him, her gaze frank and direct. "But *I'm* not a genius engineer, and I haven't more than the faintest clue of where we could possibly begin with this particular task, other than that it'll involve psychics, Feyori abilities, faster-than-light field projections, and some other odds and ends," she muttered, gesturing vaguely with the datapads in her hands. "And my brain won't stop *circling* this problem even though I need to sleep while I can, when I can.

"On the upside, you'll have over a year before it's absolutely necessary. On the downside . . . we'll only have *one* shot at getting it right," she warned him. "For that matter, I don't even know if this is something that's been considered yet in any of the *other* universes."

Harper pointed a finger in warning at her. "Except you've just thought of something, which means it now *does* exist somewhere out there. That means we *can* test it in alternate-universe possibilities, which means you need to fill your time while you're waiting in tracking down those alternate realities, and filling in what you can on those pads in your hands," he said, backing up along the walkway overlooking the banks of hydrogenerators that fed the interior ship systems, excluding the various laser cannons. "I'll be back as soon as I've overseen the last of the mods to the Tlassian scanner systems we're installing—you're damned lucky we *can* retrofit Tlassian gear into Terran sockets. And no, that is *not* a cross-species innuendo, no matter how much the Tlassian supplier xeno-smirked about it."

Ia let the corner of her mouth curl up. "That reminds me of a time when I was in the Navy, and one of my crew members got asked out for a drink by a Tlassian. He—the saurian—didn't realize the Human he was asking out was a fellow male. But I'll be just as happy if you turn this one down, thank you. I'll keep your chair warm for you."

"Keep my *ship* unharmed, and I'll be a lot happier!" he called over his shoulder, moving off toward the stairs.

Ia waved him off, retreating into his front office. *He's right about the theory of it . . . Now that I've thought of it, and have vague ideas of what to look for, I can start testing the various infinite possibilities for more solid probabilities on how to restitch the universe back together,* she thought, thumbing through some of the information she had gleaned from the timestreams. *One which would be a lot safer than just plug it up awkwardly with a miniature Big Bang . . .*

——————

Three hours later, Ia dragged herself back to her quarters. She was exhausted from cushioning Harper while he tried to read the minds of similar-but-not-himself engineers in alternate realities. But she felt satisfied that her chief engineer was going to come up with some sort of solution to the problem that had been plaguing her brain all night. She almost detoured toward the bridge galley for a snack, needing some way to make up for the energy lost from staying awake for so long, but exhaustion warred with the distaste of having to fix her own food.

As it was, at first she missed seeing the parfait bowl clipped to her office desk by its broad, flat base. Her attention was on the door to her private quarters, and the hope of at least two or three hours of sleep. The tangy-sweet scent of *ksisk* fruit caught her attention, though, making her wonder for a moment what it meant.

No source of energy in either her office or her sitting room "tasted" like the fart-fruit berry to her Feyori-altered senses, so it had to be a real scent . . . and that was when she saw the bowl. The gelatin sat in the clear-plexi goblet, piled in layers of purple and red, a spoon clipped to its side, ready to eat. Simple, yet satisfying. It drew her to her desk instead of her much-needed bed.

There was even a little card caught under the goblet's base. Pulling it out, Ia unfolded the paper. Graceful but unfamiliar handwriting—probably Private Garcia's—formed a simple, sweet message.

You're on the right track, General. Keep up the good work!

Smiling wistfully, she unclipped the spoon and dug in. *I guess Mara and I aren't the only ones working off-shift tonight. I should look up where she is and go thank her for the snack, but . . . eh, I'm too tired. And dammit, I* deserve *a little pampering,* she decided, sucking the wobbly stuff off of her spoon. Two mouthfuls later, she dug down past the purple layer to the reddish-hued one and brought it to her mouth.

I deserve *gelatin parfait gifts . . . ooh, apple-flavored? That's what the red layer is? That goes* really *well with the* ksisk . . .

Abandoning half-formed plans to track down the junior galley crew member and thank her, Ia concentrated on this unexpected but most welcome snack. It wasn't Leave on an M-class planet, and it did deprive her of ten extra minutes of badly needed sleep, but it was ten minutes all to herself, with no thoughts on her mind but the wonderful mingling of tart and sweet in a delicate, jelly-like texture. She'd just have to remember to thank Garcia at some point for the gift.

CHAPTER 4

Yes, we're getting close to the point in the chronology where the Salik issue is dealt with . . . but we're not quite there, yet.

Actually, it's funny. I didn't even think much about this at the time, other than that I had to keep him alive, but there was one man I had to ignore and treat rather normally during Basic so that I wouldn't inadvertently influence him out of the life-path he needed to take. "Happy" Harkins. I had to keep him alive, particularly in that very first battle in Ferrar's Fighters, so I could one day ask him a favor regarding his eventual civilian job, which was to help guard and guide the Terran head of the Alliance Center for Disease Control.

Lieutenant Commander Helstead once mentioned an old song about hurricanes being started by the flapping of a butterfly's wings. I cannot even count just how many butterflies I have nudged into flight . . . but I do remember each and every one. Thankfully, most of them ended in helpful hurricanes. Unfortunately . . . they were still hurricanes in the end, not exactly under my control . . . and *sometimes* not *strong enough to do the deed I needed to have done for me. Sometimes I had to step in directly.*

~Ia

JANUARY 21, 2499 T.S.
SPACE STATION *ACDC HQ*
SUGAI SYSTEM

"So. General Ia. General of the Alliance Armies, no less." Alvin Gomez, Director of the Terran branch of the Alliance Center for Disease Control, looked up through the transparent workstation screen between them. A touch of his desk controls lowered the monitor to half height. "Every time this office gets a visit from someone in the military, it means *someone* has been playing with molecules they shouldn't."

"They're not *my* molecules, meioa-o," Ia replied, keeping her tone light. Somewhere in the next few minutes, she would hit a small but dense gray patch. She didn't know what the problem would be, beyond that she would have to figure out how to get through to this man that he needed to do what *she* said was necessary, not what *he* thought was necessary. Out loud, she merely said, "Nor will it be anything the Terrans have touched."

"So, then, you claim no knowledge of, oh, releasing *Dabinian passion-moss spores* on every inhabited colonyworld out there?" he asked her, arching one dark brow in blatant skepticism. "Domeworlds as well as M-class planets?"

"The ACDC will receive the information and the counter-agents it needs to eradicate the passion-moss problem on non-Dabinian worlds *after* the Salik have been dealt with, Director," Ia countered calmly. "I'm here to discuss a completely different threat. Now, given that my ship leaves in less than two hours, I'd like to make this meeting as brief and to the point as possible. So if we could move past the political posturing and the size-comparing of our respective immune systems, I'd deeply appreciate it."

As she'd calculated, her dry-voiced quip made him smile wryly. "The 'size-comparing of our respective immune systems.'

That's funny. I'll have to remember that one. Okay, then, what disaster have you got for me today, General?" he asked, gesturing her toward the seat across from his. "I don't deal with Fire or Flood, so which is it, Famine or Pestilence? You may be touted as someone who can foresee the future, but if you're not going to give us a cure for the xenospecies invasions you've caused, then *I* have no clue why you're here."

"I am here because you and I are going to redefine 'Quarantine Extreme' today, Director Gomez," Ia stated. She offered the puzzled Director a small box before seating herself in one of the chairs across from his. "You will find a set of total self-containment protocols and procedures on those datachips, with each chip coded and labeled for every known race . . . save only the Feyori. Practicing these scenarios is not an option. It is a wartime mandate. Moreover, the ACDC will practice these procedures in conjunction with all known militaries, excepting only the Salik."

"And the Choya," Gomez pointed out, opening the case. He pulled out the first chip, labeled "TUP-QE" and slotted it into his workstation.

Ia gave him a level look through the screen rising back up into place. "No, meioa. Excepting *only* the Salik. There will come a point in time when the Choya will desperately want our help in containing the coming plague, and we will give it to them. For now, we are still at war with their race, but your people *will* practice the drills and procedures for ensuring Choyan survival under the new Quarantine Extreme measures. When the moment comes, you must be ready to save everyone from the Salik's worst mistake."

"Yeah, right," he dismissed. Turning his attention to the data flowing across the transparent screen, he narrowed his eyes. "Wait . . . this is . . ." Brows pinching together, he frowned at the screen and tapped down through the summary page. "This is insane! You're asking us to fire on our own people?"

"Technically, I'll be having the military fire on infected ships, though merchant reserve vessels will be drafted into those forces where necessary. This is *not* an option, Director Gomez," Ia repeated. "This is what *will* happen, and this is what your department will do to ensure it does not spread to the rest of sentientkind."

"This is *not* how you fight a plague!" he countered sharply, glaring at her through the text on his screen. "If you're such a precise and powerful, all-seeing precognitive, where is the information on how to *counter* this plague? Where are the details on its genome, its molecular structure, how it replicates, and how it infects its hosts? For that matter, what kind of plague *can* infect every single life-form out there, even the Chinsoiy? Is it mutagenic? Retroviral? What?"

This was the start of the fog. Ia shook her head. "There is no cure, other than to kill it in a fire hotter and longer than that required for a cremation."

"No," Gomez denied, shaking his head in turn. "I don't accept that. *Every* disease has a survival rate. *Every* disease has a cure." His finger thumped into his desk in emphasis.

"Oh, there is a survival rate," Ia told him candidly. "But it's a rate of less than one in one billion, and of those who can survive it, they already have serious health problems of their own. Even accounting for the fact that the remaining population would consist of only a few hundred people per race . . . if they were to have normal, healthy children, which rebuilding their species would require," she reminded him, her words grim, "those normal children would still die."

"Then we'll just have to prevent it from spreading in the first place," the Terran Director asserted. "Who is Patient Zero, and where are they, or where will they be? If you can see everything, like all the rumors flying out of V'Dan space claim you can, then you *can* see that, and *that* is what I demand to know. Let's stop it right here, right now, and have done with the whole thing."

Ia stared at him. Religious zealotry, she could understand. She had faced it back home on Sanctuary, after all, a level of fanaticism she still had to face when she went home for the last time before losing her homeworld behind enemy lines. *Karl Marx once decried that religion was the opiate of the masses. That it was a drug that dulled their wits and their minds, removing their ability to think rationally. But medical zealotry . . . ?*

"Tell me where and when this plague will start, and we will stop it at Patient Zero," Alvin Gomez repeated, thumping his desktop once again with a finger.

How do I get it through his head how wrong he is? He's one of those men who believes only in what he himself believes. What he himself . . . She could see it, a glimmer of a path through the fog, one which led out of the mist and into the future where she needed this moment to go. Rising from her seat, Ia stepped around the end of the bulky furniture separating them. One hand came down on the edge of his desk, the other lifted up near her shoulder. He stared up at her warily. *At least I have some of his attention. Unfortunately, I need to seize all of it.*

"Director Gomez, the entire Salik *race* is Patient Zero. They *have* to die. As. A. Species." She moved her free hand to within centimeters of his face. "Because if they do not die within the next year, *this* is what will happen, and keep happening, for the next *three hundred years.*"

Closing the distance between them, she pressed her fingertips to his brow, touching him with skin and gifts even as he tried to lean back out of range. She didn't submerge herself very deeply, but she did give him a thorough soaking.

A few years back, she had taken her 1st Platoon leader, Lieutenant Oslo Rico, into the timeplains in search of the location for the manufactories for the anti-psi machine the Salik had created. During that temporal walk, the two of them had been forced to witness a living K'Katta being torn apart and eaten one piece at a time. That was what the Salik loved to do, after all: eat sentient beings while they were still alive and aware enough to scream in pain.

Ia did not show him that exact memory. Instead, she submerged the Terran Director into the last few life-stream moments of a fellow Terran being slowly eaten alive under similar circumstances.

He didn't scream. Gomez *tried* to, but the only sounds that emerged were hissing breaths from his terror-locked throat. Ia pulled him out after only a few seconds at most of objective, real-world time. Subjectively, though, he had suffered for at least a full minute or more.

Breathing hard, the middle-aged Terran stared at her in horror. "You . . . You . . ."

"Not convinced yet? Do I need to remind you that we have *already* suffered two hundred years of *this*?" She plunged him back in again ruthlessly, into the body and mind of a Tlassian of the worker caste. Again, he suffered a subjective minute or so of torment before she pulled him out. It wasn't quite as intense since some of the alien nerve sensations didn't quite translate into Terran physiology—Humans did not have tails, for one—but it was still painful. ". . . Didn't like that, did you? No? Of course not.

"No one *sane* would enjoy such suffering. But we *have* suffered it, Director Gomez. We have suffered two hundred years of *that* for a plague, *Director* Gomez," she emphasized. "Two hundred years of *this* as a covert, hidden *cancer* on the body of the Alliance."

Again she pressed her fingers to his skin and made him suffer. A V'Dan this time, alien in that the language being thought by the victim was different, but the pain being suffered, oh, the pain translated completely. Eloquently. Brutally. She held him under for an extra half second/half minute in the waters of his fellow Human's agony, then pulled him out again.

Panting, he stared at her, brown eyes wide and wild. ". . . Will you *stop doing that*?" he finally demanded, clutching at the armrests of his chair. He flinched back when she extended her hand a second time. "Don't *do* that! Don't touch me!"

Ia lowered her hand to her hip, the other one still braced on his desk. "*That*, Director, was two hundred years of *covert* lunch. If we do not stop the Salik completely in the next year, then it will be three hundred years of that being inflicted upon everyone in what will be left of the Alliance, and it will be inflicted *openly*. Entire colonies will fall. Millions and billions will be enslaved, chained, and devoured. *That* is what the Salik have all been promised by their leaders. That even the lowliest-ranked among them will finally get to savor the sweet, bleeding screams of sentient *meat*.

"*You* need to pull your head out of your asteroid and look at the *real* plague trying to kill off the Alliance worlds." Straightening, she dropped her arms at her sides and waited for him to think his way out of the fog of secondhand pain and terror she had inflicted. "We are not going to stop the release of this plague on the Salik, but we *will* contain it so that it only kills *them*. That part is *your* job."

"Stopping *diseases* is my job," Gomez growled, rising from his chair with a glare. "*Not* genocide."

Ia matched him stare for hard stare. "The Salik population currently stands at just over fifty-three billion. If they stay alive, they will slaughter one hundred fifty *trillion* sentients. You tell me which set of deaths *needs* to be prevented."

He opened his mouth to argue.

"*Which* plague will you prevent, Director? The one that claims fifty-three billion lives in a matter of weeks, or the one that tortures and devours one hundred and fifty trillion sentient, living, thinking beings over three hundred screaming, bleeding, bred-to-be-*eaten* years?" She did not blink, did not relent. "Is *that* what you want? Do you *want* to aid the Salik in their efforts? Because *that* is what it is coming down to."

"It . . . You . . . !" Raking his hands over his short-cropped hair, he finally railed at her, "It isn't about the *math*! You can't just randomly decree that X number of lives is more valuable than X other number! It's not *just* about the math."

Relaxing her hard stare, Ia shook her head slowly. "No, meioa. It's not just about the math. It's about quality of life, and mercy. By permitting them to die by the plague, I will be giving them mild fevers, chills, some pins-and-needles sensations . . . then numbness . . . paralysis . . . and a peaceful, quiet death. It will be far more merciful a death than their victims have *ever* felt. It will be far more merciful an ending than the Salik *deserve*. But I will give it to them . . . and I will *deny* that death to the rest of the Alliance as a whole.

"But I *will not* tell you or anyone else what that plague is, where it is, or when it will start . . . because the Salik *will* turn it against us once they realize what is going wrong. We will need every single second of silence on the subject of Patient Zero we can wrench from this situation before they realize what will be happening to them, to make sure that they *don't* successfully turn that plague on *us*."

"The *easiest* way to *do* that is to stop the plague from spreading *at all*!" Gomez countered.

Mouth tight, Ia reached up and poked him in the forehead. Plunged him face-first into the life-stream of a man being eaten alive by the officers of a Salik warship just thirty light-years away, right at that very moment. She pulled her finger away, and he gasped for air, then scowled at her, smacking her hand away. "Don't *do* that!"

Ia pressed the point, literally. A plunge into the timestreams, and a release. "Three." She did it again, following him as he tried to step back. "Hundred." He tried to retreat, only to fetch up against the back wall of his office. *"Years."*

"Stop it!" he ordered.

She didn't relent, just tipped her head in acknowledgment of the irony. "Funny, but that's exactly what their *victims* keep crying."

He tried to protest one more time. This time, she clamped her whole hand over his face and ruthlessly hauled him upstream, plunging him into the body of a V'Dan from the First Salik War. She did so at a point just a day or so before the end of the man's life, and just deep enough that he could feel what that other Human had felt, though not deep enough to give it any temporal context.

It wasn't a pleasant experience, even though it was very, very mild compared to the other torture. Both she and Gomez felt how numb his borrowed limbs were, how the abdomen tingled with pinpricks, and his thoughts . . . those poor thoughts were sluggish. It was all the man could do to finish dictating a final message for his loved ones . . . and hoping that the plague would die in the intervening years of cold, dark space.

They hadn't found that ship. Ia held her fellow Human in that life as the thoughts slowed, as the heartbeat weakened . . . she brought him out before their host could actually die, but only long enough to whisper in Gomez's ear, *"The suffering induced by the plague—what you felt just now—is a mercy killing, compared to* this.*"

She plunged him into a V'Dan being carved up slice by slice, with the woman's wounds cauterized by a Salik officer who wanted his prey to last . . . and plunged Gomez into the *Salik's* mind, so that he experienced the cold, brutal amusement firsthand, the excitement and pleasure of torturing a V'Dan over and over and over.

Bringing both of them out, she pulled her fingers away from his face. He staggered and sagged back against the wall, then doubled over and retched. Nose wrinkling against the smell, Ia backed up physically, but did not back down verbally.

"What *you* don't understand is that *I* believe the Salik should have a right to live. I would *like* them to live. But in order to do that, they *must* get along with all the other races. Just as the Humans and the K'Katta and the Tlassians, and all the rest have chosen to do.

"Unfortunately, Director, the Salik *cannot* change. They are biologically incapable of changing their mind-set. They are sadistic as a *species*. Cooperation with another race is a hunting strategy, nothing more—cooperating with *each other* is a hunting strategy. They do it to lure their prey into a more favorable position for eventual attack. I learned long ago a very ugly and painful truth: if the rest of the Alliance is to live, the Salik *must die*." She turned to pace around the desk to the other side, facing him from a couple meters away. "We—the Alliance—do *not* have the resources to spare to wipe them out man-to-man. We will barely have enough as it is to contain this plague, *if* you do your job.

"And your job, Director Gomez, is to save the lives that you *can*. Alliance lives. The Salik are not a part of the Alliance, and they never have been. And before you protest that *we* are killing *them*, I will tell you this. *They* created that very same plague!" she asserted, jabbing her finger off to the side. "By the sheerest chance, it was *not* released two hundred years ago. By luck and the wits of the V'Dan, who found and destroyed the research base that created it, they *lost* every last note on how to replicate it in the two centuries since, or we would *all* be long dead and gone, our worlds barren and lifeless of *anything* with a brainstem or greater.

"But while the Alliance barely escaped annihilation as a whole two centuries ago, it is a slagging *shakk*-load of trouble that is finally going to descend on us all in *this* era . . . and I find it poetic justice that they should be slain by something they themselves created. It is poetic that, in their *greed* for the taste of sentient flesh, they will devour and spread this plague among themselves, creating their own genocide.

"*Your* job is *containment*, Director. Nothing more, nothing less. You will not send out biohazard teams to try to 'study' the plague, you will *not* take samples, and you will not permit advisors or observers to approach, for that would be a death sentence for them. You will do nothing but *burn* whatever has been contaminated. The only 'cure' is frying anything touched by that plague for twenty minutes Terran Standard at one thousand degrees Celsius *or hotter.*"

Gomez blinked at her words.

"You will not even be able to touch an infected atmosphere with the skin of a spaceship, for fear of dragging it to another world," she added bluntly. "Atmospheric reentry does *not* last long enough to destroy this plague, nor does it actually burn the hull, thanks to the hot-shockwave effect. Neither will the coldest depths of space destroy it. Rather the opposite; the coldest depths of space has preserved this plague, allowing it to lie dormant in the cold vacuum of space for two centuries. It was designed to be a weapon, one which I am turning back on its creators as the fastest means we have of stopping them before hundreds of billions of innocent sentients are slaughtered one sadistic bite at a time. *That* is more important to stop, and the only way to stop it is to stop the Salik race permanently.

"Incarceration with the Blockade did not work. You cannot isolate this patient, because the Salik will only escape to slaughter again and again. For the good of the rest of the known galaxy's body, this limb *must* be amputated to keep it from destroying all the rest of the otherwise healthy flesh. You, meioa, are trying to argue that a lethal, gangrenous cancer is more important to keep alive than all the normal, healthy cells that can still be saved if we act now with an amputation. This is that amputation. Stop trying to save the cancer, and start trying to save the rest of the patient."

He stared at her, visibly shocked and bewildered by her claims. *Now* she had him, with a clear path straight toward where the future needed to go at this stage. She didn't *like* playing the bad guy in this moment, forcing him into temporal rapport . . . but it wasn't the first time she had acted against her normal inclinations, and there were yet more points ahead where she would have to do worse. Such as the reason why she was here in the first place. Ia tipped her head in slight, ironic acknowledgment.

"As I said, Director, you and I are going to have to *redefine* 'Quarantine Extreme' today." She gestured politely toward his empty chair, glad that her ploys had worked. "Please, re-take your seat and let us make plans to ensure that the cancer of the Salik nation and the malignant dangers of their plague are *properly* eradicated from our patient, being the Alliance as a whole, and the rest of our galaxy as well."

"But, I . . ." he tried protesting one last time.

"If you do not comply, Director, I will have you removed from office on grounds of Fatality Thirty-Five, Sabotage, and Fatality Two, Grand High Treason . . . because I will hold you *personally* responsible for *this*."

One last time, she dragged him into the life-waters of someone being eaten alive by their enemy. Without touching him. Stone-faced, sick inside that she had to do this, Ia held him there until she knew he would comply, then flung him back into his body. She settled back in her seat and crossed her legs, hands clasped in her lap as if she had all the time in the world. Gomez stared at her, wide-eyed and wary.

"*That* can keep happening to the whole Alliance for the next three hundred years, Director. *Or* we can end it within one year. Do forgive me for having the compassion to prefer the latter. Now, let's get to work."

JANUARY 23, 2499 T.S.
SIC TRANSIT

Christine Benjamin studied her white-haired commanding officer. The pressure of that long, thoughtful look was almost an energy of its own, though it had no flavor. Drawing in a deep breath, Ia let it out and slouched down in the thick-cushioned easy chair bolted to one corner of the chaplain's counseling office. This was the one place where the eyes of the crew weren't upon her yet wasn't a place where she had to be alone.

Conversely—vexingly—she almost wished she were alone.

"Going to finish your caf'?" Bennie asked, picking up her own mug for a sip.

"No."

The older woman swallowed. "Got something on your mind?"

"No."

"I think 'yes,'" Bennie countered. "For the last few days, ever since we left the Gatsugi motherworld . . . No, correction," she murmured, changing her mind. "Since you came back from your visit to the ACDC, you've been . . . Oh, what's the word for it? That thing that Abraham Lincoln suffered from."

Ia frowned and slanted her friend and counselor a puzzled look. "Bipolar disorder?"

"No, no, not that," Bennie negated, fluttering her hand. "No, the *word* for it, back in the day—ah! *Melancholy.* You have been melancholic."

Ia frowned. "That sounds like 'colic,' and all I know about colic is that you increase the humidity to help ease the congestion and coughing."

The redhead snorted. ". . . You are pathetically undereducated in any area other than your calling, Ia."

Sighing, Ia rolled her eyes and slouched a bit more. "No *shakk*, Sherlock. Everything I know is on a need-to-know basis. If I don't need to know it, then I don't bother wasting my time learning it. I haven't learned more than a handful of things just for the sheer sake of learning since I was fifteen."

"I'm sure Private Tomas Orange would be disappointed to learn he'll never have the chance to teach you a French knot." Bennie weathered Ia's hard, bemused look with equanimity. "He's swapped up his duty shift—with Helstead's permission—in order to teach embroidery and card weaving to some of the meioas who are interested in it on second watch. Even Spyder's taking lessons."

"Still don't know what you're talking about," Ia dismissed. "If it doesn't harm the timelines, I don't care."

"A French knot is a stitch in embroidery, but that's not what we're talking about. Did Director Gomez know what you were talking about?" Bennie asked next, her tone quiet but pointed.

Ia flinched. Shifting her hand to her forehead, she rubbed at her eyes, the original right one and the Meddling-restored left, which felt as natural and real as ever. She knew what her friend was doing. Her confidante. Her DoI-appointed psychologist. Bennie was doing her job, which meant *she* had to do her job, too. Except . . .

"I bullied him . . . and I hate myself for it." The words were out. They were said. They were the truth, but Ia knew they weren't enough.

So did Bennie. After almost seven years of knowing each other, of talking and listening and sharing caf' after cup of caf', Christine Benjamin knew her fairly well. The chaplain sipped again at her mug and waited.

"I hate my job." The confession emerged as the barest of whispers. Warmth pooled at the corners of her eyes. Ia rubbed away the tears before they could fall free, and confessed her sins to her chaplain. "I *bullied* him into going my way, Bennie. He wasn't going to listen to reason—he's as fanatic as the damned Church! Only *his* prayer book is the Xeno-Genome Project, and his corona symbol is a molecular scanner. And I. *Bullied*. Him." She thumped her finger on the padded arm of the chair before letting it flop back into her lap.

"Did you succeed in getting him to cooperate?" Bennie asked calmly. "Without any major problems down the line coming back to bite your asteroid off? Like they did with that Feyori, Miklinn?"

"Yes, and *yes*," Ia admitted, irritated. "There will be no problems. I bullied him with images and sensations of what it's like to be eaten by a Salik . . . and what it's like to *be* a Salik taking pleasure in his victim's screams. I just want that all to end, and yet . . ."

Almost a minute ticked by. Bennie finished her cup of caf' and clipped it back into its holder on the side table set in the corner between their chairs. ". . . And?"

"And yet I can hear the relentless ticking of time." It was another quiet, too-quiet confession. She rubbed at her brow, at her eyes again.

"Why is it relentless?"

Ia flopped her hand down on the padded armrest. "Because I'm afraid to go home."

"Will the fighting be that dangerous?"

"What? No," Ia denied, frowning. "It'll be like any other fight. Difficult in trying to keep the *right* people alive, but no more or less dangerous or difficult than any other battle. Even with the Greys coming, and having to face down their greater tech, there are plenty of high probabilities I've set up in advance to see that we succeed."

"Then . . . what? Why are you afraid to go home, Ia?"

She closed her eyes. "Because once I go there, that means

I'll have to leave . . . and once I leave, I will *never* go back."
Her arm bent at the elbow, hand cupped near her ear, body
swaying faintly in pulse with her blood and her thoughts. "And
I can hear the relentless ticking of time as the seconds bleed
and bleed and bleed away, until I *have* to go home, and then
I'll *have* to leave . . . and go do everything I will *have* to do
after that . . . and never go home again. Home will be lost behind enemy lines, and will have to *stay* lost for two whole centuries, or everything—*everything*—will be ruined. As bad as,
or worse than, when we lost Private N'Keth."

". . . Melancholy," Bennie stated lightly, if assertively. "I'll
prescribe you some chocolate."

Ia sat up at that, scowling. "This is *not a joke!*"

Leveling a finger at the younger woman, Bennie spoke
flatly. "You have already used that line, young lady." At Ia's
frown of confusion, she clarified. "When Private Sung screwed
up? That big speech in front of the whole crew, with the ship in
lockdown while docked at that Battle Platform after the big
Helix Nebula fight?"

Rolling her eyes, Ia flopped back into the embrace of the
overstuffed easy chair.

"Eating chocolate will boost your serotonin levels and fill
out the hours with something more pleasant than listening to
a clock tick. If we had any clocks on board that ticked," the
redhead allowed in an aside. "I think they're all digital."

She barely even had to think about it. "Corporal Charles
Puan, 3rd Platoon, has a small collection of pocket watches.
Mechanical ones, which he knows how to fix and repair. He
only works on them at moments like these, when he knows
we'll be in transit FTL for several hours, because the little gear
thingies are too dangerous to let loose while we're maneuvering at insystem speeds. Jewels. Whatever they're called."

"Well then, you'll just have to avoid going into his quarters. Which would be a violation of the rules and regs anyway
if you didn't have just cause, so you should be covered, right?"
Bennie asked.

Ia slanted her a look, then sighed heavily. "Are we done,
here?"

"That's up to you. You're the one who scheduled this session," her friend and counselor pointed out.

Sighing again, Ia twisted onto her side, tucked up one knee, squirmed a bit more, then made each muscle group relax with a slow, deep breath. "We're done, here," she muttered between breaths. "Yeah, I'm done."

"If we're done here, then what are you doing?" Christine asked her, quirking one auburn brow.

Since her eyes were shut, Ia couldn't see the older woman's expression, but she could hear the confusion in Bennie's voice. It pleased her. She curled and wiggled a little more, pillowing her cheek on the thick-cushioned arm of the chair. "I'm going to take a nap in this chair. I've always wanted to, and so I am going to. Right now."

"Right . . . So you're going to take a nap. In my office. Shall I fetch you a blanket, then? Perhaps one of those teddy bears Private Bethu-ne' makes in his spare time?"

"Yes, please, but just the blanket."

For a long moment, the other woman didn't move. Finally, she sighed and rose, walking away. Ia kept her eyes shut, listening to one of the doors quietly hiss open and shut. Several seconds later, Bennie returned through the same door. Soft warmth draped over her. Fumbling for the edge of the afghan, Ia pulled it up over her head. Not because she was cold but because the gesture touched her, warmed her from the inside out. It also threatened to push out more tears.

"What time do you need to be awakened?"

She didn't want to think about that, but she had to. "Seventeen thirty-five . . . I'll need twenty-five minutes before supper to wake up, work out the kinks, and grab a quick shower."

"I'll set an alert on my workstation, then go tell Floathawg and Sunrise we'll be meeting in the amidships briefing room one deck up. That way you can rest in peace for the next few hours."

"I set them up, you know." Ia hadn't meant to confess that much, but there it was, out of her mouth and into the chaplain's ears. "I set up a *lot* of the pairings on this ship. A few caught me off guard—Spyder and Mishka, for one—but I knew which couples could make a go of it in the long run . . . and I set them up so they'd have some small happiness in all of this."

"I know you did. Though I'm calling *shakk-torr* on not

knowing about the lieutenant and the doctor," the chaplain quipped.

Ia flopped the edge of the afghan down out of her way, lifting her head in protest. "I didn't!"

Already on her way to the front door of her counseling office, Bennie turned and walked backwards. "*Shakk. Torr.* If I'm a two-fister, you're a manipulative bitch. Just remember, Ia," she added, tapping the controls for the door, "*yes*, you may bully some people, but you *also* set up a lot of others for love and happiness. You're not an evil monster. Melancholic, but not evil."

Debating how much energy it would take to make a rude gesture, Ia gave up and slumped back onto the armrest. *Melancholy . . . I'd cry "shakk-torr" too . . . except she's right. It's a polite word for depressed . . . and I don't want to get up and do anything right now . . .*

She flipped the knitted blanket back over her head, fussed with it a bit, then gave up with a rough sigh. Knowing that Time was ticking away, her thoughts kept trying to race to all the things she had to do, all the things she could fit into every spare second to be had.

Ruthlessly, she deliberately emptied her mind. Listened only to the rush of air in and out of her lungs, the faint thumping of her heartbeat, and the whispering of the air vents pumping fresh air from the nearest life-support bay. Focused on nothing at all, just to snatch just a few hours of rest.

"Commander Harper to General Ia. I need to speak with you about the special new project you want me to work on, sir. Do you have a spare hour or two?"

. . . Slag. She winced and buried her face in the cushions, but only for a few seconds. Giving up, she rolled face up and electrokinetically prodded her command bracer. *"I'll be there in just a few. Ia out."*

It was her own fault, too. Or rather, her instincts, her gifts. She struggled up out of the overstuffed chair and disentangled herself from the blanket. Not wanting to violate the privacy of her chaplain's quarters and mindful of the Spacer's Law, Ia settled on folding the blanket and webbing it onto Bennie's desk. *So much for my one hour of peace . . .*

Another prod of her bracer reopened the commsystem. *"General Ia to Chaplain Benjamin, that alternative location will not be necessary at this time. You are free to resume your normal schedule as I apparently have more work to do. Ia out."*

MARCH 4, 2499 T.S.
THE TOWER
KAHO'OLAWE, EARTH, SOL SYSTEM

The moment Ia boarded the shuttle and the airlock door sealed shut, closing them off from the bustling underground hangar bay built into the side of the island's caldera, she yanked at the buttons of her Dress Black coat. Two of them popped and shot across the airlock, clattering off the hard, gray-enameled surfaces. Her first officer sighed heavily and stooped to gather them off the deckplates.

"Lock and Web it, Ia. Get your temper under control," he ordered her. Around them, the ship hummed with the distinct tenor rumble of compression pumps filling the shuttle's air tanks.

In reply, she whipped off her Dress cap and flung it through the inner airlock door as it opened. It smacked into Chief Yeoman Patricia Huey's chest. The brunette caught it belatedly, one brow rising upward. "Is everything alright, sir?"

"Politicians!" Ia snapped, struggling out of her coat. Before she could fling it, too, across the room, Harper grabbed it and held on to the weighted fabric.

"Yes, he *was* obnoxious; *no*, you don't get to stay mad at the idiot. He has punishment enough ahead of him, reciting the Oath of Government Service until he sobers up," her first officer stated. "Now, let me take that from you, nice and easy . . . and I'll stow it in a cargo-hold locker . . . and *you* can repair those buttons in your spare time. You, yourself."

She shot him a dark look. He leveled a pointed one back at her. As much as she wanted to snarl at someone, Ia refrained from snarling at her first officer.

"Remember what Rzhikly said back at the Academy, Ia?" Meyun reminded her. "An officer leads by *example*. Be a *better* example."

Her smile was more tooth than charm. "And am I *not* allowed to get *angry* at being asked to perform like some sort of trained *dog*, or . . . or *circus clown*?"

"Yes, you can get angry. But not destructively." Carefully using the wadded-up, medal-lumped fabric to cushion his touch, he pushed on her back to get her to move into the rest of the ship. Their newest pilot eyed both of them warily but did back up out of the way. Harper kept talking in a soothing tone. "I know you want to string him up by his garters, plus the three that were urging him on, but *politician* isn't the dirty word it once was three or four hundred years ago. And the others did come down hard on him when they realized he was being obnoxious.

"Individuals can be asteroid heads, but he does recite the Oath every morning. After a while, it does sink into your head," he told her. "Which you'd know if you had to do it over and over and over."

She rounded on him. "That is *exactly* what I do, Harper! Every single morning, I wake up, I review where I'm supposed to be going with the timestreams, and when, and what tasks I and everyone else needs to do. If that isn't an Oath, then I don't know what is—but for God's sake!" she exclaimed, raking her hand through her neatly trimmed hair, disarranging the chin-length locks. "I told him 'no' politely over and over, and he wouldn't stop pestering me to see the future! What was I supposed to do, shove it down his mental throat?"

"Did you want to?" Both officers turned and looked at the noncommissioned pilot. Huey shrugged and folded her arms across her chest, one hand still holding on to Ia's Dress cap. She repeated herself diffidently. "You know . . . did you *want* to shove this meioa-o headfirst into those 'timestream' things you see?"

"*Yes!*" Snatching her cap, Ia turned and stalked into the cargo bay. She found an empty cupboard without more than a toe dab in the possibilities of Time, and shoved in the cap, then her jacket . . . after waiting for Harper to stuff the two loose buttons into one of its pockets. "And yes, I'll slagging well fix them myself." She looked up at Yeoman Huey, who had followed the two of them. "Does that surprise you, Yeoman? That I feel violence and rage at being harassed?"

Mouth quirking in a lopsided smile, the yeoman shook her head. "No, sir. In fact, it's actually rather reassuring. You remind me of a knight I knew back on Scadia. Loved to fight, but hated to win, because winning comes with political consequences back home. One of the best teachers I knew, but couldn't stand the pressure of being asked to win Crown.

"But he also once said it's rare for anyone to get really upset over just one thing, sir. Usually it takes a couple things to get, well . . . button-snapping mad. So, what else are you mad at?" Huey asked her, leaning her shoulder against the frame of the compartment door.

Ia stared at her, then looked at the decking. She glared at the plates, closed her eyes, dragged in a deep breath . . . and let it go. "Today . . . is my birthday . . . and the last thing I wanted was to be annoyed and pestered on my birthday."

"It's also Thorne's birthday, too, isn't it?" Meyun asked her. He tapped the side of his head at her sharp look, reminding her of his eidetic memory. "Half brother, you said, and half an hour older, but still a birthing-day twin. And we'll be there in just a few more days."

Dragging in a deep breath, she held it, then let it out slowly. That was indeed part of the problem, if only a small part. The rest, she still couldn't tell anyone. "Four days, three hours, fifty-seven minutes, meioas. Presuming you'll return to the cockpit and prepare for takeoff, Yeoman?" Ia asked their shuttle pilot. "I'd take the helm myself, but I'm a bit *angry* still. I may not be completely comfortable with the literal worship I get around the V'Dan, but even among the Terrans, my abilities are not normally considered a goddamned *party trick*."

Nodding, Huey turned to head toward the cockpit. Harper held out his arm, blocking Ia from following her. He waited until they both heard the cockpit door hiss shut, then spoke. He knew as well as Ia did that they would have at least a few more minutes before Yeoman Huey received clearance to lift off from the Tower's landing pad. "Bennie told me that you're dreading going home."

"*Shakk,*" she muttered. "Still telling tales to you, is she?"

"Don't be a two-fisting bitch, yourself," he warned her, pointing at her. "She cares, she knows that I care, and she knows that I can get through to you sometimes. Ia . . . if you don't think I don't know what you're feeling, after all these years of knowing you, of seeing the future possibilities, and being smart enough to figure out where you're aiming the future, and *why* you're herding everyone that way . . . Well, you'd be pretty damn stupid. And contrary, since *you're* the one who keeps dumping complex engineering problems in my lap."

"Oh, sweet-talk me some more," Ia retorted, rolling her eyes. She sighed and strove to let go of more of her anger, and some of her fear. The first, she managed. The second . . . not so much. Pinching the brow of her nose, Ia breathed deep. "Fine. I'm upset because of that, too. Things are snowballing on Sanctuary, slightly askew of what they should be. There's an almost even-odds chance now that Rabbit will be in serious trouble by the time we get there.

"I *want* to keep everyone but Sergeant Kardos and myself off Sanctuary, because fighting in high gravity will tax all the nonnatives even with gravity weaves, which we can't really take, which means using the telekinetics in the crew . . . but if she's captured and held for interrogation, it's going to require a fast, discreet extraction, and the best team for that job is on this ship, not on that planet. The people my family have been training are good, but they just aren't good enough, yet. That's what Kardos is for." Raking her nails through her hair, she scrubbed for a few moments, relieving the itch that had built up over the last few hours. Harper's slight, amused smile told her that he thought her actions were funny-looking. She rolled her eyes but didn't hold it against him.

"Shall we adjourn to the cockpit and squeeze ourselves in next to the chief yeoman?" he asked. "Or strap ourselves in here in the jump seats the grunts use, like so much brass-tacked cargo?"

"Brass-tacked cargo." Moving over to the doorframe, Ia palmed it shut, then hit the comm button. *"Ia to Huey, we'll be riding back here. ETA to liftoff?"*

"Since we're not in a rush, I'll be ready in five and a half minutes. I want to finish loading the tanks with fresh air. The Tower's spaceport says we can lift off in seven, so we've the time for it."

"Understood. We'll be Locked and Webbed in one. Ia and Harper out."

"Want to hold hands while we wait out the remaining minutes?" Meyun asked her, grinning mischievously as he moved over to one of the seats lining the cargo bay's bulkheads.

"Do you want to end up face-first in the timestreams?" she countered wryly, though she chose a seat with only one empty place between them. It was far enough away to avoid any accidental contact . . . but she did offer her hand, palm up, after she finished clipping the harness in place.

"I can think of more pleasant places to land, faceup or facedown," he admitted, covering her hand with his own. "Like one of the beaches here on Kaho'olawe. Southeastern, of course; the northwestern side of the island's still off-limits to nonnatives."

Thankfully, her gifts didn't activate. "You had your day of Leave yesterday, Commander."

"Yes, but it was boring going to a beach without you." He sighed. "And having to be on display today for all those politicians and top brass has soured what little relaxation I did manage to achieve. Even if I wasn't the center of all that unwelcome attention, I was still right next to the center of it."

"Welcome to my world. It's ruined what peace I garnered in my visit to the Afaso the day before . . . though I think I'm getting some of it back, now that I'm calming down." She squeezed his fingers lightly and changed the subject. "How's the special project coming along?"

"I think I'm close to figuring out what all those things have in common. But it might help if I could ask the time-plains a few questions," Harper said, holding her hand as the shuttle engines started warming up, sending a faint baritone *thrum* through the hull, adding to the noise of the compressors. "I don't know if your 'search parameter function' would work as well with *me* asking the questions, though. You've always been the one to make it work . . . but it's always been based on what *you* perceive of what I'm trying to ask. I'm not sure I can put it into words that clearly, though I know something of what I'm looking for."

"It might work that way if I was reading your thoughts telepathically as you spoke," Ia offered. These days, she felt a lot more comfortable about fraternizing with her first officer. He had conducted himself quite circumspectly, as cautiously and privately as she could have wished. "It might add that extra layer of nuance you need. But it'd be rather . . . intimate."

He smiled, leaning back against the cushioned headrest. "You know I don't have any fear of that."

There wasn't much she could safely say or do in response other than to give him a lopsided smile and draw him onto the timeplains to search for what he needed. Once they returned to the ship, she would have prophecies to write and battles to fight, all while praying Harper could find a way to not just slow but fix a gaping hole in the universe.

Her anger could wait. His task could not.

MAY 7, 2499 T.S.
INDEPENDENT COLONYWORLD SANCTUARY

She was out of time.

Ia knew it the moment the *Damnation* left the hyperrift. It felt in the back of her mind like a globule of spit flung from the mouth of a disgusted sergeant. An unpleasant image, an unpleasant thought . . . and an unpleasant reality. Her finger jabbed at the comm button.

"*Ia to all hands, we have a Plan C. I repeat, a Plan C. Commander Helstead, and Privates Yarrin and O'Taicher, meet me and Sergeant Kardos in the boardroom amidships in fifteen minutes, light armor, no weaves, weapons hot.* Teevie, get me the *Nadezhda Popova* even faster, on my left secondary. O'Keefe, helm to yours in twenty-five seconds."

"Aye, sir, helm is mine in twenty-two," Yeoman O'Keefe agreed.

Private Teevie added, "Pinging now, sir. On your left secondary."

Ia was still flying the ship at a significant fraction of Cee, coming out of the hyperrift hole. She did not take her eyes from the blips of text bursting and racing on her main screen. She still had to follow the course correction plotted by the navicomp and couldn't look immediately to her left when the dark, gray-hair-framed face of a woman in her fifties appeared.

"General Ia," Vice Commodore Brenya Attinks stated, her tone conveying a touch of censure in its increasing bite. "Last time you were in the area, you were just a Ship's Captain, and you convinced me to dismiss the charges of trespassing on two of your soldiers. I took a lot of political *shakk* for that and have been stuck here in this command ever since, when I could've been transferred to a place where I could have done some *good* in this war." She paused, smiled pleasantly, and asked, "So what can I suffer from you and yours today?"

"Transferring helm to you, O'Keefe," Ia stated.

"The helm is . . . mine, sir. Following your trajectory now," the ginger blonde pilot reassured her. "ETA to orbit, fourteen minutes."

"Good," Ia praised her. She stripped her hand out of the attitude glove, free from the task of keeping her ship in one piece and on course. *Now* she could look to her left and flicked her hands over the workstation controls, sending authorizations on a subchannel. "Vice Commodore Attinks, you are ordered to pull in everything. Every navigation buoy, every patrol fighter, every shuttle, every *scrap* of Terran military tech that is not on that planet, I want all of it pulled into the *Popova*'s bays and Locked and Webbed within thirty hours Terran Standard. If you cannot pull it in, you are to destroy it. And yes, that *includes* the hyperrelay node, but save that for last.

"Your highest salvage priority is living personnel, followed by anything with a weapon or a capacity to move. Your highest destruction priority is anything that can scan, sweep, or communicate." Leaning over to her right, she lifted up the little door that hid the prongs that gave her access to electricity, and started absorbing energy. "Your orders include temporary security clearance for accessing and commanding the personnel in the High Class 8b listening outpost on the seventh planet of this system. You will remove the twelve black boxes and the seventeen personnel on that station—by force if need be—and you will destroy their facilities from orbit with one of your hydrobombs.

"In thirty hours and two minutes, you will have the *Nadezhda Popova* back in tight orbit around Sanctuary—and by tight orbit," Ia warned her, "I mean you will park your ship in the closest orbit the navicomp can get you to the atmosphere without burning the shields. Once you have achieved that tight orbit, your pilots are to stand down at their stations, take their hands out of the gloves, and let the comp do the autopiloting until I give you the signal to break orbit and leave. Is that clear?"

"General, I do not *understand* these orders, sir," Attinks said, giving Ia a bemused look. "And this will put us behind schedule, since we were supposed to depart this system on patrol to the next in twenty more minutes . . . but . . . my crew and I will comply with your commands, sir. I also was not aware of any manned listening posts in this system . . . but then my clearance level is only High Class 7c—are you going to explain *why* we're pulling out, when we're still under contract to protect this system?"

"Just between you, me, and the daily encryption codes," Ia answered dryly, "the main government on Sanctuary is going to go *shakk n'shova* crazy. They will fire on your ship, my ship, their own space station, and anything *else* anywhere near them, just over thirty hours from now."

That startled the vice commodore. She gaped for a moment, blinked, then frowned "Uh . . . not to question my orders, sir, but if we are take up a *close* orbit, you do realize we are going to have a very hard time avoiding that incoming fire?"

"Yes, I am very much aware of it. Your shields will take it. You will not return fire, nor break orbit until I give the command to head for *Confucius* Station," Ia said, her mind aware of the ticking of time on the coming rescue party, and the fact that she needed to get herself ready for insertion, too. She was still drawing on the ship's energy grid, but now could *see* that grid, the power conduits, the glowing screens, the body heat of the others on the small, modified bridge of her elongated second ship. A slight, wry smile twisted her mouth and wrinkled her nose. "Make sure you're well rested and that everyone has a clean change of underwear, Vice Commodore. The Greys are about to invade and take over this system, and we *will* be leaving them to it."

"Ahh . . ." Attinks gaped at her. Ia didn't give her time to ask any questions.

"Now if you'll excuse me, I have to go scare up some extra personnel, then get down to my home planet in order to make sure they start their inevitable civil war on time and on schedule. Begin your countdown as thirty hours Terran Standard exactly

from . . . five, four, three, two, one . . . *mark*. General Ia out."
She cut off the channel but kept drawing energy from the con-
duit prongs. "O'Keefe, park us in a geosynchronous over Our
Blessed Mother. You have the bridge until Lieutenant Spyder
arrives."

"Aye, sir," the yeoman agreed, her gaze firmly on her own
screens.

"Sergeant Santori, get ready to shoot me."

"General, yes, sir; every time you or your guests darken, sir,"
the 2nd Platoon sergeant said. Unstrapping herself from one of
the spare workstations, the dark-haired woman unclipped the
stunner rifle from the edge of her console. Standing, Santori
flicked the weapon on and adjusted the nozzle cone, aiming it
at her commanding officer.

Drawing out a little bit more, Ia twisted the energies within
her—and popped into a silvery sphere. Santori shot her twice
with the stunner field. The electrosonic pulses tasted like bacon-
tomato sandwiches. Drinking it in, Ia swirled and headed for
the door. Santori followed her.

Out of politeness, Ia zapped the door controls, opening
them for the matter-based woman, though she didn't have to
have an opening; the huge gaps between whirling electrons
and their proton-neutron nuclei left her plenty of room to maneuver as an energy being. It wasn't far to the officers' meeting
room, just two doors forward from the bridge. As soon as the
other woman was braced in a comfortable firing stance, Ia
began.

Twisting inward, she reached for her personal cosmic
strings, the ones tying her to the Feyori who had sworn themselves in service to her. She didn't have to reach far; most of
the selected fifteen were actually on Sanctuary, having a last
snack-and-*shakk* while awaiting her call. They teleported in
ones and twos, silvery spheres the size of bridge workstations,
slightly larger than Santori could have spread her arms and
legs. They bobbed through the edges of the workstation-
embedded table, roughly occupying the spots Ia's cadre
would have used in a similar meeting. Except this wasn't anything matter-based bodies could do. Not in a timely way.

(*Thank you for coming,*) Ia stated, pitching her thoughts in
an energy format the Feyori around her could hear. (*I realize*

*the task ahead is distasteful, but it still needs to be done. I
don't have the time, and no one else has the ability. Link with
me now, so that I can share with you the exact shapes of the
satellites you will be making, in conjunction with Commander Harper's material components.*)

Curious, bored, willing, they drifted closer, until the edges
of their spheres brushed together. As soon as the last of the
fifteen linked in to the rest, Ia snapped them all into the
timestreams. There, she was still matter-based, matter-shaped,
and hauled them into a side-stream, a pocket universe wherein
she *did* have the time to do this all herself. Unfortunately, Rabbit needed rescuing ahead of schedule.

The task she had in mind was literally distasteful to the Feyori; several started, and one tried to pull herself out of the link. (*I
am* not *going to be eating and regurgitating* shit!) the offended
Meddler snapped. (*Find someone else to*— Aaaah!)

Ia relaxed her tight-dragging grip. It had only been a short
trip, but painful enough to get the Meddler's attention, nonetheless.

(*I have just abraded away one year of your life, Selula,*)
she warned the alien. (*The next among you to balk at my
commands will lose ten years. The next after that, one hundred . . . and then one thousand. After that, I start killing
you, and* then *is when I start bringing in your replacements.
But I will grant you the right to choose, either to spend your
time hauling the crysium up to this ship or spend your time
reshaping it. As this is his home territory, Albelar is in charge
of the group selecting the spray fields to be harvested. Silverstone will be in charge of the reshaping team.*

(*The two of them are in charge of your efforts in my
absence, but* do not *think my absence means my lack of
awareness. I can reach into the future, and I can reach into
the past, and from* any *point in time, I can and will chastise
you. There is no counterfaction, there is no neutral, and
there is no refusal anymore. Now. Do you understand the
tasks to which you have just been assigned?*)

Consent came. It came from them in staggered clumps,
some of it willing, some of it reluctant, but it came, and she
gained it even from the one named Selula. Pulling out of the
link, Ia swirled back, opened herself to a few more shots from

Santori's stunner rifle, and dropped back into her physical body. She staggered, still not nearly as graceful as a full-blooded and much more practiced Meddler would be, but she stayed on her feet. "Those staying on the ship will follow Sergeant Santori to the bow cargo hold, where Commander Harper's assembly team awaits.

"The rest of you, depart with my father to the far side of the planet, where the absence of so many crysium sprays will not be easily noted. Dismissed."

She didn't wait to see if they complied; her younger self from about nine hours back, before a solid bout of sleep, had taken an hour's worth of real time to watch over the Feyori for the next twenty-one hours. This side of the coming troubles would not be affected either way by the cascading chain of unpleasant, low probabilities down in the capital of her birthworld. They would comply or they would be punished, and they knew it. Knowing they would get the job done, Ia headed for the nearest lift. Helstead's team was down twelve decks, in the auditorium-sized boardroom below the core of the main gun.

Spyder was right where he'd promised to be, inside the lift, a crate of light armor opened and ready. She was already clad in her camouflage grays, colors suitable for infiltrating an urban base. As the doors slid shut, and the lift started down, Spyder crouched and snapped the legging plates into place down each thigh, while she slung on the half jacket that would protect her chest, back, and upper arms. The base material was capable of stopping bullets, though the impacts would still bruise; the polished-pewter plates were ceristeel, capable of absorbing and deflecting laserfire.

Stunners, thankfully, would not be a problem on her homeworld, or she would have had to order the team to go fully clad in mech to reduce the chance of being rendered unconscious. They had been banned long ago, leaving only the more lethal weapons at her fellow Sanctuarians' disposal. Dropping a reflection-coated helmet onto her head, Spyder waited until she fixed the chinstrap, then smacked it on the top, checking to make sure it wouldn't fall off.

"Ready check!" he barked, as if she were a raw private fresh out of Basic, and he still a Squad Sergeant in Ferrar's Fighters.

A wiggle in place as the lift car swayed to a stop let her know all the straps and snaps were secure. "Lieutenant, checked and ready, sir!"

Spyder grinned and smacked her on the back of the helmet this time. "'Ave fun killin' a few of 'em, for me," he ordered, pushing her forward through the opening doors. "But no more'n y' need to, eh?"

"No *shakk*, Lieutenant; that would be counterproductive," Ia muttered, striding down the hall. Stepping into the boardroom via the side door she usually used, she spotted the others clustered around the head table. Helstead had her hands braced on the tabletop, her eyes closed and her brow furrowed in concentration. Several bags and boxes of belongings had been stacked on the table. Straps dangled down the edges, showing they had been properly Locked and Webbed while they were in transit. Several more crates sat on the platform floor, still mostly webbed, though the two privates, Rhian O'Taicher and Iglesias Yarrin, were busy unstrapping them.

Kardos, grim-faced and silver-armored, with the visor of his helm pushed up, stood at Attention, laser rifle cradled in his arms and a pair of scimitars strapped to his hips, their golden, faintly glowing hilts spiral-wrapped with leather thongs to provide him the best possible grip.

Most of the belongings on the table were his. Most of the crates on the floor were the last of the Rings of Truth she had made to guide her homeworld in the coming centuries, boxes of blood-blended beads to allow her to craft a few more while down there, suits of armor plating on ballistic cloth—the plates were crysium, not ceristeel—and ninety-eight blades of varying styles with matching, crysium-lined sheaths she had made from the last of the sprays shipped off to the *Damnation* months ago. The last two were slung on the sergeant's hips, making for a total of one hundred if one didn't count the bracer on their leader's right wrist, waiting patiently under her uniform.

Her attention was not on the weapons, however, but rather on the crates holding them. "Lieutenant Commander. Those crates are still here."

Helstead shook her head. "I'm getting interference. It's not like it was on Dulshvwl. It's like . . . trying to push through a force-field-style fog. Whatever it is, it keeps spitting energy at me, and I lose my grasp of the drop zone."

Sighing roughly, Ia stepped up behind the other woman and wrapped her fingers around the back of Helstead's neck. Energy, memory, and telepathy poured into her. (*You know the coordinates; the fog is there for you to siphon up and lean upon, soldier.*)

Under the press of her energies and Helstead's abilities, the crates started *bamfing* out of existence, startling Yarrin and O'Taicher. They hurried to get out of the way as Helstead ported out the ones under webbing, then the ones that had been freed. Within seconds the ones on the table began vanishing as well, cluster by cluster.

Ia held out her other hand as Helstead paused for breath and to refocus her target zone. "E-clip!"

Yarrin quickly yanked one out of his ammo loop and tossed it at her. Catching it, Ia slipped her fingers into the contact points and drained the energy cell dry. That revived her energies. She tossed it back for him to stow as the last bag vanished. "The moment you land, orient yourselves, find and flank the door, and set up an ambush. We will have less than a minute before they drag in the prisoner. *Her* life is worth more than either of yours, Yarrin, O'Taicher," Ia warned them grimly. "So is the Sergeant's, here . . . and if you want to get off-world again, you keep Helstead alive as well. Is that clear?"

"Sir, yes, sir!" both men snapped, coming to Attention.

Ia nodded, acknowledging the sobriety in their eyes. "I am sorry, but that's the truth in this fight. There's a fifteen percent chance one or both of you might get hurt, but better you than one of them. Helstead, are you ready?"

"No, sir. But you feed me some more KI, we'll be on our way," she promised.

"You have twenty seconds—we'll have half a minute, down there," she warned the others. Helstead pushed away from the table, stepping back and breathing deeply, then flicked on her bracer light. Ia moved with Delia, shifting her hand from the redhead's nape to her wrist. "Grab her arms, and center your thoughts on arriving safely. Then hold yourselves still."

O'Taicher came around and grasped Helstead by the upper arm. Yarrin did the same on the right. Kardos sighed roughly, but clasped the petite woman's hand. Ia continued to feed her energies until her second officer whispered, *". . . Three . . . two . . . one . . ."*

There was a pressure differential as the universe slammed away and came back. Lungs abruptly full, then just as abruptly compressed, Ia coughed and staggered. She wasn't the only one, and not just because they came into place two centimeters off the floor. Yarrin dropped to his knees with a grunt and O'Taicher slumped against Helstead, making her stagger against Kardos and Ia. Bracing her soldiers, Ia waited three seconds for her own disorientation to pass, then used her telekinesis to haul the fallen private back onto his feet.

"Anchor your minds, support your weight, and fan out," she murmured, pushing Helstead away from the door and off to the side.

The redhead nodded and moved into the corner, pressing her back to the whitewashed wall. Everything in the unlit chamber was white: walls, floor, ceiling. There were no right angles other than the rectangular seam of the door, and what should have been the eight corners of the cube-like chamber were rounded and dimpled with glazed white domes projecting subtly into the room. Projection nodes, barely visible as glossy, reflective curves in the glow of Helstead's bracer light.

Yarrin and O'Taicher braced themselves next to her, with O'Taicher as the stronger telekinetic standing next to the tired, sagging officer, loaning her a little psychic lift against the hard pull of Sanctuary's 3.21Gs. If they slouched, it would be noticed as something unusual. Ceristeel light armor could be found through various military and peacekeeper surplus companies. Weapons were weapons, and there would always be a thriving market for such things, legal or otherwise.

Dressed as they were, they could easily be mistaken for local mercenaries. Gravity weaves and slumping postures, however, screamed off-worlder. That was something Ia did not care to shout to the loyalist troops of the Church.

Helstead had to come because she alone could get them in and out without having to fight their way through too many security layers. But though she was from Eiaven, and the *Damnation*'s gravity had been played with a little, she was no telekinetic. Yarrin and O'Taicher both were.

Ia put her own back to the wall, the door to her immediate right; Yarrin stood on the other side, of course, and Kardos took up a spot past her right elbow. A mere second later, the machinery buried in the node-bulges flared to life, projecting an illusion of a doorway leading onto an open-air platform overlooking a thronging mass of people, all of whom were shouting and screaming about "Flay the traitor!" and "Absolve her of her sins!" plus "Mercy for the repentant!" and "Why won't you recant?" sobbed in an especially emotional voice from a petite Asian woman Ia recognized: Rabbit's mother.

Quickly snapping to attention, Ia watched as her companions did the same. Helstead shut off her bracer light; two seconds after, the door swung open into the corridor. The crowd noise swelled, and guards in ceristeel-plated light armor not too dissimilar from their own quickly moved into position along the walls. Projections only, and the computer controlling them quickly compensated for their own presence, assuming in its thankfully blind way that they were to be part of the scenario.

". . . You hear *that*?" one of the approaching men demanded.

Ia didn't have to look to know he was the chief interrogator, nor that he had a fistful of Rabbit's hair, tilting her head up as she was dragged by her shoulders between the two briefly paused guards in the corridor. She didn't have to look because she had seen this moment more than once in the timestreams. Seen that pretty, moon-shaped face, bloodied at the mouth and the nose, bruised from several blows as the "Re-Education Squad" tried to break her will.

"*Do* you hear it?" the man demanded

"Hear . . . what?" Rabbit asked.

"Your friends. Your family! They're *concerned* for you, Elizabeth. They fear for your *soul*," the interrogator coaxed, utterly earnest in his concern for the woman's spiritual welfare. "Why, Mrs. Cheung, your dear, kindhearted mother, is red-eyed and trembling, nearly prostrate with her grief! With good cause, too, since if you don't recant, we're going to have to burn you alive as a warning to all others.

"Will you recant? Please, Elizabeth?"

". . . Huh?" was their captive's eloquent reply.

A disgusted noise escaped the interrogator. "Haven't you

heard a word I've said? *Tell* us who the leaders are, and your sins and your pains will be forgiven!"

"Sorry," Rabbit mumbled. "Th' music's . . . rather loud."

". . . Music? What music?"

"Music . . . in m' head . . ."

Another disgusted sigh, and the sound of hiking boots being dragged over the rubbery flooring everyone used on this world. They pulled her into the room—and Ia and Yarrin both struck; Ia, with her crysium bracer-turned-blade, and Yarrin with a service knife fetched from his boot. Both struck true, in the narrow gap between ballistics jacket and ceristeel helm. Both guards staggered, gasping in shock and pain . . . and dropped not only Rabbit's shoulders, but themselves as well. Ia yanked her target back by his shoulder and stepped over his falling body.

Crystal melted and wrapped around her fist, turning into a very brick-solid version of a boxing glove. The blow struck the interrogator and spun the neatly suited man around. He staggered, then slump-rolled to the ground, last-gasp reflexes taking over, as all Sanctuarians trained their bodies to do from early childhood onward. The rubbery plexi surface of the white-painted floor helped cushion his fall, as it had the prisoner's.

"E-clip," Ia ordered over the noise of the still-chanting projections, and held out her hand. Kardos pressed one into it. She slotted her fingers under the spring clip, against the electrodes, stripping it of energy even as she crouched over her childhood friend. Her gifts were many, and though her biokinetic skills worked best on herself, with effort she could bend it to healing others. She did so now, focusing first on the cocktail of drugs that had been pumped into the other woman's stocky, short frame. As soon as that clip was drained, she tossed it back. "Another!"

Yarrin gave her the next. That one cleared up the deeper and more painful of bruises, slaps, pinches, and even a flogging. Rabbit groaned and rolled over. Her skin still showed the mottling of her contusions, but they were reddish with fresh blood ferrying in nutrients for repairs, the capillaries fixed so they could carry out the older fluids from each hematoma. Ia still didn't know how to fix anyone else's body Feyori-style. Her crew knew she couldn't fix anything truly complicated in others, unlike her own eye, but that was alright; bruises, she had learned to heal long ago on herself and her brothers. And on her childhood friend, who pried open her eyes, squinted, then frowned.

". . . Ia?" She flopped a hand, still a little drugged from the, brainwashing cocktail. ". . . Look terr'ble. Helmet's not you."

"Deep breath, Rabbit; I need your brain functioning," Ia told her. She didn't bother to lift her faceplate to give her friend a full visual; she knew her voice would be enough. "Did you or did you not get the transceiver codes?"

Black brows lowered further. ". . . Password?"

That threw Ia for a moment, until she realized Rabbit was *not* talking about the password needed to crack into the Church's military channels. "*Glede ma glede*," she recited, naming the melody that the Free World Colony had taken as its anthem. Rabbit closed her eyes, nodding in satisfaction. Impatient, aware of the clock ticking down, Ia demanded, "Did you get the codes?"

"Shhh . . . it still hurts . . . Oh!" Her hand flopped up to her face, approximating a tap on the end of her flat, tanned nose. "Extra gear. Surv-stuff. Surveillance. Planted." She tapped her cheekbone, missing her temple by three full centimeters. "Got codes here. Think Daddy's gonna disown me . . ."

An involuntary laugh escaped Ia. "Silly Rabbit," she muttered, and heaved the short woman up off her back with muscles and mind. "You were disowned a long time ago, just two days from now, remember?"

"Fffff, was still living with 'm. When you tol' me. I'mma puke now," Rabbit groaned, slouching over as Ia struggled to balance her upright.

"I am not teleporting her if she's going to," Helstead quickly asserted. "That gives a whole new meaning to projectile vomiting, sir, and you do *not* want to go there."

Since Rabbit was short, stocky, and half-boneless from drugs, Ia couldn't exactly let her slide back down to the floor without risking a concussion. She dropped the energy-clip still in her left hand. "Give me another, Kardos—oh, and Plan D."

He pressed it into her hand and picked up the spent case, pinching the spring to clip it onto one of the loops on his waistband. Then whirled and slashed down. His scimitar *thock-chinnnged*, embedding not just in the flexible plexi below the interrogator's neck, but in the stone underneath. Plan D was, if the interrogator woke up early and faked being unconscious in order to eavesdrop, Kardos was to kill him. It was a deep measure of how much he had come to trust her in the last few months that he did so without hesitation.

While the sergeant struggled to pull the stuck blade free, Ia focused on clearing more of Rabbit's biology. Ia would rather have let the man live, as his death would have made no difference either way, but his eavesdropping would have ruined too many plans.

"Sir!" Yarrin hissed, listening from his post by the door. "Footsteps!"

"Commander," Ia grunted, pushing up to her feet. It was *not* easy, lifting Rabbit off her feet, and a cradle-carry was less than an ideal hold on her homeworld. "She'll be fine. Go."

The redhead came over to the other side. The trio of men grasped a part of her as she grabbed Ia and her cargo. Closing her eyes, Ia concentrated, projecting their next destination into the redhead's mind, then cut off her telepathy at Helstead's nod. The lieutenant commander had warned her back before the trip to Dabin that using psychic abilities—particularly the kinetics—while being teleported by someone else risked cerebral bruising, even a possible stroke. Thankfully, Helstead didn't take as long this time to gather her energies as she had up on the ship, since the distance was considerably less, even if their overall mass had increased by one half-drugged colonist.

A shout from down the corridor warned them they had been spotted. A second later, the world slammed and jerked around them. This time, there was no pressure change, no leap through the void between surface and orbit. Just an exchange of one level in the fortress-like structure that was Church Headquarters for another.

Again, they dropped roughly two centimeters. Ia staggered and quickly cushioned her knees with her mind, easing the strain of falling under her and Rabbit's combined weight. She knelt there for a moment, recovering, while Rabbit spasmed in her arms. Warned just in time by a different instinct, she tilted her friend forward, letting the older, smaller woman retch, then helped set her upright. A spin and another push sent Rabbit staggering toward a console in the new, dimly lit, blessedly quiet room.

A blessedly empty room. There had been a seventy-one percent probability that someone was either stationed inside this room, or still in the room next to it, hence bringing Yarrin and O'Taicher to keep the guards occupied while Rabbit did her job. The job she had been captured while trying to do on a mere sixteen percent chance. No one barged in, however.

The fickle randomness of Fate gives with one hand, and takes away with the other . . .

A pale green light started blinking under a nearby counter. Ia could only see it because she was on her knees, recovering. Stooping, O'Taicher pressed another clip into her hand, exchanging it for the one wedged onto her fingers. Ia stripped it of its power, and the next one he passed to her, while Rabbit braced herself on one of the workstation consoles and let the machine scan her biometric readings.

"Hurry it up, little bunny," Ia ordered. She pushed to her feet and clasped Helstead on the back of the neck, feeding the converted energies into her second officer. "The silent alarm's gone off."

"Little rabbit Foo-Foo, hoppin' through the forest," Rabbit crooned as the machine beeped, allowing her to pull her hand off the scanner and dance her short fingers over the unlocked controls. "Scoopin' up the data-packs and . . . *boppin'* 'em on the head! Console's in total-slaggin' mode!"

Spinning, the diminutive coleader of the Free World Colony shoved away from the workstation and launched herself into Ia's arms. The impact made her stagger a little, but Ia scooped her up. Elizabeth Cheung, daughter of the recently appointed Director of Biological Warfare Research. The only person in the FWC with the ability to get inside Church Headquarters one last time, and who could do so with a sample of her father's genetics carefully painted onto her left palm before starting this whole mess. Rabbit—her preferred name—wrapped her arms and legs around the taller, stronger woman in a carry-hold, her task complete.

"I wanna go home, now," she whispered in Ia's ear, her diction much clearer as her body finished flushing the drugs out of her system. The others closed in to grab them and Helstead. The smell of smoke and acid started to fill the room. "You still have to see your niece, Iulia Marie, before it's too late."

"I know." Ia hugged her friend close and squeezed her eyes shut. It was not easy, keeping her eyes tear-free. Not when crying wasn't a comfortable thing to do in the breathless jolt of one more teleportation.

"So?" her half twin, Thorne, asked Ia as she peered at the sleeping toddler in her crib. He spoke softly, so as not to wake little Iulia Marie.

Ia sighed, arms folded almost defensively across her chest. "She's healthy, she has great potential, I've already given you notes on how to gently guide her into the future . . . and I have not a single speck of maternal feelings. She's . . . not adorable," she added, shrugging helplessly. "She's not the cutest thing I've ever seen. Neither is she ugly; she's just . . . a baby. Yet another life to save."

"Wow," Fyfer murmured from the doorway. "That's pretty sad, Sis."

"That's pretty normal, actually," she reminded her younger brother. "Everyone invokes that feeling in me."

Tipping her head at the door, she followed Fyfer as he backed out, Thorne trailing in her wake. Once the door was shut and they were back in the living room of the apartment the three adults and one child shared, she could speak more normally without fear of waking her niece. Arms still crossed, she paced a little. The relentless ticking of time could still be heard in the back of her head.

"Like I said, she'll be fine; just follow my instructions and use common sense, compassion, and be willing to try different approaches when teaching her, until you hit on the styles that work best at each stage of her development . . . And that is *all* the advice I am qualified to give. I am not, nor will I ever be, a mother," Ia stated, cutting a hand through the air. "Nor do I want to be one. I have too much to do to save the galaxy."

Thorne wrapped his arms around her from behind, hugging her for a few moments. "Do you regret it?"

"Do you regret following my directives?" she countered, knowing the answer was the same as hers even as she leaned her head into his shoulder for comfort. Not for long, since she didn't want her gift to trigger. It was tempting, though, to linger as long as possible. Long past the ticking in her head. Pulling away with a sigh, Ia rubbed at her eyes. "Let's not waste what little time I have left on debating whether or not a woman *has* to have maternal instincts and needs. Did you get the last of my directives stored in the Vault?"

"Yes, and yes, they're being organized and filed as we speak," Fyfer reassured her. "The extra crystal sprays you wanted are in the storage hall behind Mom and Ma's place. I was hoping, if you finish with them early, we could throw you a little going-away party . . ."

Ia shook her head. "No parties. A final speech in the main cavern, but that's it. Are the refugee specialists in place, ready to accept everyone fleeing the surface?"

"They're in the last stages of prepping the outer strongholds to receive all the people who'll be fleeing the fighting on the surface tomorrow. Warrens," Thorne corrected himself. "I know you authorized it, but I'm not sure I like calling them that. Sometimes I think Rabbit takes her nickname and its associations a little too closely to heart."

"Well, that's because she has *me* in her life," Fyfer said, touching his chest with his fingers. At his siblings' blank looks, he added, "*Watership Down*? One of the classics of twentieth-century fiction? Oh come on, it's that long story with the rabbits that have to go traveling to find a new home, and the stories-within-the-story that Ma always read to us when we were children?"

"Oh, right, that story. I'd forgotten about that," Thorne apologized.

"It wasn't important to me, so I let it go from my memory," Ia said. She quickly raised her hand as Fyfer drew in a breath to protest. "Look, I know it's important to you. I'm glad it's important to you. I just . . . I'm running out of time, Fyfer. I have three, maybe five minutes left to say good-bye to both of you, then I'm going to have to devote every spare second to the last of the crysium shaping I need to do, before the final speech to everyone and having to leave. I've said my good-byes to Rabbit. I'm going to have to say good-bye to our mothers . . ."

Fyfer moved forward at the rising distress in her tone. Gently, he wrapped his arms around his tall sibling and hugged her. "It's okay, Ia. It's okay. We *know* this is the last time we'll see you. Aside from that speech." Releasing her, he backed up and lightly bopped her on the nose. That earned him a dirty look from her, but at least it lightened the mood. "You just go out there and take care of everything else. We've got the homeworld covered for you."

"Do you want us to be with you when you walk out to the main cavern and address everyone?" Thorne asked. "If so, we'll need the exact time to show up."

Ia shook her head quickly. "No. That would require you being on hand for when I say good-bye to our parents. Unfortunately . . . it's a gray spot. I don't know what's going to happen, but I *do* know that if either of you are there, in their apartment before I emerge, it'll disturb too many possibilities down the line."

Fyfer folded his arms across his chest. "Iantha Iulia, are you going to pick a *fight* with our mothers?"

"No?" she offered, though her uncertainty over that mist-shrouded spot made it more of a question than a statement. "At least, I don't think so, at this time?"

"Well, try not to, or I'll be very upset you didn't let me have a ringside seat for it," her younger brother teased, grinning at her.

Rolling her eyes, Ia turned to Thorne. He opened his arms one more time for her, and she went into them, hugging him back. She felt safe in his arms despite the chance that her precognition could trigger. Knowing that she would not be able to step into them again was *almost* enough to make her want to ignore the driving ticktock of time. But with a handful of seconds to spare, she pulled free. Thorne, thankfully, let her go.

"I'll see you in the timestreams," she promised, taking one last look at her siblings. "I love you both."

Thorne, tall and muscular, with thick brown hair, her rock in appearance as well as metaphysically. Fyfer, short and slender by comparison, celebrity-handsome with his curling locks and charming smile. Right now, his smile was a bit lopsided, more sad than charming. Thorne didn't even bother, though he was careful not to frown or scowl. Neither one wanted to say an actual good-bye, which was fine with Ia. She wasn't sure if she could get the words out past the lump trying to form in her throat.

". . . I'll see you in the timestreams," she repeated under her breath, as much to reassure herself as them. Backing up a few steps, she forced herself to turn and head out the front door, no backward glance. She had work to do, and only so many hours left in which to get it all done.

CHAPTER 5

Yes, I lost family when Sanctuary fell behind enemy lines. No, we cannot get them out of there. That whole system is lost to the Terran Empire, and seventeen other unoccupied star systems at this time. We'll lose a few more before it's over, but none of the others are occupied, thank God. If we stay out of Shredou—Grey—space, that is.

. . . Which god? Seriously? You're asking me now about my religious beliefs? . . . Agnostic Unigalactan. I know the Sh'nai holy texts have me quoted as saying, "There is no God but the Future, and Ia is Her Prophet," and that may be very true for the actions driving my purpose in life, but I . . . What do I think God's plan is?

Look, from my perspective, God plays poker. Dragon poker. Look it up; it's from half a millennia ago. Now, I play a form of it, too. I knew that throwing my homeworld behind enemy lines looks like I'm throwing away the three of a kind in a full house, but I know every card that's going to come up in that deck. Not just in this game, not in the next game, but every card in more than three hundred shufflings of the deck from now. I knew that throwing away a seemingly good full house in our time frame would guarantee all aces and royal flushes in every hand that would need it three centuries from now.

I'd throw Earth *behind enemy lines if I thought I could save this galaxy in doing so. I suggest you be grateful that it wasn't necessary—and be grateful again that the only ones severely affected by Sanctuary's disappearance are those very few who had actual, direct ties to its inhabitants. Like me. But then I won't let anyone suffer through something I'm not willing to endure myself.*

~*Ia*

MAY 9, 2499 T.S.

After nineteen solid hours of constant reshaping and retuning of spray after crysium spray, real food tasted odd in Ia's mouth. The orange juice was fresh-squeezed, or as fresh as a few hours ago could qualify, but it tasted like licking an e-clip on the power nodes: metallic and coppery. The ham sandwich, layered with lettuce, cheese, sauces, and tomatoes grown in the same hydroponic gardens as the oranges, reminded her of cardboard and freeze-dried emergency rations. It compared poorly to the thrumming, fresh-baked bread of crystalsong in the back of her mind, the sizzling bacon of electrical cords and the rich, spicy stir-fry of rare earth magnets.

Kardos had gone off hours ago to settle into his new quarters and integrate into his new life. O'Taicher and Yarrin had been taken back up to the ship by her second officer as soon as Helstead had finished a nap and a meal of her own. Since she no longer needed others to help manage the worst chances—bodies to throw into the fray as living shields against the slings and arrows of the most malfeasant of percentages—Ia had ordered Helstead to retreat with the other two.

Now she had just three tasks left. The first was to eat a physical, biological, matter-based meal. The last was to give a speech to everyone in less than half an hour. Her eyes felt like sandpaper from the crying she had done while she worked, her nose was still slightly stuffed, and what she wanted to do was fling aside the food and go hug her brothers. Her mothers. Her world. But no, she had to eat, and she had to give a speech.

The last speech.

She tried not to think about whatever it was she had to get through when her mothers came by.

Over two hundred light-years away, dozens of Grey ships were gathering around one of their colonyworlds, preparing to translocate from that system to this one, to begin seizing Humans for yet another attempt at preserving their truly alien, exogalactic species by infusing it with biology gleaned from this one. Those plans were laid, and the Shredou would not deviate from their path. Of course, they were also going to be receiving a message from the hyperrelay unit Ia had offered them a handful of years back, just prior to her last visit to this system. A recorded message, not a broadcast one, giving them the exact date of their attack, and the exact pattern of systems they were going to invade and claim, expanding their dying empire in search of resources and a buffer zone.

The Shredou commanders back home would spend a few days dissecting the Terran storage technology to determine it was indeed a message originally recorded on the datachips years ago, but the fleet would have already been launched. Ia sat there at her mother's age-stained but polished dining table and stared sightlessly at the fancy china cabinet they had bought and installed in their spacious underground apartment. All she could see were gray-skinned, long-lived, vaguely humanoid but *not* Human aliens deciding coldly, rationally, that Humans were still their best bet at generating another generation.

A form of hunger not too dissimilar from the Salik's, she thought, with little appetite left. *Save that the frogtopi are honest about wanting to destroy what they devour.* Looking down at the half-eaten sandwich she had made, the half-drunk glass of juice, she felt odd that there were no clips edging the table, no means of securing her family's tableware from sudden maneuvers. Shaking it off, Ia stood and bent over the table, ready to take everything back to the kitchen for composting and cleaning.

She did not know what made her glance up at the cabinet after picking up her glass, but she did. At that height, at that exact angle, she could see it. The glass slipped and *thunked* on the table, thankfully not breaking. Ia ignored the cool liquid on her fore and middle fingers, the droplets on her thumb. She stared at the rose-shaped teacup so proudly, safely displayed on the topmost shelf in her mother's glass-fronted cabinet.

The teacup. The heirloom, brought all the way from Earth. It had been shaped like a literal heirloom rose, with five thin, delicately sculpted, pink-painted porcelain petals, with a handle sculpted to look like an extra-long, curled green sepal.

It sat on a saucer that had been sculpted and painted to look like a flattened version. The saucer, she knew, had been broken on the very first planet her biomother Amelia's great-plus-grandfather had moved to, generations ago. It had been repaired in the *kintsukuroi* style, with gold lacquer spider-webbing the frail plate, holding the carefully preserved pieces together. But the reddish cup itself . . .

In her mind's eye, that cup had *always* been shattered. Broken. Perpetually left in chunks and pieces, bleeding its bone white innards along each fractured edge, instead of the deep reddish pink one would have expected from the flesh of a still-fresh wound.

Leaving her plate and glass still on the table, the latter miraculously still upright despite its short fall, Ia moved around the table to the cabinet. She stared for long, long seconds through the glazed panels, then opened the door. She had to let go of the knob because she could not bring her left hand to lift toward that top shelf. But the right one . . . yes, she could. Her right hand. Her dominant one. Her choice for action rather than reaction.

The hand-painted porcelain felt cool and glossy-smooth under the hesitant touch of her fingertips. She played them over the curves, the unchipped edges, memorizing every little detail she could without actually picking it up. She did not want to pick up the cup, did not want to risk seeing her vision come true.

But time was running out.

Determined to conquer the long-standing fears stirred by those visions from her preawakened youth, Ia gently lifted the cup out of the cabinet. Cradled it in her right palm, staring down into the depths of the bowl, where some artisan had gently painted little golden stamens and pistils at the very center. She heard footsteps approaching, and glanced over her shoulder in time to see her mothers enter the room, the slightly taller, creamy brown-skinned Aurelia, and the shorter, curly-haired Amelia, her cheeks freckled from the daily UV treatments everyone in the now underground Free World Colony endured from the light strips lining all corridors and halls.

"What are you . . . ? Ah," Aurelia said, catching sight of the painted cup gently cradled in her daughter's hand. "I see you finally picked it up." She smiled warmly, visibly pleased that her wife's family heirloom had finally been acknowledged by the last of their children to hold it.

Amelia, however, frowned. *"Kardia mou?"* she asked, briefly falling back on the Greek endearment from her mother's side of the family. The side that had preserved that teacup and saucer. The side that had given birth to her only daughter. "Are you planning on taking it with you? I . . . I could pack it for you, if you like . . ."

The gray mist of too many choices clouded her view of the timestreams, now that her parents were in the dining room. Ia returned her gaze to the cup, but her other mother spoke.

"Take it, hell!" Aurelia asserted, speaking her mind as her hands planted on her hips. "She can leave it right here, *and* come back for it, for her own dining room one day. On her world, living among her people."

"She's said she has to leave us behind!" Amelia half argued, half pleaded, touching her wife on the elbow. "Respect her wishes, *agape mou*. She is the Prophet, and we will respect our daughter for her choices."

"She's the Prophet, yes! And *that* means she could *find* a way to stay here if she looks hard enough," the taller woman shot back.

"Enough."

The barely voiced word cut off their rising argument. In the moment of silence that followed, Ia knew she'd had it wrong all along. It wasn't that this life she had followed, through blood and murder and tears, was a matter of having no choice but to do everything she had done and more. No. It *was* her choice. *By* her choice.

"You once told me all those years ago that this cup was fine," she murmured, her gaze still on the carefully preserved work of art in her hand. This *trompe l'oeil* attempt at an over-sized, half-unfurled, antique porcelain rose. She turned as she spoke. Not to face her mothers, but to face the table. To put the hand holding the cup *over* the table. "That it was intact. That it had always been intact and, with care, always would be. And if you had told me once, then you had told me a hundred thousand times. I heard you every single time. Every single word . . .

"But this cup," she said, voice gaining strength in the conviction, the *choice* she made. "This cup has *always* been broken. By. *Me*."

Her fingers clenched inward, hard and fast. The paper-thin porcelain *crunched*. Pieces immediately pattered and clattered onto the age-stained dining table. As her mothers gasped, shocked and horrified, Ia turned her hand over and gently flexed fingers and thumb, letting the remaining pieces drop. Two of the larger shards cracked further, for the surface was lightly padded for most tableware, but still far too firm for such a delicate thing in their homeworld's high gravity.

A few drops of her own blood stained the porcelain, dripping from the thin wounds on her inner two fingers and the deeper cut on her palm. Without expression, without flinching, Ia reached up with her other hand and pulled out a slender little sliver of a chip from the heel of her hand. That, too, landed on the table, coated in a deeper, darker red than anything the artist had ever used.

"What the . . . ?" Amelia breathed.

"How *could* you?" Aurelia added on the heels of her wife's words, both of them horrified.

Ia turned to face them.

"How? Because I have *always* chosen to destroy this teacup, Mothers. *Chosen*. Not by accident, not by carelessness, but by my free-willed choice. Save all the pieces," she ordered, her tone hardening in order to bring their full attention back out of their shock. Ia knew that this was a path she could add into the timestreams without ruining anything, but she had to get her parents to listen to her words, not gape at her actions. The teacup had already been broken, after all.

It had *always* been broken . . . but one day, there was a chance it could be fixed, with a level of both knowledge and understanding that she would never possess in the whole span of her current life.

"You can save them in a box, or use the same *kintsukuroi* method to hold them together like the saucer. The choice is yours. But know that this cup will remain broken, even if it is repaired, until the Savior remakes it whole, undamaged and unbroken, in a way that *I* cannot . . . and as I will *never* do. By my choice."

She moved away from the table, hand clenched to help staunch the flow of blood while waiting for her innate abilities to work. Stopping a meter away, she met her mothers' eyes, seeing the hurt feelings, the wishes and hopes she had just broken and shattered along with a simple little cup.

"I love you, Mom; I love you, Ma. I always have, and I always will. And I already know how proud you are of me . . . in spite of this momentary shock. Know that I have always been proud of you. But I do have to go, and I will *not* come back again. By. Choice.

"I've already said my good-byes to my brothers," she added, clasping her hands behind her back. Or rather, clasping the wrist of her clenched fist. The timelines had shifted just enough that her mothers would remain in this suite, rather than join her on the balcony overlooking the central cavern, but it wouldn't ruin anything; in time, they would recover. "And I've already hugged you in farewell. Now, if you'll excuse me, I need to say it to everyone else, too."

Sidestepping both women, she strode for the door. Swiftly, trying to move gracefully so it did not look like she was escaping that final, tear-streaked, recrimination-laden good-bye her instincts screamed they were going to try to give to her. A mental nudge of the doors between her and the corridors of Central Warren, burgeoning underground capital of the Free World Colony, allowed her to depart without leaving any more smears of blood on the place.

There were people in the halls, gathered as requested along all the terraces and leaning over all the balconies. Thousands of people, young and old, dark and fair, the agnostics and the atheists rubbing elbows readily and acceptingly with those who had actual faiths they followed. It was very unlike the culture the Church of the One True God wanted, and she felt a tiny bubble of pride swelling within her.

Ia *knew* these men and women, these children and elders. She knew every face, every name, every life. They parted in a path before her and kept a respectful distance of a couple meters on each side. In a crowd this large, there should have been three or five or nine *irit'zi*, the wailing cry of someone suffering from a Fire Girl Prophecy . . . but their secret source, the crystalline sprays dotting the cavern like decorative glass evergreens, were silent.

A part of her mind wondered if they—unsentient but still very much alive, however Frankensteinian from a Feyori's perspective—were silent out of respect for what their progeny was about to do. As much as Ia was the child of a Feyori named Albelar and a Human woman named Amelia, she was a child of Sanctuary. A child of the crystals.

The outward-projecting curve of the terrace her mothers lived on had been fitted with a platform, a clear-plexi podium, and a single thin wire that served as a comm pickup. Hover-cams floated and swerved in quiet *thrums* several meters away, angling for the best views to record her final farewell. Two sets of energy conduits had been brought in and snaked up the sides of the lectern, ready for her to draw upon at the end.

Thorne was already there, as was Fyfer; her half twin cradled his stepniece in his arms as he stood at his stepbrother's side. Their coleader and lover, Rabbit, was elsewhere right now, monitoring the surveillance recordings of the rising tensions in the Church leadership. The surface-side government did *not* like all the Feyori dashing down to the far side of the planet, pausing for the inexplicable harvesting of Devil's Stick sprays, and swerving back up again into orbit. They definitely did not like those silvery Meddler-spheres disappearing into the long, lean, menacing needle of a Terran warship hugging Sanctuary's atmosphere, parked geosynchronously over their precious, cathedral-graced capital.

But those things were no longer her concern. Rabbit would continue to plot and plan, thwarting the Church's attempts at discerning the exact location and highest-ranked members of the rebel government, while keeping tabs on the Church forces. Thorne would continue to calculate the needs and direct the functionality of their new lives underneath the troubled surface of their world. And Fyfer would be the face of the government, designing and discussing ways to keep the faith these colonists, these future Zenobians, would need to hold close in their heart. One day, the descendants of these people would raise the Third Human Empire as a force to be reckoned with, creating a someday home for a broken woman who desperately needed a kind of healing she would not at the time understand.

Stepping up onto the podium platform, Ia licked her lips, breathed deep, and kept her final words confined to the truth.

"I know you," she said. Her voice, amplified just loud enough that everyone quickly fell silent, echoed slightly across the cavern. "I know each and every one of you. I know your children, and your children's children, and *their* children down through the generations. Down through the centuries. Down through to the moment when *you* will make—not break—the Savior of our galaxy.

"You follow me on faith, and I thank you for it. You follow me even knowing I must leave and never return, and I thank you with deep gratitude," she said, drifting her gaze from face to face, even the ones clinging to the balconies a hundred, two hundred, five hundred meters away. Without her ceristeel armor and her silvered helm, her collar-length bob of old-woman white could be easily seen against the browns of the granite behind her, and the mottled shades of her camouflage Grays. "You follow me where I tell you to go, when I tell you, and how I tell you to go about it . . . and I thank you beyond all words for your strength, and your belief.

"I *am* going to save our galaxy with your help," she told them candidly, nodding slightly in affirmation. "Know that it *is* by your help, for I have been, and will be, beside you every step of the way. Silent and unseen for the most part . . . but for some of you, I will reach across the void of Time itself to help guide you.

"And if you do *not* hear from me," Ia added, warmth in her tone and a wry curve tilting her lips, "then take that as my sign of my absolute faith in *you*. The faith you will do what you need to do, when you need to do it, as it needs to be done.

It will take centuries of constant effort, but there will be plenty of joys mixed in with the tedium and the pain. I thank you for knowing that, as in everything, your effort is part and parcel of what makes the end result so worthwhile."

Unclasping her hands, she reached out to either side and slipped thin wires from her split-in-half crystal bracer into the recessed holes of the power cables' sockets. Her right hand still hurt, but she ignored it, choosing instead to address her neighbors, her friends, her followers.

"Everything happens for a reason," Ia stated. "Not like the Church wants you to believe, that it's for some Divine Creator's unclear and capricious-minded purpose. We are more than game pieces to be pushed around a playing board. We are more than just the cards held in our Creator's hand. But rather, because it is mostly, simply, the way that this universe works . . . and it is the culminated, interacting, interconnected efforts of *everyone* on this world, beneath and above its surface.

"The interactions of the people on all the other worlds out there will have their impact as well, though none of your great-grandchildren's children will get to see them before Sanctuary opens up to the rest of the Alliance again." She paused, watching the silent, sober people gathered around her. Watching their bodies and the power cables and even the plants lining the terraces as they started to glow, Ia dipped her head. "I know that's not the most *cheerful* of messages I can give you . . . but I swear to you, the end result will be worth everything . . . and the galaxy will know the part you have played in saving more lives than even I can take the time to know.

"You have my Prophetic Stamp on that. In the meantime . . . prepare this world for its long, slow civil war, and prepare among yourselves the home that our Savior . . . secular, stubborn, and cynical . . . will so desperately need. Thank you."

One last electrokinetic pull, and she popped into Feyori form. A metaphysical sip for a little extra boost, and she flung herself straight up, slipping through solid bedrock for a long, dark, ham-flavored span of thermally warmed rock, a flutter of cheese layers from the power conduits in a home directly overhead, and a wash of cool, tart apple juice from the slowly gathering thunderheads that bespoke the approach of yet another evening lightning storm.

One last taste of the ozone in the air, and only a taste of its chemical energy, from a body that could not smell because it could not at the moment breathe.

Ice-cold of the void invaded her energy-based senses, sapping her reserves. Highly charged particles zipped through her darkened mirror-skin, tasting like the fizzle in a carbonated drink. A shock of energy and flavor, savory and sweet, as she dove into the skin of her ship. At the last moment, she noticed the *Nadezhda Popova* slowly gliding into position a few kilometers away, nudging up close to Sanctuary's gaseous skin. Lightning jets and sprites danced up along both hulls, rife with electromagnetic power, but they were more than adequately shielded against such jolts.

Satisfied both ships were in position, she zipped to her quarters, plugged herself into the power grid in the corner of her sitting room, and popped back onto legs that trembled and staggered in the abruptly-too-light 2.3Gs of her ship. No time to rest, though. Ignoring the fact that her hand was still cut, still raw and sore despite shifting shape, Ia headed out of her sitting room physically. Psychically, she reached into the timestreams to gauge all the crystal-wrapped machines her soap bubble soldiers had made.

On schedule, and . . . every last one in perfect form. Good. Reaching out, she tapped the mind of the first Feyori she had ever spoken with as she passed through her office. Sadneczek was on duty, but the grizzled sergeant didn't look up from his task. Paperwork had to be filed on the coming breach of contract by the main Sanctuarian government against the Terran Space Force, a lot of it, and he was doing his best to fill out the many, many forms in advance. (*Doctor Silverstone, please pass along to the others my thanks for their timely and properly made constructs.*)

(*I will . . . though I am wondering what I did to get on your "shit list," as the archaic saying goes,*) the alien returned.

(*You're on it with the others because I trust each of you to get it done right, which you have. You're also on it because you are reliable witnesses to my threatening the Greys to toe the line,*) she added, passing through the short back corridor separating her office from the bridge, its two heads, and its pocket galley. (*They do know how to capture and kill your*

*kind. This is my show of my faction-protection being ex-
tended to all of* you.)

(*Perhaps. But I feel like I am being reduced to a Terran
monkey, flinging my own filth at my foes.*)

Her mouth curved in lopsided, morbid humor. (*Maybe
they'll catch a disease?*) Pulling her mind back, she hooked
her fingers in the door controls and stepped onto the bridge,
announcing herself. "General on Deck!"

The men and women of the 1st Platoon sat up straighter in
their seats, clothing rustling faintly against restraint harnesses, but did not look up from their monitoring tasks. When
they had arrived in her home system, it had been second
watch; twenty hours later, the duty shifts had cycled around
to first watch. Tired as she was, Ia was used to staying up for
long stretches of time by now. Doing so had ensured she spent
plenty of time getting to know each Platoon's bridge crews.

At the moment, what she wanted was Private Ramasa, nick-
named the Frog Prince for his generous-sized mouth, slightly
bulging eyes, and absurd sense of humor. That mouth was fixed
in a straight line at the moment, not a smile. "Ramasa, report."

"The scatter-bombs were launched promptly on time,
seventeen minutes ago," he said, calling up a set of timers on
his fourth tertiary screen. "The loading teams in the bow
have been rolling the spheres into position for launch, and . . ."
he checked his tertiary fifth, ". . . the last of them are in position now, sir. We can fire when ready, but it would help if we
either rolled the ship or lifted orbit a little, to avoid an accidental sprite jet getting into the bay."

Ia settled herself in the empty command seat, pulling the
straps into place. "Yeoman, roll the ship, coordinate the
launch of the orbs, and release them when ready."

"Aye, sir," Ishiomi said. He cleared his throat. "We had an
orbital query from the *Popova* a minute before you boarded,
sir. They wanted to know if they should go geosynchronous,
too. I told them yes, as the Lieutenant is still down in the foremost hold overseeing the special project."

"You made a good choice, Yeoman," Ia praised him. It
was something she hadn't considered herself, a little detail
that had slipped between the cracks. A looping orbit wouldn't
have changed much either way, other than made it less clear

that the Church was firing upon the TUPSF in general and not just on a ship led by one of their former citizens. "I think you just saved our Company clerk about two dozen pieces of paperwork."

"Thank you, sir." He smiled, turning his head slightly to aim it over his shoulder before returning his attention to the boards. "Rolling the ship in five . . . four . . ."

They rotated and stopped, altering the view of the planet from filling the lower half of their exterior-shot screens to filling the upper half; thanks to artificial gravity, that was the only thing that proved their position had changed. It took a few extra minutes for the Humans in the bay to clear out. Ia watched on her fifth upper tertiary screen. The others on the uppermost row should have been showing scanner feeds from the various system buoys, but those had been shut off and collected by Attinks' ship. So all she had to watch was the work of her own crew. The bow docking bay doors slid open with only a faint, distant hum, more felt than heard from as far away as the bridge.

The two shuttles in that bay had been relocated to the stern bay for this maneuver, a tight fit, but necessary. Well over a hundred golden, glowing orbs the same size as the fifteen swirling, silvery Meddler-spheres had been packed into the bay. As she watched, Ishiomi coordinated with Private Nelson at the operations station to cut gravity to that deck.

The microgravitic pull of their upside-down position in geosynchronous orbit over the planet shifted the orbs. They slowly started drifting "up" on Ia's viewscreen. The Feyori grabbed the nearest of the orbs in pairs, disappearing for a few moments only to reappear and grab another sphere. Though "grab" wasn't exactly the right word; they had no hands but instead overlapped an edge of each golden orb before lifting it out of the pack and vanishing.

"Query from the *Popova*, sir," Private Xhuge said. "They want to know what the *Damnation* is doing, and what both ships are supposed to be waiting for—ah, incoming ping from the planet," he added. "Official channels. It's the government. President Augustus Moller."

"Right on schedule. Tell the *Popova* to sit still and wait, and put Moller on my main screen," Ia ordered.

The dark-haired image of President Augustus Moller, leader of the Truth Party and third-highest-ranked member of the Church of the One True God, appeared on Ia's main screen. His hair had picked up a hint of gray and white salting through the dark strands in the years since she had last seen him. That had been during the fateful broadcast when her brother had officially received his Alliance Lottery money. Unlike back then, the President of Sanctuary was not smiling. Not even a fake one.

"You! Supposedly, you're in charge," he snapped without preamble. "And *supposedly* you used to be a Sanctuarian! What in the name of God Most Holy are you doing, threatening our capital?"

Ia raised her brows. "Threatening? Since when is a simple parking orbit a threat? On the contrary, President Moller," she stated smoothly, double-checking the timestreams, "we are here to protect Sanctuary from an incoming threat."

"Incoming threat, God's Own Foot!" he countered, flushing. "It is *your own soldiers* who have threatened the sanctity of our sovereign government!"

"President Moller, *our* intelligence sources have revealed that up until recently, members of your government were involved in clandestine biological-warfare research without an Alliance-granted permit. Of course, I am also told those research notes were destroyed by Sanctuarian citizens. Not Terran citizens. Which is just as well," she added dryly, "since I would have been forced by our contract with your government to destroy that research and take all co-conspirators into custody, up to and including yourself, if it turns out that you, too, are implicated in violating the laws governing Alliance Sentientarian Conduct Standards."

He blinked at her, his age-lined face paling, then flushing. "You—you have no jurisdiction on this world!"

She met his gaze levelly. "The Truth Party government of Sanctuary is a duly chartered member of the Alliance. The Alliance is currently at war. I am the General of the Alliance Armies, and that means I have the authority to declare martial law in any and *all* membership states of said Alliance. Be very careful with your next few words, President Moller. This may sound like a threat, but I assure you, the presence of these two

Terran warships in this system, hugging your planet's atmosphere, is not a sign of aggression against Sanctuary.

"Rather, we are following through on our duly chartered duties to protect Sanctuary."

"From *what*?" Moller snapped. "The Salik? Those amphibious abominations haven't even come within a hundred light-years of here!"

"From the *Greys*, Meioa President. Not from the Salik. As I predicted long ago, the Second Grey War is about to start in"—she checked the chronometer counting down on her lower first tertiary screen—"three . . . two . . . one."

"General, ships have just materialized at 7 by 352, sir," MacInnes asserted from her seat at the navigation console. "Five . . . seven . . . twelve ships, approximately twenty light-seconds away. They do match known Grey ship materials and configurations, sir."

"You brought the *Greys* down upon us?" Moller demanded at the same time as he registered Ia's words.

"No, but I did know they were coming," Ia replied mildly. She strapped her left hand into the attitude glove, then ghosted her right one over the controls, calling up the current trajectory of the scatter-bombs in relation to that lightwave reading of the Grey ships. They were almost in position. A check of her lower-leftmost screen showed a good number of the orbs were gone from her cargo hold, leaving roughly seventy.

The Greys were not going to attack immediately. At the moment, they were scanning the system, noting her ship's presence. The Greys were also debating not only just how accurate she was as a precognitive—having successfully predicted their presence today—but what sort of trick she was going to pull on them as a psychic.

She had a different problem to handle first, however. President Moller stared at her, eyes widening, then quickly lifted his finger to his forehead, scribing a circle on it. The mark of the Corona, symbol of his religion. "God protect me—you're that unnatural white-haired demon with the Devil's skills! The Future-Liar!"

"*God* gave me my psychic abilities, President Moller, not the Devil," she countered, still calm. Tired, but calm. Having gone over this conversation dozens, even hundreds of times in her mind, she merely gave him a level look. And a piece of her mind, of course, since this was their one and only meeting. "In fact, God gave them to me so that I could save *you*, even if you are little more than a festering pustule hidden within the scrotal folds of the Devil Himself. Unfortunately, I must now abide by the rules of the Space Force's duly chartered defense contract with your government, and tend to my duties by preventing your righteous, if premature, destruction."

"Aha!" he exclaimed, raising a finger within view of the screen's pickups. "But I am calling to tell you that my government has chosen to *cancel* your contract! So you can get the blessed *hell* out of our sovereign skies!"

"Oh, that would be just fine with me, Meioa President," Ia replied, "except that, by that very same contract, in the event a hostile enemy presence is already active within this system at the time of contract termination, we are obliged to extend that contract until said enemy presence has left. The Greys appeared *before* you informed us of the cancellation of that contract, President Moller. I will therefore protect this world from their aggressions to the best of my abilities, and *then* withdraw all Terran military support from this system."

Someone off-screen said something on his end, and the sound cut off for a few moments. President Moller looked to the side, scowled, snapped something, paled, swallowed, and returned his gaze to the comm link between them. The sound came back on.

"It seems those *are* Grey ships entering Sanctuarian orbit. But not even the full might of the entire Terran fleet would be enough to stop them from doing whatever they want."

"Not without resorting to 'Devil Powers,' no," she agreed. "Understand this, President Moller. I have just placed several satellites in orbit around this world. Touch them, or worse, try to remove them, and the Greys *will* harvest your people. Leave them in place, leave them alone, and the Greys will leave *you* alone."

"So you *are* a Daughter of the Devil, to make a bargain with His alien accomplices?" Moller accused.

"No. I am a Daughter of Sanctuary, here to save her people. Have a good life, President Moller. Or rather," she corrected herself, "as the old saying goes, 'May you one day *deserve* the good life.'" A tap of her finger ended the conversation. "Ish-iomi, helm to my control in five."

"Helm to yours . . . in . . . now, sir," Ishiomi agreed, making the switch. Since the ship was in a static orbit, and the yeoman had anticipated her request, the exchange was made swiftly and smoothly. "I hope those golden balls of yours *can* stop the Greys, General."

"I'm just hoping those scatter-bombs do the trick," Ia returned. Checking on the remaining orbs, she closed the docking bay doors and gently turned up the gravity. The heavy, tough machinery-packed spheres drifted down again. At the same time, she tipped the ship down relative to her dead-ahead, pointing the bow away from the planet at the top of her viewscreen and more toward the alien discs in the distance.

Taking her time, she lined up the attitude of the *Damnation* with the Grey vessels.

"Sir, we have a ping from the Greys on their private channel," Xhuge told her.

"Put it through."

Gray-skinned, mouse-eyed, vaguely bipedal, and disproportionate in Human eyes, the Shredou captain appeared on Ia's center screen.

"Ee Ah of the Terrans," the alien stated, with that odd, dual-larynxed, slightly-out-of-tune way of his, her, or its kind. "Your prediction accuracy is acknowledged. Your words do not stop the Shredou. Your technology does not stop the Shredou."

"*You* will stay off this world," Ia returned coldly, speaking with equally short sentences, so that there would be little room for misinterpretation. "You will obey my words. When I tell you to expand, you will expand. Where I tell you to expand, you will expand. When I tell you to stop, you will stop. Where I tell you to stop, you will stop. And when I tell you to fight, you will fight. You will fight *who* I tell you to fight."

"Irrelevant."

Ia did not take her eyes off the screen. Instead, she lifted the plexi lid on the main gun control and let the machine inside scan her identity. "Private Ramasa? Detonate."

He hit a control on his station console. Sixty handcrafted projectiles exploded in brief flashes of light, at a distance roughly eighty percent of the way to the enemy's position, transmission boosted by the hyperrelay hub the *Popova* had left in place. The Grey on the screen blinked and cocked his/its head even as Ia tapped the unlocked button on her own station console.

"Your targeting ability is flawed. Your missiles are not threatening. Your—"

"*This* is a warning shot, meioa. I suggest you pay attention," Ia told him, speaking over the alien. Deep red flashed from all the screens showing a forward view from the *Damnation*'s perspective. The bolt was short, a twentieth of a second, but the distance long, twenty full seconds. Their communication was via hyperrelay link, but the result of the attack came back after forty seconds.

Packed with thousands of shards from broken, recycled chunks of laser-focusing crystals, the scatter-bombs had exploded like fireworks. That seeded the area between her direct line of fire and the main cluster of ships with a cone. The moment that pulse from the *Damnation*'s upgraded Godstrike cannon struck, half of the beam's intensity was fragmented, fanning out in a flare of red. Over half would dissipate in interstitial space.

The rest scored straight through those alien shields. Diffused in strength, but still powerful enough to damage all twelve hulls. Damage, but not destroy. This was a warning shot, after all, even if the Godstrike, Mark II, was not something easily diffused.

Noise whistled through the comm link between the two factions: alien claxons. The expressions on a Shredou's face were hard to read, but Ia was fairly sure she was seeing alarm in the gray-skinned, black-eyed alien. Reaching out with her mind, she touched Silverstone again. (*Ready for the link?*)

(*Ready to clean the taste of shit out of our mouths,*) he sent back. (*If I'd known back then you were going to make me eat my own* shakk . . .)

(*Yes, yes, you would've killed me. And then died four hundred fifty-three years from now, instead of over two thousand.*) Pulling up a thread of awareness, she looped it around the Feyori's mind and wove it quickly along her other faction strings into the minds of the other fourteen.

The Grey snapped an order. Fifteen silvery soap bubbles

swooped into view, aggregating in a cluster and intercepting the white-hot beam that arrowed their way. In the back of her head, where Ia heard voices telepathically . . . she heard the Feyori named Silverstone belch.

(*Mm, tasty. Think we'll get any more? It doesn't go far, split fifteen different ways.*)

Lifting her right hand to her temple, Ia massaged her forehead for a moment, then addressed the Grey on the screen. "Your weapons are useless. They are food for the *shhnk-zii*. All of the Feyori are my allies."

"We will poison the *shhnk-zii*," the Grey on her screen stated.

"If you try, I will poison *you*," Ia countered.

He/it/whatever stared at her, then turned to give another order. She flicked her mind into the timestreams, activating the spheres. Ever-present as a tiny thread of melody thanks to the right-side bracer she wore, the faint, crystalline chime of crysium-song abruptly leaped into full-throated chorus. Her entire bridge crew twitched and looked up, craning their necks and darting their eyes around the room, trying to find the source of that sound. Only briefly; they did drag their attention back to their screens within a second or two, but the sudden surge of noise had definitely startled them.

It wasn't a physical noise but rather a psychic one in nature. The Grey on her viewscreen hissed and clasped his long-fingered hands around his bulbous skull, flat lips pulling back in a pained grimace to show the odd, pale, bluish knobs that served for his teeth. The greenish bolt that flashed toward the Feyori struck them, but did not scatter their formation.

(*This is very disturbing,*) Silverstone observed in the back of her mind. (*Using our own shit as a shield? I'm glad it works, but . . .*)

(*Get used to it,*) Ia told him, glad the others had agreed to filter all questions and comments through just one of their number. Silverstone had won the right to be that contact point because his particular area of Meddling influence was the Terran military; otherwise, it would have been her erstwhile father. (*You have seen enough of their construction to make more, and can use them to protect yourselves in the future from the Shredou.*)

(*True.*)

(*Whatever toxic energies they throw at you, the orbs will resonate strongly enough to counter it. The only problem is that they have a proximity effect similar to gravity,*) Ia warned him, knowing Silverstone was passing the information along to the others. (*The farther away you get, the weaker the field, in squared proportion . . . and it's best for them to be set in an orbit close enough to feed off jets and sprites from energy storms if you can't find enough portable hydrogenerators to supplement their power reserves. You'll also have to trigger them yourselves. I'm only triggering the ones we made today. I don't have time to set off the rest.*)

She reached through the timestreams and deactivated the resonances. The Grey on the screen still grimaced for a bit longer, though the chorus faded immediately. The inner machinery was based on the anti-psi devices, with a twist that allowed the resonances to be amplified by the unique ability of crysium to harness, store, and use various energies. Similar nodes had been installed all along the *Damnation*'s hull beneath concealment panels, but she did not open those panels.

The Shredou would attack again, aiming their efforts at a different Human colony in a different star system. Some, the *Damnation* would be able to deliver. The remaining crystalline balls would have to be transported to each needed system by her pack of Meddlers. Watching the Shredou leader, Ia gave him a few more moments to recover, then spoke again.

"As you can see, I can protect this world. You will not attack personally. You will be poisoned if you try. You will not send machines. Your machines will be destroyed. You can surround this system. You will stay away from this world. Two hundred three stellar cycles of this world will pass. This world will reach into space to reclaim this system. You will allow it. They will reach out to claim other nearby worlds with heavy gravity. You will allow it. If you resist? If you fight? I will aim the Zida"ya at you, as easily as I have aimed these energies.

"You will fight when I tell you. You will fight where I tell you. You will fight *who* I tell you. I am the Prophet of a Thousand Stellar Cycles. I will know when. I will know where. I will act across those thousand years," Ia told the Grey on her main screen.

"You are inferior," the alien asserted. "You will die soon!"

"Irrelevant," she returned calmly, ignoring the threat. "My accuracy will remain. My accuracy will command you, even after I am long dead and gone. You have two *kesant* to leave this system before I open fire."

Her right hand hovered over the still-uncovered access button; her left readjusted the *Damnation*'s position, since it was parked in geosynchronous orbit, which meant moving and turning as the planet did. Gauging the Grey's response in the timestreams, she hit the button and held it for two seconds. Released it, and waited, over the roughly twenty seconds of light-speed distance between them.

"Irrelevant. We refuse."

There were no buoys nearby to relay what happened in real time. It would take forty seconds from the moment of firing for the lightwave results to reach them. Ia spoke while she waited for those seconds to catch up.

"Irrelevant. You will be destroyed. You have *one kesant* to leave this system before I fire again."

The navicomp tightened and refined its view of one of the smaller ships in the alien fleet. Her beam smacked into that vessel. It was hard to see from the angle just what happened for those two full seconds, until the dark red glow vanished. In the greenish afterimage, all that was left of the Shredou ship was a brightly glowing ring of metallic composites, materials that should have been more than 120 times tougher than even the best version of Terran ceristeel.

It was rumored Grey ships could survive even the heat of a blue-white, B-class star, where the surface temperatures ranged from 10,000K–30,000K. It had not, however, survived the heat of the Godstrike Mark II.

"Sir! We have projectiles headed our way," MacInnes warned her. "They're being launched from the surface."

The Grey commander on her screen vanished, leaving her with a picture of the blue-and-silver TUPSF logo that often served as a placeholder in Terran hyperrelay channels. Ia quietly closed the dual lid on the Godstrike firing control. The Shredou had decided to leave, regroup, and consider what had just happened.

Thankfully, they had left before noticing the attack from

below; the Truth Party government of Sanctuary, backed by the fanatically xenophobic Church of the One True God, had just snapped and panicked. They would attack anything and everything within reach until it all went away.

"General, should our gunners fire flak bombs, or interceptors?" Ramasa asked her.

"Neither. Private Xhuge, warn the *Popova* to keep their shields up, add that they are not allowed to return fire, and tell them to depart only when Gateway Station has been attacked and destroyed. Send the coordinates from today's subfolder on the exact location for the *Popova* to pick up the three escape pods of surviving station personnel, and have them delivered to *Confucius* Station at their earliest convenience, along with the hyperrelay hub. Ishiomi, it's your turn to steer again."

"Helm to my control in twenty, sir," the yeoman agreed.

Ia tapped the workstation, transferring control to her backup pilot. "Make sure the *Popova* picks up those pods before breaking orbit. I'm going to go have a post-battle chat with our Feyori guests and discuss the distribution and maintenance of the remaining anti-Grey spheres across the various Human star systems. After that, I'll be asleep for a few hours. Try not to break anything on your way to System SSD-17a, where we'll have to confront them all over again. I'd like those hours to be uninterrupted."

"Aye, sir," Ishiomi agreed. "I have the helm, sir. Do I have the bridge again, as well?"

"You have the bridge until relieved by Lieutenant Rico, Yeoman Ishiomi," Ia agreed. Releasing her restraints, she paused long enough to siphon a bit of energy from the outlet built into her station, then rose and headed for the main doors. "Good job, everyone. Keep your nerves steady since we'll have to face them again three more times before we can go back to hunting down the Salik."

MAY 13, 2499 T.S.
SIC TRANSIT

Ia looked at the datapad Grizzle had handed her the moment she entered the main boardroom. The list of names and

requests was fairly extensive. She had expected this, knew it
was coming, but . . .

"Thirty-three marriage requests?" Ia asked, looking up at
the couples seated in the risers across from the head table.
Mostly male and female, some male and male, some female
and female. York and Clairmont, Teevie and Crow . . . even
Mishka and Spyder, who had chosen to sit in the tiers with the
rest.

Spyder, his left hand clasping Jesselle's right, lifted one
purple-dyed eyebrow. Instead of going back to green after
Dabin, he had started experimenting with non-Terran camouflage colors. "Y' can't tell us this's a *surprise*, 'Bloody Mary.'
Ye'r th' bleedin' Prophet!"

"Well, *your* particular pairing was an unexpected percentage, but I'll not object to it," Ia retorted. "No, my problem
is, these were supposed to trickle in over a few weeks, not
slam into one giant stack of simultaneously submitted requests.
This will look very odd to the DoI."

"Is that going to be a problem, General?" Private Davies
demanded, folding her arms across her chest. She and her
teammate Private Unger had come a long, long way from
their early, troubled partnership days. "Or are you expecting
us to back up and submit them one at a time in some preor-
dained order?"

Palms flat, leaning on the table, Ia met the other woman's
arch look. "My question is, are you asking for a *mass ceremony*? All of you, all at once, all on board this ship? With
Chaplain Benjamin presiding? Or individual services on
board? Or are you asking as a group for when we'll next have
a real Leave on some planet? Because *that* option won't be for
a long while to come; sorry, but there it is."

Over sixty pairs of eyes exchanged looks, glancing at their
partners and their neighbors. Finally, Spyder spoke up again
after craning his neck to do a face check of expressions.
"Well . . . s'a pity we won't be getting Leave soon, 'n all, but I
s'ppose onna ship's fine. Um . . . dunno about individual
versus mass, but I s'ppose we could all have a confab 'bout
that. When d'you need an answer back?"

This was throwing her schedule off. As much as she
wanted to protest that yes, they *had* to submit in the correct

order and get married like clockwork . . . frankly, nearly anything her crew did in their personal lives on board this ship would not make a damn bit of difference either way, save to make them a little happier or a little more irritable. Hurricane-causing butterfly wings lurked inside any crew's morale, true, but at least she knew she could rely on her crew to be willing to correct themselves if they started going off course.

Personally, she would rather have a happy crew. Not just because it would make her job easier in the long run but because she wanted them to have whatever happiness they could grasp, within the confines of duty, conscience, need, and precognition. Bowing her head, Ia skimmed through the timeplains.

". . . Two weeks," she said after a few seconds in reality. Straightening, she faced the couples sitting across from her. "I need to know within two weeks. Feel free to discuss this freely among the rest of the crew, in case the others want to make up their minds ahead of schedule—and you are all very lucky I have *carte blanche* strong enough to handle this mass request, too," she added, sweeping a finger along the rows. "Or else I'd have to explain to the Admiral-General the rash of happy unions among my crew.

"I'm supposed to be the Prophet of Saving This Galaxy, not the Prophet of Happily Ever After," she stated tartly. "Still, I thank you for taking the time to come talk to me all at once. See Grizzle for any further paperwork you need handled right now, and don't forget to consider carefully your individual spiritual or religious needs for any specific ceremonies. One more thing: You will *remain*, one and all, on beecee shots for the duration of your service on board this ship. That service will end when *I* say it will end, and not one pico sooner. Is that clear?"

"Sir, yes, sir!" they replied in crisp chorus, rising to their feet. Previous sessions in a boardroom very much like this one, albeit on a different ship, had taught this crew how to properly respond to their commanding officer when she used those words. Their prompt response pleased Ia.

"Good. Dismissed . . . and congratulations on each of your impending nuptials." Nodding to Sadneczek, she strode out of the boardroom. Once out of sight, she rubbed at her temple, wondering just how many *other* details were beginning to slip through her grasp.

Tired and worried that she wasn't worrying enough about the little things, she returned to her quarters. She had three hours before they were due to confront the Greys again. The ship *thrummed* with the faint rumble of hyperwarp, sucking through its artificial wormhole while wrapped in a blanket of inverted Higgs-field greasing physics.

A glance at her desk as she passed through her office showed that Garcia had struck again. This time, the gelatin had been formed in a flat disc divided into eight different-colored wedges, like a pie chart. She was more tired than she was hungry, and though it was tempting, Ia swerved to her desk to thumb the comm button, not to pick up the spoon clipped to the edge of the plate. *"Ia to Private Garcia, I appreciate the gesture, but I'd rather have it for dessert. Would you please come pick it up before it melts?"*

Several seconds passed, then Garcia responded. *"Uh, sir? What . . . what are you talking about? You want me to pick up something?"*

Ia frowned and thumbed the button for the link . . . then released it, thinking. This was . . . this was Garcia's sleep cycle. Thumbing it again, she asked, *"Did you, or did you not, arrange for another gelatin dessert to be delivered to my office?"*

"Sir, no, sir," came the crisp, prompt reply. Garcia sounded like she was waking up a bit more. *"I haven't done anything with gelatin in . . . about a week? Someone else must've done it."*

". . . Sorry to interrupt your sleep. Get some good rest," she added, frowning in puzzlement at the comm controls.

"Thanks, sir. Garcia out."

That was odd. Very odd. Taking the time to seat herself at her desk, Ia stared at the pie-chart-style dessert. It sat on a clear plate, looking neatly sculpted and smelling of nothing more than various kinds of fruit. Innocuous. *But if Garcia didn't do this one . . . I know she did the first, but did she do the layered one, with the apples and fart-fruits? Or did someone else? And if so, who?*

Who should have been easy to discern. Closing her eyes, Ia flipped in, around, and up onto the timeplains. Instead of turning to the right, however, she turned to the left, facing upstream into the past. It wasn't easy, struggling to observe a room during a time frame when there hadn't been a person physically present, but the *Damnation* was her ship. It had always been her ship, from bow to stern, dorsal to ventral, starboard to port.

Starting with the moment she had left her office to answer Sadneczek's request to gather with the others in the boardroom less than twenty minutes ago—when she knew her desk had been gelatin-free—she struggled to linger within view of her desktop. It did not help that the lights automatically dimmed a couple minutes after she had left, reducing the available lighting. The lights did not brighten, did not brighten, did not . . .

They brightened just as she—her younger self, that was—palmed open the door from the outside and stepped in, heading toward the door to her private quarters at the back of the modest-sized office. The plate was already there. Scowling, Ia reinserted herself higher in the stream, and watched carefully again. This time, it wasn't as hard to stay focused. A faint shift of shadows, a hint of movement in the last thirty seconds before her entry . . . *there*!

Except . . . it made no sense. Hands appeared out of nowhere—*out of nowhere*—and set the plate on her desk with the practiced little slide that said whoever-it-was was clipping the plate carefully in place via the slightly raised rim edging the flat surface. Then those hands retreated into nothing. *Nothing!* It did not make sense!

Sliding the plate free, she checked underneath. No note, just a rainbow of desserts. A dip into the near future showed the dessert was completely harmless, and even tasty, if the slightly puzzled but pleased look on her future self's face was any indication. Ia didn't reach into those waters close enough to consult herself, however. Instead, she skimmed back to the two-fruit version.

Hands, appearing out of nowhere, with nothing but deep darkness on the intersection plane side. *Feyori? Some new form of teleportation?* Uncertain, Ia sat there and pondered, eyeing the pie-chart gel. One of the colors was fairly close to the peach-toned hue of her crystalline bracer . . . and that gave her an idea.

Reducing its energy field via electrokinesis, she pulled off a thumbnail-sized chunk and spread it out over the surface of her desk, rubbing it flatter and flatter with her hands and her mind until it spread over her desk in a faint gold-foil-thin film. She made sure to tuck it under the edges of the clipping rim, then manually dimmed the lights in her office to double-check for any glow.

No cabin and no corridor on board a military ship was ever left completely dark; that would violate every safety regulation in the books. There were faint, phosphorescent safety strips outlining the edges of the floor, but after the bright glow of her working lights, they were very dim. With the lights out, and the paper-thin film applied, the crysium wasn't readily visible. Of course, if even the safety strips stopped working and if she stared long enough, she might just make out the rectangle where she'd spread the crysium, but it would take concentration. Satisfied, she refirmed the bracer under her gray-colored sleeve, then splayed her hands on the cool, super-hard surface, concentrating.

Crysium was not sentient, but it *was* alive in its own way. Anchored by its presence, Ia was able to skim straight through the future of her office. Minutes and hours and days blurred past, until the next dessert offering came along—she snapped the timestream to a crawl, heedless of which day it was, and grabbed those hands with her mind. Or rather, the life-energy inside those hands, as she could and would grab a Feyori encountered mid-life-stream. Hauling that person onto the timeplains was an unexpected struggle, however. With an effort more akin to pulling a mechsuit out of a mud pit by hand than simply tugging a lightworlder up onto a riverbank, she found herself sweating to pull into view . . . a waist-up image of a man with a face painted like a white snowflake on a black background.

"You!" Ia gaped at him, shocked by just who she had caught. *"But . . . you're . . ."*

He smiled and shrugged as best he could, his wrists still caught in her hands. *"I'm the Redeemer, yes. And the Savior— in* my *timeline—was quite successful."* He paused, glanced down at the waters showing the image of her desk and its spiral of polka-dot-infused gelatin, and looked up at her. *"I assure you, the desserts are harmless. Even healthy."*

It was a good question, considering what she had done . . . or would have done . . . to him and his intended life in the far-distant future. *"Why are you giving these to me?"*

Ia didn't bother asking him how. The ability to cross temporal boundaries physically, and to do so as easily as stepping into the next room, was a trick of the Savior's. Post-galactic salvation, that was. It was not something Ia could understand, for all that she knew it was possible. Nor did she have the time to learn. So the only thing that concerned her was the *why.* Particularly where this man was concerned, and her own orders regarding his life, in his past and her future.

That black-and-white-painted mouth twisted wryly. Rue-fully even, before he answered simply, *"Because I forgive you. I understand now why you did what you had to do, and I forgive you for it—but I'm still going to get you for it. Now put me back; I feel like I'm being pulled in half, here."*

"Are you going to keep forcing desserts on me?" Ia asked. She honestly wanted to know, and to know why. *"And why gelatin desserts? Why not cake, or a pastry?"*

He smiled at her. A sweet, cherubic, innocent smile that immediately put Ia on edge, wary of that halo-wreathed, wing-framed hint-of-holy aura lurking in his eyes and lips and cheeks. *"Because I know what you do not."* Pulling one hand free, he tapped her lightly on the nose. *"Your abilities, O Prophet, only extend to the ends of the universe you inhabit. Thanks to the Savior, I am not nearly so limited. My revenge will be very sweet . . . and very jiggly. Enjoy."*

Now he grinned like a devil, a cheeky, snowflake-faced devil. On the one hand, Ia was grateful he *had* forgiven her for her trespasses against him. But on the other hand, the Re-deemer had a sense of humor utterly unlike her own . . . and if he truly did know things she did not . . . No. She didn't have time to consider what *that* meant, let alone track it down. Pushing his mind back into his body, she released him from her temporal grip. He released the plate and vanished back into Somewhere Else, via a grasp of physics so profound, she could only See the first and foremost person to master it, above and beyond any of the feeble fumbling of a Feyori or the advanced mechanics of a Grey.

Dropping back into her own body, into her own time, Ia stared at the pie chart on her plate. There was literally nothing *she* could see, all the way to the ends of her life in a wide variety of possible futures, that would cause her harm if she ate the damned thing. *So whatever his "sweet, jiggly" vengeance is . . . is that a Hell made out of gelatin?*

And how is this forgiveness and vengeance in one? I don't understand. I do not understand anything of this . . . She did grasp that the several flavors of gelatin in the bowl before her were one and all perfectly safe to eat. But not the why, and not the how. Confused, Ia unclipped the spoon and poked at the stuff, watching it shimmy. *Considering what I owe him, some sort of bizarre dessert-based "vengeance" is probably a small price to pay. Like . . . I don't know . . . going to my grave never understanding why?*

That might be it. Of course, there were hundreds of thousands of mysteries in the universe she'd take to her grave without a chance to understand. Shaking her head, Ia dug into it and set aside her doubts. As far as vengeance-based punishments went, this was a very mild one to have to suffer. Downright pleasant-tasting, in fact.

Now that Ia knew where the non-Garcia desserts were coming from—however bizarre a source—she had more immediate matters to contemplate. Such as the little details that had been slipping through unseen cracks in her temporal vigilance of late. *I cannot afford to let any details slide, or the slightest deviation could send everything careening wildly off course. I cannot . . .*

An idea crossed her mind. *String theory, wormhole vibrations, universal constants, yet the multiverse lies just beyond . . . Accessing transdimensional energies is not impossible, since it does eventually get accessed, and hyperrifts are simply a crude preliminary, like how the old insystem drives were a crude preliminary to FTL, before Terrans realized it was possible to go faster-than-light without violating the constant speed of light squared. I already know the connotations of negative energy impacting on the quantum vibrations of a hyperrift opening, but where there's a negative, there's always a* positive—*!*

Inspired, Ia dug in her desk for a blank datapad. Then winced. *Not enough time, never enough time—if only I could access directly from the timestreams, but I'd have to have a way of throttling down the energy flow, some sort of psychic capacitor—* Gah! Ia smacked her forehead, then pulled off a chunk of her diminishing crysium bracer. *This is its own capacitor! If I touch only* this *while it's plugged into a datapad— I'll have to shape an appropriate plug, first—then I should be able to connect the two a lot more directly!*

Abandoning her dessert entirely, Ia shoved it under the clip edge on the side of her desk and started experimenting. She fried three datapads in just over a minute before she got a configuration on the interface that was big enough to resist the excess energies for the fourth one. She also could only use it for a few seconds at a time—real-time seconds—before those energies had to be bled off, but it worked.

It *worked*!

But those were tentative tests. She stared at the thumb-shaped bit of peach-hued crystal in her hand. The interior had turned more translucent than transparent, etched with a fine maze of striations deep inside, but it *would* work. Ia plugged it into one of the data ports on her office workstation, sank her mind into the timestreams, and plunged into a full-on prophecy culled directly from the timestreams.

Pulling back into her body, she sniffed the air, cracked open one eye . . . and sagged with relief. No smoldering wreckage from overloaded circuits. Her bracer was now a mere bracelet, reduced to a dagger's worth of crysium instead of a sword's, but that was fine. She could always reshape everything in a matter of mere seconds now that she knew how.

Excellent. Now to try to find the right alternate-universe me who knows what the hell I'm trying to think about— Meyun is going to love *this, when I show him I can drastically speed up my timestream-based search efforts . . . and none of this is something I would have thought of without that little gelatin-based visit to spur it.*

I owe you even more *now, Nuin. I'm sorry I cannot change the worst parts of your fate, but I am glad you've forgiven me for them.* She paused, thinking, then shook her head. *Even if I don't know if you came from the timeline I'm aiming for, or not. Meyun might try to blow this up, saying it's proof I succeed . . . but if there's no true paradox in shooting one's former grandfather when traveling back in time . . . then there's no paradox in his visiting me from a successful timeline when I'm actually living in a timeline where I don't succeed.*

That's the damnation of it all. "Oh, hey, just go talk to yourself in the timeline where you succeed and find out how to do it!" *As if there's no effort involved between getting from Here to There, with no need for me to police a thousand and ten hundred things. As if there's no need to depend on the whims and vagaries of others . . .*

I will have no guarantee of success until I play my final move. Not until I can see if I've dug the channels deep enough and built the levees high and long enough to withstand the floods of Time. Still . . . She eyed the dessert, then unclipped her spoon and scooped up a bite, lifting it briefly in solemn salute. *Here's to the hope that his visit means I do succeed.*

MAY 17, 2499 T.S.
GLAU
TLASSIAN COLONY 7

"The Admiral-General's on the line, sir," C'ulosc stated from the comm station. The ship swayed around them as Ia dodged Salik fire, making him grab at his console to keep his arms near his controls; the safety harness only kept his torso in its seat. "Are you busy?"

"Yes, but I'll take it anyway," Ia stated, hands shifting over the controls and in the attitude glove. "Upper third tertiary; don't shift any of my lower screens," she added, glancing down at the tactical displays. This was a messy fight; the Salik were desperate to take Glau, under the carefully planted rumor that it had no passion-moss infestation. It didn't, though there were sealed canisters on the tidally locked moon, containers waiting to be cracked open just in case the enemy's troops got through the blockade.

The Salik were desperate enough, they had brought more

than fifty ships to conquer a colony that numbered just over a quarter million. There weren't more than a dozen military ships on the Alliance side in this system, but there were a total of fifty vessels in all, thanks to the addition of merchant reserves—civilian ships outfitted and licensed for combat. Spyder had agreed to sit in on this fight even though it wasn't his shift, helping coordinate insystem maneuvers between the various factions. He worked side by side with Lieutenant Rico, who was being kept busy translating some of Spyder's more thick-accented Terranglo commands into much more intelligible versions in the makeshift fleet's various native tongues.

Her thumb graced the button for the main cannon just as Myang's face appeared over her head. "General Ia, you do realize Logistics, Strategics, and the DoI are all screaming slagging murder over how many supply movements, personnel transfers, and patrol-route changeups you've just sent through their systems?"

"Sir, yes, sir," she agreed, her gaze firmly on the lower bank of screens while the central one flashed deep red for a moment. She tapped the button again and made a course correction while the cannon recharged itself. "Over thirty-seven thousand personnel reassignments, trillions of crates of food and other supplies to be shipped ahead of schedule, thousands of hydrobombs released from cold storage . . . and all of it to be delivered on time within three weeks with a full-scale mobilization of the fleet.

"But they'll all have to get in line behind the Guardianship of the K'Katta," she added tightly, spinning her ship on its main axis, "who are having seventy thousand personnel shipped, and I'm moving over twenty thousand personnel among the Tlassians, as soon as I'm finished punching red-hot holes through this system's light-space. Plus the"—she paused while hull breach claxons blared for the amidships sector, until Darghas at the operations station cut them off—"Chinsoiy are having to move forty thousand or so around, and the V'Dan a good fifty grand . . . and the Gatsugi will have the highest number of personnel swapped in and out, at over ninety thousand bodies moved about the known galaxy."

"Is there any particular point to all of this?" Myang asked dryly.

"Yes, sir, I'm saving an additional 13,716 lives for absolute sure . . ." She fired again and sloughed her ship sideways through a set of debris that made the telltales for the ship's shields fluctuate in blips of green-turned-yellow, then thumbed the main cannon again. "And adding in a twenty-six percent chance of saving an additional fourteen percent of the Choya nation, give or take half a percent—that would be well over a billion lives," Ia stated. Red flared briefly from every forward-viewing screen. "Instead of a mere eleven percent chance."

"You're serious about saving enemy lives," Myang stated. Her tone reminded Ia of her old Platoon Lieutenant, D'Kora, who never spoke a question if she could help it.

"Very," Ia told her superior. She didn't shift her gaze upward because she was still flying through the remnants of twenty-seven Salik ships, plus the vessels from the Tlassian, K'Kattan, V'Dan, and Chinsoiy governments. Gently swapping ends, she rippled the insystem fields so that the *Damnation* was flying backwards, and fired a half-second streak of light across a swath of Salik ships while still in midturn. Near space would be awkward flying in and out of this system for the next half light-year, but better forcing everyone into strict traffic-approach lanes than to allow a single Salik ship to land its cargo of battle robots on that colonial moon.

"Is there something particularly important that's going to happen in three weeks?" the Admiral-General asked her.

"No, sir," Ia replied truthfully. "But it gives us a week's wriggle room for something in four. Still, if everyone follows the timing I've outlined to the second, it should all proceed smoothly enough. Anything else, sir?"

"Yes. I've included a set of requests from the tactical board for you to review with that precognitive juju of yours. On a personal note . . . what the hell are all those Feyori carrying around? Those golden bubble-things," Myang added in clarification. "They've been moving them into various star systems and parking them in Lagrange orbits, then asserting that they must not be touched. Telepathically, to the insystem controllers and local military heads, which has *not* been going over well. If the Feyori are *yours* to command, as you've said, then what the hell are they up to, Ia?"

"Those spheres are the property of the Third Human Empire, and as such are not to be tampered with or touched for the next 250 years. Only the Feyori are authorized to move and utilize them . . . and as this is your lucky day, Admiral-General," Ia added, firing one last brief, bright shot before closing the lid on the Godstrike button, "you are about to see the three parked in the Sol System being used to chase off the Greys. You have fifteen minutes to set up a surveillance feed from the satellites orbiting Jupiter from . . . mark."

"What are they, some sort of weapon? A bomb?" Myang asked, frowning.

"Only mentally. They're the flip-side equivalent of the Salik's anti-psi machines. The outer casing is made from crysium to protect the components within from any possible damage, since they'll have to last at least a quarter of a millennium in the irradiated vacuum of space, and the Feyori are therefore the only ones who can reach inside their impervious hulls to activate the machinery inside." Again, she rotated the ship on its main axis as a particularly stubborn Salik battlecruiser tried to sear a deeper hole in the *Damnation*'s polished hull. "You'll still want to have psychics on standby, but the Shredou will learn that a system protected by one of those spheres is a system that will not be invaded so easily."

"Then there are enough to protect every system in the Alliance?" Myang asked her.

"No, sir. But they'll be scattered throughout Terran and V'Dan space so that they can be quickly shifted by the Meddlers from one location to another whenever needed. Just leave them in orbit—if I had them stored on planets and moons, it'd take that much longer to get them into position. It's easier just to park them in space—ah sir, we're about to lose the ship's hyperrelay hub," Ia warned her superior, checking the text scrolling at the bottom of her upper third tertiary screen. "It won't be repaired for thirty-six hours . . . and I have received the data packet. I'll get back to you on that when I can. Did you have a last query?"

"What, you don't know?" Myang asked her.

"Well, I am a little busy right now—"

Another explosion rocked the ship, the claxons blared for another hull breach, and the comm signal cut off. Ia sighed. "Five seconds early, but not unexpected."

"General," Darghas called out from the operations station, wincing at the invective spewing into her ear from her headset, "Commander Harper would like to impolitely inform you that you're off his holiday shopping list yet again for what you're doing to his ship."

"Inform the Commander he is a son of a wonderful mother who should've taught him a lot more in the way of patience. C'ulosc, inform the ships on the list in your 'repair notes' folder that the battle will be over in thirteen more minutes and that I am appropriating all of the materials on each ship's sublist for the *Damnation*'s needs. I'd appropriate their repair crews, too, if it still weren't an act of Grand High Treason to let anyone else on board without permission . . . and I can't get permission for a month or two yet."

"I'm on it, sir," C'ulosc agreed.

Ia nodded, and thumbed the ship's commsystem with her right hand, her left sideslipping the ship with the attitude controls, bringing the curve of the gas giant back into view. *"All hands, this is the General. Combat will be finished in just under thirteen minutes. All hands will be required on duty to effect repairs to the* Damnation. *I repeat, all hands will be required to effect repairs, movement capacity first. We leave this system in twenty-seven hours, forty-three minutes. Doctor Mishka, break out the stimulants; no one sleeps until we're under way again. Ia out."*

CHAPTER 6

... My nickname? Yes, I suppose it's time to talk about how I truly earned it. Not that first fight, all those years ago—I did earn it in a sort of lighthearted way . . . but no. A nickname like "Bloody Mary" is best understood in the original contexts to which it applied, and no, I don't mean the drink made from tomato juice, vodka, and seasonings.

The original, of course, was Queen Mary Tudor, sister of the famous Queen Elizabeth I. Roughly three hundred Protestants died in her religious persecution in the attempt to bring the Anglican Empire back under Roman Catholic jurisdiction. Though that number isn't a lot—her father, Henry VIII, is said to have slaughtered fifty-seven thousand or so in pulling the empire away from Catholicism in the first place—the nickname she earned by it has since grown to be applied to anyone who systematically kills many while proclaiming it is their duty to do so.

Ironically, just four hundred years later, the nickname "Bloody Mary" was also used as a means of precognition in the middle of the twentieth century. It was used in a child's game by chanting the name while peering into a

*mirror under various conditions, in order to predict the fu-
ture based upon whatever apparitions the chanter might see
behind or beside their reflection after enough repetitions
were made. These apparitions were capable of being benign or malicious. They could be portents of death instead
of happiness, and could even be accompanied by attacks on
the petitioner, or attacks on their nearest friends . . . or so
people believed.*

*So, am I a psychotic, prognosticating poltergeist?
Well, I'm still alive, so we can check off my being a poltergeist. Am I a duty-deluded, mass-murdering monarch?
No one ever put a crown on my head, so one out of those
three has to go away, too.*

*Prognosticator? Oh yes, I specialize in foreseeing the
future. Psychotic? Not in the least, according to every
psych evaluation I've ever had—and I've undergone
scores over the years. I think . . . yes, sixty-three to date—
the majority in my childhood as I struggled with my
ability to foresee terrible things. So, am I duty-deluded?
Perhaps, since I believe it is my most solemn duty to act to
save as many lives as I can . . . but at the same time, I am
also forced to see in advance the consequences of each of
my decisions and their possible outcomes. So deluded
isn't the right word, not when I'm forced to see the truth of
my actions' consequences, over and over and over. Driven
maybe, but not deluded.*

*Which leaves us with the last point to consider: Am I a
mass murderer?*

                                                    ~Ia

MAY 28, 2499 T.S.
INTERSTITIAL SPACE

There were too many little details to keep track of, now. Too
many, and Ia couldn't manage it. Even with the help of her crysium transcriber whatsit wand, there were just too many details,
too many little things that could go wrong at any moment.

From the perspective she'd had as a youth—as a fifteen-
year-old, at the age of eighteen, even at the age of twenty,

twenty-two—all these details had looked manageable. Time had been on her side. Then again, Time had also pegged her to be a Commodore by now, a one-star soldier with a modicum of trust, not a five-star warleader expected to guide two full wars. The Shredou *were* starting to back down, but the Salik were growing more and more desperate.

The battle they had just fought, helping the Dlmvla take out a heavily guarded deep-space station, was just one example. At the moment, her official non-allies were chasing the last of the one- and two-manned fighter ships, ruthlessly cutting down the few survivors among the enemy, but Ia was expected to provide them with fine-chase details for not just this battle, but a good thirty more that had to be enacted before the tenth of June rolled around.

Too many details, not enough time—and her nerves tingled, warning her something was about to go wrong. Pulling her mind out of the battles the methane-breathers would have to face, Ia didn't wait for her office door chime to buzz. Thumbing the control on her desk, she unlocked the door. "Enter!"

Three women stepped inside. Not a good trio, either. Jesselle Mishka, who had a hypospray in her hand and a grim look on her face; Christine Benjamin, who had a worried, sympathetic expression on hers; and Delia Helstead, who looked wryly amused. One look at the doctor and the sprayer told Ia what she intended to do.

"No," she stated flatly. "I don't have *time* to sleep."

"You have been up for over five days straight," the blonde argued. "I don't care if you're half Feyori; five days is four days too long to be healthy."

"You really need to think about getting some rest, so that the choices and decisions you're making are the best," Bennie added.

Ia looked at Delia, to see what the petite redhead had to add. She merely shrugged, hands tucked in her back pockets. "Is this a mutiny? Because I've lasted longer on less sleep, as Bennie well knows. And I don't have time to sleep. I have allies to keep informed. It is vital that by the time we hit mid-June, the only Salik left will be the ones contained within their own star systems . . . and only I know where they all are."

"Delia?" Mishka asked, deferring to her.

Sighing, the lieutenant commander pulled something out of her back pocket. "I was hoping I wouldn't have to use this, but . . ."

Ia tensed, wary, but the former Knifeman officer didn't haul out a weapon. Nor did she use her powerful psychodominancy ability on Ia's mind, as she had once before with the force of a sledgehammer dropped from orbit. Instead, she held up a standard-issue hand mirror, wrapped in gray plexi backing, and aimed it at Ia's face.

"You look like *shakk*, sir," she stated bluntly. "You may be able to last a while longer, but your *appearance* is starting to worry the crew. When was the last time you had a decent meal, and let your *body* rest, even if your mind cannot?"

Ia looked at the mirror. The other woman's hand-eye coordination was more than good enough to have it angled just so over the three or so meters between them to reflect the image of Ia's face right back at her. But she didn't see the dark circles under her eyes, the exhaustion etching fine lines into her forehead and the corners of her mouth. She saw a round, silvery, mirror-smooth sphere, and the golden red hair of her chaplain—and made a mental leap.

Ginger. Feyori. Geas-threads woven in the tapestry.

This was going to give her a major headache in the next few days, with even less chance for sleep . . . but it would ease a huge burden off her shoulders. *If* she could find time for it.

"Sir, you will either—"

"Shh," she shushed the doctor, lifting a finger as her eyes unfocused onto the timeplains. "I'm looking for what you need."

"What *I* need?" Mishka repeated, arching her brow. "You're tipping right over into delusional, General!"

"No, no, she's got that 'I'm about to be clever' look on her face," Helstead soothed the doctor. "At least, I hope so. Either that, or she's having an aneurysm."

"Shh." She *was* tired, and the least little distraction kept threatening her concentration. But when all three women fell silent, Ia was able to see a path to what they wanted and she needed. She thumbed the comm controls on her desk workstation. *"All hands, this is the General. Change of plans. Commander Harper, reschedule the work to get this ship*

under way in three hours, not five, prioritize all external repairs; internal ones will be made sic transit. *Ia out."*

"So you'll agree you need some sleep?" Mishka asked her, lifting the hypospray.

"I won't get any for another eighteen hours. *Then* I will sleep for twenty-four straight," Ia promised. "Monitored, in one of your infirmary beds, hooked up to a nutrient drip. We'll be skipping the battle at Attenborough Epsilon 14, though I'll still have to direct it from the timestreams to make up for our absence."

"So what will we be doing instead?" Helstead asked her.

"Gathering the Feyori around the moon world of Glyker III in the Chinsoiy-held system of Glyker N-Tau. Your mirror just gave me the idea on how to answer a big problem that's been building up. I tied Ginger into the timestreams, on Dabin," Ia added, pointing at the silvered glass still in Helstead's hand. "Forced her to be aware of what to do and when to do it in an old-fashioned *geas*, or suffer the consequences of having her life-energies abraded away whenever she resisted. When the Admiral-General promoted me to General, it opened up a whole host of new possibilities for saving as many as I could . . . but that meant an exponentially greater number of details to have to keep track of . . . and as you've seen, I haven't been handling the extra workload very well. So instead, I'll be foisting it off on about a thousand Feyori to manage *for* me . . . and *they'll* do it or suffer the consequences."

"Well, at least you've *admitted* it," Mishka muttered.

"Jesselle," Bennie chided her. Then eyed Ia. "She is right, though, Ia. If you *weren't* going to admit it . . . We've been worried about you, that's all."

"I appreciate the worry—and thank you for using a mirror instead of your psychodominancy, Delia," Ia added to her second officer. Helstead shrugged and tucked her hands and her palm mirror into her back pockets again. "We'll arrive in the N-Tau System in two days. I'll have to spend about five hours summoning and binding the Feyori—even working at the speed of psychic abilities, it'll still take time to parse and bind each set of instructions for a thousand or more of them— but once that's done, then I can return to a normal work-and-sleep schedule."

"Normal for a Human, or normal for you?" Jesselle asked archly. "Because you have had a very bad habit of running a thirty-six-hour workday every few days."

"Normal for me. I'll survive," Ia countered flatly. "I'll need something to keep me going until I can sleep, though— Helstead, go to the Commander and have him unlock one of the special guns, then come back and shoot me a couple of times. I'm at the point where traditional stimulants like caf' aren't enough to keep me going."

"I'm tempted to shoot you myself," Jesselle muttered, but at a nudge from the chaplain she headed for the door. Helstead left with her. Palming it shut, Bennie came back to Ia's desk, and braced her palms on the edge.

"You really are pushing yourself too hard, Ia," the middle-aged woman warned her. "You have half the crew spying on you because nobody's seen you take more than an hour's break in the last five days. We're *worried*. And if he didn't have to keep repairing all the holes you keep putting in his ship, *and* sleep like a normal being, Meyun would be in here, too, ready to help hold you down while Jesselle shot you. Meyun and Oslo," she added, mentioning the 1st Platoon lieutenant, who was currently on duty. "I'd ask Spyder to help, but he doesn't seem to think you're in the trouble zone yet."

"I'm not . . . but I *was* getting close," Ia confessed quietly. She gripped the peach-gold wand plugged into her desk . . . then let go of it. "When I was young, I thought I could handle all of this. I had all the time back then to go slowly and be thorough in looking over all the details. But now . . . now I'm running out of time, and there's so much more to do, thanks to my promotion. I can't *not* do it, Bennie," she told her friend, her counselor, her expression sober. "It's not in my nature to ignore all the chances I have to help everybody.

"But . . . I can't do it on my own. I'm going to have to rope the Feyori into managing planet-wide details. Hopefully, by spreading it out among many of them, it won't interfere much with their normal plays in the Game, which do still have to take place." Shaking her head, she reached for the transcription wand again. "In the meantime, I still have to help the Dlmvla track down over fifteen hundred more Salik vessels that have gone astray in the depths of space. I *promise*, I'll sleep well for those twenty-four hours. *If* you'll let me get my work done right now."

Nodding, Chaplain Benjamin headed for the door. "Just remember, you promised. I'm holding you to it, young lady."

Ia nodded. The energy needed for the Gathering of so many Feyori would be provided by an ion storm, a strong magnetic field, stellar radiation, and a few shots from the *Damnation*'s guns while her ship and crew waited. She would also be able to advise the Chinsoiy government on a few extra moves they could make in the near future, too. Too many details, not enough time, but at least she *could* delegate a good chunk of it to her Meddler minions to handle and watch.

JUNE 8, 2499 T.S.
BATTLE PLATFORM *AMAZING GRACE HOPPER*

Breathing deep, Ia squared her shoulders and braced herself. The side entrance to the *Damnation*'s main boardroom was off the main corridor, but at least it did have an alcove she could partially hide in while the last of her crew entered through the main doors several meters away. Once again, the ship was on full lockdown, and every member of her crew had been ordered to attend. Not because anyone had broken a law . . . yet . . . but because this was a speech, an explanation, which Ia owed to the men and women serving under her.

When the last man had entered, and the main doors had slid shut, she counted to fifty, then took another deep breath and palmed her door open. Her Dress Black jacket had the minimum of glittery on it, but the fact she was wearing it instead of her more casual Grays pulled everyone inside onto their feet at Attention.

"At Ease, and be seated," she directed them.

A week's worth of "normal" sleep schedules—aided by drugs and monitoring at first—had removed some of the shadows from under her eyes, but she still felt the weight of Time pressing down on her. Taking her place in front of the center chair at the head table, Ia waited for the men and women around her to settle into place. She remained standing, however.

"I gave you all a promise when I first took on this crew," Ia stated, meeting a pair of eyes here, a curious gaze there. "I swore that when I had the time for it, I would let you know in advance not just what we will be doing, but *why* we will be doing it. You are all about to be aural witnesses to the worst call I will have to make in the entire span of my career. Out of *respect* for the sacrifice which is about to be made . . . you will be silent, and hold all comments, questions, and noises until after this call is finished, and I have explained that very important *why* to you."

Seating herself, she tapped the controls on her arm unit and hooked her headset over her ear. The ship's fully repaired hyperrelay hub came to life under her remote-linked command, reaching out through hundreds of light-years of distance. She tapped into the boardroom's commsystem, letting the 160 members of her crew listen in as the ping signal bounced and waited, bounced and waited.

It took a full minute to receive a reply. Ia held up her hand for patience as her crew started to move restlessly. A male voice finally answered. *"Var shou-desth, oua v'*T'tun S'Naith Qi-el, *harba voudas?"*

"—Give me that!" a female voice asserted. *"This is the Imperial Warship* T'tun S'Naith Qi-el, *and the Terran Merchant Reserve* Bee's Knees. *We are under a Quarantine Extreme lockdown. Who is calling us, and what is your position?"*

"This is General Ia, head of the combined Alliance Armies. Leftenant Na'Shouen will know of me as the Sh'nai Prophet of a Thousand Years. I am transmitting a text-based translation in High Imperial for the leftenant to read on a subchannel, since I know he doesn't speak Terranglo."

"Considering we found him in a stasis pod that was last sealed over two hundred years ago, yeah," the woman retorted. There was about four seconds of lag between them. *"No* shakk, *he doesn't speak Terranglo. He's lucky I speak V'Dan—if you're really the Prophet, do you know what the slag has infected this crew? Can it be stopped? Is there a cure? Everyone just . . . They slowed down, they lost motivation . . . they just . . . stopped. Stopped breathing. Their hearts stopped beating. They're all dead.*

"Na'Shouen says it's from some old Salik research base

his ship found and destroyed, some sort of plague that had wiped out all the researchers. He originally aimed his ship at the nearest sun to destroy it, too, but it went off course after he put himself in the stasis pod, not wanting to watch his own death. He . . . He and I both had high fevers for a few days, but that was weeks ago, and we've been limping to the nearest star system, hoping for either a cure or . . . well, it's the nearest star. Is there a cure? There is one, right?"

Ia clenched her fingers into fists. *"Second Rank Merchanter Altheen Donsett,"* she stated, keeping her voice steady. *"Your ship, the* Bee's Knees, *is a duly registered Merchant Reserve Vessel. As the head of the Terran Space Fleet—head of the entire combined Alliance military forces—I am commanding you, the surviving ranking crew member, to comply with the following wartime orders. Do you understand that you are being called to active wartime service, and that you are by license required to obey my commands?"*

"I . . . don't like the sound of that. But . . . lay it out, General. I'm listening."

"No, you won't like it. Your orders, Second Rank Merchanter, are to adjust the T'tun's *heading by fifteen degrees starboard, maintain that course, and wait. You are* not *permitted to complete Leftenant Na'Shouen's mission to destroy the* T'tun *and the attached* Bee's Knees *in the nearest star. Do you understand?"*

"No, but . . . why? This thing isn't in the medical database! We can't control it if we don't even know what it is. If . . . if you're trying to tell us there's a cure, then say *so, for starssake!"*

"Your orders, Merchanter, are to maintain the prescribed heading. You will spend the next five hours destroying all evidence of any medical emergency, particularly any and all databanks containing recordings of what happened on both ships. And you will await capture by Salik forces, which will take place in seven hours. You will not *destroy your ships. You will* not *evade pursuit."*

"—Capture?"

"Soudeg s'veth?"

Ia pressed on. *"You will also* not *kill yourselves before the Salik have synced airlocks and boarded the* T'tun. *However . . .*

at that point, I suggest cyanide caps. It will be a far better death than if you allow them to take you prisoner . . . but you will not *do so* until *you are one hundred percent sure that the Salik have been exposed to this plague, and that they will have no way of discerning that there* is *a plague on board. Do you understand?"*

She waited for a reply. A dozen seconds ticked away.

"Merchanter Donsett, you have been given wartime orders by a duly appointed member of the Terran Space Force Command Staff, and a duly appointed Grand General of the V'Dan Imperial Fleet. Do *you understand what you are required to do?"*

"Viidat cal-shoull ve'edeth, ni v'calsa ouen tu't-uul pleston gaisha v'deth!" The demand came from the V'Dan.

"Mii-stuul khanva Ki'en-qua V'Daania, n'au bistek: hetra-hetra gaina shouda vesta veshtok hetra," Ia replied, giving the name of the current Emperor, *and* an authorization code from the distant past.

"Va desz . . . ?"

She nodded, even though it was an audio-only link. *"The Emperor knows, and fully authorizes this sacrifice. You will ensure the Salik are exposed. If you do not, then your failure to follow orders will guarantee the destruction of the V'Dan and the Terrans alike. Do you understand your orders? These are not negotiable. I expect you to comply."*

Several seconds passed. Ia waited patiently while her crew sat and stared at her with a mixture of grimness and curiosity.

". . . Yes. We'll do it," the woman finally replied. *"We're as good as dead anyway, so . . . might as well take out some of the enemy, right?"*

"Meioa, you will be taking out all *of the enemy with your sacrifice,"* Ia told her. *"Within two months, there will be no Salik left anywhere . . . and no one will ever have to cower in fear of being eaten by them. I'm sorry that such a victory comes at the cost of your lives . . . but I am not sorry for all the billions you will be saving."*

"That's a cold comfort at best," the woman on the other end muttered after the lag-time seconds had passed. *"But . . . not like we can trust the aging meds on the* T'tun *to keep either of us alive, and my own supply is being used up at twice*

*the rate . . . So . . . uh . . . cyanide caps? Um . . . I'm not sure
where those are located."*

"Captain's office, left side of the desk, second drawer
down. Red box, yellow lettering, *Emergency Use Only,*" Ia
instructed her. "Pile all the bodies from your crew into one of
the T'tun's *shuttles and launch it at the star. There's a system
for remote piloting; the leftenant knows how to operate it.
You don't want any evidence left on board for the Salik to
grow alarmed. We need them to take this plague straight
back to their homeworld, and if you launch that shuttle first,
as fast as you can, it'll be too close to the star to stop and
investigate by the time the enemy catches you."*

*"If the Salik take this plague with them, it'll spread.
Na'Shouen says it's a self-replicating airborne pathogen of
some kind. It could be spread from world to world within a
matter of hours, once it hits any kind of major atmosphere."*

"That will be *my* concern to deal with, Merchanter. You
just make sure it gets into the enemy's airspace. I am sorry . . .
and I thank you for your sacrifice."

"Plessada vu she'naivu kester zhkoukel, Ia' n'kai!"

"No, Leftenant, I wasn't about to stop this from happening. Your ship going off course has handed the galaxy the
simplest way to get rid of an ongoing problem—as it says in
the Book of Autumn, 'In the waning days of the second war of
the stars, the Prophet will look upon the Enemy and know
only pity, for they shall gorge upon the flesh of Death itself, an
ancient death created by their own will. So shall the Enemy
slay themselves to the last soul in their rapacious, unceasing
hunger.' Those days are now upon us. I am sorry that anyone
has to die—even them—but it needs to be done. I thank you
both for your sacrifice . . . and yes, I know that's not what you
want to hear, but you have my gratitude anyway."

*"Yeah, well, you can take your gratitude and shove it
face-first in a Salik's mouth!"*

"If I were free to do this myself, I would, without restraint
or hesitation," Ia told her.

"Yeah, right. Donsett out!"

Tapping a command on her arm unit, Ia ended her side of
the link. She sat there for a few seconds more, then rose and

stood in modified Parade Rest, feet together and hands clasped behind her back. Ia breathed deep to steady her nerves, then began her explanation. "What you have just heard is the opening shot in the destruction of the Salik as a species. Unfortunately, the casualties on our own side will include far more than Second Rank Merchanter Donsett and Leftenant Na'Shouen.

"This 'plague' is indeed airborne-based. It is a self-replicating prionic catalyst that invades biochemical systems with electrically activated neurons—basically all forms of sentient life, including the Chinsoiy, though it propagates very slowly in their species compared to our own. It is drawn to a range of electricity found within most forms of neuro-logical networks of brain stem size or greater, which gives it the 'jolt' needed to replicate itself . . . and it will slay any-thing it infects within five weeks or less. Its own means of destruction is solely by heating the molecules to temperatures in excess of 1,000C for twenty minutes, 2,000C for five min-utes . . . and yes, we will be using the Godstrike cannon upon all infected ships, as well as every hydrobomb we carry.

"This is a very deadly disease, and I am deliberately unleashing it on the Salik. There *will* be Alliance casualties," she repeated firmly, giving her officers a grim look as well as the noncoms and enlisted across from her. "We will have to fire upon our own vessels, both military and civilian. We may even have to destroy a colonyworld or two—luck willing, we won't *have* to, but that threat is very real. The lives we will *save*, however, will outweigh the lives lost in ratios exceeding ten million to one . . . and that is not hyperbole, meioas.

"It is vital that we contain this plague strictly to Salik worlds alone. It would take the Chinsoiy twenty-five months to develop a binding counteragent . . . and they might survive that long, if they ruthlessly close their borders. It will take only five weeks for the Salik—and most other races—to die. Six and a half weeks, technically, for the plague to be spread, and for the remaining Salik forces to be contained on their colonyworlds, infected, and destroyed." She let that grim statement hang in the air a few moments, then added, "But it will guarantee that seven weeks from now, we will never have to deal with them again. No one will be eaten, no colony will be invaded, and there will be nothing left for us to do but burn their worlds to slag.

"This course of action is *not* open to negotiation," Ia asserted. "I will not destroy the septillions of lives that will otherwise be saved by trying to salvage a foe that refuses to change their uncivilized ways. They have been given the best warning I could give them, without fear of them trying to find and turn this plague upon us. With that in mind, you will *not* discuss the nature of this plague anywhere other than this boardroom, in this hour . . . and you will not resist my orders when I command this crew to open fire if and when one of our ships—or even a colonyworld—has been infected with the catalyst.

"I will have enough trouble getting the other ships in the Alliance to open fire as it is," she added grimly. "This hour is given to you to ask questions, and to give you an opportunity to see for yourself the differences this course of action will make in the timelines between the Salik dying as a race, and the Salik being allowed to continue to plague and plunder the other sentient races . . . and this time, Private Theam," she added to one of the women sitting in the second row, the one who had asked a few years back if there was a way for Ia to show everyone at once what she could foresee, "I have developed a way that can connect these timestream visions to the ship's monitors without the risk of destroying anything.

"However, it'll still be racing past at compressed time, so what you'll be seeing is a slowed-down recording of what will be viewed, which is not the same as a real-time, interactive experience. If any of you wish to see the *why* of Merchanter Donsett's and Leftenant Na'Shouen's sacrifices . . . now is the time to line up, or to wait patiently for a transcribed recording. Otherwise, you are under standing orders to stay silent outside of this hour in this room on all particulars of this discussion, until such time as you are given direct permission by me to speak of it."

Theam raised her hand as the others stirred, murmuring among themselves. Ia pointed at her. She stood and spoke, and the others fell quiet again. "Does the Admiral-General know about this plague and course of action, sir?"

"Yes, she does. Admiral-General Christine Myang has known for several months. She does not know exactly what the plague is, but she does know that the Salik are about to be destroyed."

Absorbing that, Theam hesitated, looking around at the others. She gauged their expressions, then squared her shoulders and faced Ia again. ". . . I guess I can speak for most of the crew when I say that we'll follow your orders, sir. We've seen too much not to keep putting our trust and faith in you."

Ia bowed her head. "Thank you, Nadja. I promise you, I wouldn't do this if it weren't the best way to handle the Salik with the least—literally, the least—loss of lives over the long run. Even if it means destroying several worlds, and several billion lives, in the short term." She looked at the others and tested her mental toes in the timestreams. "So . . . no one else has any questions?"

Spyder uncurled himself from his seat. He stretched as he rose, and sighed. "Nope. 'M goin' back t' bed, sir. Wit'*out* seein' anythin' in th' streams," the lieutenant added pointedly. He scratched his belly with one hand and his short-cropped, pattern-dyed hair with the other. "I'd like t' get a *good* night's sleep, 'f's'all th' same."

She spread her hands and shrugged. "Dismissed."

The others started rising and moving toward the doors as well. There was a little bit of conversation, a few murmurs here and there, a number of sober expressions, but for the most part, they seemed to just accept her word on the whole matter. Ia sank down onto her chair, unsure what to make of that broad of an acceptance. Crossing behind her, Lieutenant Rico paused long enough to clasp her shoulder with one large hand.

"We do trust you, sir. Just stay worthy of that trust, and that's all we'll ask." Squeezing briefly in comfort, he headed out the door.

Stumped, Ia sat there and tried to comprehend her crew's acceptance. It was possible; it had clearly happened, but . . . she had come here expecting protests, a struggle, a fight to get at least some of them to understand . . .

"Everything alright?" Harper asked her, leaning close.

"I . . . think so?" she said, looking up at him. "Actually,

everything just went . . . really well. Too well. I think I may need to worry about this for a while."

He chuckled and shook his head. "Just accept it, Ia. If you said it's necessary, this crew would follow you into Hell itself, no questions asked."

"Excuse me, but *I'd* ask questions," Helstead argued from his other side. "Like how many demons are we taking out, which ones we're supposed to leave in place, and whether or not we're taking over permanently or just visiting, and if so, for how long?"

That woke her up from her daze. "This crew is *not* going into Hell," Ia asserted, pushing to her feet. "Not if I have anything to say about it. But if the lot of you don't need me today, I have a mountain of work waiting for me, to make sure you *do* stay out of Hell—Sergeant Grizzle, don't forget we're boarding a shipment of hydrobombs from the *Amazing Grace* at 1700."

The aging clerk nodded, though he didn't lift his attention from the datapad in his hands. "Got most a' th' paperwork squared away. Just needs yer signature, sir. Sittin' on yer desk in the In bin."

"I'm on it," she promised.

JUNE 16, 2499 T.S.
CHO VA ORBIT
CHO CHSHIEN SYSTEM

Despite having departed last, the *Damnation* was the first to arrive. Ia brought the long, narrow ship out of the hyperrift tunnel and braked quickly with pulses from the insystem field. The ship halted just beyond the outer orbit range of the Choyan homeworld. It was a predominantly water-based world, with tens of thousands of islands and several smallish continents, wreathed in wisps and streaks of grayish white clouds to the right and the darkness of city-sprinkled night to the left. Of course, they had also arrived upside down compared to what the natives thought of as north versus south. She didn't bother rotating the ship, however.

"Huey?" Ia ordered. "Aquinar? Belini?"

"Already calling," the pixie-shaped Meddler murmured. She had dressed herself in a strapless top and high-waisted tights marked with large triangles and diamonds of pale yellow on black, and stood out a bit against the shades of gray everyone and everything else wore, on the bridge.

"On backup, sir," the third watch pilot murmured. She wasn't taking over Ia's job of manning the helm, per se, but she was watching to make sure nothing surprised them and would make minor course corrections if needed because Ia was not going to be watching their heading directly for the next little while.

"We are . . . launched, sir," the gunnery tech stated, as a *whump* echoed faintly through the deck. "Navcomp says . . . on time and on target, achieving a stable orbit in three minutes."

Mysuri spoke from the comm station. "Sir, I have pingback from the Cho Home System Fleet, and a broadband light-speed recast ready. The Choya are demanding we surrender or they'll destroy us. Status on all hyperrelay bandwidths is wide open and green for go."

"Acknowledged, Private. Light 'er up," Ia ordered.

"Activating general broadcast on your primary in three . . ."

She lifted her finger on a silent *two . . . one*, and slashed it off to the side on *zero*. A yellow-skinned, gill-pack-strapped Choya female appeared on the screen, but Ia didn't give the admiral a chance to speak first.

"I am Ia, General of the Alliance Armies, Prophet of a Thousand Years. By joint agreement of all the heads of state of the Alliance nations, I am hereby declaring Martial Law throughout known space, and enacting a full-stop Quarantine Extreme on *all* known systems. You will cease all attempts at invasion, trade, commerce, travel, and exchanges of any sort whatsoever. You will close your borders, and you will cease all battle actions. You will refuse any packages, couriers, shuttles, escape pods, merchant vessels, battle ships, *anything* that has touched Salik airspace, even *rocks* lobbed your way by the Salik nation, or face destruction on grounds of Alliance Center for Disease Control Quarantine Extreme Protocol 99alpha. Everyone outside of the Choya nation has one Alliance Standard day to pull in everyone who cannot survive for six weeks on their own."

"You will ssssurrender or be dess—" the Choyan commander of the home fleet began to counter. Ia continued speaking firmly, cutting her off.

"These orders will be applied to the Choya nation as well, but *you* do not have one day. You will immediately pull in every worker taking a spacewalk, every shuttle, every courier ship across *all* known Choyan occupied worlds, moons, stations, and ships, and seal yourselves for the next six weeks Alliance Standard. You will destroy any ship, package, or item that attempts to touch your surfaces, whether that's an atmosphere or a ship hull, and you will do so using extreme force and extreme heat in excess of 2700 degrees Alliance Standard."

On Ia's left secondary screen, the one that showed real space instead of a tactical schematic, silver spheres started popping and streaking into existence around her ship. Some used translocation tesseracts; some swooped in at faster-than-light speeds. Ia held her gaze on the screen pickups.

"This will require the detonation of hydrobombs. If you do not have any, or refuse to use any, the Alliance and the Feyori are here to ensure that the infected zones are thoroughly destroyed for you," she explained.

"Feyori . . ." the alien admiral repeated, slit pupils widening in shock as she turned her gaze to the side, staring at a secondary screen of her own.

"You have exactly 137 *zvikmah* Choyan Standard from . . . three . . . two . . . one . . . *mark*, to pull in your people and prepare to sit tight for six weeks Alliance Standard. This is Quarantine Extreme, meioas. No one in; no one out; no exchange of contaminated surfaces or atmospheres; *no* exceptions. Failure to comply will result in the infected ship, station, moon, or *world* being destroyed.

"This is not a threat, meioas," she clarified bluntly, as ships started blipping into view on the tactical grid being displayed on her right secondary screen. "We don't care that you have been allied with the Salik until now. We are here today to do whatever it takes to ensure your species survives. I suggest you cooperate."

The admiral started to speak—and the screen flickered,

shifting to an image of a brownish-hued Choyan male, his fine-scaled skin tinted slightly green in the lighting around him. He sat in a silver-gilt throne, his shoulders collared in gem-studded links crafted from platinum.

"I am Fshau, Son of Cho, Ruler of the Thirteen Chshien," the new alien stated in the same flat, firm tone Ia had used. His Trade Tongue was flawless, lacking the usual sibilant hisses and drawled soft consonants of his race. "You have no authority here. Human. You will be destroyed."

"I greet you in neutrality, Son of Cho," Ia replied, dredging up what she remembered from her xenoprotocol lessons. "Your allies have released and spread a plague that will destroy all sentient life. I warned them not to go to war. I told them that if they did, their entire species would perish. They went to war anyway . . . and that plague has been released. One hundred thirty-six and a half *zvikmah* from now, the first infected ship will reach Choyan airspace. We will destroy it rather than allow it to destroy your people."

"You will not be alive. Attack them!" the leader of the Choyan nation ordered, glancing off-screen.

"Feyori. Counter it," Ia ordered.

A telepathic pulse from Belini flashed through her mind— and the first wave of silver soap bubbles scattered. Hundreds more were still arriving, but those first arrivals swerved outward by the scores, intercepting the ships that had started moving into firing positions as soon as the *Damnation* had first appeared. They turned dark and blocked and swallowed projectile missiles, laser fire, even enveloped single-pilot fighters.

Laser fire brightened the spheres, returning them to bright silvery shades. The fighters they spat back out, pointed back the way they had come, their engines dead and drained. The projectiles . . . remained within the depths of each Meddler. Some brightened, as if absorbing the energy stripped from the missiles. Some of the Feyori remained dark, as if merely holding on to their captured payloads, or perhaps slowly digesting them somehow.

The Choyan bared his teeth, displeased. "Cease the attack," he ordered whoever was off-screen, and returned his gaze to Ia's. "We do not surrender. But we acknowledge the impasssse.

We acknowledge you have a reputation for truth-speaking. Speak now the truth, General."

Ia dipped her head, knowing the Son of Cho had to be furious to let his diction slip like that, even if only briefly.

(*Just as you warned me, we do have our first conscientious objector,*) Belini told Ia. (*Here, grab him. A fellow named Dunkun.*) She handed over her tie to the Feyori in question. It was a tenuous thread of purposed kinetic inergy, psi-stuff, but that was all Ia needed to track down and identify exactly which Meddler was not willing to play along. Eighteen different individuals could have spoken up first, which was why Ia had turned over the task of looking for them to her cofaction.

"Son of Cho, two and a half Terran years ago, I told the leaders of the forty Choyan ships sent to attack the Terran homeworld that they should not attack. That they should stand down. They refused. I destroyed thirty-three of those ships. I did so while they were traveling faster-than-light, and while my ship was at a standstill.

"I say to you, as I said to them: 'Turn back, Son of Cho. Turn back, and let go the burdens of your anger,'" she invoked, repeating the same cultural quote she had given those ships years ago. "'Or your people will never reach the far shore.' *Turn back*, Son of Cho. Surrender, cooperate, and your people will live. This I swear to you as the Prophet of a Thousand Years."

"And if I refuse?" Fshau asked. His voice remained flat, neutral, and firm.

Ia subtly tucked her right hand into the little alcove holding the energy outlet for her station. "My ship is at a standstill. Your exact location is *not* traveling faster-than-light. If I need to, Fshau, I will target you, destroy you, and apologize to the survivors of the resulting blast and firestorm that will engulf your capital city. *After* I have saved the rest of your race from this plague. I would rather not have to do that, but I am no longer playing by the soft-touch rules I used before. Your life is nothing. The lives of the billions around you are everything, and I am here to save as many as I can. I do not care about your nation's actions in the Second Salik War right now, save whether it means having to find someone to replace you as leader."

Holding his gaze, she raised her left arm, wrapped her hand around the KI-link Belini had handed her, and *pulled* the resisting Feyori through several star systems. The Son of Cho flinched at the silver bubble that flashed into existence at her side, visible on her end of the comm broadcast. Without looking at the energy-based alien, Ia laid down the law. Her law, regarding the Feyori.

(*You will* all *do as I say, when I say, and how I say, or I will remove you from the Game and appoint a new Meddler in your place. There is no neutral. There is no counterfaction. There is only obedience to the Prophet, or death.*) Seizing his energies, she pulled, twisted, and *dragged* the Feyori through the timeplains, abrading five years off his life. He screeched, sparks hissing off his sphere. Ignoring them, she looped a net of purpose around the Feyori's energy matrices, then dragged him on the timeplains to the squared speed of light. (*This is your punishment for disobeying my first command. Do not seek the next level of punishment with a second offense.*)

Linked with Belini, Ia stuffed him into a Choyan body, then braced him with her hand around his scaled, slightly damp wrist as he landed and stumbled, trapped next to her workstation in matter-form. Addressing the other alien in front of her, the one on her primary workscreen, she lifted her chin a little.

"As you can see, Son of Cho, I have many more allies than you. Terran. V'Dan. K'Kattan. Tlassian. Gatsugi. Chinsoiy. Solaricans. Dlmvla. *Feyori.* Let *go* the burden of your ambitions. Sever your ties with the dying Salik race. Surrender, and you will be saved.

"I send *this* Meddler to you to instruct you on exactly what to do to survive the coming storm." Ia pushed the Choyan-shaped alien forward, releasing his wrist. *She* didn't have this ability, and didn't have the time to study it, but Belini was ready. The Feyori seated at the backup comm station teleported her fellow Meddler down to the planet, landing him right next to the Choyan leader's throne.

The yellowish green Meddler stumbled a second time, then straightened, regaining his matter-based dignity. He wrinkled the muscles of his face in an odd way—clearly not used to Choyan physiology—and hissed in pain. A quick peek at the timestreams told Ia he had just tried to resist his new assignment. A second struggle, a second hiss . . . He broadcast telepathically, (*I do not like you, Prophet. You should never have been born.*)

Ia knew he had sent that to the Choyan leader as well as to her. Unfortunately, her own telepathy—and her xenopathy—were a bit too weak to bridge orbital distance, even with a direct line of sight to the Son of Cho. She spoke instead. "I do not care whether or not the Feyori likes me. Dunkun is bound to my will, and he will serve. *You*, Fshau, Son of Cho, have two choices before you. Which do you choose?"

He studied her a long moment. "What are the terms of surrender?"

"Unconditional. You will sever all ties immediately with the Salik; you will cease firing upon any and all Alliance ships, save only at my direct command, or by command relayed through my Meddler, there; and you will immediately recall every ship to defend your own worlds and colonies from future contamination, excepting only those that are within Salik atmospheres as we speak. You will encourage every Salik on your worlds to leave immediately. I know *exactly* where every last one of them is, and where they will be, should they try to move. If they are not evacuated, I will know, and will direct Alliance troops to invade, search, and destroy.

"As for every Choyan who is on a Salik world or a Salik vessel at this point in time . . . unfortunately, they will perish," Ia told him, softening her tone only a little in compassion. A velvet glove to her underlying ceristeel. "They cannot be allowed to leave and rejoin your people. That would spread the plague. Everyone else can be salvaged if you implement the new Quarantine Extreme 99alpha protocol immediately. When the Quarantine period has ended six weeks from now, your people's various actions in the Second Salik War will be reviewed by a combined Alliance military tribunal. However, your full cooperation right now will go a long way toward reducing any punishments or repayments the tribunals will impose upon the Choyan nation. This is why representatives from the militaries of all Alliance nations are here, to witness for themselves how well you choose to cooperate."

"Hyperrift, General," Private Ng called out from her seat at the navigation station. "347 by 27."

A courier ship spat out of the not-quite-funnel-shaped hole down and to the right from Ia's relative dead-ahead. It swerved abruptly, catching sight of the long needle that was the *Damnation*, the thousands of silvery Feyori-spheres, and the twoscore Alliance ships in a standoff against the Choyan Home Fleet. That instinctive course correction shifted the Salik ship on a near-collision course with the hydrobomb launched as soon as they had reached outer orbit.

"Aquinar," Ia ordered her gunnery crewman. "Detonate when in range."

"Aye, sir. Three . . . two . . . *boom*," the private murmured. Light flashed in a bright double pulse from all the screens.

Ia squinted, prepared for it, then quickly checked the timestreams for lingering traces of the plague prion. "Well done, Private; no traces of the plague remain."

The Son of Cho eyed her, baring his teeth once more. The incisors were sharp, meant for tearing meat into chunks so that the molars in back could grind it to paste. "That was a hydrobomb, General. That was excessive force."

"Where this plague is concerned, there is no overkill," Ia told him. "There is only fire, detonate, and reload. The cold vacuum of space will not destroy this burden, Son of Cho; only vaporization will end the threat against your people. Do you surrender?"

He regarded her a long moment more, then lifted his chin and his wrists. "'. . . I release the burden of my rage, so my people will live.' *Cho Ya Va-Shien naho*. The Choyan Nation chooses to surrender. You know our legends well . . . and you know you xenopsychology, Prophet General, as I was warned."

"I know which path through the many possibilities of the future will preserve the greatest number of lives, Son of Cho," Ia corrected him. "That includes the many lives of the Choya nation. I am placing Royal Sector War Prince K'sennshin of the Solarican Empire in charge of directing the defense of your homeworld and outlying colonies. You will follow all of his instructions and directions as if they were my own, excepting only the corrections stated by your Feyori advisor," she continued. "The Solarican capital ship *Niien Rra* will remain in orbit to coordinate your defenses, as will one each of the other nations, to act as observers. Be advised that any attack against an Alliance vessel will be a breach of contract with your nation and will result in the Son of Cho being removed from office . . . one way or another. Begin the immediate extraction to a safe location of everyone who cannot survive for the next six weeks on their own. You have 130 *zvikmah* to comply."

The Son of Cho narrowed his eyes, squinting a little, but lifted his chin. "We will comply. We would need more time, though."

"Do what you can." Ia quickly skimmed the timestreams. Mostly, the Choyans would comply. The Son of Cho had heard her reputation for accuracy . . . and for telling the truth. Not always all of it, but the truth nonetheless. "Thank you, Son of Cho. You will be remembered for your wisdom . . . and most of your people will reach the far shore if you and your people heed and follow the steps outlined in Quarantine Extreme Protocol 99alpha. No contact with anything Salik or Salik-tainted, including your own people; no exceptions.

"These exact same restrictions are in effect for the entire Alliance. Follow them, and we will do everything we can to save your people, Son of Cho. You have my Prophetic Stamp on that. Thank you for your cooperation; General Ia out."

She tapped a control on her console, switching the view of the Son of Cho to a forward view of Cho Va near space, and started turning the *Damnation* away from the Choyan motherworld.

"Ng, plot a course for the Choyan colony on Sellvis IV. Look sharp, everyone; it's only five minutes away by hyperwarp, so we'll be there in under fifteen . . . and the next one after that is in one hour. Sorry, but we won't be stopping for rest anytime soon."

A chorus of, "Aye, sir," met her words.

(*Belini, bring the bubble-troops on board,*) she ordered. (*No need to make them exhaust themselves in following us.*

Tell them to pack themselves into Decks 2, 3, 4, 19, 20, and 21 . . . and to leave our belongings alone. They can sup on the ship's thermal and electrical energy on those decks, but that's it.)

(*Aye aye, Captain General, sir!*) Belini flicked her a mental flourish, the telepathic equivalent of an extra-fanciful salute.

Ia refrained from rolling her eyes. She had too much to do and too little time to get it all done.

JUNE 22, 2499 T.S.
CONFUCIUS STATION
XKC-DELTA SYSTEM

Too many battles. Too many prophecies to oversee. Too many hours with not enough sleep. Too many emotions and not enough time to express them. Ia felt like an archaic pressure cooker. She could only hope there wasn't a flaw or a crack within her. Once again, they faced the Shredou, the Greys, and once again, she was trying to get through their alien mind-set that their current course was suicidal.

Save for her ship's main laser, the psis on board, and a pair of crystalsong broadcasting spheres still carried on board for emergency backup, the Alliance members in this system were hopelessly outclassed compared to the Greys and their technology. It was very much an uphill struggle. At least the triple threat of the *Damnation*'s presence did make their invasion fleet stop while it was still several hundred thousand klicks from the great wheel-shaped station, the hub and the heart of the mining efforts in this ore-and-gas-rich system. Stop, and listen. Cooperate . . . that was another matter.

"No," Ia denied. Off-screen, her hand eased up the lid on the main gun control. Splaying her fingers on the palm reader, she let it accept her biometrics. "You will not take this system. This whole system is denied to you. The people in this system are denied to you. Humans are denied to you. Tlassians are denied to you. Solaricans are denied to you. K'Katta are denied to you. Chinsoiy are denied to you. Dlmvla are denied to you. Gatsugi are denied to you. Choyans are denied to you. You will go elsewhere. Leave now, before I lose my patience with you."

The Choyans were not actually in this system. Their miners had long since withdrawn from the region back before the start of the Salik war, but they would return. Ia had put them firmly on the denial list for that reason. By the time another sentient, sufficiently advanced species was found, the Greys would no longer be a threat.

"We will not leave. You will not give us orders. You will not stop us. You cannot stop us," the Grey equivalent of an admiral informed Ia. His—her?—dual-toned voice was flat, dissonant. "You will leave. If you do not leave, we will destroy you."

"If you fire your precious new weapon," Ia warned the Grey, checking the streams one last time, "you will puncture a hole in the universe. *When* you do that, you will cause the destruction of this universe. You go to war by your choice. You fire your weapons by your choice. You will carry the blame, and the shame. I will stop that. I will save you. You will owe me. You will do as I say, when I say, where I say."

"You boast. You say you see. You know nothing," the admiral retorted even as her thumb shifted. "We will destroy you."

Sterling engines *thrummed* and *whumped* down the length of the ship. Her left secondary showed the Grey ships shifting into attack formation, just as she'd predicted. "*You* do not listen. But don't worry. I will eventually find someone among your people who does. And then I will save the rest of you . . ."

Bright red lanced forward, a blip of a streak. Grey shielding was good, the materials tough, but very little in the universe could withstand the equivalent of a thermonuclear blast reduced to a column only twenty meters wide. Of course, the beam chewed up several hundred chunks of rock between her and them, but that only ensured the beam didn't keep going past a handful more of asteroids beyond the lead invading ship.

". . . From yourselves," Ia finished in a mutter. "Al-Aboudwa, ping me the next ship."

"I have the one to the upper left and the one to the lower right on the line, sir," the unflappable private stated. He lifted his chin at his screen. "Which one you want?"

"Upper right. He or she doesn't speak Terranglo, but they do have a translation program running." As soon as the new alien appeared on her screen, Ia sighed. "Let's try this again, gentlebeings. You will leave this system alone. You will not attack its people." The timestreams soured, so she slipped her gloved hand up and to the left, shifting the ship slightly, and tapped the firing button with her right. ". . . Wrong answer, Shredou," Ia stated, as energy crackled through the space where the *Damnation* had just been. "You will not attack this ship. You will not attack this system. I will continue to destroy you, ship by ship, until I get to the one who *will* listen."

Once again, deep crimson flared briefly from every screen. Al-Aboudwa cleared his throat. "And . . . lower right is firmly online, sir."

The third alien had a slightly different head shape, and the voice was a little deeper on its lower note, a little higher on the upper, more harmonious than the not-quite-tone-deaf voices of the other two. But still, there was no indication of gender, though she or he tipped their head, big black eyes regarding Ia steadily while the alien spoke. "I listen."

"Good. Inform your superiors that this war between us is to be paused. You will not attack, you will not press, you will not invade. This war will not continue until the worlds infested with the Salik plague are destroyed. If you attack, if you press, if you invade . . . I will infect *your* worlds with the Salik plague. You will die in just three weeks instead of five hundred years from now, when your biology and your technology will fail the last of you. If you do not wish to die in three weeks, you will do as I say. No fighting. No captures. Nothing. Do you understand?"

"Understanding is not needed. Compliance is needed," the Grey pointed out.

Impatient, Ia struggled to hide her irritation. Semantics was politics, and she hated dancing those steps. But she did know what would happen in the next twelve seconds, and carefully closed both lids on her console. "Do you comply?"

"We will comply. In this system," the alien clarified. "Others will decide elsewhere."

"Good. Carry this warning to them. *Dulshuwuuul sh-wie-ehh nn gnaa-k lluun znin ni-i-iven doon,*" she half sang, half stated, her voice pitched more or less low. Then repeated the phrase a little higher, her vocal cords shifting and modulating. "Run *that* through your translators and suck on it."

The alien officer studied her in silence. Ia didn't really grasp how the Greys thought, but she did know that "sucking" on something was an insult in Terranglo, whereas it was a cautionary bit of wisdom in their mind-set. Of course, the Greys knew more about Terran culture than the Terrans knew about theirs, but that was more because Terrans still used light-speed communications for many things. A sensitive scanner probe parked at the edge of a star system could gather quite a lot of information about the Second Human Empire.

Faintly, she heard her short message being repeated on the alien's end of the link, both versions layered together so that her words came across in proper Grey harmonics. The Grey quickly twisted to glance at whoever off-screen had replayed the message, then turned back to her.

Ia spoke before s/he could. "Leave. Take your damaged ships with you. These people do not need to get their hands on Grey technology at this time. Leave."

"We comply. In this system," the Grey stated, and ended the link.

For five precious seconds, Ia allowed herself a deep breath and a slump of her shoulders and spine against the padded back of the command seat. A second breath, and she ordered, "Next call, Private."

". . . We have ping on the MRV *Bjelik*, General," Al-Aboudwa told her. "Two-second delay."

The screen to the left of her primary showed the Grey ships popping out of existence, leaving as promised. The tactical screen to the right showed the navicomp markers for each ship also vanishing. Between them, the holding screen pattern, soothing shades of blue with the TUPSF logo in metallic black, shifted to an image of a bridge with control panels that looked as if they had been repaired more than once by whatever parts the crew could scavenge.

"This is Captain Bran Verse of the *Bjelik*," the dark-haired, dark-skinned man occupying the center of the screen stated. "We're in the middle of a salvage op. Who are you, and what do you want?"

"This is General Ia of the Alliance Armies. You have just begun salvaging a recently destroyed Salik courier, despite Alliance-wide orders to cease all such operations. You have two minutes to reprogram all salvage robots to reroute that salvage into a combat bundle and send it *away* from your ship by ten thousand kilometers, or *your* ship as well as that wreckage will be destroyed by the Redhawk Class carrier ship TUPSF *Dai-Lo*.

"The *Dai-Lo* will arrive insystem in twenty minutes. At that time, I will *know* if you have complied and will transmit orders that will either save you or destroy you. The choice as to how long you and your crew will live is entirely up to you, Captain Verse," Ia told him. "But I *will* enforce Quarantine Extreme, and that cargo is contaminated, which means you are about to be destroyed if you choose greed over safety.

"I suggest you rethink the thoughts running through your head. This is not a negotiation. General Ia out." She cut the connection and thumbed the ship's intercom. *"All hands, fifteen minutes to OTL. I repeat, fifteen minutes to other-than-light transit. We will be stringing four jumps in a row, so this is your reminder to have your space-sickness bags on hand."* Shutting it off, she checked her two secondary screens to make sure all of the Grey vessels had left, and nodded to herself. "Next on the list, Private."

"High Nestor Zul . . . Zubwuh . . . Zulbwuhvuh?" Al-Aboudwa tried. "She or he is pinging us. Six-second delay."

Ia nodded. "High Nestor Zlbwvvh, put her through."

The brownish-skinned alien had hints of purple along her half-scaled skin, but the iridescent gleam of her multifaceted eyes was bright, and the gesture she gave was a common, if abbreviated, Gatsugi-style greeting between allies. She also did not speak Terranglo herself, but relied upon a translation program that printed her words along the bottom of Ia's primary screen. *"Bright days and warm nights, General of Ia-ness. I give you cheese of admirations."*

"Please tell me the translator's not broke," Al-Aboudwa muttered from his station, monitoring the call on one of his lower tertiary screens. "It's working on the outgoing, I *know* it is, but the incoming . . ."

"Relax, Private," Ia murmured. Speaking up, she addressed

the larger alien. "Greetings, Zlbwvwh; I accept your cheeses and offer you half-used coloring sticks," Ia returned. "May your nestlings always draw you large and dark with wisdom."

She had to wait a few seconds while the translator worked on the Dlmvlan end of things, as well as for the timing delay, given the vast distance between the two ships. The High Nestor did respond, however. *"Please, for calling this one Zulby is easiest. We have reached the end of prognosticated locations. What our next target is, we seek advice from the soft-skinned, fart-breathing Prophet—may you ever elude the Room."*

"The Room for the Dead will always have an extra space awaiting me," Ia returned dryly, referencing their culture's greatest piece of poetry. "But I will not leap into it before it is time. Your particular region's next job is to take a two-week break, Alliance Standard. More instructions will arrive at the end of that time. On behalf of the whole Alliance, we thank you beyond words for taking care of the Salik hideouts in deep and interstitial space. I trust you have not lost too many ships?"

The alien shrugged, a gesture that was more Human than Gatsugi. *"Losing, lost, won, fought, folding like nesting sheets with wrinkled corners. It is far fewer with our thanks than attempting on our own to have produced. Your elucidations were accurate and awe-summed. Elucidation addendum— this two Alliance weeks for ourselves alone is, or fleetwide?"*

"Sorry, High Nestor," Ia apologized. "It's only for the fleet under your personal command, with the exception of a few ships still fulfilling last-minute instructions on their way back to base. You will need to load hydrobombs and other high-yield thermal explosives onto every ship during your vacation from mayhem, before beginning it again."

"This was stated in the elegance of your notes. Query of personal-ness," Zulby added, leaning forward a little. It was a slightly aggressive stance from a xenopsychological point of view, but Ia didn't take offense at the translated words scrolling along the bottom of the screen. *"In such exactitude and elucidity, does anything surprise the Prophet?"*

"Unfortunately, yes," Ia admitted, wrinkling her nose. "Even the lowest of probabilities is still a probability. But I bend and reshape like a cloud in the wind. Very little will stop me from scudding along."

The High Nestor relaxed. *"May your scuddings fruitful and purposed be, like a berry picked and packed for persons."*

Ia smiled briefly, keeping her lips closed so that her teeth wouldn't offend. "Next time we're out that way again, we'd be happy to trade far better than a child's toy for a canister of fart-fruits. Enjoy your two weeks, Zulby. Ia out."

"Next, sir?" the comm tech asked her.

She nodded. "We need to squeeze in three more on that list before making the run to OTL. Speaking of which, Yeoman Ishiomi, you want the helm?"

"No, sir, but I'll take it anyway," he quipped. "Give me a minute to warm up my station and strap my hand in."

"Take it when ready, Yeoman; we're not going anywhere just yet. I'm ready for the next call when you are, Al-Aboudwa."

"Aye, sir. You'll have a ten-second one-way delay for Grand High General Pwish-Pwish-Pok-Gnath. Can't be helped, at this distance."

Nodding, Ia eyed her center screen. One of the bridge doors slid open, admitting Lieutenant Rico. He took a seat at the spare operations station, lifting a hand in greeting to Ia, who returned it briefly. As soon as the Salik came onscreen, she smiled. Smiled, and waited, lips closed, expression blandly pleasant. And waited, quite patient, while his eyes on their stubby stalks rotated and studied her.

Finally, he spoke. "Hhew are cleverr for a Hhhewman, Gennneral Ee Ah. Redusssscing usss to Blockade worldsss. Accurate, too. Annnd topmost hhhunter. Innn charge," he added, curling two of his microtentacles into range of the screen, though the rest of his half-bone, half-boneless arm remained down below the screen's edge. His broad, froggish mouth curved slightly in a tooth-hidden version of a smile. "We wisssh to dissscusss the termmms of our ssurrender."

Never losing her smile for a moment, Ia simply replied, "I don't eat pity-meat." Not waiting for his reaction, because the round-trip was twenty seconds for the signal to get there and back, plus the seconds it would take for him to register her words, she continued smoothly. "I warned your predecessor, the previous Grand High General—in person, no less—that any attempt to go to war against the Alliance would end in the death of your entire species.

"Tadpoles, crones, teens, and adults, everyone will die. This death is spreading exponentially fast on your home-world, and has already infected nearly every colonyworld you have." He reared back, in reaction to her first word, then leaned forward again, slit pupils widening into a hunter's rage as she continued. "And by the time this conversation is over, even the last one will be plagued . . . and you will truly have only yourselves to blame. Had you stayed home, had you given up your plans of galactic conquest and *lunch*," Ia scorned, before resuming her polite smile, "then your race would have survived, and Sallha would have continued to be the ever-flowing Fountain of the galaxy.

"So, yes, I do accept your surrender . . . your uncondi-tional, total surrender . . . but I will not eat the pity-meat you offer. Of course, I do realize you are lying when you say you will surrender," she added lightly, watching his pupils con-tract to slits as he listened to her words from twenty seconds ago. "You will realize that the Quarantine Extreme is indeed necessary, and you will attempt to launch everything you have in order to infect every world, *any* world . . . but you do not face a mere hunter, Grand High General. You do not even face a hunter-mother. You face the Prophet of a Thousand Years, and *every* scrap of this plague will be destroyed.

"I directed the Dlmvla to the *exact* locations of every single one of your bases hidden deep in interstitial space, in the vast void between stars. No matter how many ships you launch, no matter how many rocks you throw, each and every single one will be tracked down and destroyed. At most, you will take with you roughly 112 million members of the Alli-ance . . . but I will do my best to deny you even that much. Still, compared to the trillions still out there . . . I'm willing to face what little remaining risk you pose to their lives. Even as it dies, a *gnarp-pwish-tar*—forgive my accent—can still thrash around and knock one or two hunters out of the water . . . but it cannot kill the whole hunting pack. Accept your fate with the grace to acknowledge you have done this entirely to yourselves.

"Now, do you have any final message to give before you do

the galaxy one last favor and die?" she offered, still polite, still calm.

Seconds ticked by, as he listened and reacted with growing rage to her words, spread across far too many light-years for even a pinprick-sized hyperrift to conquer quickly. Finally, he replied. ". . . Drink *sssshakk*."

The link terminated on his end. Rubbing at her forehead, Ia lifted her chin at Al-Aboudwa. "Next call, Private."

"Are you sure it's wise to goad him, Ia?" Lieutenant Rico asked her. "He'll have his people look for the plague, infect everything they can, and launch everything they've got."

"TUPSF *Arkhipov VII* online, sir," Al-Aboudwa warned her. "Six and a half seconds."

Ia held off answering Rico. "Commodore Mikhale Baltrush, you are instructed to begin the harvesting of as much purified water as you can across the 1st Cordon, 5th Brigade, 7th Battalion hydrotanker fleet. Pull in every ship with detachable tanks that you have and start parking the filled tanks at the locations my comm tech is sending to you on subchannel alpha, along with the necessary paperwork. These orders take priority over everything. You may hold up to one-third of your nondetachable tankers in reserve for topping off the ships in your jurisdiction, but otherwise you are to instruct the majority of them to fill their own tanks."

Baltrush nodded, listening to her as the hyperrelay lag caught up to him. "General, yes, sir. I'll get my meioas on it right away. Though given we're all supposed to be parked in orbits, watching for stray Salik ships trying to breach the Quarantine, nobody's supposed to be expending a lot of fuel right now."

"There will be some fighting in a week or two, but there are a couple of carriers already en route to help you guard those tanks from sabotage," she told him. "Thank you for your cooperation, Commodore. I know it'll be a tight schedule to get it all done in time."

"My pleasure, General. I was told the Quarantine would get rid of the frogtopi," Baltrush added, tipping his head. "If this helps, I'm all for it."

"Personally, I'm sorry they have to go away. They created a lot of wonderful things," Ia told him. "But their whole mind-set as a species won't change. They won't stop trying to fight and eat the rest of us . . . and I am not going to put up with another *shakk-torr* Blockade. Anyway, good luck. Ia out." She glanced over at Rico while Al-Aboudwa worked on calling up the next contact on the list. "To answer your question, Rico, by goading him, he'll do what I want, when I want.

"Even when he double-checks his actions versus his knowledge that I know what he'll be doing . . . the Salik will still be doing what I want them to do, which is what I have planned for them to do. So long as everyone else involved follows the checklist logic-trees I made, every single scrap of the plague will be accounted for," she finished.

"We're cleared for departure, General," Yeoman First Class Ishiomi warned her. "Departing *Confucius* Station far orbit . . . now, sir. Transiting to clearspace above the system plane."

The stars on the viewscreens started shifting as the *Damnation* turned away from the last major mining hub on the back side of Terran space. Al-Aboudwa spoke up. "Still trying to raise the MRV *Mary Jane in the Rain*, sir," he said. "*Confucius* is pinging us; they want to know if the Greys are coming back once you leave."

"Tell them yes, but not for several more weeks. They'll have better protection at that time. You have two more minutes to raise the *Mary Jane*," she told the comm tech. "If you can't, then fire off the automated message, and we'll try again after we've strung our four OTL jumps."

"My sickbag's on standby, sir," Al-Aboudwa promised her. "It's a good thing there's a shift change coming up soon."

JUNE 28, 2499 T.S.
V'DARSHET, V'DAN SYSTEM

"But you haven't slept in four days, and only then for five hours when you last did, Ia," Jesselle argued with her commanding officer. "And not for the three days before that. I don't care if you're half-Meddler; that's not healthy for a Human."

Ia didn't break stride. "So long as Harper keeps shooting

me with the psi-guns we made, I can keep going for another
eight days if need be, Commander."

"Will you *need* to?" the blonde challenged her. Taller, if
more slender, she moved to block Ia's path, arms folding
across her chest.

"For the next seven of them, yes. I promise to get two hours
of sleep later today."

"In one of my infirmary beds," the doctor asserted. "So I
can monitor you."

"No." Ia pointed at her. "*You* only want me in your infirmary so you can hit me with a hypospray of some sort of
sleeping serum. I don't have time for that, and *you* would be
hauled up on charges of Grand High Treason for allowing
that many people to be infected and die."

A voice on the hall comm interrupted them, as the ship's
interior sensors located their target. *"Yeoman O'Keefe to the
General. We are fully fueled and cleared for departure."*

Ia tapped her arm unit. *"Acknowledged, Yeoman. Depart
when ready."* She released the button and stepped around the
doctor. "As soon as I'm done giving my next message, I'll go
down to Engineering, get shot again, and be fine."

Opening the door to her office, she nodded to the quartet
of clerks on duty. There was now so much paperwork coming
through the front office that it required all the workstations to
be manned. Retreating to her office—Doctor Mishka still following her—she didn't bother retreating all the way to her
cabin, where the currently Human-shaped Feyori, Belini, was
still lounging in Ia's bed, indulging in the "quaint downtime
of sleep." It wasn't as if there was anywhere else on board the
ship to stick the Meddler.

Instead, she stripped out of her sweat-stained T-shirt, used
it to wipe her face dry, and opened the drawer where she had
stuffed a change of outer clothes, namely a set of Dress Blacks.
Moving swiftly, she changed into the shirt and coat, leaving
the pants in the drawer for the moment. "How do I look?" she
asked as she buttoned up the gray shirt to the collar, then
adjusted the lapels on the jacket. "Presentable?"

Jesselle tugged a couple of the medals into better alignment, then grimaced and raked her fingers through Ia's hair.

"You'll do. You're picking up shadows under your eyes again . . . and you don't look twenty-seven. You look closer to forty-two."

"Private Teevie to the General, twenty seconds to airtime."

"I'll live." Ia sat at her desk, adjusting her knee-length coat one more time. She activated the main workscreen, and thumbed the comm. *"Acknowledge, Teevie, thank you."*

"You're going to kill yourself at this rate," Mishka warned her.

Ia flicked her an annoyed, determined look. "I will *not* die before my work is done, Commander. I'll drop up to ten million lives if I have to, at this point. But I am trying not to. That's the whole point of this."

"Right." Jesselle started to say more, but the older woman clamped her mouth shut as the workscreen flashed, showing the TUPSF map-within-a-laurel-wreath logo.

"This is General Ia of the Alliance Armies, and Prophet of a Thousand Years. I apologize for interrupting all broadcast channels, but this warning is necessary. You are all about to receive a series of messages from the Salik Empire," Ia stated without much preamble. "They will tell you that they have identified the few patients who have suffered from the plague infecting their world, and that those patients have one and all recovered. They will try to convince you that this Quarantine Extreme which I have imposed across the entire Alliance is not necessary. They will try to claim I am exaggerating the threat of the plague in order to damage the health of each nation's economy, due to the closure of all travel, trade, and atmospheric interactions.

"Please do not be fooled by these claims. The handful of survivors they have identified are just that. They are the only ones who *can* survive this plague . . . but as they are now permanent carriers of it, they must not be permitted to leave their colonyworlds alive. The last of the Salik will be dead within one month. Make no mistake, citizens of the Alliance: The Salik *created* this plague two hundred years ago. Only by the grace of pure luck did they not wipe out all sentient life back during the First Salik War.

"I have been unable to see the Salik *ever* ending their hunger for our flesh, no matter which way I try to include them alive in our future," Ia continued, wrinkling her nose briefly. "So I have chosen to allow them to rediscover this lost plague of theirs and spread it among themselves. What they would have unleashed upon all others has merely been returned to them unchecked. By the end of July, the Salik will devour nothing and no one. They will not wage another war. They will merely be a sad footnote in our histories.

"But they are not dead yet, and they are still quite cunning. Do not believe them, and do not be fooled. I would like to get out of this without having to destroy any of our own colonies, just to contain the plague and prevent its further spread." She hardened her tone, staring into the pickups that would broadcast and rebroadcast her message everywhere in the known galaxy. "If it does, the infected ship, station, dome, or colony *will* be destroyed, even if I have to do it myself. Please continue to cooperate with the Quarantine Extreme, so that it will not become necessary.

"I know several of you think this is a joke. I wish it were, but it is not," she continued soberly. "The reason for this Quarantine Extreme is so that it will be very obvious when the Salik start trying to contaminate our worlds in earnest . . . which they will start doing shortly.

"Just be patient, meioas, trust in me to make sure the plague is stopped, continue to follow my commands, ignore the lies of the Salik, and avoid anything they try to send your way. For those of you who will need to send out or receive needed supplies, individual orders will be sent shortly before that point authorizing exactly how to go about it without risk of contamination. Other than that . . . try to have a good day and ignore the Salik. I'll let everyone in the Alliance know when the danger has finally passed. General Ia out."

Tapping the comm control on her workstation, she held her square-shouldered, confident pose for a moment more while the link shut down. Once it was closed, she untied her boots and pulled the slacks out of the drawer, exchanging her mottled gray workout pants for higher-quality black ones with four narrow stripes down each side.

"Right, I have twenty-three minutes to thumbprint sign all the paperwork in Grizzle's 'Requires Formal Authorization' pile," she muttered. "Then it's down to Engineering to get an energy shot, then back up to the aft-galley lunch . . . breakfast?

Food," Ia dismissed, relacing her boots. "Food with the 2nd Platoon while I discuss repair priorities coming up with Harper and listen to *him* telling me I'm not getting enough sleep. Then we join the Dlmvla 3.723 light-months from the V'Dan colony of Pa-Ren to destroy an attempted Salik stockpiling point, and I spend half of that battle chatting with would-be Quarantine breakers, trying to convince them not to kill off their own side out of greed or whatever.

"The same as I spent most of my workout just now, speaking on the comm with sentients across the known galaxy—if you really want to do something to help, Jesselle?" Ia added, standing so she could tuck in her shirt and fasten her trousers. "Get me something to drink to keep me from going hoarse with all this talking I've been doing. I can feel my throat getting a little sore, in spite of my biokinetics."

Jesselle sighed. "You are going to kill yourself at this pace, you know . . ."

"Not today, and not anytime soon," Ia said, heading for the door. "I have far too much work to do."

CHAPTER 7

That is the question, isn't it? Am I a mass murderer?

I know what my head says. Every time I use my pre-cognitive abilities, I am forced to remember that I am a soldier and an officer. That I am trying to do my damnedest to save the most lives and waste the least resources in doing so. If there were another way that could save as many lives, I'd take it in a heartbeat. But as a soldier and an officer, I have an objective—the saving of as many Alliance lives as possible, and the lives of civilizations we haven't met, and won't meet for hundreds of years—and I have to follow through on that, even if it means having to kill. The objective is too important for the good of all.

Am I a murderer? My head solidly says, "No," and it points to all the reference matter for the legality, morality, and ethics of everything I've been trying to accomplish. No, no, and no.

I am not a murderer; I am a soldier.

~Ia

JULY 14, 2499 T.S.
SELDUN IV
ISC 197 SYSTEM

There wasn't much left of the original domes, but the Salik
had dug in, establishing a base for a little while. Bombard-
ment had broken up most of that, leaving the rock surface
pockmarked with craters visible on high resolution. But Ia
wasn't here just to destroy the deeply buried colony of only
two thousand or so Salik. While that makeshift settlement
was not yet infected, buried deep as it was in the bedrock-dug
caverns that were required for emergency retreats beneath all
domes by Alliance-wide law, their leaders back on Sallha had
decided that "revenge seeding" was in order.

They had sent a ship with launch drones to drop canisters
on the surface, Tlassian-style pressure-sealed barrels marked
in Tlassian and Trade Tongue as relief supplies, rare ores—
anything the Salik thought would entice a salvage team in the
future into bringing the canister into an atmosphere and open
it up. The refugees would have to be burned out with the main
cannon, but Spyder had taken a team down to an abandoned
ore-mining base to use the few intact drones to find and col-
lect the canisters into a single location easily destroyed by
hydrobomb.

They had been here for seven hours now, and while Ia continued to make and field calls across the known galaxy, the
rest of her crew had been given a mini-Wake, taking three
hours in rotation for each duty shift—minus Spyder's group—
to party and relax.

"Eyah, Ia," Spyder's voice came over the comm. "We're jes'
'bout ready fer yer lil' light-'n-fire show. ETA four minnits."

"The bomb's already been launched," Ia relayed.

Helstead, lounging with her feet on the pilot's console,
since they were parked in a stable orbit, joined the conversation. "Navicomp says we'll see the light show from here, too.
That's a quadruple-load tank on that hydrobomb."

"Eh . . . I'm feelin' paranoid, down 'ere. Ready-check that
we got 'em all, eh?" he asked.

Nodding—he couldn't see her, since the mining base
didn't have functioning vid at the moment—she dipped her

mind into the timestreams . . . just in time to see a probability levee collapse along the channels she had painstakingly dug. On a world that should have remained safe. A reddish world, close to many others. A world with an atmosphere, even if everyone on it lived in domes.

"No . . . no no no *no*— MARS!" (*BELINI!*) Ia shouted, panic boosting her broadcast.

Helstead flinched, clapping her hands to her head. "Muckin' *shakk*, sir!"

The air *popped* next to Ia's command station. Clad in a skimpy, leaf-patterned dress that made her look even more like a faerie creature, a margarita glass in her hand, Belini scowled at Ia. "Excuse me, but I was in the middle of chatting up—"

(*Shut up!*) Ia snapped. Reaching up, she snagged the other woman's wrist, ignoring the flavored, alcohol-laced ice that splashed onto her sleeve in favor of pushing the exact problem and its coordinates on the Meddler. (*We're about to lose Mars! Grab that hydrobomb and* go!)

"*Shakk.*" Eyes wide, Belini slapped the console with her other hand to grab enough electrical energy and accepted the kinetic inergy Ia shoved into her. In two seconds flat, she glowed and popped into a silvery soap bubble, then vanished from the bridge.

Ia didn't care that the margarita glass dropped and cracked, its contents splattering on the deck; it could be cleaned up later. Mars had to be cleaned up *now*. She closed her eyes and reached out through the timeplains to the trio of Feyori in the Sol System nearest the red planet. That wouldn't be enough to protect the nearest dome from the force of a bomb that strong, so she shifted the streams into a tangled skein of Feyori-style anchor points, and *tugged* on fifteen more, all of whom had anchors near enough to help.

Not to pull them to Seldun IV but to *push* them to Mars. Only because they were already in their energy forms could she make this work. The moment they arrived, disoriented, Ia swept their minds into a single group and relayed their instructions, then let them go. One and all, the eighteen spheres raced down into the atmosphere.

"*Sir*, what's happening on Mars?" Helstead snapped.

"Everything within fifty klicks of Red Castle 53 is—" Ia started to explain.

"I'm on it!" Mysuri called out from the comm station. "Routing . . . routing . . . ping! *Red Castle Region, emergency override, Martial Law authorization India Alpha. Evacuate, Evacuate! Everyone within fifty kilometers of Dome 53, Evacuate, Evacuate! This is not a drill! I repeat, Martial Law authorization India Alpha, subauthorization Sierra Mike. Evacuate, Evacuate! This is not a drill!*"

Caught off guard, Ia checked the timestreams . . . and clasped her hands over her mouth, stifling a sob of relief. Sixteen of the nineteen Feyori were spreading themselves thin over the curve of Dome 53 that faced the epicenter; it was too late to grab the artificial prions themselves, because they had already made it to the atmosphere and were using the thin light of the system's sun to start breaking down and reassembling the local molecules. The winds weren't storm strong, but they were carrying those dangerous molecules along too fast and too chaotically for Ia to pinpoint exactly which bits of air to nab by the energy-based species.

They were dangerously near an atmospheric processor as it was, a processor that had far too many of the right materials for prion-replication. It would be a race to see if Belini or the prions got there first. It would also be a race to see if the other two Meddlers managed to get the two dozen technicians manning the processor to safety. At least seven of them *had* to survive, or Ia's plans would start collapsing as the floodwaters broke through the channels she had carefully laid farther downstream.

"Satellite, satellite . . . got it!" Private Mysuri added, popping several screens around the bridge into showing a three-second-delayed view of the Red Castle region.

It was just a geosynchronous, somewhat static view of a span of Mars' surface from close orbit, maybe only two, three hundred kilometers wide. Nothing happened . . . and nothing happened . . . and nothing . . . A sharp, double-pulsed light flashed halfway to the upper right corner of their view. Seconds later, a dark bright pimple grew on the surface of Mars.

"Did we get it, sir?" Mysuri asked.

Dipping into the timestreams, Ia checked. The domes were cracked from the force of the explosion . . . but they *were* holding, including the one closest to the blast, the one sheltered by the Meddlers she had sent. There were now eighteen *very* overfull Feyori, and twenty-one shook-up atmospheric miners who had found themselves abruptly teleported to an emergency bunker twenty kilometers away. The remaining three . . . didn't make it. There hadn't been time. But they weren't absolutely necessary to the timestreams, and the timestreams *could* be repaired from the damage this shake-up had caused. Pulling out, she nodded, lowering her fingers from her mouth.

"Private Mysuri? You are officially my hero," Ia told the other woman. "You did *exactly* what needed to be done. Only three casualties. The rest will finish evacuating before the cracks in the domes cause any real safety concerns."

"Don't let our pet Meddler hear you saying that, sir," Rammstein told Ia. He twisted to look at her since there wasn't much his operations station needed to monitor when the ship wasn't going anywhere or doing anything taxing. "She's the one who nabbed that hydrobomb and teleported it over three hundred light-years away."

"True," Ia admitted.

"Speaking of which, sir," Private Sung spoke up from the gunnery position. "That was *my* hydrobomb. What the hell am I going to destroy the plague on *this* world with? 'Cause the loss of that one is *not* coming out of my paycheck, and I am *not* going through another caning for something I didn't do."

Relief made Ia chuckle, though she tried to stifle it. Canings were very serious business—and she had been there right with him, stroke for stroke—but she was just too relieved not to feel a little giddy. "Relax, Goré. This one's on me. I'll use the main cannon. We'll just have to pick up a little extra fuel on our next stop."

"Sir, *how* did the plague get past your defenses?" Helstead asked pointedly, craning her neck to look at Ia. "You have the fleet in the Sol System scanning for everything bigger than a baseball, and the Feyori tracking everything else on top of that, and I *know* you gave them details on what to look for and where to find it."

Realizing she didn't know, Ia tipped her head and dipped her mind into the timestreams. Not into the immediate future, but into the immediate past. It wasn't easy tracking a molecule, but . . . *ah. Eighteen fat-and-fed Feyori. Not nineteen. That's what happened.* "We lost a Feyori."

"Huh?" Helstead asked. She pulled her boots off the edge of the console so she could turn and look at Ia fully. "How do you lose a Feyori?"

"Nunsen. He was old, over seven thousand years Terran Standard," Ia explained, mental fingers still trailing through the past. "They *do* eventually get so old, so worn in their energy matrices, that they get the equivalent of dementia. He missed a small pocket of the plague during the missile crisis from the ninth of July. Just a scrap on a chunk of missile plating large enough to survive the heat-shock of entering Mars' thin atmosphere once its orbit decayed.

"But he *thought* he had gotten it . . . and he was a past master of the timeplains. For a Feyori," she allowed dryly. "So . . . his belief clouded my view until it was too strong a probability for his belief to occlude. Then . . . he just took in too much energy when the bomb went off, and lost control of his matrices. The bubble popped one last time . . . and now there's nothing left of him. I have to find a replacement from outside the known galaxy, because everyone else is . . . yep, on schedule," Ia reported, catching up with the present and slightly into the future, over on Mars. "The others, fat and full, are popping back to their original positions, which means our personal Meddler will be back in less than a minute."

"Well, I'm not cleanin' up the mess she made, dropping her margarita like that," Delia told her, turning back to settle in her seat and prop her heels up on the pilot's workstation. She held up a hand, forestalling any argument from her CO. "I'm not saying I'd prefer Belini had been delayed, ruining the saving of everything and everyone; I'm just sayin' *I'm* not cleaning it up."

"Just for that, you *are* cleaning it up," Ia ordered.

Head thumping against the padded rest of her seat, Delia whined, "Awww, *muck* it!"

Sighing, the redheaded psi scowled at the ceiling of the bridge, then swirled her hand. Air *popped* on Ia's right.

Leaning over, Ia peered at the floor. Every last scrap of the drink, from stray salt crystals to the cracked rim of the plexi glass, had vanished. "Dare I ask what you did with all of that?"

"I gave the planet a margarita," Helstead said flippantly. "Something to kill the pain of being shot with the Godstrike laser cannon. Mark II, no less."

"You did *not*," Private Balle stated, watching her screens at the navigation post. "You gave the planet's *orbit* a margarita. Tracking trajectory now . . . and . . . yeah, we'd better be gone in about ninety minutes, or it's going to smack us in the aft, sirs."

"Oy! Bloody Mary! Did we get all th' canisters, 'r what?" Spyder asked, reminding everyone that his comm link was still active. *"Or d'y' got more confabbin' an' arm-flappin' t' do, up there? We got limited breath on our mechsuits, in case y'don't remember, yakkos."*

Ia quickly checked the local timestreams, and nodded. *"Lieutenant, you are free to leave the colonyworld,"* she confirmed. *"All hands, this is the General. We will be breaking our stationary orbit to get into position to destroy the plague on Seldun IV, then moving to destroy the final Salik base on this world. This means we will be behind schedule, so everyone is going to have to double-time it on repairs and refueling after the fight around the Salik colonyworld of Nuk-Pwish'Gwan in three hours. Ia out."*

"Sir . . . I'm sorry, but the Premiere is calling," Mysuri stated as soon as she finished.

"Bottom third tertiary," Ia directed, fitting her hand into the attitude glove and tightening the straps with two practiced tugs. The Premiere's face appeared on her lower-center screen. She spared him a glance, taking note of the lines that had started to crease his dark brow and the gray hairs salting the edges of his tight black curls, and spoke without preamble. "Premiere, yes, sir, I know why you are calling, sir."

At the same time, he said, "I want to know *exactly* what just . . . Go on," Mandella stated as her lag time caught up to him, 2.7 seconds according to the ping mark in the lower-right corner of the screen. "Explain to me what happened . . . and make it good, so that I can hopefully explain it to everyone else here at home."

"Premiere Mandella, I apologize for the damage to the Red Castle region domes on Mars, but it was absolutely necessary, sir. One of my subordinates dropped the ball on tracking a piece of the plague. As soon as I found out about it, the only materials available to stop it were a quad-sized hydrobomb and a handful of Feyori." Her right hand flicked the controls, opening an untouched data folder. "I am sending you . . . on subchannel beta . . . information and an authorization code for using an account registered in my brother's name. It has been earmarked with his permission specifically for paying for repairs and reparations for any damages made by mistake."

"Your brother? . . . Right, the famous Meioa Fyfer Quentin-Jones, the lottery winner," he recalled. "Who was lost behind enemy lines, and who will be declared dead in ten years. Nice to know he'll be returning the money early."

"No, he will not, sir. Most of his money has been earmarked for his lawfully designated heir, who will appear two hundred years from now . . . and as the Alliance Lottery is adjudicated and enforced by the V'Dan Empire, they are taking my word very seriously that there *will* be a lawfully designated heir in two centuries. For now, sir, you will have access to fourteen million credits. Twelve of those need to be earmarked specifically for repairing the domes and rebuilding the atmospheric processing tower."

Another tap of the controls nudged the *Damnation* into motion and shifted the view of that slowly diffusing cloud on Mars to a view of the curve of the rocky, purplish surface of Seldun IV. Ia kept her eyes on what she was doing with the ship, though she continued to speak to the head of the Terran government.

"Those people will need their jobs stable and steady four years from now. If you get going on the paperwork and the red tape right now, construction will be cleared and funded to begin one week after the Quarantine Extreme ends." She checked the navigation information which Balle, as efficient as Private Mysuri, fed to her on the location of the gathered canisters. "In the meantime, I wish to officially commend Private First Class Suriya Mysuri of E Beta, 3rd Platoon, A Company, 1st Legion through Division, 9th Cordon Special

Forces. Her quick thinking in ordering the evacuation before I could even think to do it has saved the lives of over fifty-three thousand Martian colonists from troubles and dangers related to the local domes cracking and failing."

"She did, did she?" Mandella asked.

Ia met his gaze and nodded. "She's not the only one who has shown initiative, innovation, and competency above and beyond even my expectations, either. I am increasingly proud of this crew, sir," she stated, knowing the bridge crew, sparse though it was, would spread her words to the others on board. "They have pulled together and shaped themselves into far better soldiers in these positions than in any other duty post they have ever held, or could ever have held. Every single soldier on this ship has been absolutely outstanding. As soon as the Quarantine is over, I'll be sending in a stack of recommendations taller than my 3rd Platoon lieutenant."

"Hey, I resemble that!"

Ia ignored Helstead's quip. The Premiere blinked, but nodded. "I'll ask the DoI for a summary of it all."

"You do that, sir. Now if you'll excuse me, I have to go shoot two holes in this planet so it'll be ready for recolonization once the current wars are through."

"I'll do my best to keep the regional governor on Mars from screaming at you," Mandella promised her. "Premiere out."

Ia nodded and flipped open the outer lid on the main gun control. Rammstein cleared his throat. "Energy spike in your cabin, General. We have our Feyori guest back on board."

"Acknowledged," Ia murmured, guiding the ship with tiny adjustments from her left hand, her mind seeking the right moment to fire so that the beam incinerated every last scrap of the plague. Private Smitt might not ever return to this world. He wouldn't even look at a viewscreen while they were here, not wanting to remember where his father and sister died, just so a Gatsugi halfway across the known galaxy could convince the methane-breathing Dlmvla to join the war. But one day, it would be inhabited again.

After she burned out that nest of technically plague-free but still-dangerous frogtopi lurking beneath the ruddy violet rocks of its surface. No survivors. No exceptions.

JULY 25, 2499 T.S.
BEAUTIFUL-BLUE, SUGAI SYSTEM

"Ia . . . I need to talk to you about something," Harper stated.

Ia finished shifting another pin up by a few millimeters and carefully stuck the next one in that row through the thankfully sturdy gabardine of her new, knee-length Dress Blacks coat. As usual, she didn't know what Meyun wanted to talk to her about. The timestreams were still cloaked in patchy fog around him, but she could tell that, whatever the outcome of this conversation, it wouldn't impact the future by too much.

"I'm listening," she told him. "I'm pinning too many damned medals in place—this thing practically counts as armor by now—but I am listening."

"Yes, you do have too many medals."

Like her, the commander was clad in Dress Blacks. They'd both acquire more commendations before the end of the wars—and the Second Salik War was almost over—but Ia had been issued a new jacket to try to space out her awards. The Terran Space Force firmly believed in the carrot-and-stick approach. Caning was literally the stick, along with incarceration, scutwork punishments and the like; pay raises, medals, and ranks earned were the carrots. Both were handed out firmly; if a soldier earned it, if someone wrote up a verifiable report about it, that soldier received it, praise and punishment alike.

Most soldiers in combat zones went home with a dozen medals. She had hundreds. Meyun himself had a hundred-plus, many of which she had requested he receive based on all the repairs he had made, often literally on the fly to her two main ships. "So what did you want to talk about in the fraction of time I have left before the Premiere and the Admiral-General board, and I have to have this coat on and myself at the airlock door?"

"Your lack of emotions."

Her head came up in surprise at his choice of topic—and the pin in her fingers slipped, stabbing her. Wincing, she pulled her hand free, eyeing the tiny drop of blood that welled up. Concentrating, Ia focused her biokinesis to seal the wound, then stuck her finger in her mouth as the quickest way to get the blood off, so it wouldn't stain any of the remaining ribbons she was transferring from one coat to the other.

". . . What do you mean, my lack of emotions?" she asked, returning her attention to fastening the pin's clasp.

"I was talking with Bennie, and—"

"Oh, with Bennie," Ia quipped, rolling her eyes. She shifted another Target Star, earned for accurate shooting, from the thigh-length coat to the duster-length one. "Of course. And what does our resident psychologist say?"

"Don't be a two-fisting bitch," Meyun ordered her. "That's what *I* say. And *she* says that once the plague started being spread, you just haven't . . . You've shown some emotions, but before you were showing grief, depression, anger, irritation— mood swings that, while a bit strong, were understandable. But now? It's all been shut down to the bare minimum. And she's right."

"That's because I've been too busy since then to indulge in mood swings, Harper. Nothing more," she added, fastening the next pin. Just forty or fifty more to go, and she would be done.

"Yes, but when was the last time we made love?" he challenged her. "Do you even remember?"

That made her blush. She quickly let go of the pin she was placing on the coat, too, not wanting to jab herself a second time. Straightening, Ia gave his question serious thought. Not because she didn't remember—she did—but because this wasn't a subject either of them discussed out loud very much. "Not since before . . . Sanctuary."

"Sanctuary, exactly," he agreed, moving around to stand beside her, next to her bed. Meyun spread his hands slightly. "Ia . . . you know I don't press, and I'm *not* pressing for that. I'm not even asking. But I am trying to point out the fact that you're . . . closing down. Shutting off parts of your life that you should still be enjoying. Yes, even the mood swings." He gave her a frank look, slightly helpless and worried. "What is going on inside your mind? Your heart?"

They might have settled their relationship more or less, both work-based and personal . . . but he was still dangerous to her. Dangerous because she felt compelled to answer him with the truth. Unhappy, knowing she needed to keep working on her coat, Ia stooped over it again. "I've shut most of it down because I don't have time for it."

"Don't have time for what?" he challenged her. "Laughter? Love? Enjoyment of life?"

"Grief. Rage," she stated. "Regret. That's the big one," Ia added. "We'll have nine hours in transit after we're done with the last of the Salik problem. Nine hours in which I have allotted myself four of them to howl in grief and five to sleep . . . and then we'll have to face the Greys. And face the Greys, and face the Greys. And I'll have to lock it all down again when we do because I'll need every scrap of wit and concentration I can muster to keep ahead, or even just abreast, of everything they will try to do to us."

"They've scanned the plague, by now. They've manipulated it virtually. They've *learned* from it . . . and they will have captured it via their translocational technology before we're done eradicating it. They have done so with the thought of using transloc to transport it onto *this* ship, to threaten and destroy *me*. And I don't have time to quiver over that, either."

"*Shakk*, Ia," Harper breathed, eyeing her warily. "How do we stop *that*?"

"I'll have the dubious joy of informing the Feyori they aren't free to go. Instead, they'll be conscripted into a vanguard for invading Shredou territory, tracking down every piece of the plague, its calculations, and destroying it all." She looked up at him, her mouth twisted in a mild, wry smile. "A task made that much easier by the fact that I can now punish them directly if they refuse. But while I can wield the stick well enough against the Meddlers, I still have yet to provide a decent carrot. I'll be distributing the appropriate prophecies to each Meddler where necessary . . . but still, I can't exactly pin a plethora of medals to a soap bubble's chest, and I can't give all of them prophetic advice without screwing things up even worse along the way."

"No, you can't," he agreed, still a bit stunned by her revelation. "Ia . . ."

"I will also have to deal with the aftermath of slaughtering the Salik into extinction. I already have a pair of legal teams worked up for that," she said, transferring another Target Star. "One team was put together in advance by Grizzle from his contacts in the Judge Advocate General's branch of the Special Forces. The other has been assembled by the Afaso, thanks to the ever-wonderful Grandmaster Ssarra, to handle all the civil cases that will be flung my way.

"So tell me, Commander. *When* will I have time, other than those four hours I've already scheduled—which I might just add to the five for extra sleeping time—to have a chance to express myself emotionally?" Ia asked. "I can't do it right now, or I'll stab my fingers into Swiss cheese, and stain all these ribbons with blood and tears, neither of which I am inclined to shed needlessly."

"Ia," he started to argue.

Her hand clenched on the pin—and again, she pricked herself. "Dammit!" she swore, jerking her hand free. "I don't have time for this—And *no*, I am not going to display any more anger for you," she added, forcing herself to calm down. Pausing just long enough to suck the faint trace of blood from her skin, she resumed working on the last of the transfers. "I will be *fine*, Meyun."

"Functional, maybe," he told her. "But fine, I very much doubt."

She didn't look up from her work. "Until the war with the Greys ends, and this damned war with the Salik, I will not have a single moment of peace. The coming days will be spent with the Admiral-General *and* the Premiere on board, along with two of her attachés, and five of his, and us tripping over Denora de Marco, who is dazzled with the thought of being able to record our next session live. Even if she'll have to be content with the in-ship security cameras since hers will be forbidden from this ship.

"I wouldn't even let the Admiral-General on board," she added in a mutter, "if the Premiere and the other heads of state hadn't all gotten together to insist on personally witnessing the destruction of Sallha. A fact which is going to raise some very awkward questions when the Admiral-General realizes she cannot *remember* how the Godstrike cannon was made. Yet another military court-martial I'm going to have to dodge just so I can keep fighting and keep the Greys out of Terran space."

He fell silent for a couple minutes. Finally, Harper spoke

again. "You keep saying there will be an end to the Second Grey War. Do I at least get to know *what* causes them to stop?"

"They'll make a mistake, we'll make a mistake, and the combined timing and collision of those two mistakes will rip a hole in space. All those fancy new nodes you've been designing and installing will stitch the fabric of reality back together again . . . but not until after the Shredou have scanned that rift and realized just how horrifically they *shakked* up the universe. It's also a very, very common technology on our end of the combination, which means they'll have to scrap their fancy new weapon or risk it happening again, and again, and again."

"And I will threaten them with flooding their home territory with that mistake if need be, so that *their* worlds are the first to go," Ia warned him.

"That sounds a bit vicious," Meyun remarked dryly.

"Territorial, fierce, uncivilized of me . . . another big stick. And while I can find carrots for the Feyori, it's very difficult to find carrots for the Greys. What they want . . . I cannot even give them because it's just not possible. They're in the wrong galaxy, the flow of energies are all wrong, and they're being slowly poisoned to death. And the worst part is . . . they should've left eighteen thousand years ago. Preferably twenty thousand or more," she added, sighing. Fifteen more pins remained to be transferred, and she worked doggedly on them. "Unfortunately, that would take far too many Feyori lives to throw them back far enough to warn the Shredou . . . and I wouldn't order it anyway."

"You wouldn't?" he asked her.

"It would destroy our ability to be in the right place at the right time with the right people to thwart their ancient enemy. They'll die as a race . . . but the last of them will die *after* seeing the Savior destroy the Zida"ya. I cannot save them, but I can offer them vengeance. *If* everything goes just right. I will not make a promise to them that I cannot personally keep." Ia took a few more moments to finish the last of the pinning, then straightened and sighed, rubbing at the small of her back. "Done. Toss the shorter one in the sonic cleaner, will you? I have to find the strength to don this thing."

"I *did* have engineering dial back the gravity plates over

the last three days, you know," he told her. Harper raised his voice as he retreated to her head and stuffed the jacket into the cleaner, doing as she asked so that she could shrug into the heavy coat. "No matter how many medals you have, that thing will not weigh anywhere what your weight suit wears— how many *do* you have by now, anyway?"

"I don't know . . . over five hundred? Most of them are Target Stars," she said, nodding at the distinctive golden stars with their arced red stripes forming concentric rings. They covered most of the lower panels of her coat. "I have personally shot down a lot of enemy stations and ships. Next-most are a heavy chunk of Skulls and Crossbones for confirmed kills of officers and noncoms—most of the recent ones were from the Dabin debacle."

"Dabin debacle. I like it." He wrinkled his nose as he came back into view, no doubt remembering the crew members killed under his command. "I do wish all those needless injuries and deaths could've been avoided—and I *know* you tried your best. It wasn't your fault, Ia."

"No, it wasn't," she agreed, buttoning the heavy, colorfully pinned coat, which now showed a bit more black than the previous, overcrowded version. "But I still feel far too many regrets. I just don't have time to express them. As it is, our guests are at the airlock and—"

"Lieutenant Rico to General Ia; we have guests at the portside Deck 16 airlock."

Ia adjusted the fit of the headset hooked over her ear and spoke into it. *"I know, Lieutenant; the Commander and I are on our way to the fore section. Ia out.* As I was saying, they're there and waiting impatiently for us."

Nodding, he palmed open her bedroom door. They passed from her sitting room to her office, to the Company clerk's office, where the still ever-efficient ex-Knifeman, Mara Sunrise, rose from her seat, pulling several datapads out from under the clips lining the edge of her workstation.

"I have all the paperwork ready, sirs," she stated, and moved to join them as the two officers continued through to the corridor outside. The other clerks on duty kept working; unlike them in their casual Grays, Sunrise had donned Dress Blacks, striped down the sides of jacket and trousers with a single gray ribbon; the only difference between her and Harper's uniform was that Ia had ordered the full range of medals to be displayed, which meant the majority of hers were Skulls and Crossbones, while his were Compass Roses.

"General," Rico's voice sounded in her ear. *"The Admiral-General is getting impatient that you are not there to greet her and the rest. She's also a bit testy that we're refusing to let them board."*

"I'm well aware of that, Lieutenant. Please kindly remind the Admiral-General of her standing orders regarding unauthorized personnel and the Damnation.*"* She caught sight of Meyun glancing at her out of the corner of her eye but kept walking. He was smart enough he didn't need to hear the other half of this conversation to guess what his fellow officer was saying. Same with Mara.

"Oh hell no," Rico countered. *"You* tell *her why even she can't come on board just yet."*

"Then just tell her to be patient. They'll be on board before we leave orbit."

"I'll try. Rico out."

"Tell the Admiral-General to be patient?" Sunrise echoed, hearing her side of the conversation.

"More like, 'Thank you for your patience,'" Ia replied. "Oslo Rico can be quite diplomatic."

Sunrise snorted. "You should've seen him on Dabin. Somehow, I don't think using an unarmored Salik as a club to beat off other frogtopi is found inside the Alliance Diplomatic Corps' 'how to' manual."

"Oh, come now," Harper countered. "I'm sure I remember him saying 'please' and 'thank you' during that fight."

Caught off guard by the first officer's dry wit, Sunrise snorted, hastily covered her mouth, then had to slow down and juggle her slipping pile of datapads so they wouldn't clatter to the ground. Ia reached the lift and pressed the button. She wanted to smile since it was funny in a morbid sort of way . . . but Meyun was right. She wasn't *feeling* much at the moment.

Sort of like those five stages of grief and loss. Though I'm not sure I've gone through a denial phase . . . unless . . . no, my blind acceptance of my belief that Mattox would obey, that was denial, particularly in the face of the doctor's assessment of the patient. She stepped into the lift with the other two, riding it down several decks. *Anger? Off and on throughout the years. Bargaining's easy: my entire existence is a massive round of bargains against time and the fickle nature of sentient beings caught in the waters of fate.*

I think I've already gone through acceptance, taking on the heavy burden of responsibility for everything I've done . . . which leaves depression. And while the classic model doesn't quite cover it since it's an aversion to activities . . . I am in a sense mired in an aversion to feeling *anything, not doing anything.*

"By the way, sir," Sunrise stated quietly as they stepped out of the lift onto Deck 19. "I wanted to thank you for not making Floathawg and me bunk with someone else."

"You have too many lethal surprises scattered around your cabin to make you shift quarters. It'd take too long to disassemble all your hiding holes," Ia said. "I'd rather not any of the civilians hurt themselves out of accident or ignorance."

Sunrise shrugged . . . then gave Ia a sly sidelong look. "I noticed you didn't object to them hurting themselves deliberately."

"That's because I have a chaplain psychologist to handle that. I'm only responsible for their physical well-being."

They passed through the section seal and approached the airlock that connected their ship to the capital ship that had carried the Premiere this far. Ia tucked her fingers into the control niche for the airlock and tapped the keys to unlock the inner door. The new airlocks on the *Damnation* were an improvement from those on the *Hellfire*, in the sense that there were two actual airlock chambers. Both were long and broad, both with heavily armored doors, with the outermost one tucked behind yet more layers of external ceristeel plating when not in use.

Lieutenant Spyder stood at Attention in the outermost airlock with a stunner rifle in his hands, even though it wasn't his duty shift. Once again, he was filling in for the role of Military Peacekeeper of his own volition, simply because the Damned didn't have anything of the sort. Normally, they never needed it. Ia made a mental note to recommend him for another Honor Cross, for attention to details, anticipating a need, the initiative to carry it out, and the willingness to attend to it personally.

Another detail that slipped through the cracks. Rico was talking about Spyder, not whoever is manning Operations right now . . . Dinyadah? Yeah, the duty swap relieving Nelson was twenty minutes ago.

Nodding to him, she moved to tuck her fingers into the last set of controls . . . and realized the timestreams were converging on a lower-than-expected probability. Hesitating, she glanced over her shoulder. Glen flashed her a grin, then raised a violet-dyed brow. His hair had been redyed in shades of blue and purple, but though the buzz-cut strands were starting to grow out enough to show off his sandy brown roots, things like dyed eyebrows took longer to replace.

She knew why he arched it. Coupled with the slight, questioning shrug of his shoulders, he was asking, *Well, should I?* She wasn't sure if she should. Taking a split second, she probed the timestreams . . . and found his reason for why.

He wanted to make her laugh. Ia almost winced. *Hell, the whole crew thinks I'm headed toward being a robot, not just Meyun. Little details, slipping through my grasp. I still need my crew.*

Though it might cause her a few problems, Ia acknowledged that crew morale was important. So was her long friendship with Glen Spyder. Instead of shaking her head, she dipped it in permission, and merely said, "Clear the line of fire, meioas."

The commander and the private exchanged hasty, startled looks, then quickly split to either side, putting their backs to the airlock walls. Her first officer eyed her even as he moved to at Attention opposite the equally stiff-bodied Sunrise. "I hope you know what you're doing, Ia . . ."

"She has only herself to blame for laying down the rules." Tucking her fingers into the controls, she manipulated them, then stepped back and to the side as the airlock door hissed slightly from the pressure differential and slid open.

Her 2nd Platoon lieutenant quickly lifted the stunner to his shoulder, barking out, "*Halt!* This is a restricted zone, sir, and you are not authorized to enter it."

Caught with one foot touching the rim of the capital ship's airlock threshold, Admiral-General Christine Myang froze and peered through the opening at him. Behind her, her two aides eyed the gray-clad Spyder and his white-and-black weapon. Beyond them, the Premiere's Agents, highly trained security specialists, sprang into action: two pushed him back against the sidewall of the airlock, while the other three drew laser pistols. At the back by the hoversled packed with their luggage, the Dabinian reporter froze in her tracks.

There was a little red light on the gun, bright enough to display that it was charged and ready to fire, a visual warning for anyone the wielder faced. It was almost obscured by the wide-open cone of the nozzle, but it was visible. The Admiral-General eyed it, then looked at Ia, who indeed found the tableau amusing.

"What the . . . ? General Ia, what the *shakk* is going on here?" Myang demanded, her startled look snapping into a scowl. "Why are you smiling?"

"Paperwork, sir." Oh, it hurt physically to keep herself from bursting into laughter. She held out her left arm, medals swinging and clanking faintly. Sunrise quickly tucked the first datapad in her stack into her hand. "As per *your* standing order, Admiral-General, *no one* is to be allowed on board the TUPSF *Damnation*, Harasser Class Mark II, without the proper authorization and clearance."

Myang opened her mouth to protest, then shut it. She sighed. "You think this was funny? *Threatening* the Premiere, as well as your superior?"

"Lieutenant Spyder is standing six meters back from the airlock entrance, Admiral-General; the standard issue 40-MA he is wielding has been set to the five-and-five, as per airlock guard detail regulations," Ia explained patiently. She looked past Myang, the aides, and the suited men guarding the Premiere. "That means, gentlebeings, that the effective stunning distance is at most five meters long, for a duration of only five minutes. *I* am within range of his weapons fire, but none of you are, unless and until you step across the threshold. As per regulations, sirs."

"Stand down. Everyone," Justinn Mandella ordered his aides. He straightened his jacket as the two stopped shielding him with their bodies, and the other three lowered their weapons. "An interesting ploy, General Ia."

"Ploy?" Myang asked him, twisting to look back at the chief Councilor.

Ia relaxed subtly, following his line of thought in the timestreams. She'd picked the right way to explain, and he had picked the right interpretation to cause the least amount of trouble.

"She knows there will be a tribunal called to question her choice to slay the entire Salik race. This is her way of demonstrating palpably she is still following all possible rules and regulations. Paperwork, as you said," Mandella added, nodding at her.

"Precisely, Premiere. Admiral-General Myang," Ia offered, holding out her hand again. Sunrise passed a second datapad, allowing Ia to turn both pads in her hands to face their military leader. "You have two choices of paperwork before you: We do have the time to fill out every single form required for authorizing the ten of you to come on board for this specific mission . . . or you can cancel the order entirely and sweep it under the rug of my *carte blanche* discretionary powers. I will comply with either, and in each circumstance, I will continue to defend the sanctity of this ship and its secrets. It's your choice, sir."

Myang eyed her, eyed the pads, looked back and forth twice more, and grabbed the one on Ia's left, the one that canceled the standing order and put everything under her *carte blanche*. "Pain in the asteroid . . ." she muttered, scrolling through the text and scanning her thumbprint in every box that called for it to initialize each part of the orders. "It's almost arbitrary, which orders you'll obey and which you'll bend or break."

"Actually, I try follow almost every single one of them," Ia countered lightly. "And for the most part, I succeed."

"Well, it *feels* arbitrary. There are your orders, General," Myang countered, scrawling her signature with her fingernail, not bothering to pull out the stylus for that part. "Now let us on board."

"Lieutenant Spyder," Ia called out as she accepted the

datapad back and held it out to Sunrise. "Stand down and let these ten meioas and their luggage pass."

"General, yes, sir!" Spyder confirmed, snapping his rifle vertical. "Welcome aboard, Admiral-General."

"I ought to court-martial the lot of you," Myang muttered as she crossed the threshold.

Sunrise stepped forward. "Welcome aboard, Admiral-General Myang. Colonel Lars Sofrens, Lieutenant Commander Dasha Talpur," she added with a polite nod to each of the officers. "If you'll come with me, I'll show you to your quarters once you have your luggage in hand."

"Wait, isn't that . . . ?" Mandella asked, frowning and pointing at Mara. "Aren't you supposed to be in a military prison? For that incident with Counci—"

"—She's been given a full pardon, so none of that matters," Ia countered, interrupting him before he could name any names.

At his frown, she flicked her gaze pointedly to the reporter, who was still hanging back by the luggage. Mandella followed her gaze and lifted his head slightly. "Right. It doesn't matter. Not that it should have mattered in the way it did originally, either. Now, can we please board?"

"Welcome aboard, Premiere Mandella. Bravo! Sierra!" she snapped, startling Denora de Marco and the five security agents who were accompanying the Premiere. "Fetch the luggage off the sled. That machine stays with the *Kuribayashi*, and does not touch this deck. This is still a restricted vessel and shall remain so."

"We don't take orders from *you*," Agent Bravo growled, clearly still upset that her lieutenant had threatened to shoot his charge.

Ia stared him down. This was the downside to letting Spyder have his fun. "The entire Alliance, and with it, the Terran United Planets, is still engaged in wartime under the rules of Martial Law. I am the General of the Alliance Armies and am in charge of that rule of Martial Law. I am also the captain-and-commander of this starship, *and* its chief pilot. You will do what I say, when I say it. Be glad that all I am asking is that you bring the damned luggage on board . . . because I have every legal power in the book to say who gets to board and who gets left *behind*."

"Bravo, Sierra, get the luggage. All of you get it," Mandella added to the other three. "And you *do* take orders from General Ia, so long as they do not conflict with my personal, immediate safety."

All five Agents scowled in similar ways, though they ran the gamut of ethnicities, from sandy blond and spotted with cinnamon freckles, to skin so dark, chocolate would look pale in comparison. But they did turn to the sled. Looking rather out of her depth, de Marco quickly grabbed her two allotted bags from the sled and hefted them over the threshold.

"You're going to have to make it up to them, you know," Mandella added dryly to Ia. "And to me. I was not expecting to be threatened."

"Technically, we only threatened the Admiral-General . . . but yes, I do apologize," Ia replied lightly. "My crew has been concerned with the level of tension I've been under. Lieutenant Spyder, having known me from my Basic days, thought his strictly-by-the-book actions might amuse me—legally, he had every right to act exactly as he did, following his orders to the letter."

The Premiere eyed her and arched a dark brow. "Presuming you foresaw his intent, is that why you let it happen? Because it amused you?"

Now she smiled, letting her humor show. "Yes. It actually did cheer me up a little . . . but then my sense of humor has always been a bit *noir*." Gesturing at her first officer, she introduced them. "Premiere, this is Commander Meyun Harper. Harper, this is Premiere Justinn Mandella."

"Welcome aboard, sir," Harper greeted him. "If you and your Agents will come with me, once you all have your luggage sorted, I will show you to your quarters, just as Private Sunrise will show the Admiral-General and her attachés to theirs."

"Meioa de Marco, you're with me," Ia told the reporter before de Marco could feel left out or forgotten. She gestured for the Dabinian woman to move over to her side in the long airlock, and watched as the Agents moved luggage over.

As soon as it was on their side, Myang, her two officers,

Denora, and the five security specialists sorted through and grabbed their own gear. Ia touched the airlock buttons, first on the *Kuribayashi* side, which had extended its gantry to the *Damnation*'s airlock, then on her own side. Agent Whiskey hefted the Premiere's luggage as well until the Premiere eyed him, held out his hands, and accepted the two cases from the grudging hands of his aide.

Satisfied everything was on board, Ia checked the lights that confirmed the airlock door had sealed tight, then lifted her chin at Spyder. As he moved to cycle the middle door, she touched her comm button on her arm unit. *"General Ia to Private Dinyadah, kindly inform the* Kuribayashi *that our passengers have fully boarded, the airlock seals are green on our side, and they are now free to disengage when ready. Then call Sugai Traffic Control to let them know our intent to decouple and depart. General Ia to Yeoman Fielle; permit the flagship to disengage and move first. When they are at least five klicks off, set course for Sallha at FTL speeds."*

"Aye, sir." "Sir, yes, sir!"

"FTL speeds?" Premiere Mandella asked, eyeing her over his shoulder. "Aren't we using that secret faster-than-FTL ability of yours to get there?"

She shook her head, gesturing for Denora to follow her as the last two out of the outer airlock. "Premiere, no, sir. We do have a dedicated vacuum hub on board for using the comms while traveling faster-than-light, and I know you'll need to be in touch with several people for the next six hours. We cannot enter any hyperrifts while doing so because it does involve using an other-than-light hyperrift itself. When you sign off to go to sleep, that's when we'll switch to hyperwarp and finish the trip.

"Going slow will also give Meioa de Marco a chance to see what the survey drones are recording on Sallha," she added, glancing at the other woman, who had finally recovered from her wide-eyed state.

"I wish we could have a dozen years sifting via remote robotics through the treasures of Sallha," de Marco admitted. She held up her hand quickly, "I know, you explained off the record that every second spent *not* destroying the planet is a second someone could slip through and grab a bit of the plague to threaten the other worlds with, but . . . we're going to lose a lot of their history, their culture . . ."

"I know," Ia agreed. "You have no idea how much I regret having to do all of this."

"The xenoanthropologists are going to have to content themselves with studying lightwave and hyperrelay transmissions," Mandella stated, stepping through the innermost airlock door. "Those robots the Alliance sent down this last week have been turning on every broadcasting system available and hooking them into the Salik databanks."

"I'd be happy to give them more time to study," Myang said, "but the battle reports state there have been several attempts of criminals trying to send drones into the atmospheres of the infected worlds to capture the plague, no doubt to try to hold whole planets hostage for ransom demands." She glanced back at Ia. "Though I would like to have captured more than a few of their parent ships, on top of knowing exactly where and when to destroy those drones. I should order you to tell me."

"Unfortunately, sir, my personal philosophy insists that if they do not absolutely have to die, for the betterment of all, I have to give them the chance to continue living," Ia said. "I know, or can find out within a single second, the identity and location of any murderer, serial killer, terrorist, rapist, or whatever out there.

"I could even coerce the Feyori into sending someone back in time to stop Vladinsky's followers from destroying Vladistad with that nuclear bomb, and I know I'd be saving well over a million lives if I did so. But I *know* that letting that event happen prevented the destruction of many *more* lives," she told Myang, knowing that Mandella, the two aides, the Agents, and especially de Marco were listening to her words. "Yes, letting a serial killer roam free is an immoral act on the surface. But they are butterfly wings; some will flap and create a devastating hurricane through a chain of events which only I can foresee. Many others will flap, and not stir anything but the faintest breeze."

"S'not our place as sojers t' decide who lives 'r dies," Spyder added, speaking up from the back of the group. "S'our place t' decide if'n enemy lives or dies, and enemies aren't everybody. We identify an enemy, we take that enemy down. Sometimes that means wi' a stunner; sometimes that means wi' a knife. Sometimes wi' an 'ydrobomb, and God damn us f'r killin' so much, but our job *ain'* rampant destruction in every lil' instance, meioas. It's gettin' th' job *done*, frugally, efficiently, an' hopefully gettin' ourselves back out again alive."

"It's getting the job done, and done right, so we can have peace," Ia agreed. One of the two men who had pulled his laser pistol, Agent Tango, frowned at her. "Gentlemeioas, I want to put half the Space Force out of business." Her words earned her a sharp look and a thoughtful frown from Myang. Ia continued. "I want to send those men and women home. Without the need for a massive Blockade effort, there isn't a need for a massive Blockade task force, and those meioas will finally get to go home. There will always be a need for the Space Force, period, but we won't need it to be nearly so big, nor so psychologically taxing as Blockade Patrol has been."

"Here is where we part company, sirs," Private Sunrise interjected politely, and held out a datapad. "Admiral-General, you've been assigned to share a cabin in Lieutenant Spyder's old quarters with the lieutenant commander, as she's your aide-de-camp; Colonel, you have quarters across from them in Sergeant Santori's cabin. Please apply your thumbprints to the scanner on the pad, so your quarters can be locked for your use."

"Former cabin?" Myang asked, glancing at the former Marine. "You're not quartered there . . . ? Oh, right. You married someone, didn't you?"

"Ship's doc, Jesselle Mishka," he confirmed. "Santori's moved in wi' Lieutenant Helstead, 3rd Platoon. Makes f'r easier sleepin' if they don' hafta share a bed at th' same time."

"Your suite, Premiere Mandella, is up on Deck 6," Harper stated. "You'll be taking over our chaplain's quarters, since that gives you an office to work from. The couch in the office and the one in the private sitting room are convertible into beds with all the standard Lock and Web features, so we're quartering two of your Agents in there as well, presuming that Agents Bravo and Sierra will not be sleeping in shifts. The other three,

Agents Whiskey, Tango, and Foxtrot, will be bunking next door in Private Warden's and Hardon's quarters."

"And where did those privates get shuffled off to?" Mandella asked.

"Quarters for Privates Dhargas and Doedig," Ia answered him. "They're in the 1st Platoon, so they don't share the same sleep schedule."

"If you're such a big precognitive, and have a *carte blanche* budget," Agent Sierra said, "I'm surprised you didn't build extra quarters into the ship for us. You knew we'd be here."

"That would be a waste of resources and space. You'll only be on board for a couple of weeks," Ia told him, gesturing to head toward the lift now that Myang and the other two were accessing their quarters. Sunrise passed Harper a datapad and held out one to Ia as well before stepping into the colorfully haired lieutenant's old quarters.

"But you knew this guy was marrying and moving," Sierra pointed out, flipping a hand at Spyder.

"Actually, I didn't consider it, as it was a very low probability that those two would fall in love and get along so well," Ia told him. "As it is, his quarters have only been empty for a little while—and by empty, I mean, being used as a storage area, up until yesterday when it was cleaned out and refurnished as living quarters. Most of the others who have paired up, it's simply been a matter of swapping bunks with their respective teammates."

"What about me?" de Marco asked her. "Where am I sleeping?"

"Deck 10 fore section, with Privates Aggie Wildheart and Morgan van de Kamp; they're 3rd Platoon. Wildheart is one of the four bridge techs for navigation and scanners for that shift, so she'll be able to answer several questions firsthand for you on my combat skills and leadership styles. They have a couch that's been converted into a bed as well."

"So I would stick to 3rd Platoon areas, such as the common rooms, rec facilities, and the galley they use, right?" Denora wanted to confirm. It was clear she had done some reading up on psychological needs for space and territory.

"Nope," Spyder told her as the lift arrived, and they boarded. "Crew's small 'nuff. Ia said, whole ship's one big happy fam'ly. Galley's wherever y' getcher food. Most sign up fer a specific meal 'n go t' that 'un ferra nosh, but addin' ten randomly won' strain th' cookin' crews."

"If a door opens for you—any of you," Ia added, swaying with the slightly sideways curve of the lift as it moved, "—then you can go in there and have a look around. The ship's internal security system has been programmed for your appropriate clearance levels. Once you've put your thumbprint in the system for your quarters, you're in the system for everything. I'm afraid you'll find a lot of places are restricted access, though some of them you can ask, and if it's safe enough with an escort, you can have a quick look under supervision."

Mandella eyed her. "So what areas am *I* restricted from?"

"Anything to do with the main cannon, sir. You are also absolutely forbidden to touch the command console in any way, which is the foremost rule for all personnel on board."

The doors to the lift slid open for Deck 9, and she stepped out. The reporter followed her. Mandella blocked the opening with his arm. "Why is it forbidden to touch the command console?"

"Because if anyone tampers with the control for the main gun, this entire ship will blow up in one minute, with no way to stop it," Ia told him bluntly. "I have too much work left to do to allow anyone to *shakk* it all away, so as much as I like and respect you, I would have to shoot you dead first before you got within half a meter of it—of course, since I know you and your Agents are smart," she added as they bristled around their charge, "I'm glad that won't likely happen. Enjoy your quarters, sir, gentlemeoas. Don't worry about ousting Chaplain Benjamin; she's been moved into my quarters for the time being, and she'll be using one of the smaller meeting rooms for her counseling sessions."

"All hands, this is Yeoman Fielle; we are now departing orbit from Beautiful-Blue and will be transiting to FTL in fifteen minutes. Lock and Web until we've made the transition just in case, meioas."

Mandella removed his hand from the lift opening, allowing

the panels to slide shut. As soon as they were out of sight, Ia sighed and let her shoulders slump. Denora eyed her. "Tired, General?"

"Exhausted. I run thirty-two-hour days, most of the time. Plus, we've cut the gravity back to 1.01Gs Standard, which is screwing with my physical reactions," she confessed.

The reporter nodded. "Oh, I know that feeling—you'd think it'd be easier and safer to move in a lighter gravity, but you're having to tense up and move slowly and carefully, over and over, so you don't overact and then over*react* in all this light gravity. On the trip out from Dabin, the other heavy-worlders and I had so many bruises in the first week, the infirmary on board almost ran out of contusion crème. Ahh . . . about my *recording* our interviews . . ."

"That's the other reason why you're bunking with Private van de Kamp," Ia told her, palming open the section-seal air-lock door. "She knows how to take professional-quality images—flatpic, holography, videography, you name it. She'll be your camera operator and your footage editor while you're on board since she knows exactly what is, and isn't, allowed to leave this ship in an archived format. You'll also get all the nonsensitive raw data when you leave, to do with as you please, but she has some nice editing equipment and will be able to put together some good-quality interviews for transmission between now and then."

"How far in advance did you know you'd need her for her holocamera and editing skills?" Denora asked her.

She didn't reply immediately, but opened the section-seal doors so they could pass through. Finally, she asked, "On the record, or off?"

"I don't have a camera to record anything yet, so off," the reporter reminded her.

"I knew back when I was fifteen. And yes, I knew you'd ask me for an interview on Dabin, and yes, I knew you'd be invited here by the Admiral-General. She likes how well you've interviewed herself and other military personnel, not just me," Ia added.

She stopped in front of the woman's temporary quarters and held out the datapad Sunrise had given her. Denora used her thumb to sign in and looked at Ia. "I know you've said over and over that everything started when you were young, but . . . I guess I just want to know *when*, exactly, you started seeing all the details. Or rather, each detail."

"I saw the outlines and the key points on the first morning, and spent the rest of the day arguing with my mothers that I *had* to do what I foresaw, and in dealing with what I saw. I took that week off from school to look at all of the details. I went back to school, convinced my teachers that I was bored and wanted to study for my general equivalency degree, and split my time studying for that and studying the timestreams. I declared emancipation at sixteen and continued studying the timestreams, adding in physical as well as psychic training."

"Yes, but—"

Ia held up her hand. "Please, meioa. I saw *all* of it. When I was fifteen. Everything you are about to see, I have already seen, and more. A lot more, because I have also seen many of the alternative outcomes. Now, here are your quarters. It's first watch right now, but neither meioa-e has gone to sleep yet. You're welcome to stay inside and get some sleep when they do; otherwise, there'll be a review of the plans for Sallha and the other colonies in the officers' meeting room at 1000, Deck 6, amidships, forward from the bridge. Wildheart will teach you how to navigate the ship."

"I learned how to navigate military ships on my way out here, meioa," Denora returned dryly. "I was on the *Aitzaz Hasan* before transferring to the *Kuribayashi*. I do know a thing or two about nameplate colors and corridor designations."

"Yes, but this ship isn't built like other vessels in the fleet," Ia cautioned her. "The central core, which runs from Deck 7 to Deck 17, bow to stern, disconnects the starboard and port sides, and the way to get from one side to the other efficiently depends on which sector you're in; you can always refuse, of course, but it's a courtesy Wildheart is willing to extend. Now, if you'll excuse me, I'm going to get out of this mountebank's coat and go get things ready for the meeting. Either I'll see you there, or I'll see you later on."

"What, you don't know which I'm going to pick?" Denora asked skeptically.

"It isn't overly critical for anything," Ia told her. She turned and started up the corridor. "Lives aren't hanging in the balance, so you are very free to choose . . . which is what I prefer, whenever possible. That's why I'm doing all this, so that everyone will have better choices than just 'die now,' or 'die a few minutes or hours or days from now.' Sleep well, if you choose that. If not, I'll see you soon."

"Sleep well, when you get there," Denora called out after her.

Waving, Ia headed for the lift to get back to work.

The Admiral-General was already waiting for her in her office. Myang had claimed Ia's chair, though she had not activated the console nor scrolled up the screens into working position. Letting the door slide shut, Ia stepped up between the two chairs and stood in modified Attention, hands clasped behind her back.

"Admiral-General, yes, sir," she stated briskly, shoulders and chin level, gaze affixed to the back wall behind Myang's head.

"Is that an acknowledgment of my presence, soldier?" Myang asked, eyeing her. "Or is that a confession of your guilt?"

"Ask your questions, sir. I will answer honestly," Ia stated. This was an unpleasant moment she had to face, but most every pathway out of here would continue on the correct course. Of course, there was always that three percent chance that she'd get shot in the shoulder anyway. Figuratively speaking.

Myang eyed her, and nodded. "Very well, General. The problem is, I cannot *remember* how the main cannon on this ship was built. Nothing about its specs, nothing about its capacity. I *know* what it can do, for I've seen all the footage of your battles . . . and I know it was built on Oberon. But no one *else* on Oberon remembers how it was made . . . and all the data files, all of their research notes, have mysteriously vanished. What did you do?"

"I gave an order, sir."

Myang narrowed her brown eyes. "You gave an order. What order?"

"Admiral-General. I ordered the Feyori to selectively wipe

all traces of how to re-create the Godstrike cannon, including the suppression of logic chains and leaps of intuition that would allow the original creators to re-create how they did it, sir."

"Why?" The single word was a warning, a soft-voiced, wary growl. It was not necessary for the Admiral-General to shout at Ia in order to get her underlying threat across.

Ia tried not to shiver openly. "That cannon is too damned dangerous for anyone to attempt to re-create. I spent more than a dozen rescue missions on and around Oberon's Rock, just trying to keep that information out of the hands of the criminal elements of the known galaxy. I knew that I would not be free to continue to perform precision countermeasures for years, decades, and even centuries. Expediency and the safety of the Alliance worlds demanded that the information on how to re-create the cannon be removed from our collective awareness.

"After considering the implications, and the sheer power of the laser in its Mark II version, the Feyori agreed it was necessary."

"That was *not* your call to make!" Myang snapped, rising and slapping her hands on Ia's crysium-plated desktop.

Ia dropped her gaze from the wall to the shorter woman's face. "I will *not* always be on a ship that would be free to intercept another such theft attempt," she countered firmly. "And I would *not* leave it up to the vagaries of Fate. I had Grandmaster Ssarra *ensure* I would be assigned to Ferrar's Fighters as a fresh-out-of-Basic grunt, just so I *could* be there the first few of those dozen tries, and I arranged for the Lyebariko of undergalactic lords to be *disrupted* long enough to stay away while I was on Blockade patrol . . . but I still had to go back after the *Hellfire* was commissioned.

"The problem, Admiral-General, is that I will not always be *able* to be there. And this cannon is too damned powerful to allow anyone else to use it in my place." She held Myang's gaze steadily, and stated, "At the end of the Second Grey War, I fully intend to destroy *this* ship as the last relic of that technological advancement in extreme, laser-based caloric efficiency. Sir. Because the Alliance is *not* ready, nor capable, of handling the repercussions of every would-be planet pirate or mass murderer being capable of building their own version and holding whole worlds hostage."

"So you *say*," Myang sneered.

Ia slapped her own hands on the edge of her desk, glad her workstation screens were scrolled down below the edge. She leaned over, not quite nose to nose with her superior, and growled, *"So I know."*

Myang narrowed her eyes. She clearly wanted to say more, but she had also been working with Ia for nearly four years, she had seen the strength of Ia's precognition, and both of them knew it.

"I will not waste one more life than absolutely necessary . . . and you, *sir,* do not yet comprehend just how powerful the Mark II version is, compared to the Mark I. You will hold your tongue, and hold your orders, until the destruction of Sallha and the other infected colonies."

"You do not give *me* orders," Myang countered, lifting her chin.

"*I* am still the General of the Alliance Armies, and we are still under Martial Law, because we are *still* at war, soldier," Ia returned sternly. Exercising the power that had been given to her. "Until both the Salik *and* the Grey threats are dealt with, I will remain in charge . . . and if you try to remove me from command, I have the authority of all the *other* governments in the Alliance to have you removed and thrown in a brig for attempted treason. Grand High Treason.

"I will *not* allow this technology to fall into the wrong hands, and if that requires removing it from the *right* hands to prevent it, then that is what I will do. I will fight these wars to the best of my ability, with every scrap of duty and conscience I carry within me, and I will not let you flaunt your rank as a *carte blanche* pass to be an idiot. I respect you *too* much to allow that piece of asteroid-headedness to pass on my watch."

"You *respect* me?" Myang scoffed.

"Yes, sir. I still do. But until you know the lay of the local terrain, stop trying to lead from a thousand light-years away. Sir."

"Are you *comparing* me to Brigadier General Mattox?" the Admiral-General asked, rearing back with a scowl.

"If *you* think that, sir, then you just might be a little too close to *being* it. I am giving you an order, soldier," Ia repeated. "Stand down, hold your tongue, and *watch*, so that you will see just how dangerous what you are trying to grasp is, before you actually touch it and burn yourself—and if you cannot trust my precognition and my sense of ethics after nearly four damned years of working with me, then you had *better* shut up and watch, because time is the only thing left I have to prove my words are true."

Pushing away from her desk, she stepped around the desk. Myang frowned. "Where are you going?"

"To get out of this damned coat. I feel like a court jester in it." She slapped open the door to her private quarters, stepped through, and turned to face Myang. "Our next meeting is at 1000 hours, Deck 6 officers' meeting room, amidships, forward of the bridge, sir. I'll see you there."

The door slid shut between them. It was not going to be an entirely peaceful flight to the Salik homeworld.

CHAPTER 8

My heart . . . is a bit harder to convince.

~Ia

Sallha was a beautiful blue-and-white world when seen from orbit. The defense satellites had been shot down earlier, and orbital-sweeper robots had been sent—and sacrificed—to sweep the debris out of orbit, aiming it down into the atmosphere to burn up or crash, depending on the size, the angle of reentry, and the composition of each errant mass. More than that, thousands upon thousands of Feyori soap bubbles still swooped through the atmosphere, checking for plague particles and stray scraps the sweepers had missed.

Every once in a while, a silvery sphere would swoop down into the atmosphere, do something, and swoop back up again. Some were dumping matter; some were snacking on the natural radiations bouncing off the planet's magnetosphere or issuing up from the atmosphere in the form of electrical jets and sprites.

Ia herself wasn't sure of the numbers, but knew they numbered somewhere above fifty, sixty thousand, not counting the ones at the other colonyworlds. More were still coming in from beyond the edges of the known galaxy, drawn as much by the promise of Ia's precognitive help in their own positions as by the threat of the consequences of failure to appear. Carrot-and-stick.

With the middle and highest orbits cleared, the flagships and escort vessels of every Alliance member sat and waited in extreme far orbit, including a token ship from the Choya. They were still essentially war prisoners, and their government officials awaited trial for crimes against the Alliance, but it was deemed important for them to have a delegation here to witness the death of the Salik nation. But they, too, had seen the broadcasts from the Salik and knew how close they themselves had come to this death.

First, the boasts, the threats, the promises. Then, the pleading, sly at first, then more and more sincere as the reality of their predicament became more and more real to them. Then . . . the panic, from those that still had the energy to be panicked by their fellows slumping and sagging and barely breathing. Ia had banned most of it from being broadcast on the ship. Recorded, yes, but openly played, no; she knew it would be too depressing. Nor were the Salik images the only ones banned from being played over and over by her crew.

There were other starships out there. Most of them were hydrotankers, but—flying here in defiance of the Quarantine Extreme—various well-meaning but poor-thinking "Save the Salik!" groups had banded together to protest what was happening. They had tried legal channels, trying to force the governments of the Alliance to end the destruction of the Salik race, only to be blocked at the highest levels by the Terran Premiere, the Gatsugi President, the V'Dan Emperor, all the Queen Nestors . . .

The ones who had tried to save the Salik as a species were now trying to broadcast messages that General Ia was a monster, that her crew were psychopaths for following her, that she would turn the plague on all of them next. Others were trying to protest the restriction of just how many surveillance drones were allowed to descend and record everything on the Salik motherworld one last time. Still more were only pretending to be protestors and conscientious objectors; they were here to try to sneak in and snag a bit of the plague, or maybe to find a way to grab a bit of Salik wealth and figure a way to cleanse it for resale.

Ia didn't want to hear any of that invective aimed her way. On one level, she knew she very much deserved it. She was damned for everything she did. But on every other level, she had heard it and endured it long, long ago, and knew there was no better way. No path that she could live with. Not when compared to all the deaths her murderous choices had prevented. Ia knew the other military ships were threatening to shoot and tow them for being in a restricted space, but that was up to them to handle. Her mind was elsewhere.

This time, when she paused for a deep breath to steady her nerves, it was while standing outside the back door to the bridge, in the corridor that contained the two heads, the minigalley, the door into the main corridor as well as into the bridge, and the side door into her clerk's office. Rather than wearing formal Dress Blacks, she had donned a gray Special Forces shirt, black slacks with the four colors of each Branch down the seams, and a gray headband that hopefully would keep her sweat out of her eyes. Her shoulder boards and collar points bore the five stars of her rank, and she had attached to her rolled-up shirtsleeves the flashpatch for the Terran United Planets Space Force on one shoulder, and the flashpatch of the Damned on the other: a pale blue and gray snowflake on dull red and orange flames.

This time, it wasn't the entire crew that awaited her, but rather, her bridge crew: Lieutenant Rico, whose watch it was; Yeoman Ishiomi, who would serve as her backup pilot; Private Shim, who would be plotting her course and all corrections needed; C'ulosc, who would be manning the comms; Nelson at operations; and Ramasa at gunnery, though unless things went terribly wrong, his teams would not be needed. The others in the bridge were her witnesses: Denora de Marco, Admiral-General Myang, her two aides, the Premiere, and two of his five watchdogs, Tango and Sierra. Seven guests were all they could fit into the bridge comfortably since there were only twelve seats: five primary workstations, the command seat, and a backup for each.

Her vision kept threatening to blur. Scrubbing at her lashes, she firmed her will. She knew what she was destroying, knew every beautiful island, lagoon, lake, river, fjord, waterfall, isthmus . . . every water feature, natural and artificial, which had prompted the Salik in one of their rare poetic moments to dub their world *Fountain*, an ironic contrast to the plebian, dull, Terran *Earth*. By the time she was done, though . . .

Squaring her shoulders, she sniffed hard to clear her nose, set her jaw, and opened the door.

"General on Deck!" Rico called out. Unclipping his harness, he gained his feet, faced her, and saluted formally. "General Ia, crew and ship are ready for maneuvers."

His formality was for posterity. Ia preferred to run a casual crew, limiting salutes and requiring only that everyone be in uniform most of the time, without having to specify what quality of uniform, whether it was camouflage casuals or formal Dress. But this moment, on the bridge of her ship, was being recorded for history's sake, and that meant running at least some of this moment by the book. Her casual-seeming attire was a necessity, as were the light layers she had ordered her bridge crew—her entire crew—to wear. Her advice to the Admiral-General, the Premiere, the Agents and aides to do the same had gone unheeded, but the reporter, she noted out of the corner of her eye, had donned a lightweight dress in somber navy.

Returning Rico's salute, she spoke, keeping her diction crisp and clear. "Lieutenant Rico, you are relieved of bridge duty. Report to your secondary post."

"Aye, sir." Stepping down from the raised platform, he gave her room to step up in his place. The seat automatically adjusted its distance from the console to accommodate her shorter legs as soon as she sat down and clipped the straps in place. She listened to the bridge door hiss shut as her third officer left but did not look up to watch him go. Instead, she called up a chronometer and calculated how much time had passed.

"Status report," Ia ordered.

"Orbit is holding steady, sir," Ishiomi said, keeping his hand steady in the glove and his eyes on the screens in front of him.

"Courses plotted and laid," Shim told her. "Stage one ready to execute at your command, General."

"All ships on standby, and the Alliance is ready for broadcast, sir," C'ulosc added.

"Gunnery teams on standby, sir," Ramasa stated. "Bored but ready.

"All systems operational, and all systems normal, sir. Ambient temperature 20C," Nelson reported.

"Private Nelson, let me know when it reaches 35C, counted off on the fives," Ia instructed.

"Aye, sir."

"Open the broadcast, Private C'ulosc."

"Aye, sir. In three, two . . ."

Ia didn't speak immediately. Instead, she let the silence stretch on the bridge. There were several variations of this speech she could give, but she wanted to give not just the right one, but the one from her heart. It was hard to find the right words, though. Not when her heart was in turmoil over all the things she had done, and all the things she had still left to do. Still, she had to say something.

". . . I know this is being recorded for posterity. I know that everyone has questioned, and will continue to question, all of my choices. Particularly the ones leading up to this point in time." Her voice sounded steady, which relieved her. She didn't want her emotions to break loose now, not when she had too much to do in the next handful of days. "I want you all to know, from now until far into the future, just how much I regret the necessity of this act.

"I will not do so by explaining how many lives I have saved. The numbers are so large, they are rendered meaningless to most everyone but me. Instead, I want you to know how long I have been working on this problem." She looked up at the cloud-wreathed planet before her on her main viewscreen, just far enough away that the full curve of Sallha barely filled the screen at zero magnification. "Twelve years, one month, twenty-two days, twenty-three hours, and forty-six minutes ago, Terran Standard time units, I realized that for the rest of the galaxy to live past three hundred years from now, when the ancient enemy of the Greys would come to try to destroy us . . . the Salik would have to die.

"One month, eighteen days, eighteen hours, three minutes ago was the deadline for deciding their fate. In the intervening time between that moment of realization and that deadline, in the twelve years, five days, eighteen hours, and . . . now four minutes," she allowed, checking the chronometer, "I strove every single day, even several times a day—for 4,388 days Terran Standard—in the effort to find another way that would keep the Salik alive while also keeping the majority of the members of the Alliance alive . . . and keeping the rest of the galaxy alive more than three hundred years from now.

"I did not find any." She let her words hang in the quiet of the bridge. No one spoke, though Myang gave her a grim look, and Mandella a sad one. The two Agents eyed her warily, the two aides looked almost as grim as their superior, and de Marco swallowed, looking away. "My job as a soldier is to stand between my people and all that would bring them harm. To use my body, weapons, skills, and even my life if necessary to prevent my people, my home, from being devastated by war.

"My job as an officer is to do all of that and more, to do so with the least expenditure of resources wherever possible, and the least loss of lives . . . on both sides, ironically. But I will point out that for two hundred years, the Alliance has tried to Blockade the Salik . . . and that for two hundred years, they consistently slipped past our best efforts, rebuilt their war machines, and tried to shove us into, as the Dlmvla put it, the Room for the Dead. I have chosen instead to close that door upon them.

"In an attempt to warn them not to go to war, I arranged for myself to be captured by the Salik, and was nearly eaten alive three years, ten months, thirty days, ten hours, and fifty-two minutes ago. They refused to deviate from their course . . . so I destroyed their top military leaders and gave them time to reconsider. They did not reconsider. One month, five days, eighteen hours, and six minutes ago . . . I allowed the plague, created by the Salik in the first war, to infect the Salik nation here in the second. Another point of irony, but then I do admit I have a strange sense of humor."

She touched her workstation console, warming it up for piloting. Strapping her left hand into the controls, she checked the complex navigation program her bridge navigators had painstakingly created over the last five hours, ever since arriving in this system. Checking the fit for comfort, she adjusted her headband, drew a deep breath, and nodded to herself.

"Yeoman Ishiomi. Helm to my control in thirty."

"Aye, sir. Helm to yours in twenty-seven," he replied promptly.

Her right hand flipped up the outer lid, and pressed to the scanner. "Navigation, ETA to target."

"Two minutes thirty-eight seconds, sir," Private Shim reported.

"Noted. Comms, inform the fleet I am moving into position in twenty seconds. Alert Commodore Baltrush to have the Navy 1st Cordon, 5th Division, 7th Battalion begin moving into position for refueling procedure."

"Aye, sir," Private C'ulosc agreed, and spoke into his headset in the low tones that were easy for the rest of the bridge crew to ignore, even as it remained crisp enough for the other comm techs across the system to understand.

". . . Helm to yours," Ishiomi stated several seconds later.

"The helm is mine," she confirmed, as telltales lit up on her console and on her screens. "Moving to intercept target."

She had to have her hand in the attitude glove in order to be the pilot, but Ia didn't have to actively guide the ship. Not this time. The ship's insystem thrusters pulsed, and the *Damnation* swept forward, still following an orbital curve but exchanging speed for altitude in a carefully pre-choreographed dance. A dozen hydrotanker vessels broke position as well, trailing after her ship like Terran ducklings in the wake of their parent.

The swirling mass of tiny, mirror-bright beads shifted, several hundred peeling off from the rest to flank the ship, with several hundred more peeling off and popping instantly out of view in handfuls of a dozen or more at a time. Plenty remained to keep up their sharp vigil, though; they were still acting as the thin, silver, soap-bubble shield between the plague and the ships of the Alliance.

"I admit freely that I allowed this plague to happen," Ia stated for the record. For the recordings. "I did so under carefully controlled circumstances . . . for I will also state, for the record, that it has always been my intention to clean up the

messes I have made. I shall begin doing so now. Private Shim,
Private C'ulosc, coordinate the broadcast of the destruction of
Sallha with the surveillance drones and the fleet."

"Aye, sir." "Sir, yes, sir." They murmured among themselves, until Shim nodded at C'ulosc, who announced, ". . .
Broadcasting now, sir."

Ia's primary screen remained focused on the surface of
Sallha, but that screen-filling image of the predominantly
watery world shifted to the left secondary for every other station watching the dead-ahead view. On the nonoperational
workstations, every screen filled with a different view, some
from space, some from ground level. There were dead bodies
in view, exploded from the force of the gasses stirred by the
bacterial colonies multiplying inside, decomposing slowly as
lowly insects and various fungi devoured the rotting remains
of the Salik who had been trying to move across plazas and
streets when the last of their strength, their willpower, had
given out.

Most of the remains were covered in a faint, fuzzy white
sheen. That was the mark of the plague in its dormant state,
now that there weren't any creatures with sufficiently electrically active neurological systems left to feed the artificial,
virus-like prions. Trillions of prionic filaments crammed into
a single square centimeter of sagging, dried-out flesh.

"I am deeply sorry that I had to step aside and allow the
Salik to destroy themselves." She lifted the final cover standing between her conscience and her duty. "Giorgi Mishka
knew that testifying would permit a terrible tragedy to
occur . . . but he did not know the wonderful things that followed in the wake of that tragedy—the formation of the Terran United Planets government, so on and so forth.

"I, on the other hand, know exactly what I do, in all of its
permutations and possible consequences. And while I am
very sorry for the death of the Salik race . . ." She paused long
enough to press the button with her littlest finger, while sliding her thumb, index, and middle fingers across the controls
to lock the weapon on, not an original part of the ship's design
but rather a specification of her own, ". . . I am not sorry for
all the other lives being saved.

"'Thus the Ever-Light of the God-Being smote through

their enemy, piercing the Room . . . the *World*,'" Ia amended, altering the original line from the famous poem as she spoke up over the encroaching *thrum* and *whoosh* of the Sterling engines, "'. . . for the Dead.'" Bright crimson leaped forward on her final words. It did not stop pouring out of the bow of the *Damnation*, either. Around the red-bathed bridge, the forward-facing scanners quickly blacked out the majority of the beam, and kept it blacked out. Over at Private Nelson's station, what had once been a series of elegant green and yellow lines immediately shrank to tiny pinpricks as the rest of the overall chart followed the spike of power being produced and used by the main gun.

Ia's main screen shifted to an extrapolated third-person view of the *Damnation*'s position over the planet, allowing her to check that the ship was still firmly on its preprogrammed course. Three of her five top tertiary screens had shifted to views from the drones on the ground, as had the left secondary.

The initial view was awe-striking; a great, rich red lance of focused light struck the ground near the heart of one of the lifeless Salik cities. Instantly, the ground flashed double-bright, for the impact was as powerful as some of the hydro-bombs the *Damnation* had recently carried. Clouds billowed outward from the impact zone, white-hot, mushroom orange, boiling red as bodies and buildings and other objects vaporized, charred, and burned.

The ship continued on its path, settling into a stable midaltitude orbit. That single mushroom cloud rapidly turned into a line of mushrooms. A wall of flaring light, billowing heat, and roiling clouds of ash.

The first shockwave caught up to the nearest drone recording all of this in the distance. It slammed into the camera, shaking the view with streaked and flickering images for a second, before that firewall caught up with the machine. The camera's new view of the sky, peaceful with scudding wisps of clouds, vanished as the second, stronger shockwave reached the drone and obliterated it. Static filled that screen, until C'ulosc switched broadcasts.

One by one, other images from other drones near the blast zone were also hit, and destroyed. Only those who were high in the sky from hundreds of kilometers away survived; as the last of the close-range cameras vanished within ten seconds, all they were left with was a distant, haze-blurred view of a great, bright, thin beam of bloodred light slicing down through the atmosphere, at the forefront of a wall-shaped inferno that spewed smoke, ash, fire, and darkness into the sky, all trailing in the Godstrike's wake.

Back near the beginning point, not only was there the distinctive, ringed remnants of a mushroom cloud, but there were now great fiery columns rising and twisting. Firestorm tornadoes, whipping the winds inward to fuel the conflagration that had begun. The base of the boiling clouds still rising in the wake of the laser's path glowed white-gold, and the ground rippled in a queasy pattern. Not just in a concentric circle running outward from the strike zone, but in several arcs that overlapped. Buildings toppled, destroyed by the ground-quakes.

"Fuel at ninety-six percent, sir," Nelson stated, her voice steady despite the awe-striking images. She had to raise it slightly over the *thump*-and-*whoosh* of the Sterling engines trying to convert the excess heat of the ongoing strike.

"Commodore Baltrush, begin refueling procedures now," C'ulosc ordered over his headset. The bridge was starting to feel warm; the Sterling engines did their best to reconvert what little waste heat was being produced by the main cannon, but it was not originally designed to keep running so long.

"Ah . . . How deep is that laser going?" Premiere Mandella asked. He turned his head slightly from his screen, but could not pull his gaze away long enough to actually look at Ia. In the wake of the laser fire, ash and fury were now lined by dozens of twisting, dancing, spiraling infernos, like a line of living, flame-made columns decorating a grim and gritty, billowing wall.

"At this location, where the surface rock is slightly less dense than in others . . . this ship's main cannon is vaporizing the crust to a depth of just over five kilometers, Terran Standard," Ia explained grimly. "The beam is traveling at a rate of roughly 6.8 kilometers per second across the surface, and the local crustal depth is seven to eight kilometers. The density of the crust of Sallha ranges from five kilometers to one hundred and fifty . . . but we're not going through the mountains on this pass."

"You never said anything about this in any of the briefings," he accused her.

"I did tell you that this ship's main cannon could vaporize Grey ships, Premiere, sir. A planet's crust is considerably less tough," she replied calmly.

"Ambient temperature 25C and rising," Nelson announced.

"Thank you, Private."

Several improvements had been made to the efficiency of the Godstrike Mark II. Thermal retention had been one of them, but there was still some bleed-through. As the seconds and minutes stretched on, as the *Damnation* swung through its ninety-minute arc, the Godstrike continued to fire, and the ship continued to heat up.

At the edge of her vision, Ia could see the Admiral-General shifting restlessly in her seat. One of the Agents, the one code-named Tango, pulled out a kerchief and wiped his freckled brow when Nelson announced, "Ambient temperature 30C and rising."

Elsewhere on the ship, out by the water tanks that shielded the inner cabins from the hull, Ia's crew were overseeing the automatic shunting of purified water from the tankers to the ship, and from the ship's tanks to its hardworking main engines. In the vast majority of probabilities, everything worked fine, but Ia didn't want to take any chances. Along the entire length of the main cannon, running at full power, only a maximum of four hydroengines out of the hundreds spanning the length of the kilometer-plus-long ship could be safely shut down before it destabilized the beam.

Those engines were in top shape, barely used for more than fractions of a second until now. Not even during the testing phases had the Terran engineers who created it used the Godstrike Mark II for so long. This, however, was the ultimate stress test.

On her lower fifth tertiary screen, the one showing a view from orbit at an angle to the *Damnation*'s path, the tranquil blue-and-white swirl of Sallha was now marred by a horrid dark line, as well as that bright spear lancing down from her ship. While the upper winds were still doing their best to carry the clouds off to the right along the local jet-stream direction, the lower winds were marring those streaks with the slowly forming swirls of massive vortices. Lightning flared in the roiling clouds, stirred up by the polarity differences churning between scarred surface and superheated air.

The Godstrike reached the edge of the largest landmass and dipped into the semishallow seas of Sallha. The ship slowed fractionally, thrusters correcting automatically to keep their orbit at a steady distance rather than dipping closer to the surface. Water distorted the beam; by slowing down, the same depth could be scored in the rocks at a speed of 6.2 kilometers per second instead of 6.8.

The bridge continued to heat up. Sweat now sheened Ia's skin, making the headband necessary to keep the salty stuff out of her eyes. Nelson cleared her throat. "Ambient temperature is now 35C, sir."

(*Group One*,) Ia projected carefully, telepathically. (*Dinnertime*.)

Their escort group of five hundred Feyori swerved abruptly from their broad, ring-shaped formation into a much narrower, straw-like stream aimed straight at the *Damnation*'s bow. They swooped in through the hull, some peeling off before they reached the first section; others delved deeper, each one's path designed to cover a different strip of the ship.

Carefully, they avoided the actual core of the main laser and its engines. The Godstrike was too strong for any one single Feyori to withstand. Just as carefully, they avoided the multitudes of small but still-nasty-flavored crysium nodes Harper had buried just beneath the skin of her ship. Crysium was what they preferred to leave behind in the way of matter-based residue after returning to their natural energy-based state. It was refuse, excrement, *v'shova v'shakk* to them, so they avoided it.

Within seconds, three dark pewter spheres streaked through the bridge, enlarged to cover as much area as they could. There was no actual, physical sensation to their swift passage, though the Premiere yelped in startlement and the two Agents groped reflexively for their guns. Myang, Sofrens, and Talpur flinched, while Denora flung up her arms. The Meddlers passed without harming anyone; indeed, they left in their wake a refreshing, even somewhat shocking level of coolness.

Nelson eyed her monitors. "Ambient temperature on the bridge is . . . 19C . . . overall ambient temperature of the ship . . . is an average of 20C, sir," she reported as the last of the Feyori exited the stern. They swirled out to join the others around the planet, while a new group, Group Two, swerved in to form the escort ring not far from the bow of the ship. "We are back to normal temperatures."

"Keep counting it off on the fives," Ia said, repeating her order. "We have a long way to go."

"Aye, sir."

Silence filled the bridge, which slowly began heating up again. Finally, Admiral-General Myang spoke. "I owe you an apology, General Ia. You are right. This technology should not be replicated."

"Apology accepted, sir. For those of you still watching," Ia stated, mindful of the broadcast still being sent out of everything happening on the bridge, "you are now seeing the full might of the TUPSF *Damnation*'s main cannon. It is capable of piercing enemy ships at a fraction of a second . . . and it is capable of carving up a world. However, *I* am at the helm of this planet-killer. It is by my hand, and mine alone, that I destroy this planet. By my own hand, the other geothermically active colonies of the Salik race will also be destroyed in the next few days, eradicating the last traces of the plague.

"I will *never* allow this ship to be turned on any of you, by my hand or any other. It will be used to destroy the plague, and it will be used to halt the Greys, nothing more. You have my Prophetic Stamp on that."

Silence filled the bridge, until Nelson reported, "Ambient temperature 25C, sir."

"Fuel?" Ia asked her.

"Fuel reserves have stabilized at an average of eighty-seven percent, General."

"Private C'ulosc, send my compliments to the 7th Battalion, 5th Division, 1st Cordon Navy," Ia directed.

"Aye, sir," he agreed. He murmured into his headset, then

hesitated. "General, sir . . . we are being pinged by several of the, ah, civilian ships in this system. They are demanding to speak with you. They've opened so many channels, they're starting to interfere."

Admiral-General Myang fielded that one. "Private. Kindly inform them that they are in gross violation of Martial Law and the rules of Quarantine Extreme by having invaded a severely restricted and quarantined system, and that if they do not remove themselves immediately, I will give the order to have them blown out of the night."

"Admiral-General," Premiere Mandella corrected her, "it is by *my* order that they are *not* being blown out of the night."

"They are in violation of—"

"Sirs," C'ulosc asserted, cutting through their argument. "One of the vessels, the Tlassian Civilian Cruiser *Ssu-Sienth Tlakk*, is claiming it is being pinged by survivors on the planet. Salik, Choya, *and* other race members. They're apparently in a sealed bunker on the major southern isle, and are demanding to know what you are going to do about rescuing them."

"There are no survivors," Ia asserted flatly. "That entire atmosphere is contaminated. Only the Feyori can fly in and out of it, and even they have to be cautious. There will *be* no survivors." She could feel the tears welling in her eyes and tried her best to ignore them. "We tried for over two hundred years to get the Salik to cooperate and play nice with the rest of the known galaxy, and for *two hundred years*, they lied to us, laying plans and building up massive forces in the hopes that they could overwhelm, crush, and devour us.

"Whoever thinks that the Salik would have changed in even as much as three hundred years more is deluded beyond all grasp of truth and reality."

". . . What if there *are* non-Salik down there?" Agent Sierra asked her.

The tears spilled over. She ignored them, blinking hard to clear her vision so she could keep an eye on the autopilot program guiding the *Damnation*. "Three years, ten months, thirty days, eleven hours, and seven minutes ago, I was the last Human to leave Sallha alive, meioa. Everyone else has been tortured and eaten by now. Any so-called 'survivors' are nothing more than sophisticated traps laid by the Salik in the hopes that we would be *stupid* enough to risk contaminating ourselves in some misguided attempt at rescuing them.

"Between my precognitive timing efforts and the effects of this plague, I have ended this war three years early and saved countless trillions of lives in doing so. I will not risk one more life in any rescue attempts. Anyone else who tries will simply be stupidly throwing their life away for nothing. Private C'ulosc. Inform the fleet of the following: If *any* of those civilian ships comes within ten Alliance Standard planetary diameters of Sallha, its moon, or its neighboring planets, they are to be, to quote the Admiral-General, shot out of the night," she ordered. "And if they *v'charok* about that, remind them that they still have free will, but that it is my hope they also still have the capacity to think things through to all possible consequences *before* they choose to act. Anyone or anything touching a contaminated atmosphere that is not a Feyori *will not be coming back*."

"Sir, yes, sir," C'ulosc confirmed. He worked a few moments with the ongoing recordings on the bridge. ". . . Message transmitted."

"Let us hope it is also a message *received*."

Silence descended once again, if one did not count the noise of the conversion engines trying to recapture and drain the thermal energy from the main laser. When Nelson announced, "35C, sir," Ia once again broadcast psychic permission to Group Two to sweep the ship, devouring thermal energy as they went. Group Three lined up in their wake to await the thermal buffet being offered.

The *Damnation* continued its graceful glide through orbital space. Only it, the hydrotankers, and the Feyori dared to move from their parked positions. Crossing mostly over ocean, including a near-arctic climate as the beam passed close to the axial pole, the Godstrike was now leaving boiling clouds of vaporized water in its wake, in a long cloud that was still black back on land, and white in the laser's immediate wake. They crossed the occultation line from day into night, and within moments it was clear from the reddish glow and the spider-crawl flashes of lightning that there was still a lot of heat and ion imbalances bleeding away in the main laser's immediate wake.

———————

One hundred seventeen minutes after the first cut had begun, the diagonal circle was complete. Ia unlocked the main cannon and shut it off, closing the double lid to secure the control button. The Feyori currently on standby took that as their cue to sweep through the ship one more time, siphoning up the excess thermal energy. In the wake of their passing, the Sterling engines shut down, bringing a blessed level of quiet that soothed aching, overstimulated nerves.

"Yeoman Ishiomi. Helm to your control in thirty."

"Aye, sir. Helm to mine in . . . twenty-six," he confirmed. He restrapped his hand into the attitude control and woke up his console. ". . . Taking the helm . . . now, sir. I have the helm."

"The helm is yours," she confirmed. "Move the ship into position for phase two. *All hands, this is the General. Duty-swap in five minutes. I repeat, duty-swap in five minutes.*" Unbuckling her harness, she stood and flexed her shoulders. "Yeoman, you have the bridge until my return."

"Aye, sir, I have the bridge."

There was virtually no chance of anyone trying to take over her bridge, now. Not when the sheer destruction wrought by the main cannon, and Ia's carefully controlled wielding of it, had been so amply demonstrated. That, and long-standing tradition insisted that the pilot of a vessel always had the final say, as they had the final responsibility for the safety of that ship.

Just as well. Ia had to use the head and needed to stretch fully. She was also hungry. Retreating into the back corridor, she found Lieutenant Rico inside, putting the finishing touches on a pasta dish. He nodded at her. "Two minutes to food, sir. The doctor insisted you should eat, and I'm tired of watching you fix sandwiches."

She knew what he was not saying, what he wanted to say. The burden of all of this was on her, and her crew was concerned.

"I'll enjoy it when I get back," she promised, and ducked into the nearest head. When she emerged, hands washed and stiff muscles somewhat stretched, he handed her a bowl layered with noodles, meat, vegetables, and a sprinkling of cheese. He delivered it with a warning.

"Myang has been interrogating me in her spare time," Rico told her. He was the chief spy for the Admiral-General, so this was not too surprising. "I think she suspects I have been covering up several subjects for you."

"She would be a fool not to suspect that," Ia agreed, reflexively checking the timestreams. When she did, she relaxed a little and dug her fork into the layers of the dish while she leaned against the galley counter. "It'll be okay."

Her warning about the need to control, and destroy, all information regarding the Godstrike weaponry had sunk in deep in the other woman's psyche. The canals and levees she had struggled to build over the years now seemed to be laid too deep to easily disturb, though Ia had no intention of letting down her guard even now. The Miklinn mess had proved that to be a necessity. Little details were still slipping through, yes, but the majority of her plans were now solidly in place. All she had left to do was—

"Sir? You know I respect you," Rico told her, interrupting her train of thought. "But either you move so I can get to work, or *you* will have to scrub these dishes."

"Lieutenant, yes, sir," she quipped, shifting to lean against a cabinet he wouldn't need. By the time her meal was finished, the bowl and fork were the last bits in need of scrubbing. Handing them over, she fetched a bottle of water out of the bottom of the cooler. "See you in a few more hours."

"And you."

Checking herself quickly in the mirror in the nearest head, Ia made sure she hadn't spilled anything, wiped her mouth, and headed back to the bridge. C'ulosc at communications had been replaced by Xhuge, Ramasa by Hong at the gunnery station, ship's operations were being watched by the vigilant Dinyadah, and Hulio had replaced Shim at navigation. Yeoman Fielle had taken over her seat at the command console at the back of the bridge; in deference to the solemnity of the moment, he was not pulling a Helstead with his boots on the console edge but instead had his feet flat on the floor.

Glancing her way, he released his harness and stood. "General on Deck."

Since she was not relieving him of watch—that was still Ishiomi's job—she didn't bother to salute. The two of them just traded places. Strapping herself in, she fitted the glove onto her hand. "ETA to target two?"

"Coming up in two minutes seventeen seconds, sir," Private Hulio told her.

"Helm to yours in twenty, sir," Ishiomi added as she sat down and clipped her water bottle into place.

"Helm to mine in . . . twenty—let me adjust my seat, first," Ia confirmed, pausing briefly to push at the levers. Its sensors knew her usual configurations, but the tension of watching over the Godstrike had warned her she needed the back to sit more upright, so that she could relax into it while remaining alert. Various acceleration forces weren't pressing her into it, as they more normally did when she was at the helm, which was usually during moments of combat. There were none, this time. ". . . I have the helm."

"Helm is yours, sir. Permission to stand down, General?" the yeoman in the pilot's seat asked.

"Permission granted. Yeoman Fielle, take your seat and prepare to stand by. Private Dinyadah, what is our fuel status?"

"Aye, sir."

Dinyadah checked her screens. "One hundred percent, with three tankers connected and more on standby."

"Excellent."

While the two men changed places, Ia checked their altitude, speed, and orbital path. Yeoman First Class Ishiomi Hatsue had done a good job of aligning the ship with the correct orbital path for phase two, set at an angle to the original diagonal ring cut around the world. On the monitors showing the curve of the planet, a ragged, dark red-gray line was coming into view, still molten-hot, spewing up steam from the shallow oceans and scorching the land with ongoing firestorms.

She unlocked the control box, watching the countdown timer. The destruction of Sallha required precisely timed stresses applied to the planet's tectonic plates in specific locations. "Beginning phase two in ten . . . nine . . ."

Eight seconds later, she activated the cannon, locking it on. The sensors on board the *Damnation* blacked out the forward-pointing view, switching to incoming camera angles from other ships. Once again, the beam struck land first, erupting in an initial mushroom cloud that quickly sprouted into an elongated shockwave.

There were still surveillance drones in the atmosphere, and their images were similar to the first set: those close to the blast were obliterated; those farther out showed the ash clouds in the distance, and the quaking of the ground, the toppling of plants and buildings, even a landslide or two. A view from a ship in far orbit, showing three-quarters of the world's curve, displayed a few dark spots in the clouds, blotches of ash and smoke that were nowhere near the lines being carved in Sallha's skin.

"What are those spots?" Denora asked, pointing. "Does anybody know?"

"Volcanoes," Ia told her. "You slept through the planning session that first day. The objective is to create points of grave weakness in Sallha's crust, disrupting the delicate balance of stress shared by all its tectonic plates. This ship will carve five sets of rings around the world, then assume geostationary orbit and bore seven holes in the greatest mountain chain.

"Some of the Feyori will then bring in an asteroid roughly the length of this ship, and sling it at the center of those seven boreholes. This will break off a wedge of the crust and drive it deep into the mantle. Other groups of Feyori will sling smaller asteroids at the intersection points of the cuts the *Damnation* will have made. This will cause chunks of the crust to collapse and subduct in those areas, while the shock forces will push tsunami-like waves through the magma, causing it to burst through the weakened crust at other points.

"The last of the five rings will be carved approximately nine hours from now. The boreholes will be finished in just ten hours, and it will take fifteen minutes at most to sling the rocks. Within twenty-seven hours, this world will be suffering the kind of catastrophic crustal subduction failure that geoscientists believe caused the surface of Venus, in the Sol System, to look like it now does. At that point, the coldest spot on Sallha, at the uppermost edge of its atmosphere, will be over twenty-three hundred Celsius. More than hot enough to destroy the plague," Ia finished.

The reporter blinked at Ia, then looked back at her screen.

"That's . . . impressive. And frightening. But . . . Sallha's moon has a thin nitrogen-and-carbon-dioxide atmosphere, which means it's contaminated, but it's not geothermally active. How are you going to destroy it? How *can* you?"

"The Feyori will envelop it in what they call the Great Gathering. My crew will launch a thick screen of scatter-bombs—they have a payload of diffraction prisms—and I will shoot the Meddlers with the main cannon. With that much energy at their command, they will shift Sallha's natural satellite out of orbit and sling it toward its parent star . . . the same as they will do for all the other plague-infested, gas-covered, but otherwise thermally inert worlds and moons."

Denora's jaw dropped.

"For the five other worlds the Salik colonized, ones that are thermally active, we will carve them up, break them down, and let them burn. Navigation over the next three millennia will be a bit tricky, while Sallha adjusts to lacking a moon . . . but then most everyone will be wanting to park themselves in interstitial space, or in other star systems, to catch the last of the data streams sent out.

"Once it's been slagged, and the plague has been destroyed, there won't be any reason to actually visit this world . . . unless you're a geophysicist," she allowed lightly. "But just to be safe, a rear guard of Meddlers will stay on hand to keep plague-seekers away for a full ten Terran days while the planet burns at temperatures above the plague killing threshold."

"Won't the churning of the atmosphere kick some of the plague into space?" de Marco asked next, looking at the screens.

"That's what the other Meddlers out there are doing," Ia said, lifting her chin at the screens. "They're spotting and snagging the plague, then dragging it back down into the lower atmosphere, where they release it so it can burn."

"Ambient temperature is now 25C, sir," Dinyadah announced quietly.

"Thank you, Private."

"But . . . if they can do that, what's stopping them from taking the plague to other worlds, and threatening us?" the reporter asked, twisting once again in her harness-strapped seat so she could peer at Ia.

"The most important reason why they won't ever do that to

us is because it is against their own rules to wipe out each other's pawns," Ia patiently explained. "The other main reason is that they know I will not let them."

"That does bring up a good question, General," Myang stated. "*How* are you controlling the Feyori?"

"Fear, and respect. They know I value each of *their* lives. They may push and prod us, even breed with us for their own manipulative ends . . . but they are in their own way a civilized race. They can and do get along with the rest of us. Unlike the Salik," Ia added in a grim aside. She reached one-handed for the cap of the bottle, twisting it to open the mouth before tugging it out of its clip on the side of her workstation console. "I have attained player status among them, as one of them, with more than enough strength to have gained their respect."

"And the fear?" Agent Tango asked, mopping his freckled brow again as the warmth of the bridge continued to rise.

"They know now that I can kill them. Any place, any distance, any*time* I desire." Tipping her head back, but keeping her left hand steady and her eyes on the ship's course, Ia drank.

"How *do* you kill a . . . ? No," Myang corrected herself, closing her eyes and shaking her head. "No, I do *not* need to know that information. I'm not a half-breed, and I wouldn't be able to stop them from killing me, first."

"You are very wise, sir," Ia praised politely, returning the bottle to its holder. "The next group of Humans to figure out how to kill a Feyori won't come along for nearly four hundred years. I assure you, that won't turn out very well for them."

Dinyadah shifted abruptly in her seat. "Ah . . . we have a broken pipe on Deck 12, aft, near cross-corridor Papa, sir. It's just a small leak . . . looks like a seal blew its gasket. The crew are already rerouting . . . and repair teams are on their way from Engineering."

"Deck 12, aft, near Papa?" Private Hong asked from his seat at the gunnery post. "I'll bet you it was that patch we did after the fight at that K'Katta outpost back in mid-March. The Commander wasn't fully happy on the rush job we had to do."

"You'd win that bet," Dinyadah confirmed, checking the repair logs.

"There will be no actual betting," Colonel Sofrens ordered

them, speaking up from his position at the spare operations station. He flicked a glance at his superior. "That's against the rules and regs."

"Colonel, I am well aware that betting for things *other* than cold, hard credits goes on all over the Space Force," Myang told him. "I used to bet scutwork detail with my junior officers when I served as a first officer in the TUPSF Navy, on board the *Aitzaz Hasan*. Lost a few, too, before I got better at picking my bets. It is only betting for *wealth* that is frowned upon by the rules and regs. Money or other valuable goods. If we tried to outlaw all forms of betting, the whole Human race would be up in arms against us."

"Do you ever bet on anything, General Ia?" the freckled Agent asked her. "Or rather, does anyone allow you to bet? With your precognitive knowledge of the probabilities . . ."

She lifted her right hand from the edge of the console, indicating the various views of the planet visible on most of her thirteen major, medium, and minor workscreens with her upturned hand. "You're looking at it right now, meioa-o. I am betting I can save the Alliance from the Salik, the plague, the Greys, *and* the ancient enemy of the Greys three hundred years from now. Long after all of us on this ship are dead and gone."

". . . I think I'd rather clean the life-support filters," he muttered.

"So would I, meioa," Ia agreed. "*Very* much so. But that's not the hand I was dealt for this particular game."

JULY 28, 2499 T.S.
LLGKH-PWOK
T'UN SHIEN-SWISH 1271

The silver-wrapped planet centered on the *Damnation*'s viewscreens was the last of the infested colonies with an atmosphere. Technically an M-*beta*-class world since it had a cold core, Pwok sat halfway between the size of Mars and Earth, dusty and dry near the equator but wet and temperate at its poles. Plague-infested and lacking a hot mantle to draw to the surface, it required being flung out of orbit.

The Premiere and his Agents had already disembarked. He had personally overseen the destruction of the Salik home-world, as was only fitting, but his position as the chief Coun-cilor required him to get back to work. Admiral-General Myang was still on board, but it was her sleep cycle. Colonel Sofrens sat in one of the spare seats, as did Denora de Marco, but nei-ther had anything to say.

Ia sighted through the blur of tempered prisms scattered between her and the thumb-length planet, and fired the main cannon. Just for a split second, but it was enough to diffuse through the scatter-bomb clouds and strike the mass of Feyori enveloping the world. Nearly a million of them, the Meddlers had finally convened from every corner of the galaxy two days ago, to begin tossing worlds at their parent suns. Locked in the group-mind of the Gathering, they absorbed and shared the energy she tossed at them.

With an effort that felt like a subtle pressure against her inner senses at this distance, the aliens shifted the planet a little more out of orbit. Ia patiently waited a full minute and a half, then pulsed the main gun again. Each time she did this, the scattering effect diminished as the power of the laser chewed through the prisms.

Miniscule dots—Feyori who were on patrol instead of partaking in the Great Gathering—swept and swerved, herd-ing the prisms more or less back into the center to fill in the gaps that had been made by the Godstrike. A few moments after they shifted away—nearly a minute after, at light-speed relativity—several missiles streaked past the *Damnation*, shooting from stern to bow.

"And . . . the *Lauri Torni* reports they are now out of scatter-bombs, sir," Private Kirkman stated, sitting back in his seat. "That's the last of them."

Ia fired again, eking one more shot through the current mass of prisms before the missiles reached their target zone and exploded. "Acknowledged."

"Three more pushes should send Pwok spiraling into T'un Shien-swish," Wildheart stated, manning the navigation post. Her main screen was running a real-time calculation of the planet's speed and trajectory in the network of planets and their moons circling the local star. Llgkh-Pwok didn't have a moon, thankfully, but it was a heavy mass to move. "But you'd be better off making it four."

"Acknowledged." Sighting again, Ia waited for the right moment, then fired. Though she could not see the prisms, as from her end of things the scatter-bombs had not yet exploded, she knew the beam chewed through a knot of them, spreading out to saturate the planet far beyond.

However, rather than keeping the ship pointed at her original target, she shifted the nose of the *Damnation* to the right and up a little. Mental toes in the timestreams, she adjusted her aim with tiny touches from the thrusters, then tapped the button. Ten seconds later, bright red snapped out from the nose in a twentieth-of-a-second burst. Swinging the *Damnation*'s nose back to the planet, she waited while the Feyori on herding patrol gathered up the straying crystals once more.

"Ah—sir, we're being pinged. Salik vessel," Kirkman stated, sitting up once again. "An actual Salik vessel."

"Put her through."

"Her?" Aquinar murmured. The gunnery lead twisted in his seat, eyeing Ia in bemusement. A moment later, his eyes widened. "The Squid! You're telling us the Squid survived?"

"I don't know, but wherever they are, it's insystem; there's no lag on the signal," Kirkman said. "Connecting it now, sir."

The bulging eyes, broad mouth, and bared teeth of an angry Salik appeared on Ia's upper third tertiary screen. The use of it required her to tip her head back. It was subtly ironic, since the stubby eyestalks of the amphibian race had meant their own viewscreens were almost always angled overhead on their ships.

"Hhheww have been a worthhy foe, Ee-Ah. I, G'nathg'pish, am the lasssst Ssssalik alive. I demannd to be eatenn by you *persssssonnally."*

"You have been a worthy foe, G'nathg'pish," Ia replied, stumbling a little over the glottals, and the nose-whistle. "However, I'm afraid I cannot oblige." She returned her attention to her center screen, and made another subtle adjustment before tapping the main cannon button again. "I am in the middle of destroying Colonyworld Pwok."

That, she managed to pronounce correctly, since in Sallhash, it was a sort of indrawn lip-smack sound, one similar to the lip-smacking noise they made when mocking a potential sentient meal. Rumor had it that when the Salik first settled there over three centuries before, there had been a primitive sentient race on the world—the Alliance insisted on keeping advanced civilizations away from primitive ones, and the Salik had known this. They, of course, had denied it, claiming their "herd beasts" from this world had been nothing more than brute animals.

Either way, it was moot; the natives had been devoured long ago . . . and the devourers were now quite dead. All but this last one. "I have, however, honored you by being the last to die," Ia told the Squid, the hunter-female who had repeatedly chased her ship over the last few years. "I knew you would survive that last ambush, and that you would run silent for a while. I didn't bother to have anyone chase you down because I knew you would come to me."

". . . Asss all prey mussst," the female agreed. She bared her sharp teeth for a moment in a not-smile. "I demannnd you kill mmme perssonally. There isss a sssmall but habitable—"

"I'm sorry; I'm afraid I can't do that," Ia apologized, looking up once again. Her finger tapped the button, shooting the Feyori through the dwindling prism-cloud one more time. "I'm also sorry I did have to destroy your race. I wish you could've learned to get along, to be genuinely compassionate toward others, rather than deceptive. You should have treated all sentient life as though they were your own pond-brood . . . but your people did not, could not, and never would. The only thing I can give you is a salute for being a worthy foe and a swift death."

Lifting her right hand from the controls, Ia touched her fingers formally to her brow.

The Squid narrowed her pupils and opened her mouth to speak. The signal cut off abruptly.

"On target, and on time, quick and painless," Ia murmured. She lowered her arm, then bowed her head for a moment. "And may God grant me the same."

"What was that?" Denora asked. The reporter perked up her seat. "Are you expecting to die soon?"

Ia didn't answer. She gauged the timestreams, then tapped the button one last time. Again, that pulse of mass kinetic inergy washed over her, a distant pulse of intent from the Gathering wrapped around the infected world. "Wildheart, how does the trajectory look now?"

"It . . . looks good. Very good. A fifth pulse . . . would . . . *definitely* run the risk of the planet pulling a slingshot around the sun, according to the navicomp," the tech stated, running the simulation through the navicomp one more time to verify. "Confirmed, sir?"

Ia turned her attention inward, checked, and nodded. "Confirmed. Everything else has been killed by hydrobombing it to death . . . and with the Feyori standing guard over each world, no one is getting a single scrap of the plague between now and that planet being devoured by its star."

"I'll go tell the Admiral-General it's done," Colonel Sofrens offered. He unbuckled his restraints and rose, smothering a yawn. "Or as done as it's going to get."

Beside him, Denora hastily raised her own hand, her own mouth gaping. "Ohhh . . . don't do that! Don't yawn . . . I'm so ready for my bed. If this is all, I'll let the recordings cover the rest. I don't need to be an eyewitness to a mudball moving slowing toward the local sun—I'd rather make an eyewitness report on watching paint dry. It'd be faster."

"Sleep well," Ia told them, resisting the urge to yawn herself as the oddly contagious act spread to the rest of her bridge crew. Hundreds of years with all manner of advances in biomedicine, and doctors still couldn't tell a meioa why a yawn was so contagious among Humans. "Our next stop will be Battle Platform *Warcraft IX* in five days. I'll see you tomorrow, de Marco, for our wrap-up interview."

Denora fluttered her fingers as she left. Ia waited until her last two witnesses had left the bridge, then gathered her strength. Focusing her mind, she reached out to the Great Gathering. It was . . . dangerous. Their group-mind was strong. Powerful. But her weak telepathic abilities—tele*pathetic*, according to the late Miklinn—were an advantage because it didn't give the Meddlers much to grab onto and pull her in.

(*The planet is now on course for the local star. It is time to disperse. Those who were selected to guard shall remain behind; the rest of you . . . I have one more shot to give you, to pay you in the energy needed to leave. Do not use it on the*

*planet, or I will have to call you back within a year to correct
its course.*)

(*UNDERSTOOD.*)

Disengaging quickly, she shuddered in revulsion only
after she was out from under the weight of their group-mind.
It wasn't so much a single thought-word, as an entire concept
pulsed wordlessly, with thousands of undertones. The vast
majority were in full compliance with her wishes, however. In
this state, with nearly a million of them in gestalt, they were
far too powerful. But she had Time literally on her side.

If they didn't kill her now, while they could, they wouldn't
be able to kill her, ever. Individually, and in small groups of
up to a couple thousand, Ia could face them down and win
from *her* high ground, the timeplains. Like this . . . not a
chance. Great Gatherings were rare occurrences, however,
particularly as this one would result in a spate of pairs and
triads and even a few quartets splitting off together, until
baby-sized matrices were budded free, spinning into newborn
Feyori.

New players always upset the Game, but Ia had the advantage; she had instructed the gestalt-mind how to deal with
each newborn, the same as she had instructed the former
Salik players on which new territories to claim for their
pawns. As she had promised, she had increased the play between the various players, enhancing the Game in ways that
would help her allies. The Game would be very well balanced
for the next four hundred years. But five hundred years from
now—and the Feyori were a very patient, long-lived race—
the Game would start getting rather interesting for them.

After the Savior saved everybody, when it would be too
late for the Meddlers to realize they had been Meddled with.
It was a very long Rite of Simmerings, with a lot of deep-laid
plans, all generated from carefully placed butterfly wings. Ia
was very glad she would not be around to see it happening.
That was a level of irritation, fury, and respect she did not
want to have to face.

Still, they needed to be fed. Ia tapped the Godstrike button. Ten seconds later, a brief bolt shot out and impacted the
giant silvery sphere. As the energy was shared out around the
globe, the envelope shimmered, shattered, and darted off in

hundreds, thousands of directions. Most winked out—many stringing their jumps like beads, using the hyperrift created by the ones in the front to get that much farther without having to expend quite so much food.

One—two—spheres broke off from the rest. Not conjoined like clinging soap bubbles, but separate entities. Something had shifted. Ia frowned, tracking it down. When she realized what it was, she winced, sighed, and waited. Sure enough, the sphere that was Belini Baiyah zipped into her bridge, dipped briefly through an unused station to siphon off a bit of energy, and popped into her pixie form. Short-haired and blonde, petite body, a charming little skirt and a halter-vest top. No shoes, of course.

Ia seized the recordings of the bridge with her electrokinesis as the other Feyori arrived and did the same. He popped into a tall, handsome, clean-shaven fellow with distinct Asian features not too dissimilar from Ia's own. He smiled at her and held up a golden, faintly glowing orb the size of a softball. Albelar. Her father-progenitor. "A gift, Daughter Dearest. For you."

He lobbed it at her with a smile. Ia caught it with a scowl, listening as the sphere-within-a-sphere chimed on impact, the smaller ball clanging and rolling inside the larger shell. It sang, too, in the way of all crysium, charged as the biomineral was with its matter-based matrix of psychic energy. But to her, it sang of death, despair, and failure. "I would rather refuse."

Albelar's smile tightened. "*Would* is a conditional phrase, Daughter. It means something is preventing you."

She narrowed her gaze, but only because he was right. A tiny fraction of a possibility that her warnings to the Greys would not be enough. Carefully, delicately, she reshaped the outermost sphere, carefully tweaking the mix of crystalline colors until script emerged, garnet red embedded in pale gold.

DO NOT OPEN UNLESS CONTACTED BY ME DIRECTLY.
CONTAINS SALIK DEATH PLAGUE. ~IA

Her progenitor mock-pouted, watching while Ia added her trademark "wax seal stamp" of an arrow within a circle, drawing a line in from the right.

"You're no fun . . . but I knew you'd do that," he allowed.

Belini peered at the sphere, then at her fellow Feyori. "*Eww!* You crapped in your daughter's hand?"

Ia flung the doubled ball back at him. He caught it easily, making it chime again, and arched a brow at her.

"Deliver it to your progeny-son, on Sanctuary," she instructed. "Inform my brother to stick it in the Vault under the heaviest lock and key. If it is to be used, it will be used eight hundred years from now. And then leave him the hell alone. This is the *last* task I need from you. Anything else you choose to do—so long as you are smart and stay out of my way—will not have any effect either way on the outcome of my moves in the Game. Good-bye, 'Father.' I'll admit it was good to finally meet you, and I'm glad you chose to faction with me, but beyond that and this last task, our interactions are through."

With an eloquent bow, Albelar popped back into a soap bubble and darted away.

Ia eased back on the bridge recordings, allowing them to record normally now that Albelar and his package were gone. She had already left a note for the Savior to keep an eye on it, and to peer into the timestreams, borrowing Ia's abilities as she had once borrowed Jack's. It hadn't been an overly high probability that her progenitor would offer that little scrap of the plague, but it hadn't been a small chance, either.

Kirkman, at the comm, cleared his throat. "Are we done being threatened by megalomaniacal beings?"

"Awww, you're cute," Belini purred, crossing over to stand behind him and tousle his sandy brown hair. He winced.

"Back off, Belini," Ia ordered. "He's not into alien women."

"Oh, hell no," Kirkman muttered, flinching again when she tried to touch him a second time. "Definitely not!"

Pouting, the Meddler sighed and moved away. "I really should be going, too; my pawns are getting a bit unruly. And you'll need me to quell the rising riots being broadcast back home—you do know you're being blamed not only for the Salik dying, but for their going to war in the first place? There are even some scurrilous rumors that you even had a hand in *creating* the Salik race as rapaciously hungry for sentient flesh."

Ia frowned in puzzlement; she had no clue what the archaic word *scurrilous* meant, though she could guess a bit from context. Dismissing it with a shake of her head, she made sure the cover on the main gun control was securely latched. "I don't know, and I don't care. I have three days to get ready for being slapped with a summons to a military tribunal, fifteen criminal lawsuits, and over two hundred civil suits . . . none of which I can afford to take the time to attend in person."

"Huh?" Belini asked, raising her brows. She thought a moment, then nodded. "Oh, right . . . the tunnel-visioned idiocy of the shortsighted. Well, I'll leave you to it. And as your first and foremost lieutenant in the Game—whatever Kierfando or that silvery bastard who swears he's your father might say—I promise to turn the tide of Terran entertainment and its related media in your favor."

"I appreciate it. Have a last snack before you go," Ia added, gesturing at the untended console near the Human-shaped Meddler.

Belini patted her slender belly, sticking it out a little. "Ouf! No, thank you. I'm quite full. I'll just use the anchor point in our quarters."

"*My* quarters," Ia muttered. "Not yours."

With a flutter of her fingers, the pixie-shaped alien disappeared through the back door. Slumping in her seat—mindful of the hand still tucked in the attitude glove—Ia rubbed at her temple with two of her free fingers.

"Wildheart . . . got that course plotted yet?" she asked.

"Sir, yes, sir," the private confirmed. "One course, plotted and laid, for SJ 723, where we will rendezvous with the *Warcraft IX*. Ready when you are. Will you be keeping the helm, sir?"

"Actually, I'm scheduled to go have a nervous breakdown in the privacy of my quarters for a few hours, then I'll get to sleep like the dead for several more," Ia countered. "Sangwan, it's your turn . . . Sang . . . ? *Sangwan!*"

"—What? Wait, wha . . . ?" Limbs flailing, body jerking against the restraint harness, the Yeoman First Class swore under his breath, floundering a bit as he came fully awake from his nap at her shout. "*Shakk* me . . . General, yes, sir! I'm sorry, I didn't mean to fall asleep at my post, sir. *Shakking* hell . . . *seriously* sorry here, sir," he added, knuckling grit from the corners of his eyes.

"No harm done, Ching," Ia told him, sitting up so she could begin turning the *Damnation* onto the course Wildheart had passed to her main screen. "Take a few moments to wake up, get a cup of caf', and visit the head. I'll get the ship under way. A few minutes either way won't put a dent in my schedule today."

He unstrapped himself, yawning, but shook his head. "I shouldn't be depriving you of any sleep, sir. I'm sorry."

"It's not a loss of any sleep, Yeoman. It's only grief," Ia countered mildly, "and I started grieving well over twelve years ago."

He eyed her as he passed her console, on his way to the heads in the back passage. "Twelve years? No disrespect, sir . . . and I mean it, but . . . aren't you done, yet?"

"Actually, the odds are high that I'll just sit on my bed and write prophecies until I fall asleep, which is what I do every night. But I might grieve one last time. I'll let you know if anything unusual happens in my routine," she mock-promised.

He nodded and left. Silence reigned for the next minute or so, broken only by the occasional murmur of Private Zedon at the operations console, and the faint *thrum* of the ship's engines.

"Admiral-General Myang to General Ia," she finally heard in her headset.

"Ia here; go," she told the sleepy-sounding Myang.

"Is that it? Is that the last threat to the Alliance from the plague?"

"Technically, the plague won't vanish until this last planet hits its local sun on April 28, 2501, sir," Ia corrected, *"but I can see on the timestreams that the Feyori will capture and deal with all attempts to gain control of it by outside forces. Each planet and moon will have an honor guard of at least three hundred Meddlers orbiting it while it's inbound, and they all have been tied into the timestreams by me to keep track of every scrap of the plague. With that in mind as a caveat . . . yes, the Alliance is safe, sir."*

Except one last scrap, but Ia kept her mouth shut on that. If it wasn't going to be needed in eight hundred years—and that was the greatest probability—then one of her far-flung descendants would pitch the thing personally into Sanctuary's sun, to get rid of it once and for all.

"*Right, then. As per our joint Alliance leadership's operational guidelines, you are hereby directed to lift the Quarantine Extreme immediately, blah blah, legalese, I'm damned tired and it's the middle of my sleep cycle, Sofrens, so stop looking at me like that. Ia knows all the necessary paperwork . . .*" She paused for a conversation Ia couldn't hear, then added, "*He wants me to remind you to remove the Martial Law.*"

"*Please remind the colonel that I cannot do that, as we are still very much at war, sir,*" Ia returned politely.

"*She says* v'shova sh'tiel, *Lars—my phraseology, not hers—and points out we're still at war . . . With who? With the Greys! Out! Get out, and let an old soldier get some badly needed sleep.*" More silence, then Myang stated, "*Sorry about that. He's a good soldier, but he doesn't always think on several levels.*"

"*It's okay, sir,*" Ia promised. "*A lot of people have forgotten we're still at war with the Greys. I only negotiated a temporary cease-fire. The true end of the war won't be for a few months yet. Go back to sleep. I'll call you on second watch.*"

"*Ia?*" Myang asked, her voice tinged with a hint of concern. "*Get some sleep, yourself? You stay up way too long for a Human, even if you're a half-breed.*"

"*I know, sir. That's why it'll be second watch. Ia out.*" Speaking above a headset murmur, Ia addressed James Kirkman. "Get me an Alliance-wide broadcast, Private. I need to tell them the Quarantine Extreme is finally over . . . save only for the interdicted Salik systems. And get me the Alliance military leaders—other than the Terrans, I mean; don't wake up the Admiral-General again. I need to tell the others they'll need to keep the Blockade going for two more years, but this time directed to keep other people *out* of the Salik systems. Adding them to the Feyori as a matter-based defense line will help ensure the plague stays out of everyone's reach."

"Aye, sir. I'm on it," he promised.

She increased the thruster field, aiming the ship on an

FTL course. The tankers of the 1st Cordon Navy had long since parted company, and her ship didn't have quite enough fuel left after firing the Godstrike several times to expend it on the water-hogging version of hyperwarp travel, but neither did they have the time to seek out the ice fragments of the local Kuiper belt. The Salik had tried seeding those proto-comets with bits of the plague, in this and other areas, but Ia and her allies had stopped and destroyed every last one long before they had reached any system's edge.

It was a good day's fight. A sad day's fight. The last day of the last member of the Salik race, whose ship now drifted aimlessly somewhere out past the second gas giant of this system, punctured straight through the bridge by a God-sized spear of light.

CHAPTER 9

This will be our last interview in person—at least for the duration of the war, of course. I'll try to sneak in a couple more sessions after you've left the ship, but I wanted to thank you, Meioa de Marco, for being such a pleasant guest, and an excellent reporter. I know many others, Human and otherwise, wanted to be on board as well, but between your insights and your integrity, you have represented the journalism community well. Thank you . . . You're welcome, too.

Now that we've caught up with current events . . . we need to start talking about what'll happen next. Everyone else may have forgotten that the Greys came out of hiding to attempt a second war of xenobiological experimentation upon Humans as their next-nearest version of potential kin . . . but I have not. This is why, with the permission of each government's leader, I have kept the rule of Martial Law in place. The Greys—the Shredou, as they call themselves—are as far beyond our capacity in technology as we are from a primitive tribe that knows how to rub dry sticks together to make a fire. Yet somehow, we must draw the line and stop them.

My intent, as it has been all along, is to make it too psychically painful and costly for the Shredou to continue to pick upon Humans for their attempts to revive their biology with cellular infusions and breeding experiments. There is another way that will stop them—and it will end the war—but it is extremely risky. I would rather they brought everything to an end before I'm forced to use that to put a stop to their predations. I've always been interested in the path that is plotted both ethically and expediently, with the least loss of resources and lives.

... No, I cannot speak for the Shredou, as to whether or not they understand such concepts. I'm afraid I've always understood the Feyori and even the Salik viewpoints a lot more. The Greys . . . are truly alien.

~Ia

AUGUST 3, 2499 T.S.
BATTLE PLATFORM *WARCRAFT IX*
ALBEDO ICE STATION SJ 723 SYSTEM

"You may be seated," Admiral Ioseph Leonidovich directed all the members attending the tribunal. He had a slight accent from his home in the Western Russia Prefecture back on Earth, but not nearly as thick as some Terrans possessed. Nothing like the accent of one of her old Naval Academy instructors, for sure.

As the highest-ranked officer of the Special Forces Judge Advocate General's Office, Leonidovich had to preside over any tribunal involving a member of the Command Staff, save only instances of clear personal involvement in a particular case. Thankfully, Ia had never run across him in the entire span of her career. Lesser officers working in conjunction with the JAG division, but never him personally. Leonidovich was renowned to be impartial, thoughtful, blunt, and fairly even-handed in digging for the truth and dispensing appropriate justice.

He was also a skeptical soul. Tapping the workscreen buried in his bench, he read its contents, then glanced at the admiral on his right and the general on his left. ". . . There has been a motion requested by the defense for General Ia to make a preliminary statement before this tribunal hearing begins. She insists it is temporally sensitive."

"That would be highly irregular, sirs," General Somatel, prosecutor for the case, asserted. "The prosecution always presents its case first. I must lodge a protest."

Leonidovich frowned down at his screen, looked up sharply at Somatel, then eyed Ia. "That, General, is precisely the wording she used when quoting you in her request. I am inclined to give her leave to speak. Please be seated. General Ia, you may make your opening statement."

Clad in her heavy, ribbon-decked overcoat, Ia rose. She tried not to make too much noise as she did so, but a couple of the medals clinked against the edge of the table assigned to the defense team. Most of her attention was on going over the warnings of both her defense attorney, Rear Admiral Hemet Johns, and her own examinations of the timestreams. *I am not to address the prosecutor directly, no matter what he says. I am not to levy any accusations, however rightful. I am not to display any sarcasm, impatience, or arrogance . . . no matter how much I hate the fact the idiots at the other table delayed these proceedings for* lunch, *of all things.*

"Thank you, sirs," she stated. "While the Second Salik War has ended—and is the subject of this tribunal—we are still very much at war with the Greys, who are a vastly superior foe in terms of technology, armor, and armament. We are low on hydrobombs, and the only other weapon that can penetrate their ship hulls is the Godstrike cannon, which is DNA-code-locked to my hand. Those codes cannot be changed without destroying the ship, a safety feature installed by order of the Command Staff, leaving myself as the only person who can safely wield it.

"My defense counsel has advised me that, if these proceedings are arranged so that all witnesses and evidence are presented first, the sheer amount of testimony the prosecution wishes to bring to light in these proceedings will ensure that I myself will not be needed to take the stand for several weeks."

If not months, since if the defense stalls for time by

presenting everything else on my side first, then I won't be needed on the stand until next year, she thought, but kept those words silent.

"Admiral, in the light of the ongoing and very immediate threat which the Greys are against the Terran United Planets and its allies," Ia stated, keeping her gaze on the eldest of the three men seated on the bench across from her, rather than the white-haired man off to her right, "I must request that those testimonies and evidence be presented first, and for myself to be granted leave to resume combat against our remaining enemy. I understand that this will severely limit my direct responses to all allegations against me, and that it will require me to review these hearings by hyperrelay proxy until such time as I am physically required to take the stand.

"However, the Greys *are* a major threat to the safety of the Terran Empire. They have acquired the Salik anti-psi machinery and are able to block out most counterattacks by members of the PsiLeague and other associated psychic organizations. My ship, under my command and my precognitively directed control, is therefore our best current weapon. At least until such time as more hydrobombs can be created and amassed for combat, which I have been informed will take at least another two months. Do I have your permission, sirs, to continue to defend the Terran United Planets in our ongoing and very real hour of need?"

"Objection, Your Honor. The defendant's *use* of the Godstrike cannon is what is under investigation, here," the chief prosecutor, General Somatel, argued dryly. "Along with her many orders which led to the xenocidal extinction of an entire race. Admiral Leonidovich, I don't think it's appropriate for General Ia, as the defendant, to ask permission to go forth and kill even more."

"Objection, Your Honor," Admiral Johns stated, raising his hand. "This is a military tribunal, not a civilian case. Being a soldier is, unfortunately, all about defending one's home territory. Up to and including the possibility of enacting the deaths of any enemy aggressors. Which the Greys clearly still are. Furthermore, my client has given me a detailed list of every single colonist whose life will be affected by her ability, or inability, to resume combat against the enemy in a timely manner."

"And what, exactly, constitutes a 'timely manner'?" General Somatel challenged him.

"Why don't you ask the *duly recognized* precognitive in our midst?" Admiral Johns countered.

"Gentlemeioas," Admiral Leonidovich stated flatly. It quelled their budding argument. "We will have the rule of law in this courtroom." They subsided. He turned his attention back to Ia. "The prosecution raises a good point. General Ia, what constitutes a 'timely manner' in this instance?"

"Admiral, sir, I would need to have your judgment on my request rendered within the next eight minutes forty-six seconds Terran Standard, in order to get myself and my ship to Parker's World in order to defend it and its colonists from the predations of the Greys," Ia told him. "Arriving on time will prevent the translocated kidnapping of 652 colonists. Failure to arrive on time will end with the Judge Advocate General's office being sued for deliberate and malicious negligence to properly defend a Joint Colonyworld in the face of forewarned enemy aggressions, which my statement in this court qualifies as. This ability to bring suit falls under the established precedent of Johns and Mishka versus the United Nations."

"General Ia, are you threatening to *sue* the JAG office if you're not allowed to go haring off to battle?" Somatel challenged her.

This, she had to answer directly. Turning, she looked at the white-haired military lawyer. "Sir, no, sir. *That* charge would be filed by the government of Parker's World as a violation of the Terran Space Force's responsibility to respond to a fully identified and known-in-advance threat to their colonial safety. Article III, Section K, clauses 3–5, and in particular clause 8, paragraph 2, subparagraph d, which clearly states the Terran United Planets Space Force is required to respond to all precognitively known-in-advance threats as issued by duly recognized precognitives. Such as myself. The main charge levied by the government of Parker's World would be Fatality Four: Dereliction of Duty."

"Something which you would have told them to do in advance," Somatel argued.

Ia returned her attention to Leonidovich. "Admiral, Generals, the Colonial Charter for Parker's Paradise was filed with the Alliance in early April of 2417 and ratified after it was formally settled on June 14 of that same year. I was not born until 2472. My only involvement in the matter, sirs, would be whether or not I and my ship show up. *That* decision rests entirely in your hands, sirs.

"Before you make up your mind, however, I would respectfully remind the court that any decision in this particular matter comes with consequences: Refuse to let me go, and hundreds, even thousands of civilians will be kidnapped for alien experimentation, which will include their torture and eventual deaths. Grant me leave to go, and many sentients will die, both allies and enemies, in the coming conflicts—no matter how hard I may strive to reduce the number of casualties involved, there *will* be injuries and deaths," she stressed. "Either way the court chooses, like every other soldier, I will have to abide with, or suffer, whatever consequences come from that decision."

Leonidovich studied her, his brow furrowed in a thoughtful frown. Leaning over, he consulted with the general on his right, both men hiding their mouths behind their hands, their voices pitched too low to easily overhear. The admiral then leaned over and consulted with the other four-star general. The first general checked his arm unit, gesturing at it, which stirred a bit more conversation. The admiral even scooted his chair back so that all three could lean in close for a direct discussion. Faint ripples of static in the air above the front edge of the judicial bench suggested they had raised a force field to help muffle their debate.

Finally, Leonidovich leaned his arms on his bench, dropped the field, and studied Ia.

"The question has been raised, General Ia, as to whether or not you already know the outcome of this tribunal. Do you?" he asked her. "Is that why you're trying to avoid being here? To avoid being bored?"

"Sirs, I deal in percentages. There are eight possible outcomes to this tribunal which are greater than one percent in their probability, and fifty-two possible outcomes that are less than one percent, most being less than one-*tenth* of one percent. However small those minor possibilities are, I cannot rule them out as an outcome. I was shot in the shoulder with a handheld laser cannon on a less than three percent probability, which most people would consider to be a highly unlikely outcome. I was also elevated to the rank of a four-star General, never mind that I am now a five-star, on a less than one-hundred-*thousandth* of a percent, when the largest percentile, forty-seven percent, was that I should have been elevated only to the rank of Rear Admiral.

"As for being bored . . . I actually would prefer to be here because that means nobody would be attacking our colonies. But they are, and that means my preferences must take second place to my sense of duty. I will admit I have sat through this tribunal around eight or nine times in the timestreams, examining those eight largest percentiles," Ia added candidly. "This has left me very familiar with the majority of all evidence the prosecution will be presenting against me . . . but again, the outcome is never one hundred percent certain, until it has actually come to pass. I do take this tribunal seriously, but I also take the ongoing threat to Terran civilians equally seriously, sirs."

The general on the admiral's right tapped his arm unit. Leonidovich glanced at his fellow judge, and sighed. "Very well. With the understanding that you *will* review all hyperrelay-transmitted recordings of these tribunal proceedings in a timely manner, that you will keep this court apprised of every bit of free time you may have available to return to testify and answer any and all questions in person, and with the understanding that any and all actions you undertake in the coming days will *also* be considered as eligible for submission by both the prosecution and the defense in this ongoing case . . . you are dismissed to return to combat at this time."

"Objection, Your Honor!" Somatel called out even as Ia raised her hand to her brow in salute.

"Overruled," the general with the arm unit stated. "There are ample precedents already set in prior cases for the defendant's not being present for the majority of their tribunals. The meioa-e is not being tried *in absentia* in the sense that she isn't going to attend or even hear about these proceedings at all. There is nothing illegal in her request."

"General Ia, you are indeed dismissed," Admiral Leoni-dovich repeated. He lifted his hand to his brow, returning Ia's salute.

Formally dismissed, Ia turned and stooped over the shoulder of the man she and Sadneczek had selected to be her JAG-trained defense attorney. Rear Admiral Hemet Johns was not related to the famous attorney John Johns, who had defended Giorgi Mishka centuries before . . . but his name would still draw attention to the parallels in the two cases, a subtle reminder that everything Ia did was bound under the statute governing that famous case. She squeezed Johns' shoulder as she murmured in his ear, "Try not to be bored over the next several weeks, will you?"

"I *live* for courtroom minutiae," Johns muttered back. "Try not to get killed between now and when I'll need you on the witness stand. I'll do whatever I can to put it off to give you more time to win the war, but eventually I *will* need you here."

"Trust me, I would *love* to be free, so I could be seated here for the whole damned thing. I'll let you all know when and where I can return." Squeezing his shoulder, she edged out from behind the table and headed for the side door.

She was running late, and had known she would be running late from the moment the prosecution had decided to choose a prolonged, early lunch over justice. Forewarned, Ia had already sent the rest of her crew back to their ship, permitting no witnesses to delay her departure from the courtroom. Reshaping the thin bracer on her right arm, she crouched by the first power outlet she spotted in the hall outside the court chamber and shoved a set of golden translucent prongs into the sockets.

Five electrokinetically charged heartbeats later, she zipped as a silvery soap bubble through the bulkheads and layers of the Battle Platform, arrowing up and out, and into the hull of her ship. Staggering a little as she regained Human shape on the bridge, she braced herself on the edge of the piloting station and nodded to Yeoman Huey. "Huey, since I know everyone is back on board, you have leave to depart. Get us under way."

"Aye, sir," the ex-Scadian agreed, and nodded at Mysuri to

start the comm procedures for decoupling from the Battle Platform. "Will you be wanting the helm, sir?"

"No, I have several more prophecies to write. I'd rather have done some of them while sitting around, kicking my heels and waiting on *lunch*," she half growled, still irritated at the prosecution, "but that would have been seen as disrespectful—did I ever tell you how much I hate politics, Patricia?"

"Did you ever resew those buttons back onto your coat, sir?" she returned dryly.

"Indeed I did," Ia admitted. "Telekinetically while composing prophecies, but I did."

"Then I know how much you hate politics, sir," Huey said.

". . . *Warcraft IX* says we are clear to depart," Private Mysuri informed both of them.

"Then I'm getting the ship under way, sir," Huey confirmed.

Nodding, Ia crossed through the back corridor and the clerk's office to her own . . . and stopped at the sight of the dish clipped onto her desk. Carefully crafted in a swirling helix spiral of grape purple, topado blue, and lime green, the gelatin dessert awaited her. Not five minutes before—while she was still back in the courtroom, listening to Somatel's accusations—her younger self had confronted a certain snowflake-faced man from one of the possible futures. Back then, she hadn't even considered that today was the day he had chosen to gift her with the tart-sweet colloidal dish.

The day her trial began.

Ia moved to her chair and settled herself in it, eyeing the dessert in its clear plexi cup. A scrap of white proved a note had been slipped under the base, back when he had placed it. She hadn't noticed at the time, but there it was, a message from the Redeemer . . . one possible version of the Redeemer. Easing it free, she unfolded the sheet and read the neat script.

"Something sweet, to get your mind off your many troubles."

Her vision blurred. Ia knew why, even though she hadn't planned on doing this now. Not now. It was such a caring, compassionate gesture . . . from a man whose young life she would ruin, whose heart she would break . . . on a day when she would have given anything to have been able to stay behind and be *bored* in a courtroom full of accusations and presentations that would paint her over and over as a murderer.

Instead, she had to head off to face an implacable, technologically accelerated enemy over the next few months. Some of whom would be armed with a weapon that scared her witless if she couldn't manage to outpilot her ship and crew around that lethal future beam.

Ia didn't have time for dessert or despair, and she wouldn't have time. Giving in only meant that she would have to stint herself yet again on an hour or two of sleep just to catch up, exhausting herself further in the relentless ticking of the seconds slipping past, one by one, ten by ten . . .

She had work to do. She *had* work to . . . She bowed her head and let her tears fall onto the desktop and her latest parfait, unable to get her mind off all her many troubles for a few moments more.

AUGUST 29, 2499 T.S.
DLC 718 TORPETTI'S SYSTEM

The waiting was the worst part. Not the first fight, nor the second, nor even the fifth. The Greys were attacking more than one system at a time, but between the Feyori and their crysium psi-enhancement spheres, some of the psychics who lived within each system, the various other psis brought in on board various Alliance ships to help out, and Ia's own ship, which darted from battle to battle to cover the spots that were thin on resources, the Greys were being kept at bay.

But the waiting for that damned gun to be fired was the worst of it. Even-odds possibilities meant they could use it at any time, in any of these confrontations. That required constant vigilance, and constant vigilance was exhausting. The only good news was that it had a very short range, even in space. Maneuvering her ship, not just moving it, increased the odds that they wouldn't fire, for even Shredou translocation technology required relatively empty space to teleport a ship. If the *Damnation* was fishtailing and changing course abruptly—

She had half a second of warning, and slapped the FTL panels open down the port side of the ship. That greased and shot the *Damnation* to the left. A Grey ship appeared on the starboard, rapidly receding. She quickly cut off the field— and another appeared to the port. Eight more portaled in, matching the *Damnation*'s speed and trajectory. They swerved together, boxing her in with a ring formation that pressed dangerously close.

That also brought in the anti-psi devices, clamping around her mind like a headache-sized vise. Ia didn't have many options; she *could* accelerate faster than a Shredou vessel, at max speed. That would put her up to half Cee, which was fast enough to safely use OTL . . . but opening a hyperrift *now* was far, far too dangerous.

"All hands, impact!" she snapped, activating her headset electrokinetically; her fingers were too busy cutting speed abruptly. Very abruptly—bodies jolted with grunts into their harnesses, heads snapping forward. Not fast enough; the Grey ships shot forward relative to the *Damnation*, unable to react fast enough . . . but one of the ships managed to fire, and tagged near the bow.

Ba-HOOM!

The force of the explosion skewed the ship, spinning it downward. Warned precognitively, Ia cut all forward thrust and focused on gently—*gently*—correcting the force of that spin. Telltales at the operations console were blinking bright yellows and even a couple reds. Corporal Crow looked at all the stress indicators and whipped his head around to stare at Ia. "What the hell was *that*? What hit us? I can't even see a hole!"

"Nothing hit us! By Buddha's breath, I swear, *nothing hit us!*" Ateah protested, flinging up her hands at the gunnery seat, her eyes locked on her screens.

"Quiet!" Ia snapped, finally getting their torque under control. Facing backwards. "That was a ranging shot. The next one will kill us."

Shocked silence met her words. Again, the Grey ships popped out of their previous location and popped into formation around her ship. In a split second of intuition, Ia realized how they knew what she was doing. She held herself still, seized the controls electrokinetically, and activated the interior safety fields a split second before shifting to FTL. Forward, not backward.

The safety field only fully covered the inner cabins and the fuel tanks; the rest of the ship groaned in partially protected protest in the fractional gap before the faster-than-light field fully enveloped the ship, greasing the palm of physics. More yellow lit up across Crow's screens, but wrapped in FTL's inertia-canceling field, they darted forward, away from the rapidly retreating Grey ships. *Now* she opened an OTL rift, retreating from the fight by about eight light-minutes. A careful curve, a second tunnel, and she shifted them somewhat to port by another two minutes, along the curve and slightly above the system's plane.

Spat out the other side of the second tunnel, Ia switched back to insystem thrusters. Mind racing, she tried to think of how to counter their new tactics.

". . . Sir?" Private York asked her. "*Are* we going to die?"

"Not on my watch," she denied grimly, still thinking. The problem was, she could only do so many things at once. She needed her psis free to do more than just tend their normal duties—like her, they had grown used to the pains of the machines used by the Saliks, and could work normal, nonpsychic tasks while the things were active, but the emanations had to be shut off before their extrasensory abilities could be put fully to work. The anti-psi machines would have to be destroyed.

"What *was* that?" Crow asked her, checking his screens. "The ship's stressed from bow to stern, as if someone tried to bend us like a bow, but the sensors say we only lost a chunk of the hull half the size of a credit chit!"

"That, Corporal—for lack of a better name for it—is the entropy gun," Ia told her bridge crew. "The Greys have figured out a way to dissolve nuclear forces, introducing chaos into whatever it strikes—in other words, disorder on a level that renders protons, neutrons, electrons, even quarks, gluons, and so forth equal to each other. Explosive power. It has no visible component, so there's no telling when it's being fired; we can only suffer when it hits.

"Their technology is so advanced, they can blink their ships out of range before we've more than begun exploding from the sheer fission of it."

Yes . . . the anti-psi machines are the key to getting out of this. I've been focusing too much on physical attacks and counters. She double-checked the timestreams. She hit the switch for the interior comms.

"All psis, report to the boardroom double-time! Douglas, get to the bridge." Shutting it off, she lifted her chin at her current operations tech, who was still in his seat. "Crow, as soon as Douglas gets up here, race down and get everyone ready to focus on KI-streaming straight into the Greys' minds. Link with your mate and lead the gestalt. I'm going to take out their anti-psi field, but I *won't* be able to help you smack their arrogant brains. I'll be too busy keeping us alive for most of the fight."

He looked up at his screens and slowly shook his head. "I don't think we can withstand a prolonged fight like that last one, sir. Not if we get spun again, or have to do vector maneuvers—in fact, I think the only thing that kept us from snapping in half is whatever material makes up the God-strike's core, and I don't know its tensile strength."

Ia frowned and checked in the timestreams. He was right; while there was no such thing as wind resistance or a strong enough pull of gravity in the depths of insystem space, far from the immediacy of an actual planet, spinning the ship had put centripetal strain on the frame. More than she had realized, and all from a tiny fission explosion. Even if they weren't tagged again, just maneuvering would worsen the effects of shear-force strain on the frame of her ship.

They couldn't retreat, however. Torpetti's System had an ice-processing station and two protocolonies, both oversized research-dome complexes. One lay on an L-Class planet with an atmosphere similar to Mars', but with more oxygen, and the other had been established on its barren, airless, geosynchronously locked moon. Whatever they were researching was unimportant; what mattered was the fact they were sitting ducks for the Greys to swoop in and teleport out as many of their own research subjects as they wanted.

The only grace of God in this moment is that they're too

*busy popping around the system, trying to quarter it looking
for my ship. They know they have to destroy us to keep us
from stopping them. No surrender, no retreat. Shakk, I'm
going to have to mess up interstellar travel for months ...
and then figure out how to fix my ship without sticking it in
dry dock for several months so the techs can take it apart and
put it back together again ...*

She hit her intercom button again. *"All hands, stand down
and return to stations."*

Scrubbing her face with her free hand, she checked the
timestreams. The Greys were still popping in and out in
search patterns, trying to check the lightwave signatures for
signs of her ship. Since they were still traveling at half Cee,
she sparked another hyperrift and wrapped the ship in faster-
than-light—straight OTL would have shaken the ship too
much. Skipping forward by three more light-minutes along
the middle reaches bought them a few more minutes of time.

"Prudhomme," she stated after drawing in a deep, bracing
breath. Her hands shifted the ship, dropping speed. Though it
would make them a sitting target, the *Damnation* had to be
relatively still to make it a lot easier for her to line up her
shots in the timestreams. "I am going to fire the Godstrike
several times. I want you tracking every single beam that
passes through this system and into interstitial space, and I
want that data packaged up for York to send to System Control to be rebroadcast to all adjacent systems. We have an
overshoot of nearly a full light-year with the Godstrike Mark
II. I don't want any ships running into any of those beams."

"Aye, sir," Prudhomme agreed, subdued.

"Are you sure we're not going to die today, sir?" York
asked, glancing briefly at her. Ia frowned, and the comm tech
shrugged. "I wouldn't be so concerned if we could see them
coming, but that damned teleport tech of theirs is like being
blind in one eye—we know they're out there, but we have no
clue how close or far away."

Blind in one eye ... of course! "York, if you weren't married to Clairmont, I'd kiss you."

He craned his neck again, this time his expression baffled
instead of worried. "Ahh ..."

"Crow, inform Harper that I'm going to have the Feyori fix

the damned ship," she ordered. At his own uncertain look, she explained. "The main cannon is fine, but we don't have time to take the ship apart and replace all the systemically stressed structures. So I'm going to make the Meddlers do it for us. If I can fix my own eye, and they can change one of our crew members into Private Joseph N'Keth, they can fix a damned ship.

"I don't want to have to disrupt interstellar shipping lanes for months to come, but better a minor disruption or nine than to have us die before the Greys are stopped. How much fuel have we got?"

"Over seventy-five percent, sir," Crow reported. "I'm trusting you when you say the main cannon's fine. I don't want to know what would happen to all that power if there's a microfracture somewhere in its path. I certainly don't want to die."

The others nodded as well, echoing the sentiment. Ia tightened her jaw. Their agreement only solidified a decision she had made long ago. Pushing open the upper lid, she scanned her palm, opened the inner one, and sunk her mind into the timestreams. Left hand twitching, turning the ship in slow, easy movements, she lined up her first shot. Fired. Lined up the second. Fired. Lined up the third, fourth, and fifth. The rest required swapping ends.

Carefully, she did so. Fired a sixth time. Since the Greys were still looking for her, that was a solid probability as to where their ships would relocate next after each scan-and-hop. It wasn't a case of will-they-won't-they-fire. Holding off on firing at the last four ships, she opened her eyes. "York, ping me the Greys."

"Ah . . . yes, sir," he agreed. "They are hot to answer; we have pingback."

The moment the black-eyed, gray-skinned, bald alien appeared on the screen, Ia spoke. "I warned you not to use that weapon. You used it. I will not tolerate its use. If you keep using it, you will cause a terrible hole in the universe. If you keep attacking Humans and the other Alliance members, I will destroy you. If you attack me, I will destroy you."

"You are nothing. You are tiny life-form," the alien retorted, uncurling her or his longish fingers. "You are stain on surface."

"Tell that to your *other* ships. I always know *where* they appear. I always know *when* they will appear. I am Death," she asserted, knowing that in that moment, two of her shots were tagging their targets. "Understand this, Shredou: *I do not need you to live.* Your lives are immaterial. Your deaths are immaterial. I will save this galaxy from the Zida"ya with or without you. I let you live as a *kindness.* As a form of courtesy. But I do not *need* you to live.

"Now, get out of Terran space," she ordered, repeating herself one more time to drive her point home. "*I do not need you to live.* So you will leave now. Before I *end* this courtesy."

Two more beams slammed into the alien ships in the distance as she spoke; Ia could see it in the timestreams. They were closing in on her position, having caught lightwave readings as they translocated to within light-seconds of her position . . . and another shot destroyed the fifth ship. The sixth abruptly changed course, translocating straight out of the system, so that the Godstrike shot that would have intercepted it kept going without interruption.

The Grey on the screen vanished, cutting the communication link. York eyed his own screen, then glanced warily at her. ". . . Did we win, sir?"

"This time. And . . . we've put off a couple of fights between now and the next engagement," she added, checking the streams. The remaining four ships had vanished when the link had been dropped, removing themselves from the local system. As she peered into the waters in the back of her mind, the damaged ships vanished, too; the Greys were not going to leave any scraps of their technology behind for the jumped-up insects to study. They would be back, though. "But we did not scare off all of them, and we'll need to hurry after we get refueled so we can get into position to start shooting up the skies in other places."

"Speaking of which, sir," Prudhomme announced, her gaze still on her calculations, "the navicomp's done calculating the worst-case path of those shots. If the Godstrike didn't hit anything, then we know exactly how far into the future it'll affect the shipping lanes. If you'll give me the stats on how much each connecting shot was absorbed, I can crunch those numbers for you."

"Don't bother. Just transmit the full-strength data. Rerouting ships slightly won't affect the timestreams by that much, in most cases. O'Keefe, take the helm, and take us in to the ice station to top up the tanks," Ia ordered. "Nice and easy. I'm going to trance and look for engineering-minded Feyori who know how to 'rewrite' flawed starship structures."

"Helm to my control in twenty, sir," O'Keefe agreed, getting herself ready. "Here we go . . . nice and easy, so we don't stress anything else . . . because I can't afford to have the ship fall apart on my watch."

"None of us can, Yeoman," Ia agreed grimly. "Not your watch, and not mine."

SEPTEMBER 17, 2499 T.S.
SIC TRANSIT

Never-ending battle, never-ending battle . . . I know exactly how Helstead felt, the day Sung shot the wrong ship. Her comm unit chimed. Ia saved her current round of prophecies and activated the link. "Good evening, Admiral-General. You're lucky I knew this call was coming, and slowed to FTL speeds."

The timing-lag stamp in the lower-right corner showed there was a two-second delay at each end. Four seconds round-trip. Myang eyed her a few seconds, nodded as she listened, and spoke. "I'm glad you did, because even if you know what's coming, it all still has to go through official channels. Admiral Ioseph Leonidovich has called off the tribunal . . . and strongly suggested you cancel the Martial Law over all but the last of the plagued systems. We'll need the Blockade to continue to protect those inbound planetary bodies your soap-bubble buddies sent on their merry way.

"And as you probably *also* know, the civil suits are still pending," the older woman warned her. "That defense lawyer of yours is rather sharp; I've looked over some of the proceedings and have been admiring his clear-cut counterpoints."

"Feel free to borrow Admiral Johns when this is all over, sir," Ia offered lightly. "The civil suits can start whenever they're ready. However, I'm still very much needed out here, so they'll just have to start without me. I've instructed the rear admiral to inform the next court of the reasons behind my continuing absence. As for the Martial Law, now that I don't have to worry about being dragged into a courtroom anytime soon, go ahead and inform the Premiere and the other leaders to lift it, save for in those interdicted systems. I'm sending the confirmation orders on a subchannel now, sir."

"I'm so glad you're usually so well prepared. Speaking of being needed somewhere, the TUP Council wants to commend your entire crew in a special ceremony," Myang told her. "They want it to take place on Earth, at the capital on Kaho'olawe. I'm supposed to order you to show up on October 30."

"Like hell we will, sir," Ia retorted. "We can't take the time off for a trip all the way back to Earth. But I can arrange for a nine-hour layover at Battle Platform *Osceola* on October 29. It'll be in System Gliese 505 at that point for reprovisioning from the farms and mines on Haskin's World."

"I figured you wouldn't want to come in," the Admiral-General said dryly. She leveled Ia a stern look. "We're going to have to have a little talk about your devotion to combat duty. After the war ends, of course . . . but you haven't said *when* the war ends. Not yet. I'd like to know. Are you *ever* going to tell me?"

"The first of November," Ia answered promptly.

Four seconds later, she watched the head of the Terran military choke on her own spit. Spyder might have chosen to amuse her by playing hard-and-fast with military rules and orders, but this was her own choice moment of levity; it wasn't every day that the most powerful, unflappable person in the whole Terran military was so visibly flapped by fate. Ia smiled only briefly, though, and schooled her expression into a sober one.

". . . That is, *if* everything goes right. If not, it'll take several weeks to several months more to set up another round of circumstances that are just right to force the Greys into surrendering and standing down . . . so I'd appreciate it if you kept that date to yourself. I'd rather not promise openly when this war ends, only to have the probabilities roll the wrong percentile on the dice and disappoint everyone."

Myang cleared her throat. "So. November 1. Where will it take place, if and when you pull it off?"

"I'm sorry, sir, but I can't tell you that. I can't tell you any of the details because much like the Salik plague, I don't dare let any outside influences screw up this play. All I can say is, it's a matter of very delicate timing," Ia stated. Honest words, if only a small fraction of the truth. She had spent every single day since that fateful morning at the age of fifteen planning for the end of the Second Grey War. "There's also a percentage chance that some of my crew may die in the attempt, even with my best efforts . . . so I'd rather not put off the commendation ceremony. It's better to pin a medal on a live hero's chest than to send it home in a box to their next of kin."

"True," Myang allowed. She studied Ia a long moment, then sighed. "You know, you *are* a major pain in my asteroid. A loose cannon I cannot control . . . though I have tried. Either you are the luckiest woman alive, or the smartest who will ever live, and I cannot help but wonder if I should envy you for either one of that."

Ia wrinkled her nose. "I'm not lucky, and I'm not the smartest, sir. I've been *cheating* my way through life from day one. My only defense is that I recognized I was *able* to cheat and decided I'd do my best to cheat in a way that benefited the greatest number of lives, not just my own—in fact, if you haven't noticed from my latest mission reports, I don't even dare get *close* to the Greys in the latest confrontations. Whatever that entropic fission ray-gun-thing they have is, I have to sniper them with the Godstrike from several lightminutes away, or risk losing everything, because if they get close enough to scan my ship, then they know exactly what moves my hands make.

"That's how they nearly caught me the first time with that ray-thing, analyzing my own movements to predict my ship's movements. It's scary to think the Greys can penetrate ceristeel with their scanners so easily, but there it is. So yeah, I'm not lucky, and I'm not smart," she repeated. "I'm just cheating my way as best I can, to help keep everyone else alive."

Myang nodded. "Well, for your sense of conscience and your sense of duty, I salute you, soldier. And you're smarter than you think. I'm sure you've foreseen this, too, but I'm going to make it very clear to you right here and now: When this Second Grey War is over—however long it takes—I expect you to be reassigned to my office—*office*, not a starship—to help the Space Force clean up all the postwar messes that are left. And you'll have to pick a training camp or an academy, or maybe even a flight school that you'll want to teach at for a year.

"While I do still have a few years left in me to give to the Service, I am finally getting too old for this *shakk*," the Admiral-General stated, "and I am picking you to be my successor. I don't care what precognitive *shakk-torr* you think makes you qualified for this job, you will jump through the rules hoops and climb over the regulation hurdles to do it all by the book. Is that clear?"

"Crystal clear, sir," Ia replied. "And for the record, I've given some thought to creating a system of boot camps for psychics, so they can learn to focus and use their abilities midcombat, rather than wrapping them up in space insulation and hull plating fifty meters deep."

"Well, your credit is damned high in the Command Staff and the Council alike, even if the civilian idiots are trying to revile you for a mass murderer in the press. And if we can train more psis to be as effective as you . . ."

"Not everyone will be able to master using their abilities in the midst of a fight, sir," Ia cautioned her. "But it is a necessary skill I would like to see trained . . . and it's one of the few areas where I did *not* cheat. I had to learn how to do it from the ground up and managed to invent and learn most of it before I joined up. The rest was just practice, practice, practice."

"I'll start prodding the budget committees into figuring out how to apportion some facilities. Once the last of those plague planets hit their stars, we won't need the Blockade funds anymore. It'll be a smaller military, and I don't know how the civilian sector is going to employ all those dismissed soldiers, but it will be a huge fiscal relief not to have to support a two-hundred-year war."

"Amen to that, sir. I couldn't agree more. I'll leave you to set up the commendation ceremony on Battle Platform *Osceola* on the twenty-ninth. If you'll excuse me, I need to go tell my bridge crew to step it back up to hyperwarp speed to go shoot down a few more enemy ships," Ia said.

"Are you ever going to tell us how you're managing near-OTL speeds?" Myang asked.

Ia shook her head. "You'll figure it out in about two hundred years. Or rather, our descendants will. Ia out." Touching the control that ended the call, she hung her head for a moment. *One month, twelve days, three hours . . . and one month, fifteen days, seven hours to go. Then the damned war will be over.* Scrubbing at her tired, stinging eyes, she activated the comm. *"General Ia to Yeoman Huey, resume hyperwarp transit when ready."*

"Aye, sir. Huey out."

OCTOBER 15, 2499 T.S.
SIC TRANSIT

Ia stared one last time at the list on the datapad in her hand and pinched the bridge of her nose. This was not going to be pleasant. Shifting her hand to the intercom button between her personal office and the Company office, she said, *"Ia to Sadneczek, please come into my office."*

It wasn't exactly common for her to call him in to meet her when she could just get up, walk through the door, and speak to her Company clerk in person. But this was not a conversation she wanted shared with the other clerks. It took him a full minute to get into her office, but then she hadn't specified time was of the essence, and the aging master sergeant was a methodical, tidy man.

When he entered, Ia realized that his salt-and-pepper hair had turned completely white at some point in the past few years. She searched his face for other signs of change, noting the heavy five o'clock shadow had also turned white on his jaw. Deep lines etched his face, many of them worry lines along his nose and his brow where he had frowned a lot . . . but there were also wrinkles at the corners of his eyes and his lips from where he had also smiled.

He stood tall and proud in his plain gray slacks and button

shirt, body still strong despite all the signs of age. She suspected some of that was helped by the fact the ship now ran at 1.51Gs Standard since they didn't need to be quite as physical-combat-ready as before. *He'll be retiring in two, maybe three more years,* she thought. *Thank God he'll be able to.*

"You wanted t' see me, sir?" Grizzle asked her.

Ia held out the datapad in her left hand. "This is a list of various transfer forms, honorable-discharge papers, and related civilian-integration appointments. I want you to fill these out personally; don't share the work with the other clerks, and don't talk about them. I don't want the crew to waste their time speculating. To that end, you will transmit and file them with the *Osceola*'s personnel department the moment we return from the commendation ceremony on the twenty-ninth. Got that?"

He gave her a wary look but accepted the datapad from her. "I got 't, sir. Don't understand, but that never . . ." His gaze dropped to the pad, and his white-tufted brows pinched together in a frown. His thumb scrolled through the list. Head snapping up, he scowled at her, lifting the pad. "This is *horseshit*!"

Yep, not a pleasant conversation. Ia held her ground, her expression sober and firm. "These are your orders, Sergeant. You will carry them out to the letter. Is that clear?"

He drew in a breath to protest.

"You will not disobey my orders, Sergeant," she warned him. "This is what I want done. You will comply, or I will lie to the Company about why you're taking a nap in the brig."

Grizzle glared at her but growled, "Still a load a' *horseshit*. Sir."

Turning on his heel, he strode out of her office, still scowling at the datapad. Tense, Ia checked the timestreams and cursed under her breath. The tangle of possible reactions had turned into a gray spot, one that covered the next few days. The only good thing was that most every single path leading *out* of that undecided blankness had Henry Sadneczek dutifully—if begrudgingly—filling out every single form on that list. Neatly, properly, and fully.

It would be done, and she would be able to attend the commendation ceremony without any problems over it. That was all that mattered.

OCTOBER 17, 2499 T.S.
INTERSTITIAL SPACE

Something was wrong. Something was dreadfully wrong. Clawing her way out of badly needed sleep, Ia strained all six of her senses in an attempt to figure out what had gone wrong.

Her bedsheets were clean, warm wherever her body had rested, cool where it had not. The cabin was remarkably quiet, the only noises the faint hush of air coming through the ventilation duct, and the sound of her own breath. It was dark, save for the faint green emergency lighting strips on the floor and the red numerals on her bedside chronometer. There were no miscellaneous smells—her mouth had that early morning *bleh* to it, but otherwise taste wasn't a matter for concern—and her precogni—

Eyes snapping wide, she stared at the chrono. There were no engine sounds. It was the middle of her allotted sleep cycle, and there *were no engines.* No *thrum* from the FTL panel, no *thrum* and faint rumble from hyperwarp. Alarmed, she tried to look into the timestreams, but everything was a thick fog, tainted with an odd bitterness. Ia strained her mind to the bridge, to see what the operations screens said . . . and froze breathless in shock.

No one was on the bridge.

Her mind swept over the ship, trying to find someone, *anyone*, wondering if this was some sort of horrific, realistic nightmare . . .

The comm chimed. *"Commander Harper to General Ia."*

She jumped at the noise, twitching under the covers as her heart pounded. Batting the sheet and blanket out of her way, she slapped the comm button under the chronometer. *"Ia here! Why the hell is the ship stopped, and why is* no one *on that bridge?"*

"General, please dress and come to the boardroom, sir. Harper out."

Of all the—!

Furious, she battled her way out of the bed and grabbed for the first set of clothes that came to hand. Then changed her mind and tossed the camouflage Grays back into their drawers unused. If Harper was in the boardroom, if *everyone* was in the boardroom, she was going to dress to *remind* them who she was! Only the habit of nearly ten years made her remember to press the button that would web the bed for safety's sake, caging the rumpled fabrics against any abrupt vector or velocity changes.

Clad in the armor of her Dress Blacks—her short coat, the one with the bare minimum of glittery—she debated adding her cap to her head, then dismissed it. She didn't need to be *that* formal when facing down this . . . this *insurrection* in her crew. Stalking out of her quarters, she headed for the boardroom, located down on Deck 19, directly beneath the— *empty*—bridge, on the other side of the Godstrike's core.

It was a longer trip to access the side door to the platform, but she was not going to enter like an enlisted soldier. This was her ship, her boardroom, her crew . . . who were all gathered, she saw, the moment she strode onto the officer's stage. Every single seat was filled, in the sense that all 160 crew members were on hand. Over half of them were standing and talking with each other, some arguing, some glowering, most of them visibly upset to some degree.

They also fell silent the moment she came into view. One and all, they turned to face her, wearing near-identical scowls. Ia did not let herself falter. She stopped only when she reached her first officer, facing him with a glare of her own. Meyun Harper. The one man whose moves and choices—even now!— she still couldn't predict more than a quarter of the time.

"What the *hell* is going on here, Commander?" she demanded.

"Is the ship in danger?" he asked her bluntly.

". . . What?" It was not the reply she had expected, though a corner of her mind was grateful he *had* considered that stopping in the middle of nowhere, even in the vastness of space, could not guarantee their safety. "No, it's not, but we *should* be under way. This ship is to be manned at all times, save by my direct order."

"What, like *these* orders?" he demanded, snatching a datapad out from under the clip edge of the table. Harper smacked it into her chest, forcing her to take it or let it drop. "And don't tell me we're falling behind schedule. We were traveling FTL, so we can easily make up the fuel cost at Battle Platform *Mosin*. In fact, I've already put in an order for extra fuel to be shipped out to meet us. So what the *hell* is going on with *those orders*?"

Ia glanced at the screen and the familiar list. She stepped to the side just far enough to glare at her Company clerk. "I ordered you to keep your mouth shut, *Sergeant*."

"I did," he replied, lifting his chin defiantly. "I didn't say a word. I jes' *showed* 'im what was on that pad."

Sadneczek had showed . . . Harper. The one move which he, a canny noncom officer of far too many years, *knew* Ia would not be able to predict. The whole crew knew she couldn't always predict Harper's moves, and her Company clerk had chosen to use that knowledge against her.

Closing her eyes for a brief, headache-filled moment, Ia opened them, and asked, *"Why?"*

"S'not right," Grizzle told her, leveling a hard look at his CO. "After all these years, you know we'd choose t' follow you int' Hell, sir. But *those* orders ain't givin' us a right ta *choose*!"

A glance up at the men and women in the tiers showed that, by their expressions, they knew very well what was on the tablet in her hand. This was not good. Not good at all.

"That's because they're *not* orders to follow me into Hell!" she asserted, returning her gaze to her chief sergeant. "These are orders that assign some of you to new duty posts, but the rest of them are honorable-discharge papers! That is *not* the same as sending you into Hell!" Ia shifted so she could look at Harper again. "Meyun . . . this is tantamount to a *mutiny*—and over nothing!"

"Nothing?" he countered. "You think this is *nothing*?" He shifted position, too, so that he didn't block the others' view of her, and swept his hand out, indicating their crew. "You're sending away every last one of us before the end of this month, and this is *nothing*? When you haven't *once* told us when or where this war will end?"

"That's because it's going to end soon!" she told him, flinging up her hands. "I can't believe you're risking a Fatality Seven over this. Mutiny is a serious offense!"

He snatched the tablet from the left one and shook it at her. "All of these transfer orders take place within *three hours* of that commendation ceremony, which is barely enough time to pack and evacuate the ship. That's not the end of a war, Ia. That's a commander *getting rid of her crew*. Which makes *all* of us wonder *why* you're getting rid of us, and doing it in a way that we will have no time to protest or try to sway or change your mind."

Mishka spoke while Ia was still trying to figure out what to say that would defuse the tension in her crew. "In the event a junior officer—or even a noncom or an enlisted soldier— suspects a superior of undertaking a course of action that will be harmful, even detrimental, to the chain of command, the missions at stake, or the lives and well-being of a particular group, it is a requirement that such courses of action be queried before any harm can occur." The doctor rose from her seat at the head table and folded her arms across her gray dress shirt. "*I* am questioning these orders. Sir. And I am questioning your sanity in making them."

"I'm with her," Helstead agreed, though she remained seated in her usual boots-on-the-table stance. "All I can see is that this is a steaming pile of *shova v'shakk*."

"All *I* see is that she's not givin' us a *choice*," Sadneczek argued. "I think we've *earned* a choice on what t' do. We've followed you blindly, Ia, but we *deserve* th' right to *choose*."

"*I* think it's bloody dangerous," Spyder stated, rising to stand next to his wife, his own arms folded across his chest. He wore nothing but the camouflage tank shirt and shorts which he used to guide physical training sessions—a match to the outfits worn by several others, proof that Harper had called this meeting very abruptly.

"It is *not* dangerous," Ia countered, wondering where and how she had lost control of her own damned—her own Damned crew. "It is the exact *opposite* of dangerous. Every assignment I'm giving you will lead you to happy, healthy, *safe* lives."

"It *is* dangerous!" Spyder snapped, stepping up to her, muscles standing out on his lean, whipcord frame. "Don't you lie t' *me*, Bloody Mary—this *is* bloody dangerous of you, and you're endangerin' everybody *because* yer doin' it!"

"No, it is not! I am *trying* to get you *out of danger*!"

Ia stopped, shocked that she had revealed that much in her stress . . . but the words were out. They were out, they could

not be unsaid, and the wide-eyed silence in the tiered levels of
the boardroom let her know everyone knew.

"It's a suicide mission."

She turned to look at Harper. Meyun, her first officer, her
confidant, and more. He stared back at her, pain and a need
for unmet denial lost in his brown eyes. He repeated himself,
pain winning over the denial.

"This is a *suicide* mission, and *that's* why you're getting
rid of us." He held her gaze, pain in his voice, in his words.
"Why didn't I ever *see* this? I've seen your death, my death,
their deaths over the years, in the visions I saw in your head—
but those were always accidents, or random battles, or
moments in time that we've long since passed! Did you block
this from me? Did you . . . did you *erase* it from my memory?"

Wincing from the finger he poked at her, Ia didn't have a
good answer. She had *an* answer, but not a good one. "I didn't
have to. You were never *in* my destiny."

He flinched back from her.

"You two-fisting *bitch*."

Ia paled and looked at her chaplain. Bennie tightened her
mouth, hands fisting and thrusting downward in front of her,
visual insult added to the verbal. She opened her mouth to say
more—a lot more, and none of it meant to be pleasant, gauging by the red coloring the older woman's face—but Harper
cut her off.

"*Enough!* General," he stated coldly, "you promised us
that if we ever came to you *before* an event happened, and
asked you what was going to be, you'd tell us if you had the
time. Well, right now, we *have* the time, and *we are asking*.
What is going to happen after that commendation ceremony
that makes you so damned *eager* to get rid of us?"

A glance around the boardroom showed that every single
one of her crew was staring straight at her. Silently demanding
the same. There was no getting out of this, no avoiding the
stubborn determination in every face she saw. It was the same
determination, the same dedication that had seen her crew
through far too many difficult battles, and they were not
going to stop or back down just because this one was a verbal
war waged on their own CO.

Blinking, she considered what to say and how to say it. Stalled for the time to think by stepping up to the head table. The other members of the cadre who were standing moved out of habit as well, drifting to their own habitual chairs. She tucked the datapad under the clip edge and raised her gaze to the enlisted and yeomen across from her.

"Be seated."

Reluctantly, grimly, they settled into their chairs on the risers.

"Many of you know by now the danger of the Greys' entropic gun. You've felt it, you've seen the danger to the ship, and you have an inkling of what it means. It . . . dissolves the energy bonds of the very substances that make up our existence. It scatters everything, ripping apart not only molecules into its component atoms, but the atoms into their subatomic particles. An instant fission on the subatomic level. But what most of you don't know is that this . . . entropy weapon . . . dissolves energy, not just matter.

"It isn't quite an antimatter beam—it's something else. I'm not a theoretical physicist. I'm not a xenotech. I have *no* idea how the damned thing works. I do know—I have *always* known—that when that beam impacts the edge of an OTL hyperrift . . . *when* it impacts that rift . . . it will tear a hole in reality. Not into hyperspace, but *beyond* it. Beyond everything. Beyond wormholes and string theory and quantum fluctuations and who knows what else."

She looked around the room, meeting the eyes of her rotation groups of bridge crew, her life-support techs, her engineers and gunners, and her officers, too. Good meioas who should not have needed to hear any of this.

"That rift will widen slowly. And if the ancient enemies of the Greys weren't going to come out of the black of intergalactic space in roughly three hundred years . . . in just over five thousand, that rift will have grown to wipe out one-tenth of the Milky Way . . . including all the stars of what everyone but the Solaricans like to call the known galaxy. It will dissolve stars and planets in a way utterly unlike the ray that exploded a tiny chunk of our ship with enough force to damage its integrity—you all know the Feyori came out at my command to fix it, but this will not be like that.

"The stars, the planets, they will not explode, they will not fall apart in fission. They will simply . . . dissolve. Through analyzing and realizing what they will have created, in just two months, the Greys will call off their attacks and retreat. They will keep an expanded set of boundaries, but they will finally leave Humans alone. Unfortunately, by then it will be far too late."

"Wait," Harper interrupted her. He had taken a seat with the others and tapped the table in front of him. "I thought all those fancy crysium components you had me design, which you then crafted and I installed, were to *stop* the Greys from doing something that sounds very much like this."

"If enough matter and energy fills that hole in the universe within a handful of seconds of its creation," Ia explained patiently, "then the edges of that hole will seal over and end the rift. Space in that region will have to be interdicted for any and all future hyperrifts, even the tiny, pinpoint, communication rifts, but the patch would hold. That is, when my *original* plan was to simply fire the Godstrike while driving the ship into it.

"With the additional types of energy radiated by those crysium nodes—kinetic inergy, exo-EM as well as regular forms of electromagnetic energy, and all that—the hole will be sealed fully. You could drive a natural, cosmic-sized wormhole over it, and nothing would tear it open again. I have foreseen that much, and that it will still stop the Greys in their version of horror and shame . . . and I *don't* need anybody else on board to do that!"

"That ain't yer call, *sir*," her Company clerk growled. "That's not yer choice t' make."

"You're not leaving the *Osceola* without us, Ia," Harper warned her.

"Yes, you *are*. You don't *have* to die!" Ia argued back, leaning over him with her hands on her hips. Her eyes stung, but she knew if she blinked them, she would start crying. "And if you don't *have* to die, then you are *not* going to die!"

He shoved out of his chair, towering over her by the few centimeters of difference in their heights. "I would rather spend one hour in Hell with you, than a *hundred* years in Heaven without!"

It was hard, but she knew she had to do it. She sneered at him, trying not to let her tears fall. He was being so stubborn, so blind—! "I don't care what you *think* you feel for me. I am *not* taking some lovesick *stubbie* with me."

He slashed his hand between them, scowling at her. "This has *nothing* to do with that! This is about me being a soldier, and an officer! This is about me doing what is *right!*"

"I would rather be damned for what I do," Christine Benjamin asserted, while Ia was still drawing in a sharp breath. The chaplain's words—a direct quote—cut her off before she could speak. *"Than be damned for what I didn't do.* Is that not what you have always said, Ia? Isn't it? All these years of talking with and listening to you?" She rose from her seat, hands this time fisted at her sides, her hazel eyes brimming with unshed tears. "Well, guess what? You don't have the *exclusive right* to feeling that way!"

"Dammit, Bennie*!"* Ia yelled at her chaplain, her friend. *"Do you* want *to die?"*

"SIR, YES, SIR!"

Startled, Ia jumped and whirled, facing the tiers . . . where every last one of her crew had jumped to their feet, at Attention, chins raised proudly. Ready to serve.

Ready to die. With her.

The tears fell, with a sob she couldn't contain, couldn't control. Huddling in on herself, feeling as horrible as she hadn't felt since that damned, damnable morning, Ia cried. She felt arms wrapping around her and flinched from their touch, fearing a mind-quake, but Harper hung on anyway, pulling her against his chest.

He held her as she cried, as steady as her lost brother, as solid as her lost homeworld. Ready and willing as the rest to die. She didn't lose control of her gifts; rather, the more Meyun cradled her, the more she felt grounded instead of cast adrift. He had no psychic training, no abilities beyond basic gut-level instincts, but he grounded her as solidly as stone in the face of a storm.

A voice spoke up from the ranks as her sobbing died down. Julia Garcia. She recognized the voice, and quelled the last of her tears with a hard sniff. At some point most of the others had reseated themselves, she didn't know when, but Garcia was on her feet.

"I once called and asked my old CO back on the *Leo*, why me? Why 'Wrong-Way Garcia' out of all the billions of soldiers you could've picked? And you know what he said?" she asked. "He said that *you* told him you didn't dare pull away anyone else who was *needed* in their original post. That my life—*our* lives—wouldn't make a damn bit of difference spent anywhere else. But that on your ship, he said, we *would* make a difference. That we'll finally count for something.

"Well, on board this ship, sir, I *have* made a difference," Garcia asserted, no longer the breathless, rambling young private she had been when Ia first brought her on board. "I have shot down the enemy as a gunner, and I have repaired this ship as an engineer, and I have been a member of the finest Company in the known galaxy because we *have* been doing what you needed us to do. An' like Bennie says, sir, I'd rather be damned for dying doing what's *right* than for living doing nothin' at all!"

Ia pushed Harper away, scowling up at the defiant brunette. She opened her mouth to counter that argument, but Helstead cut her off.

"Oh, *do* shut up, sir," the ex-Knifeman drawled in a disgusted tone. She arched her neck and back so that she could look Ia in the face behind Harper's back, but true to her nature, didn't bother to sit up, let alone stand. "If you try to throw us off this ship by force, not only will we *not* go, we will toss *you* off the ship and go do it ourselves—and you *know* we'll muck it up without you. But you know what? That's a risk we're willing to take if you continue being a mucking *fool!*"

A glance at Harper showed one of his dark brows rising, silently daring her to argue. Turning away from him, Ia braced her hands on the table, head bowed. Her first officer pressed further.

"Answer us this: Are you *sure* you'll die, if you take this ship through that rift you described?" he challenged her. "Absolutely, one hundred percent sure?"

"Harper, I *don't* come out the other side. Not in any percentile even close to the miniscule chance it took for the Admiral-General to make me a Command Staff General instead of a mere Rear Admiral—and I'll remind you I did *not* foresee that promotion coming."

"But there *is* still a chance?" he pressed. He lifted his chin at her. "How would it work?

She rolled her eyes. "It involves a Feyori somehow, because somehow, it involves *time travel*. But virtually every last one of them is needed exactly where they are, and not a single one of them would volunteer for the job. I've looked. For over twelve *years*, I have looked. Nor would I sacrifice a single one of them. I may command them, but I will not destroy them when it is not necessary, and it is *not*. I go. I go alone. I die. Because *no one else* has to. That is *final*."

"No, it isn't," Harper asserted.

Ia bowed her head in frustration. This argument was going nowhere.

"You are not *needed* to be on board." It was all she could think of to say. "That means I have to set you free, so you can live, and do whatever you want. And some of you *have* to leave this ship. I have to stay, and die, because the future needs me as a martyr. But some of you *have lives* ahead of you. Important paths that you must undertake, if all of my efforts to save this galaxy are going to come true. The rest of you *deserve* long and happy lives . . . so *all* of you will leave."

"*Horseshit*," her Company Sergeant repeated, echoing his words from two days before. "Now, I'll still fill out all that paperwork, sir," he told her, "an' some of it *might* be needed . . . but you *are* going to give the rest of us other choices as well. *Including staying on this ship*. You don't treat the people who've been watching your back like something to scrape your barn-mucking boots over."

"Grizzle—"

Harper caught her arm. "How many of us are *must-leaves*?" he asked her. "How many of us *must* take certain paths? Ignore everything else, and just give us the truth. Who absolutely *has* to leave and survive, at the bare minimum?"

Ia stared at him, then looked down at the fingers gripping her black-sleeved arm. Pointedly. He released her, and she sighed, closing her eyes. A flip inward, outward . . . The time-plains were clear now, but while she could see each stream and river, each bush and blade of tall, golden-bleached grass, there were storm clouds gathering in the distance. Shifting the view into a chart, she checked the flow of time for those needs.

"Chief Yeoman Patricia Huey. You'll go on to first train, and then teach for a while at the Shikoku Yama Flight Academy. You'll then head back to Scadia and teach what you've learned there. Your people will need those skills, and they'll need to know that I'm a woman of my word. Your kings and queens will continue to have and hold to that treaty I signed, as will the Third Human Empire when it rises.

"Private First Grade Moira MacArroc, and Private Second Grade Wade Redrock. You talked about settling down and raising kids, if you got off of Dabin alive—and you did get married—so that's what you're going to do. Not because I want you to have a happy ending, though I do, but because two of your great-plus-granddaughters are going to be inspired by their family legends about the two of you, and go into the military. One will be a Special Forces General, and the other, her sister, will be the Admiral-General three hundred years from now.

"You wouldn't have been selected for this task," Ia stated dryly, opening her eyes to look up at the blushing pair, "but you'll be settling on Dabin and your offspring will help fill in the gaps of a dozen or so people who would've otherwise influenced everyone down the line. I've already arranged for my *favorite* Meddler, Ginger, to ensure your family line helps fill in those holes she and her idiot partner tore in my plans for that world.

"Private First Class Angel Ng, you have been a fine navigator and scan tech," Ia continued, seeking the woman's face in the tiers of seats. "You will also have a role to play. You'll retire after a few more years, enjoy your civilian life, and eventually be asked to become a councilor for your hometown. You can rise as high as councilor for your regional prefecture, but don't rise any higher, and resist becoming an advisor. I won't tell you which way to vote, other than to listen to your fellow citizens, and listen to your heart, but that is your task.

"Corporal D'ouw Deschamps," she named next, closing her eyes briefly. "You will spend a year or two learning how to be a civilian again . . . and then you will join the Afaso, where you will train to your fullest extent, and work your way up the ranks of monks who guard my Vault of Prophecies. After the corporal . . . York and Clairmont. You both have to leave, so you can become the twenty-sixth century's equivalent of Gilbert and Sullivan."

The two men eyed each other, brows lifting and shoulders shrugging. Ia knew it was because both men had considered doing just that, turning their talent for music into a career, post-Service.

"And the last one . . . is Commander Christine Benjamin," she finished, knowing that this one was going to get the strongest protest.

"Like hell I will," the chaplain retorted. "I'm not leaving."

"You *have* to leave ship, Commander," Ia told her. She faced her longtime friend. "You are the one person who knows me best. You are the one person who knows my *motives* the best, and you will be tapped time and again to explain my decisions, to expound upon my directives, and to enforce my prophecies. You are as important to the future as Grandmaster Ssarra of the Afaso was to my initial assignment to the *Liu Ji* . . . where I knew I would meet you, and that you would get to know me, and eventually be in a position to do *damage control* to everyone who will want to turn me into either a martyred saint or a sacrificed monster.

"You will advise the Command Staff, you will become a living military historian of my past, and you will do your job, the same as the other five. The rest of you . . . have already had your impact. There'd be some fame for a while as a surviving member of the Damned . . . but fame is fickle, and basking too much in the glory days of the past will lead many of you into soured lives. You'll be better off either continuing to serve in the military until your careers end and you can retire with honor, or blending into civilian society, and getting on with your lives."

"Well, that's *still* not yer choice to make," Grizzle pointed out to her.

"*You* could have happiness and peace, and that *is* the best choice to make," she argued.

"Sir," Rico said, finally speaking up. Quiet, thoughtful,

analytical, he was well respected by the rest of the crew, and his question held their attention as well as hers. "Will it ruin the future if we *don't* leave this ship? The crew members you didn't name? Be honest, sir. Don't lie. *Will* it ruin the future?"

Sighing, Ia knew the answer to that without having to do more than dabble her toes in the back of her mind. ". . . No. Not if Bennie goes willingly and steps up to her task. Not if Redrock and MacArroc, and Huey and Ng and Deschamps, Clairmont and York all step up and speak out from time to time, as the . . ." Her voice threatened to waver. She firmed her gut. "Not if they speak up from time to time as the surviving members of the Damned."

"Then that's settled," Grizzle asserted, rubbing his hands together. Ia turned back to him, only to be given a shooing motion with a flip of his fingers. "Go back t' bed, sir," he told her. "Th' eight you outlined'll take yer orders on how their lives should turn out, an' th' rest of us'll spend our time between now an' that medal ceremony figurin' out what we should do with our lives."

"That's not how this works! This *isn't* a democracy," Ia argued, frowning at him. "This is the military. And you will do as you're told!"

"Oh, like *you* have?" Helstead quipped sarcastically. "Way to lead by example, sir."

Ia wanted to keep arguing, but the fog had lifted from the streams. When she looked at her own efforts, at the path she was trying to carve, and not just at individual lives . . . the results were clear. The future wouldn't be affected too badly if they voluntarily stayed . . . but it might be affected for the worse if she forced them to go. Very much for the worse.

Her vision wavered with more tears. Swiping at them, she glared at her crew and her cadre, then let out a hard sigh. "So be it. You will take the next eleven days to sort out what you want to do with your lives. I will even spend several hours I could've spent sleeping, just so I can write up a set of *tailored* pathways which each of you could choose—*with* multiple options, Sergeant," she added, before Sadneczek could protest. "Things that you can select to do, instead of throwing away your lives. I will have them ready for each of you by the time the 2nd Platoon comes on duty later today, and each one of you will take the intervening days to consider what you will do.

"There will be *no* harassing of anyone who chooses a different path from the others. *No* pressure on any of you to choose one way or another . . . and you will *not* breathe one word to anyone about this conversation until one month *after* this ship and I are gone. Is that clear?"

One and all, they again snapped to Attention, even the normally laconic Helstead. *"Sir, yes, sir!"*

Ia eyed each of her crew. She blinked to get the sting out of her eyes, and set her jaw. "I want this ship back on course, and gauged to be *on time* to reach the *Mosin*, as per the schedule I outlined before. The Wake planned for later today will take place on time and on schedule, and I do not want to hear a single *word* of this conversation within the Wake Zone, either in person or via the timestreams. Is *that* clear?"

"Sir, yes, sir!" the Damned asserted in unison.

They were hers.

Castaways, nobodies, useless, forgotten souls, former wretched scutworkers with only a couple dozen among them of any value elsewhere in the universe. Stubborn as hellfire, tempered by hardships, and headed for damnation . . . and they were *hers*: the Damned, the Space Force's finest crew.

It hurt, accepting that fact. Her chest hurt as if a hundred-meter leafer beast had decided to park on her sternum for a nap. Ia clenched her teeth and curled her fingers into fists for a long moment, struggling to breathe, just breathe, in the aching, awful, awe-filled glory of it. When she could speak again, she nodded curtly.

". . . Good. Now, I am going to go back to my quarters to go back to sleep, but I will leave you with one more thing to carefully consider: I had to come to terms *long* ago with the fact that, in order to save the galaxy long after the normal Human life span of around a hundred years, I had to end mine before my twenty-eighth birthday. However you look at it, even a famous martyr like me is someone who will be *dead*. The rest of you have the right to live out your lives, and I never will . . . and that is what I want for each of you.

"I am not demanding you leave and abandon me because I

am a selfish monster. I demanding you leave and *live* because I *care* about you." The tears she had tried to stave off came back again. Ia ignored them as they trickled down her face and dripped onto her clothes. Salt water would wash out in the sonic cleaners. The stains on her conscience would never fade. "Now, get back to your posts and get us under way. We have far too much to do, and very little time left for doing it. Dismissed."

"*Sir, yes, sir!*"

Carefully not looking at Harper—if she did, she knew on instinct her tears would only fall harder and faster—Ia made her way out the side door. With luck, she would never have to enter it again, nor be forced to feel this strange mix of pride, grief, and pain.

CHAPTER 10

. . . How do I stay sane? What kind of a question is . . . ? No, of course I understand very well what you saw in all that footage from Sallha—you were on my ship, meioa. I know what you had access to. Yes, I understand that you finally realize I have been seeing those corpses ever since I was fifteen, and that you've realized I made the decision that I would have to aim at ending all of their lives, for all that I tried to find a way out of it. But you have to ask me how I stay sane?

How do you people stay sane?

When you walk down a street in your hometown or city, or along a corridor on whatever station you visit, how do you stay sane when you see a fellow sentient being who is homeless and hungry, and in need of sanitation and fresh clothes, food and a warm bed, things that you get to enjoy? How do you stay sane when you hear about your neighbor having lost their job, and they're mired in debt, unable to pay their bills, when you have plenty to spare? How do you stay sane whenever you see an injured stray dog who needs a trip to the nearest vet, with no

*owner in sight and no one else but you aware of his pain
and his plight?*

How, *meioa, do you and your viewers stay sane when
there are so many things you can* do *to make this universe
a better place, day by day, step by step, kindness by kindness, instead of just sitting there complaining about its
awful state? How can you and your viewers stay* sane
*whenever you stay silent on matters of social injustice,
oppression, and bigotry?*

You ask me how do I *stay sane? I stay sane because I*
act. *Because I would rather be damned for something I*
do, *rather than something I* can *do but don't otherwise
bother to try. And that, meioa, is the* only *difference
between the vast majority of your viewers and someone
like me. My precognition gives me an advantage, yes . . .
but even without it, I would* still *be faced every single day
with the choices to be kind, negligent, or cruel!*

You get one *guess as to which I'd choose—and you
dare to ask, how do* I *stay sane?*

~Ia

OCTOBER 29, 2499 T.S.
BATTLE PLATFORM *OSCEOLA*
HASKIN'S WORLD, GLIESE 505 SYSTEM

Standing in the wings of the stage that served the inhabitants
of the *Osceola* for moments of commendation and corporal
discipline alike, Ia waited patiently for the last of the presenters to arrive and the ceremony to begin. Almost every single
member of her crew was waiting in the front rows of the audience, seated in front of dozens of Terran United Planets
Councilors who had made the trip to this system, in part to
attend this ceremony, but also as an official visit to the Joint
Colonyworld the *Osceola* orbited.

The few who weren't attending this ceremony consisted of
a skeleton crew of the five bodies needed to man the bridge at
all times, plus one life-support tech, one of the engineering
leads, and Lieutenant Rico, who had volunteered to stand

guard over the airlock attached to the *Osceola*. All of them were from the 1st Platoon. Helstead would be the first to receive her award, followed by a set of bridge crew, engineering, and life-support techs, who would all hurry out of the ceremony to take their crewmates' places so that they, too, could attend and receive their awards, without the *Damnation* being left completely unmanned.

Ia was not seated with them; she was going to be one of the presenters, by special request. The medals she herself would receive—technically just one—would come at the end of the hours-long ceremony. All she had to do was wait for Helstead to be the first across the stage, to receive all her other commendations, and present her second officer with a very poignant choice.

"General Ia!"

She turned and mustered a smile for Admiral John Genibes, her former direct superior, and now her equal on the Command Staff . . . if one ignored she was still the General of the Alliance Armies. That title and rank would not end until the Second Grey War ended. Though the Greys weren't going after any other race, they were still attempting to steal test subjects from the Terran worlds nearest their territory, and from the occasional Joint Colonyworld, which meant the V'Dan were involved in the war as well. The others were loaning what forces they could—mostly psis to project acidic kinetic energy at the invaders since their ships and weaponry were nearly useless—in solidarity as Alliance members, but this was still much more of a Terran war than the Salik one had been. The Terran generals and admirals present for this ceremony outnumbered the entire V'Dan delegation.

Since they were both wearing full formal Dress Blacks, replete with caps, the admiral saluted her as the technically junior officer to her senior position as the General of the Alliance Armies. But he grinned as he did so, since the formality of the occasion was not technically meant for both of them.

"I wasn't completely sure if you'd make it, Admiral," Ia told Genibes, clasping his hand. At the arch of his graying brow, she dipped her head. "Seventy-five percent sure, but not one hundred percent."

He chuckled. "I've actually missed being interrupted in

my meetings by you and your precognitive nitpickings. But I can live with it, given all the good you've done now that you're my superior."

"Equals, when we're not actually navigating a battlefield," she countered. "Like every other resource, I don't use any more of my rank than I have to."

"There you are, John. Welcome aboard the *Osceola*," Myang stated, drifting over to join them. She was in a very good mood about Ia's precognitive warning on when the war was ending. The head of the Space Force clasped the admiral's hand with a warm smile, then gestured at Ia. "I overheard your comments about rank, and it reminded me of something: I am having a spot of trouble with our youngest Staff member, here."

"Oh?" Admiral Genibes asked, glancing between the two women.

Ia bit her tongue and turned partially away, trying to hide her amusement. Unlike Myang's genuine good mood, hers was a slightly desperate sense of mirth, one that was trying to cling to these last few pleasant moments. Instead of giving in, she looked over at the tables arrayed across the stage, especially the one laden with carefully arranged black boxes stamped in silver with the names of each crew member who had their final choice to make. The sight of that stack at the end of the tables sobered her sufficiently to steady her nerves.

"She refuses to call me by my first name," the Admiral-General complained, while Ia focused on calming herself. "Even when she outranked *me*, it was 'Admiral-General' this, 'Sir' that, and almost never even so much as a simple, straightforward 'Myang'—what do you think it'll take for her to call me 'Christine'?"

"That's my chaplain's name, sir," Ia interjected. "I'd feel kind of awkward about calling you that."

Myang favored her with a mock-stern look. "In a military over two billion strong, there are *hundreds of thousands* of meioas named Christine. Deal with it."

"It wouldn't be respectful. Sir. Deal with *that*," she retorted lightly.

"She's got you cornered, there," Genibes chuckled. "Can't fault a meioa for trying to be respectful."

"I can try. So, Ia, what's in all those boxes?" Myang prodded, gesturing at the endmost table. "I heard a rumor that they're not anything that's on the DoI's commendations list. Everything else has been accounted for."

"John, there you are—and Christine, and of course the meioa-e of the hour," a familiar voice called out.

Grateful for General Sranna's interruption, she turned to meet his smile with one of her own and clasped his hand. "General, it's good to see you again. How's Tumseh working out for you, on Dabin?"

"What, you don't know?" he asked, raising his age-whitened brows. "I thought you knew everything."

She shook her head. "I've been so busy with the Greys, I didn't bother to check in on that. I only have so many hours and minutes in a day. I know he's competent enough to have stayed with the Division, but that's it."

"Well, he's done an outstanding job. One of his junior officers translated a tracking algorithm that can pinpoint all those damned not-cats with high-altitude drones salvaged from the Salik war machines, and he's been using it to hunt down the damned things. Apparently, they wanted to keep track of their little pets."

Wincing at the memory of the ground slamming into her back and of claws scrabbling over her half-armored chest, she shook her head. "I'd rather not think about that, sir. I came a little too close to being eaten by two of them."

"Better that than the Salik, eh?" he offered.

"Back to what we were talking about," Myang asserted. "Ia, about those boxes—"

"*Thsstitch'h, Ia'n ssdh'dah, suweh neh mok'kathh stha tchiah.*"

The Admiral-General flicked up her hands, eyes rolling in a silent bid for patience. Composing herself, she turned to watch Ia greet the Grandmaster of the Afaso.

"*Mok'kathh suweh nehh khunnssswearahh, Ssarra,*" Ia replied, lips closed but curved in a smile and her arms opening wide. The batik-clad Tlassian curled up the corners of his broad, scaled lips and turned his green-clothed back to her. She wrapped her arms around his chest in friendly greeting, then turned her back to the saurian so that he could do the same . . . and bent over, lifting him off the ground with a chuckle at his hiss of surprise.

"*Nnghah, Ia!* Ssso you thinnk you are ssstrong?" he challenged her as she set him back down and turned to face him. She had to adjust her Dress cap, since the move had dislodged it a little. The Grandmaster held up his three-fingered hand, palm out and thumb up in the common Tlassian-Human gesture of forestalling extra comments. "I knnow you are *phhyssically*, my *mok'kathh*. Thisss is a philosssophical questionn."

"I am now stronger than I have ever been, *mok'kathh*," Ia replied, giving him a polite, respectful bow, hands interlaced Tlassian-style in front of her chest. "And the path I take next is the strongest of steps."

The alien monk eyed her, his scaled expression not easy to read for Humans. This was the tail end of a conversation they had started a very long time ago, back at the Afaso Headquarters just a few days before she had left for Australia Province and a certain recruitment office. Bowing, he accepted her words. "Then I shall pray that you shall have everything you need when you finish your journey."

"That's rather cryptic," Myang muttered, eyeing the Grandmaster. "Still, it is good to meet you again, Grandmaster. I believe we last met before the wars started, on Mars? You were overseeing an exhibition of Afaso skills, versus the best of the best at that Army base."

"Yesss . . . it was a good commpetitionn, as I recalll. A pleassure to ssee you again, Admirrral-Genneral," Ssarra agreed.

"Quite. Now, Ia, about those boxes," Myang reasserted, turning back to her. "What's in them, if it's not on the DoI's list of approved commendations?"

"It's something private for my crew," Ia demurred. General Sranna came to her rescue, as she knew he would.

"Something for your crew? *I* think I know what it is," he said. At the blank, curious looks from Admiral Genibes and the Grandmaster, he dug into his pocket and pulled out a metal disc. "Challenge coins! They're all over the Army. I was making a bet with that blue-haired fellow of yours, the one with the thick accent—Lieutenant Spyder?—on how many awards he'd get, and told him to haul out his challenge coin. That was when I heard you didn't have any—Genibes, how could *you*, at least, not have heard of them?"

"He's heard of them, but they're almost never found in the Marines or the Navy," Ia told him, answering for her former CO. "The Army is often stationed on a planet, save for when they're traveling. Both the Marines and the Navy are almost always in space, and a coin is an unsecured projectile on a ship. Ferrar's Fighters served entirely on board the *Liu Ji*, except for a few colonial-rescue missions. And when I was in the Navy, I was always on the Blockade, where such things are even more likely to get left out of shipboard life. Ever since then . . . I've been stuck on a ship in multiple high-speed combat zones, save for our brief tour on Dabin. I never bothered to issue any because it'd just be one more thing to keep track of and make sure it was Locked and Webbed in case of a sudden vector change."

"That makes it sound like they're not challenge coins, then," Myang said, lifting her chin at the black boxes. "So what are they?"

"A little something I decided to issue as one of my last few official acts as General of the Alliance Armies," Ia hedged mildly.

"Oh?" Genibes asked her. "You make it sound like you won't be, for much longer."

"Well, I don't like abusing my power, so I rarely *use* it," Ia pointed out. "That means my official acts as the General of the Alliance Armies are few and far between . . . but the Second Grey War *is* going to come to an end at some point, and that means I won't be needed as said General of the Alliance Armies after a while. Call it a little indulgence, if you want—and it looks like they're about to start the ceremony, so we need to take our places, meioas."

Myang caught Ia's elbow, holding her back for a moment. She murmured in the taller woman's ear. "*Is* everything on schedule?"

Ia knew what she meant. "With luck, yes. But I'm not taking any chances, so *no* announcements, sir."

Myang sighed. "*Christine*. Once you're in my office, training under me, I'll insist you call me by my given name. When we're not being formal."

"It would be an honor to call you by your given name," Ia agreed under her breath as they strode out onto the stage together, to the applause of the people gathered in the auditorium, "but this is still very much a formal moment. Sir."

"Pain in the asteroid," Myang muttered. She clung to Ia's medal-covered elbow a moment more. "You do know that your defense team is doing an outstanding job of defending you so far, right?"

"Of course, sir. I do listen to all the depositions while I'm filling out the klicks and klicks of paperwork that continue to cross my desk," Ia not quite lied. She did play the recordings, but she had the sound turned down so low, it was a bare murmur at best.

"Well, you're still a pain in the asteroid, but at the rate Admiral Johns is defending you, you'll still be *my* pain in the asteroid." Releasing her, Myang continued forward.

Mildly amused by her superior's attitude, Ia stopped by her table of boxes, located near the steps that would be used as the exiting point for her crew. The Admiral-General strode across the stage to the podium, met briefly with her chief aide, Colonel Sofrens, then gestured for him to move to the far set of stairs, the ones the members of Ia's Damned would use to mount the stage. Behind them, the senior generals and admirals who had traveled to witness the ceremony took their seats on the stage. So did the Premiere, and the dignitaries from the other members of the Alliance, the equivalents of generals, admirals, and leaders or their representatives.

Rather than wearing a bulky breather pack and their version of a pressure-suit, the Dlmvla had appointed a Human delegate to represent them physically on the stage, along with a vidlinked presenter on one of the screens at the back of the platform. Equally wisely, the Chinsoiy had appointed a Human delegate to represent them physically as well; such courtesies were not uncommon, given their different environmental needs.

As soon as everyone had settled, the head of the Space Force began. "Soldiers, dignitaries, and civilians. Today, we celebrate and commend an extraordinary collection of Human beings. Though we are still at war with one of our most implacable foes, our other great enemy has been vanquished . . . and it has come to the attention not only of the Command Staff of the Terran United Planets Space Force, but to the attention of our Council, and to the attention of our fellow members of military and civilian authority that the greatest source of our many victories can be attributed to a single Company in the Terran Space Force.

"This force, this group, has acted not only for the good of our sovereign interstellar nation, but for the good of our many sentient neighbors and Imperial kin. They have done so time and again with little rest, and virtually no Leave, no breaks or stays in their unceasing efforts to defend our borders, our worlds, and our friends . . ."

It was going to be a very long ceremony.

Ia settled herself into Parade Rest, legs slightly bent and relaxed enough to ensure proper circulation, though thankfully the gravity was Earth Standard and not nearly so taxing on the knees. Behind her back, under the cover of her knee-length Dress Black overcoat, she extruded a thin crysium cable, socketed it into her arm unit, and began composing prophecies.

Her first award ceremony once she got beyond Basic had been a treasured memory. This one . . . was occupying some of her last precious moments of time, minutes and hours she could put to better use. Far too many events had wobbled off course in the last twelve-plus years for her liking, and the only things that had saved her plans were contingencies and improvisations. So she stood, smiled and nodded faintly at all the right points, and worked on making sure those potential improvisations in the distant future would become yet more well-plotted contingencies.

". . . And lastly, Lieutenant Commander, it is my honor to bestow upon you the Medal of Honor," Premiere Mandella stated, "for the unswerving, unwavering performance of valorous and courageous deeds, both those listed here, and for others beyond number."

Applause burst out across the auditorium. Waking herself up from her prophecy trance, Ia pulled her attention firmly into the present and unhooked her bracer. She watched Mandella pin the last medal onto the lapel of Helstead's Dress Blacks. The Premiere shook hands with her, speaking some private message for her under his breath, and the pair paused briefly for the hovering cameras to record their images together. Then he gestured for Helstead to cross the stage to where Ia waited. Stopping in front of her CO, Delia saluted Ia.

"Sir. Requesting permission to report back to the *Damnation* to relieve Lieutenant Rico, sir."

"Not yet, Helstead," Ia told her, returning the salute. Crisply, she turned to the table, selected the topmost box—all arranged in proper order by her earlier, via telekinesis—and turned back with the container in her hands. Opening the lid, she angled the contents so that only Helstead could see it. "Is *this* what you truly want, soldier? Think carefully, for this is your last chance."

Helstead stared down at the interior of the black box. A soft frown creased her freckled brow, and she looked up at Ia. One of the hovercameras swerved closer; Ia closed the lid to hide the contents. "I was thinking, sir. You need something to speak eloquently about the Damned, right?"

"Right," Ia agreed, wondering what, of all the many possibilities, was running through her second officer's mind.

"Well, how about we donate our coats to the TUPSF museum?" Delia asked. "Medal for medal, kilo for kilo, we're the heaviest of award-bearing Companies based on all we have done . . . but people won't *know* it unless they *see* it, sir."

Blinking, Ia quickly skimmed through the timelines. It was not an expected canal . . . but it would alleviate several potential floodwaters in the future. She nodded. "That's a very good idea. It'll help cover what the others won't be able to do, which is to spread the message for longer than a Human lifetime—I'll inform the rest. But *only* the coats of those who accept this offer."

"Then pin it on me, sir, for I accept all that it means with a free and loving heart."

A free and loving . . . ? Ia eyed the redhead. "Delia? In the words of your fellow Eivaneners . . . you're mucking *crazy*."

Helstead flashed her a grin. "Thank you, sir!"

Mindful of the hovercameras, Ia reached out and shifted

them back behind her 3rd Platoon officer by several meters. Only then did she pull out the pin and carefully fix it on the lapel across from Helstead's Medal of Honor. Black enameled metal strung on a black ribbon, it blended in with the satin lapel, not very visible . . . but it was heartrending to see it there all the same.

"Lieutenant Commander . . ." There was so much she wanted to say about Helstead's choice, but all of it was lengthy and some of it would have been either tear-streaked and morose or shouted irritably at the top of her lungs. Instead, Ia tightened her gut and merely said, "In the name of all you have done, and especially for what you *choose* to do . . . however insane . . . thank you."

Helstead unbuttoned her jacket, folded it so that the Medal of Honor side was pointed up and her three K'Katta sashes of Honor, Valor, and Sentientarian Aid were tucked inside so that just a tuft of color from each could be seen, turned crisply, and set the bundle on the floor next to the table. She returned to Ia and saluted one last time. "Sir. Again, I request permission to return to the ship and relieve Lieutenant Rico of his duties, sir."

"Permission granted." Ia saluted her back. "Dismissed."

Bemused and unsure what had just happened, the audience in the stands and on the stage applauded politely as the short redhead strode off the stage and up the aisle, heading for the nearest set of doors that would lead her through the massive labyrinth of Battle Platform *Osceola* and back to her own ship. Ia watched her go, then tucked her arms behind her back again. Colonel Sofrens called up the next member, Huey, who would be following in Helstead's tracks back to the *Damnation* to relieve Fielle so that he could come receive his own rewards as well.

Tucking her arms behind her back, Ia slipped back into her light timestream trance, pausing every few seconds to "cool off" the excess kinetic inergy building up in her translation bracer. At the end of Mandella's presentation and the pinning of her Medal of Honor, she crossed the stage to Ia and saluted, much as Helstead had done.

"Sir! Requesting permission to report to the *Damnation*

for piloting duty, sir," Huey stated. She eyed the pile of boxes under the cover of her upraised hand, curiosity in her gaze.

Ia saluted her back. "Permission granted, Yeoman . . . and no, those aren't for you. Remember to be ready to move out as soon as you are relieved in turn." She held out her hand. "Thank you very much for serving with my crew, Patricia, and for being willing to go next where I need you to go."

"The honor was mine, sir. My things are packed and ready to go. Ah . . . why did the Commander remove her coat?" she added under her breath, glancing at the jacket on the platform floor.

"Posterity. Yours is not needed. Thank you for standing watch through the rest of this, Yeoman. Dismissed."

"Aye, sir." Turning, she headed down the stairs and up the nearest aisle, following Helstead's route.

Next up was Private First Class Valya Dubsnjiadeb, backup navigation tech and a fine cloisonné artist, who would be replacing Phaenon on the bridge. When she reached Ia, she saluted without a word and glanced at the boxes. Ia fetched hers from the stack.

"Is *this* what you want, soldier?" she challenged, opening and displaying it for the other woman's eyes only. "Because this is your last chance to change your mind."

Dubsnjiadeb closed her blue eyes for a moment, swallowed, and nodded. When she opened them, she gave Ia a fierce stare. "Sir, yes, sir!"

Pulling the pin from the box, Ia pinned it to her lapel. "As you have accepted this, soldier, you will remove your jacket, fold it like the Lieutenant Commander's with your Medal of Honor face up, sashes tucked inside, and report to the bridge."

"Aye, sir." Unbuttoning her coat, she turned, eyed the jacket on the floor, folded hers with a few flips into a similar half-faced stack with her sashes between the dark folds, and set it next to Helstead's. Turning back to Ia, she saluted once more and left for the ship. Up next would be Dorsen, who would relieve Sutrara at the comms station, then Gasnme— Kastanoupotonoulis, whose full, Grecian-style name even she admitted was ridiculously long and complicated for most Terranglo speakers to say—who would relieve Rammstein at operations, and then the gunnery position, engineering, life support, and finally those who were supposed to be here for the full length of the ceremony.

Thankfully, each delegate delivering awards had made one single speech commending all of the recipients as a group rather than an individual speech for each soldier. All except for the lone Choya ambassador; he had spent his time delivering an apology for entering into war against Ia's very successful, victorious Company, a brief speech of gratitude for saving his species from xenocide as per the dictates of his race's main culture, and otherwise had no medals or honoraria to give. Beyond those group-aimed speeches, the medals were simply announced and applied, with the Medals of Honor given a brief listing of the actions taken that had earned them.

———————

They finally reached the end of the 3rd Platoon with the awards for Private Second Class Gowan Inakkar, a skillful gunner and manufactory technician who had earned several Target Stars and Compass Roses along with his Medal of Honor and handful of alien honoraria. As he saluted Ia, folded his Black Dress jacket onto the growing pile, and returned to his seat in his black, gray-striped pants and gray dress shirt, Admiral-General Myang stepped up to the podium.

"There will be a ten-minute Terran Standard break before we begin again with the commendations for the 2nd Platoon, A Company, 1st Legion, 1st Battalion, 1st Brigade, 1st Division, 9th Cordon Special Forces. The next break after that will come between the ceremonies for the 2nd and 1st Platoons, 9th Cordon."

The majority of people in the Battle Platform's main auditorium stood and stretched, many turning to their neighbors to start up a conversation. Some left the tiers and balconies, seeking out nearby restrooms. Since she had been standing all this time, Ia took the opportunity to perch herself on the partially emptied table at her back, between the stacks of black boxes to her right and the piles of Dress jackets on the floor to her left.

The only drawback to Helstead's wonderful idea strolled over to stand in front of her. Myang eyed the boxes, the coats, and Ia. "What the hell is going on, here? Why are most of your people leaving their coats, and all of their new medals, on the floor? Do you know what this looks like to our allies?"

"They're assuming it's an odd Terran military custom," Ia told her. "And for all it's one that has just been invented by my Company, it is the truth."

Myang frowned in confusion. Her brown eyes flicked to the coats, then back to Ia's face. She looked at the boxes, then back again. "What were you handing to them? I couldn't see, and the hovercameras never got a good angle . . . which I'll presume was your intent?"

"Sir, yes, sir, because it's none of their damn business at this point in time. The medal I offered was one step in a choice I gave to them. Donating their jackets was the other step."

"Explain," Myang ordered as the Premiere wandered over.

"Premiere, sir, please don't touch those," Ia told Mandella as he started to stoop, hand extended toward the topmost coat nearest to him. "If you disturb them, they'll slide out of formation, and they will look messy on the stage. I'd rather not waste everyone's time by calling my soldiers back up to fix them for the hovercameras before we go on."

He straightened and joined her, eyeing both women in curiosity. "So why are they on the floor?"

"The General was just about to tell me that," Myang prodded, looking at Ia.

"Because there's no room on the table. Once this ceremony is over, they will be donated to the Terran United Planets Space Force Museum of Military History on Earth. There are still a few more tough fights against the Greys, and . . . some nasty odds on just how much of my ship will remain intact. Lieutenant Commander Helstead wisely asked if it would be easier to send them back home from here, rather than risk the probabilities that some might be destroyed." She smiled slightly and lied by using the truth conditionally. "Of course, I'll be busy striving to get my crew and ship safely through all those fights, but I was shot on a less than three percent chance as a noncom, so I'm not blindfolding myself to the other possible outcomes."

"But your soldiers *will* come through alive?" Mandella pressed.

"Sir," she told him, reaching out to touch his arm for a moment, "believe me when I say I have been keeping my Company clerk very busy in the last few days filling out transfer orders and retirement papers for *all* of my crew members in conjunction with the end of the Second Grey War, which will end very soon. *If* everything goes the way it rightfully should. But I am not a Rear Admiral, so no percentage, however low, can be easily dismissed just yet. I don't want to jinx the end of the war."

"What can we do to help make sure everything does go right?" the Premiere asked her, lifting his chin.

"All you have to do, sir, is step back, relax, and don't interfere," she told him. Ia included Myang in her look. "It's taken me over twelve years, but I have finally set up everything. We'll even be able to stop the Greys, very soon. They'll have expanded their territory, but that is a concession—including the loss of my own homeworld—which I am willing to endure giving up, to soothe their soon-to-be highly bruised egos."

"You're going to bruise the *Greys'* egos?" Myang echoed skeptically. "How?"

"Don't interfere, sir," Ia repeated. "They're going to make a terrible mistake. I will step in and fix it, and they will stop fighting out of whatever passes for their version of embarrassment and shame. So just step back, relax, and watch the war end. When it does, my people would very much like to retire into quiet lives, rather than be paraded around as war heroes. Which is one of the reasons why Helstead suggested donating our jackets in our stead here and now rather than suffer from endless rounds of intrusive interviews and pointless parades."

"Well, I suppose I can't blame them about getting out of the spotlight," Mandella muttered. "I'll be glad when my term is up next year, and I can retire and let my Secondaire take over. So what are you going to do?"

"I've been ordered to report to the Admiral-General's office," Ia confessed wryly. "And there was something in there about having to teach for a year at some camp or academy. The exact details of my retirement from active combat zones will sort themselves out in due time, I'm sure. In the meantime, I still have a few last alien not-cats to herd . . . and our break is almost over."

Nodding, the head of the TUP Council strolled off. Myang studied the jackets on the stage floor. She shifted her weight slightly toward them.

"I wouldn't do it," Ia warned her. "You mess them up, I'll make *you* refold them."

"You wouldn't dare." Myang did turn away from the coats, though.

"Until the Second Grey War ends, I still technically out-rank you in any combat zone, sir. This system still qualifies as a valid combat zone because the Greys will be back here to try attacking one more time in just a few more days."

That earned her a sharp look, but Myang's aide approached, clearing his throat. "It's almost time to begin again, sir."

"Relax, sit back, and don't interfere," Ia repeated under her breath. She touched Myang's elbow as she had the Premiere's. "You know how accurate and needful my precognition-backed actions have been. Trust in me to *always* do the right thing, Christine. Short-term or long-term."

Myang narrowed her eyes at Ia's use of her given name now of all moments, but it was time to restart the commenda-tions. Sighing roughly, she turned to walk back to her place on the stage. Ia stood up from the table, resumed her place, and settled back into Parade Rest.

She had made room on her overcoat for the new alien-bestowed medals. Under the Terran Standard gravity of the *Osceola*, and compared to the standard-and-a-half of her own ship, the weight of her coat was bearable. Crowded but bear-able, with the K'Katta sashes—new and old—carefully looped cordon style around each arm, tucked under the shoulder boards, and all the rest pinned in place. It felt almost like armor when she stopped next to Mandella. She tucked her hands behind her back, but out of respect for the end of the long ceremony, did not try composing any prophecies.

Mandella eyed her coat, sighed, and addressed the watch-ing crowd. "One Terran month ago, I sat in a meeting with my Secondaire, twenty fellow Councilors, the Admiral-General, twenty senior officers of the Command Staff, and one dozen noncommissioned and enlisted members of the Department of Innovations, the cornerstone of the strength of the Terran Space Force.

"We had gone through the list of names and associated actions of all the meioas you have just seen and applauded today. We had come to quick agreement on what awards to give to the 160 members of A Company, 9th Cordon Special Forces . . . but debated and even argued for over half an hour on what to award General Ia. Half the camp insisted that this soldier had earned a second Medal of Honor—more than earned it, for her repeated actions of personal effort and bravery have consistently gone above and beyond the call of even extraordinary duty.

"Those efforts have been aided by her abilities, yes . . . but we were all in agreement that she *chose* to act. That this Human turned her hand and her mind and her skill to saving her fellow sentients' lives. The other half of the special commendations committee," the Premiere confessed, "did *not* want to give her a Medal of Honor."

Scowls, puzzled frowns, and dark looks sprang up on the faces of Ia's crew. They stirred in their seats. She shifted her hand from behind her back in a brief, subtle gesture for them to abide. Her crew members respectfully settled themselves. They weren't the only ones upset at that thought, but they were the most important ones to soothe. The rest of the audience murmured a bit, then fell quiet when Mandella raised his own hand for silence.

"It's not what you think. There was no doubt in our mind that she deserved recognition—in fact, from her records of combat, her entire uniform should be covered in medals for taking down individual enemy officers, noncoms, ships, vehicles, and the rescue of so many of our Alliance allies and native civilians, all things which the Department of Innovation decided to award as acts lumped under a single medal per battle, per type, even for battles that were several hours long. So it was not that she did not deserve in their eyes—and mine—a second Medal of Honor. We simply thought that it was not, and never would be, enough."

Turning to the last box in sight, a white satin one larger than usual, the Premiere picked it up, pulled up the lid, and displayed it to the dignitaries seated behind them in the risers at the back of the stage. Moving to face the front, he allowed one of the hovering cameras to zoom in and display a close-up of the brooch that rested inside, which the cameras dutifully projected onto the screens set high over the stage.

Wrought in platinum and gold, the oval map-projection of the surface of Earth, the Terran motherworld, had been outlined in metal and inlaid with semiprecious stones: lapis for the oceans, tigereye, jade, and more for the continents. Each branch of the laurel wreath, one in pale platinum, the other in rich yellow gold, had been filled in with tiny teardrop-shaped tourmaline, with one quarter of the leaves colored Marines Brown, one quarter in Army Green, one quarter in Navy Blue, and the remaining quarter in an almost pewter-shaded but still clear and cleanly faceted Special Forces Gray.

The whole piece was about ten centimeters in length, six in height, and was mostly flat, save for a gold five-point star that rose up out of the Pacific Ocean toward the left edge of the map. That star marked the capital of the Terran United Planets, Aloha City, located in the tropical splendor of the Hawaiian Islands. Ia swallowed down her emotions, looking at that raised bit of gold; it had not really registered that she would never again return to Earth. Never again to her own birthworld, but not to Earth. Not until just now.

"When it finally occurred to us that we could *create* a medal specifically for honoring all that General Ia has done for us as a fellow Terran Human . . . we stopped arguing and started planning what it would look like. As you can see . . . I think we did a good job. Gentlemeioas," Mandella stated, turning to face Ia and gently lifting out the brooch, "it is my deepest honor to award to General Ia the one and only Terran Star."

He lifted it toward her chest, and hesitated. Mandella eyed her medal-covered coat, then lifted his hand and swirled his finger, point down. Obligingly, Ia turned in a circle. Military style, of course, crisp quarter turns learned all the way back in endless drills during her Marines Basic days. When she faced him again, she tucked her hands behind her back in modified Attention once more.

This time, Mandella's sigh was a bit more exasperated than a breath to brace himself for his speech. ". . . I think we should have stopped giving her medals long ago. No offense, General, but I have no idea where to pin it. Could you please stop being so efficiently heroic?"

"Sorry, sir, but I can't do that," Ia countered lightly as a chuckle rippled across the crowd. The pickups caught her words and projected them, same as they had everyone else's. "It's not in my nature to be less than efficient. The heroic bit is just me doing my job, sir. However, I can make a suggestion, Meioa Premiere."

"And that would be . . . ?" he asked.

Her left lapel bore her two Stars of Service from before the start of the wars, and her Medal of Honor. She tapped the untouched right one. It was the side reserved strictly and solely for the Black Heart, the one pin a soldier never wanted to earn, and a superior never wanted to give.

"That's a little unusual, soldier," Premiere Mandella reminded her. He eyed her chest, covered as it was with neat row after row, save for the ones most recently applied by the other presenters, and gave in with a shrug. "But, given the crowding of your coat . . . it'll have to do. Thank God I'm not a superstitious man. This is normally reserved for the Black Heart. As far as I know, you're not dead, yet."

"Well, back in 2490 Terran Standard, I was briefly considered to be dead right here in this very system. My Marines Company thought I'd drowned in a flood on Haskin's World," she explained, holding still so he could slot the pin through the fabric. Then smiled. "I'm still not dead yet, sir."

They turned slightly as he clasped her hand, allowing the cameras and the soldiers and handful of civilian contractors sitting in the audience a chance to have a good look.

"Kindly keep doing whatever you can to avoid dying anytime soon, General. That's an order from your Commander in Chief," he added under his breath, giving her a pointed look. The pickups didn't broadcast his subvocalized words, since they were too quietly spoken.

"I will do whatever I must, sir. That's a promise from the Prophet," she replied in kind, holding her slight smile. "May I address the hall?"

Releasing her hand, he stepped back, gesturing her toward the clear plexi podium. "Be my guest."

Nodding, Ia faced the main part of the multilayered hall. Concerts were held in here, lectures, and theatrical performances. It was far more than just a place where the military versions of carrot and stick were applied. It was also, at this moment, her last chance to speak to the Alliance at large. Her first chance to speak was still yet to come, ironically, though it was still a couple days away.

"You have all come to know me as General Ia . . . and I think I can safely say I'm now the single-most-decorated soldier in Terran history. In the other's too . . . You have also come to know of me as Bloody Mary, the xenocidal militant who insisted on causing weeks' worth of economic crashes, health panics, transport shutdowns, and many other problems. And you have come to know me as the Prophet of a Thousand Years, seeing for yourself just how temporally accurate I can be.

"A Human only lives about a hundred Terran Standard years on average—around 113 in Alliance Standard. But while the Second Salik War is gone, and technically the Blockade is no longer needed to keep the Salik contained, it will still remain in effect in all Salik Interdicted Zones for the next five years. This is to ensure that the atmosphere-bearing planets and moons which are still contaminated with the plague they created have the time needed to sail into their local suns for a final round of eradication. The Feyori—normally a collective pain in the asteroid—have pledged themselves to ensure that no scrap of it will escape those colonies and their fates.

"A Human only lives about a hundred Terran Standard years," she repeated. "And for the moment, we are still embroiled in a Second Grey War. They have figured out how to live for thousands of years, but the means by which they have succeeded have several serious flaws, including genetic sterility. They will not be allowed to attempt to use Humans in an effort to revive their dying race. Continue to follow my orders, seek out and train new psis, and together we will continue to keep them at bay.

"I am mostly Human—fully so in my mind and heart—and my longest possible life span would be only a hundred or so years. Yet I know that roughly three hundred from now, the implacable, ancient enemy of the Greys will reach out toward this galaxy with the intent to steal all of its resources, its planets, nebulae, and stars, like a swarm of locusts on Earth stealing all the plant life they can eat. I will not live to see that day—none of the matter-based races have natural life spans that long, not even the Chinsoiy, though they may come the closest at two centuries for their eldest. But if you encourage your children, and your children's children, to continue following their prophecies, I promise you I will guide the Alliance and its future allies into stopping them. Even after I, too, am long dead and gone.

"I can do this, and will do this, by doing it with *your* help. We have won against the Salik, we are winning against the Greys, and we will win against the Zida"ya. Even after I am personally long dead and gone." She swept her gaze over the somber, listening crowd. "As you have seen by the efforts of my crew, who were recognized today for their many, many efforts . . . I cannot do it alone. I need you, and I will continue to need you down through the ages. I hope you are willing to help make our galaxy a better place for our descendants, and not just for ourselves. It will take work, but it can be done, and it will be worthwhile. I have foreseen it ahead of you.

"Speaking of my crew," Ia continued, lightening her tone. "Some of them are going to be able to retire shortly into civilian lives, while others will continue in the Service for a little while more. However, as much as we are all deeply honored and humbled by these accolades and recognitions . . . we one and all, from myself down to my juniormost private, believe that we are simply doing our jobs, and we know that we do not need any further singling out for special recognitions.

"Once the Second Grey War is over, if my crew wishes to speak about their experiences, they are free to do so, within the bounds of their oaths to maintain the secrets of the Terran military and so forth," she allowed. "But if they do not wish to speak, or if they wish to go do something else with the rest of their lives, please respect that. With that in mind, I know many of you have wondered why most of my crew took off their Dress jackets."

Ia paused and carefully unbuttoned hers. She folded the medal-covered garment into a neat bundle with a little help from her telekinesis, and held it out to the Premiere. Mandella blinked, his hands coming up automatically to accept the weight. Removing her Dress cap, she set it neatly on top, then faced the main half of the audience again.

"We are honored to receive these things, as I have said . . . but we don't need honors to motivate us to do what must be done. We are fellow soldiers, enlisted through officer, and the only thing that separates us from anyone else is that when we see a job that needs doing, our conscience and our sense of duty compels us to get it done. Our sense of honor and our pride ensures that we do so to the best of our abilities. So all these coats are being donated to the TUPSF Military Museum back on Earth. Because we'd still be doing every single thing we have ever done in the name of saving the Alliance and the galaxy, even if we had never *once* received a single speck of recognition, for all that we are humbled and grateful that we have."

While she had spoken, Mandella had set the heavy bundle of her overcoat and cap on one of the now-empty tables between the two of them and the risers of seats at the back of the stage. Ia turned crisply to face him as he returned to her side and raised her hand to her brow in salute.

"Commander in Chief," she asserted firmly, hand held at her brow. "A Company, 1st Legion, 1st Battalion, 1st Brigade, 1st Division, 9th Cordon Special Forces requests permission to return immediately to the next battle zone, sir."

He returned the salute. "Permission granted, General. Go kick those Greys out of our sovereign space . . . and then come back to tell us all about it. We'll throw you one last big party, before letting you get on with your lives."

"I would like that very much, sir." She held out her hand instead of lowering her arm to her side. He clasped it for a moment, nodding to her, then let her go. Turning in a crisp About-Face, Ia addressed her troops. "A Company, 9th Cordon!"

They surged to their feet, a handful still in their Dress Black jackets, the rest in their shirtsleeves, and every last one of them standing at Attention in under two seconds flat, ready to move.

"We have fifteen minutes to be back on board, and thirty-seven to get under way. Move out!" she ordered, pointing up the aisle on her right at the same doorway which Helstead, Rico, and the other swapped-out crew members had used. The aisle on the other side of the center seating section would also have to be used, but it was convenient to point to her right.

Turning crisply, her crew split themselves down the middle of each row and peeled out of the seats, heading up the aisles with Spyder in the lead on one side and the equally gray-shirted Rico on the other. Ia descended the steps in their wake and took up position at the rear. On the stage, she heard the Admiral-General thanking everyone for coming, and looked not at the audience, who were one and all rising to their feet, applauding, but at her crew.

They didn't react openly to the standing ovation, but they did walk a little taller, shoulders back and chins level, filled with determination. Most of them in their shirtsleeves. Most of them. Not some of them, or none of them, or only a few.

Ia kept her eyes dry by sheer willpower all the way back to the ship. The sight of eight bodies in Dress Blacks lining up along the side of the airlock attached to the *Osceola*'s boarding gantry, awaiting the transfer of their personal belongings packed in crates from the depths of the ship by their crewmates . . . that spilled the tears over. Mindful of the surveillance system, Ia kept her back to the gantry's cameras as the rest of her crew formed a Human chain, passing boxes and bags from ship to Battle Platform deck, to the sleds which someone had thoughtfully ordered for the departing crew members.

Her arm unit chimed. Slipping her headset out of her pocket, she accepted the call. *"Yes, Admiral-General; you wanted to speak with me?"*

"Ia, what the hell are all these Black Hearts doing on all these jackets?" Myang snapped in her ear. *"Genibes and I found the pins the moment we started looking at 'em. Those medals are* only *given out postmortem."*

"Sir, the probabilities are running rather high that some portion of my ship will be destroyed in the final fight. This means it's highly likely that, no matter what I do to stave it off, some of my crew will die. But as they have served me loyally for over four years, I have given them the choice *of*

whether or not they wish to face that high risk to their lives. Giving them those Black Hearts was my way of shoving that potential death right in their faces, in the hopes that some might choose to stay behind—and for the record, some are *staying behind.*

"I don't need a full crew for the final battle, and I can run the Damnation *with twenty or less if need be. Or even just one, just as I ran the* Hellfire . . . *though I'll admit that would not be nearly as easy, since this will be a full-on running fight, and not just laying in wait as a trap."*

She heard Myang sigh in disgust. *"General, I am* not *happy with the thought of* any *of your crew being at risk. I certainly am not happy at the thought of* you *being at high risk."*

"Neither am I, sir. If it's any consolation, I would be happy to personally revoke each and every Black Heart that turns out to be unnecessary—hell, I would gladly unpin them from all those jackets myself, if you like, though of late every time I transfer any pins from coat to coat, I keep pricking my damned fingers."

"Yes, *I'd like that,"* Myang snapped.

"Then I'll keep that in mind and see what can be arranged. If you'll excuse me, sir; I have to finish getting my crew on board and our ship undocked. We still have at least four fights to go before the final battle . . . and I do have an interview with Meioa de Marco scheduled to begin in less than an hour."

"I swear to God and my ancestors, you are a true pain in the asteroid, Ia. I'm going to order these Dress jackets held until after you get back, so that hopefully no rumors about the damned Black Hearts get out to the press. You're lucky the hovercams were shut off before Sranna and I started rummaging through the stacks."

"Thank you, sir; I appreciate your sense of discretion. I'll see how many I can save on my end of things. Now, if you'll excuse us, we still have a war to get back to. Ia out."

Ending the link, she stuffed the headset back into her pants pocket and checked on the progress of her departing crew. As the last bag was passed, the line of makeshift stevedores turned into a farewell line of hugs, backslaps, tears, and even some laughter.

Some of it was spurred by the first of her departing crew. Clairmont hugged her briefly, and promised to ". . . compose a scandalous, libelous libretto about you, sir." York hugged her tightly, whispering how much he would regret not getting to sing with her again, while Ia struggled not to let her gifts trigger. MacArroc and Redrock each saluted, then hugged her. Huey saluted, then swept Ia a Scadian-style bow before clasping hands. Ng and Deschamps each shook her hand—then group-hugged Ia together. Her throat ached, and her eyes stung.

Commander Christine Benjamin was the last one in the line. The two women shook hands, but then the normally very physically reserved Ia wrapped her arms around her friend rather than waiting for Bennie to hug her first.

"Thank you for taking care of me," she whispered, shaking a little with the need to control her pain. For a moment, her voice simply wouldn't work. Not since hugging her twin good-bye had she felt this much suppressed grief, and only now acknowledged just how much she cared for her chaplain, psychologist, and friend. Clearing her throat, she tried again. "Thank you."

"You're making me *verklempt*, and despite the last name, I'm not even Jewish," Bennie muttered. "And you're welcome. Thank you for letting me."

Ia had one more thing to say. Not out loud, but in another whisper. "Watch over *them*," she ordered, meaning Deschamps and the rest. Pulling back, she gripped her chaplain by the shoulders. "You get into *any* trouble, you call on Silverstone. He still owes me for that double play I gave him, and I'm handing you his leash. Don't use him unless you have to, but don't hesitate if there's true need."

"Understood," Bennie agreed, nodding. She adjusted her Dress cap on her neatly bunned red hair, and breathed deep. "Dorsen caught the transmissions from your arm unit during the ceremony and copied them for me. I'll get the last of the prophecies to the Grandmaster for you."

"Thank you. God bless you, Commander Benjamin," Ia wished her friend, letting go. The airlock was almost clear as everyone finished filing on board. "You deserve every bit of the happiness that lies ahead."

"Tinged with bitter sadness, to remind me of the sweet,"

she agreed. "God bless you, too . . . and since you believe in reincarnation, may God give you a much better time of it in your next life."

Ia merely shrugged. "Well, divine or not, the two-fisting bitch *does* owe me."

Chuckling, Bennie headed for the hoversled holding her things. Turning toward her ship, Ia stepped on board, wiped her eyes dry, and did not look back.

NOVEMBER 1, 2499 T.S.
GLIESE 505, ONE LAST TIME

Three days later, the Greys turned up, just as Ia had promised. So did the *Damnation*. So did three hundred Feyori, in one last battle-gathering under the Prophet's command.

The Grey vessels, bulky but sleek in their curves, teleported into place around the *Osceola*, placed so close to the Battle Platform that Ia was pretty damned sure even without checking the timestreams that the *Osceola*'s entire bridge crew and command staff needed a full change below the waist. The only problem from Ia's point of view was that their half-shell formation, snugged tight against the station, meant that any angle where she had a shot at their ships either ran the risk of slamming her target into that station if the explosive force of the Godstrike vaporizing that ship made it tumble askew, or hitting the planet with the overshoot.

Some of the Feyori had the crysium spheres on hand, swooping them around the alien ship at a range Ia had determined was outside the effects of that damned entropic ray. The spheres were blaring KI as hard as they could, trying to sting the aliens into leaving. The Greys in turn had cranked up their anti-psi generators in the hopes of poisoning the Feyori. They also kept trying to translocate Humans off the *Osceola*, and off Haskin's World itself since it was in range for their technology . . . but every time they tried that, a couple of Feyori swooped in, grabbed the prisoners, and popped them completely out of that star system, dropping them on a colonyworld far enough away that the Greys had no hope of getting any of them back.

The Feyori, she knew, were rather upset that the Greys were trying to steal away their comrades' pawns and were determined to evacuate every last colonist if need be. Sometimes it was good that a Meddler liked the color red, when one just happened to be a red-colored game piece. They were also expecting their half-breed fellow player to end this fight in full today. Ia had already laid plans, with funds from her younger brother's hidden accounts, to ensure the translocated victims would have food, lodgings, resources, and travel plans to get them back home again when it was safe to do so.

As for the fight, the insystem buoys were broadcasting it onto her left secondary screen, since her dead-ahead course was on the primary. At least, she was watching what there was of the fight that was actually visible. Mostly it was just tiny specks of gold-and-silver water molecules flying around lumpy blackish things hovering close to a mirror-polished thistle burr floating above a blue-green-brown orb, one-quarter shadowed in night, and the remaining three-quarters of the visible hemisphere swathed in streaks and swirls of gray and white.

Her lower third tertiary screen showed the exact same countdown timer as every other third tertiary screen on the bridge. The same as at virtually every active workstation across the overgrown needle of a ship, from bow to stern, engineering to life support, gunnery pods to recreation decks. Not that anyone was relaxing at the moment; all hands were on deck.

"Sir," Xhuge said, his eyes on his communication screens, "Meioa de Marco is calling. She wants another interview. She says the last one ended a bit . . . vigorously yesterday, and she'd like the chance at recording a different, preferably calmer one."

"Inform her we are entering combat, and that I'll send her a prerecorded one in a moment. Let her know that she's still free to transmit the previous one in whole, unedited. I think it might be enlightening for everyone."

"Aye, sir," he said. "The Greys are trying to hijack the local relay hubs in an effort to ping you. They definitely want you to respond. I suspect it's so they can translocate to your current location, wherever that might be in the Alliance."

Her mouth curved up slightly on one side. "I suspect you're

right. Please contact Afaso Headquarters on Earth instead, and inform them to begin broadcasting file . . . 117a. And rebroadcast it when you get it, all channels, hyper and lightwave."

"File 117 A-as-in-alpha, got it, sir." He made the connection and murmured into his headset pickup. "Incoming on the hyper, and outgoing on the hyper and in the light . . . now, sir."

An image appeared on the screen. The Human centered on what looked like padded practice mats in some sort of martial arts classroom was both familiar and odd. She was quite young, still in her late teens though her long, wavy hair was old-woman white. Her clothes consisted of medium blue pants, slip-on blue shoes, white socks, and a light blue, flower-sprigged, long-sleeved blouse. She stared straight into the camera pickup with amber-colored eyes framed by dark blonde lashes and brows, her expression serious, even a little sad on her naturally tanned, Asiatic face.

"'Ey! I know tha' outfit," Spyder exclaimed softly from his backup gunnery seat. "Innat th' one you wore in Darwin?"

"I also wore it at Afaso Headquarters outside Antananarivo, Madagascar prefecture, Earth. Shh," the much-older-looking, short-haired, gray-clad Ia hushed her oldest military friend. "I have something to say."

Young Ia nodded, and began speaking. "My name is Ia. Most of you will have come to know me as General Ia, Bloody Mary, or the Prophet of a Thousand Years . . . but today . . . my name is just plain Ia. Today's date is March 1, 2490 Terran Standard, and in three more days from my point in time, I will be arriving in Melbourne, Australia Province, to sign up for a long and harrowing career in the Terran Space Force. From *your* point in time, you are hearing this message on November 1, 2499.

"To the Shredou who are trying to find your timeline's version of me, I already told you what will happen. You will, in your desperate arrogance, rip a chunk out of the universe. I, who have the power to destroy every last one of your worlds . . . will save everyone in this galaxy. Including you.

"You will stop fighting. You will stop trying to grab Humans," Youngest Ia recited, her voice hard, her sentences short and clipped so there was no room for reinterpretation or misunderstanding. "You will analyze what you did. You will shut off your new weapon. You will apologize. You will go home. You will *stay there*. I have given you the new boundaries of your space and Terran space. If you violate those borders, my followers among both the Humans and the *shhnk-zii* will aim the Zida"ya straight at you.

"You have heard my words. You have had time to analyze them. You have analyzed their timing. You have seen my words come true. You *know* how accurate I am," she asserted fiercely, hands fisting at her sides in youthful, stubborn determination to be obeyed. "You will do as I say, or you will be the first to die when your ancient enemy comes to this galaxy. My Prophetic Stamp on that. You know how accurate I am. I will still be that accurate for *ten* thousand Terran Standard years."

Ia—the one on the ship—palmed open the lock on the main cannon as her younger self spoke. She tapped the button thrice, strafing the ship slightly as it sliced through the night. The ship's engines charged up and fired the briefest of shots three times just as she adjusted their trajectory by the tiniest bit. A dark lump translocated straight into their previous path—and the *Damnation* strafed red death through the Grey ship that popped into close proximity and streaked past before anyone could blink.

"Ah, yeah, about that, sir," Xhuge drawled, eyeing the glowing wreckage now visible on a rearward-facing screen. "I meant to tell you that these *ri shao gou shi bing* have managed to triangulate our position based on our broadcast signal."

"*Sheh sheh*, Xhuge," Ia replied, sideslipping the ship to starboard to prevent return fire. The numbers on the countdown timer were getting distressingly smaller. "I know it's the thought that counts."

The camera angle on the broadcast switched. The youngest version of Ia turned to face the new vid pickup. Back then, Ia had broken down all possible speeches into different segments and had repeated them for the recordings, saving each portion as soon as she had a good enough version—within two or three tries, usually—just so she wouldn't have to say the same things over and over and over with each new subtle change. Contingencies within contingencies, all planned and accounted for even back then.

"For the rest of the known galaxy," Youngest Ia stated from her position in the past, "I wanted to thank you one last time for trusting me. I also need to apologize to my superiors in the Space Force . . . and to my legal defense." She smiled wryly, sadly, at her unseen future viewers. "In five more days, when I take the Oath of Service, I will lie. I will lie so perfectly that your fancy machines will never detect it. I will lie to my superiors about obeying all their orders. I will lie about giving up my citizenship with the Free World Colony on long-lost Sanctuary, I will lie by implication about upholding the Charter of the Terran United Planets, because I will break the laws for which that Charter stands, and I will lie about performing my sworn duties in solely lawful ways.

"I will conduct covert communications with alien nations and broker secret treaties. I will agree to carve up and deliver an Alliance member state on a damned *platter*, being my own homeworld . . . and I will commit murder. Over, and over," she asserted, pointing off to the side as if pointing at a mounting pile of bodies just beyond the camera's range, "up to and including the destruction of the entire Salik race."

Ia wrapped her ship in FTL, gently swapped ends, tapped the button, and dropped the warp field long enough to fire before enveloping it again so that she could straighten out her course. Another Grey ship burned in the star-strewn night. Young Ia lifted her chin slightly.

"I apologize for lying to you. For concealing what I will have done. I do *not* apologize for all the things I know I must do, the stains I must take upon my soul, in order to save the majority of you."

"Harper to Ia, I have a confession to make."

Naturally the one man she could not predict just had to throw a wrench into her plans. *"Ia here. Go."*

"Whoa!" Private Mellow muttered from his post at navigation. Bright light flared briefly near the view of the Battle Platform and its unwanted companions. "We have an explosion fifty klicks out, system upstream from Haskin's orbit, just off the *Osceola*. Looks like the Greys brought in an extra ship and have successfully tagged one of the crystal balls the Meddlers are flying around with, by using the new weapon."

"I kinda took that information you gave me, about the

Feyori somehow being involved in time-traveling our way out of the upcoming mess?" Harper reminded her.

"Mostly, I am telling you this right now because I want you to understand that I am going into all of this, the next nine-plus years, with my eyes wide open . . . and my heart and mind fully aware of what tasks and terrors lie ahead," Young Ia stated, squaring her floral-printed shoulders. She looked odd, compared to the older, short-haired version, no shadows under her eyes, no lines of weariness marring her youthful face. The sober, determined look in her gaze was the same, however. "And I will tell you that *all* of these things I do, the fighting, the slaying, and arranging that people will *die* . . ."

"Well, I contacted that Silverstone fellow. I asked him to ask around, to look for a Feyori volunteer who could come on board. After all, they don't always *die when time travel is involved, right?"*

Ia frowned at the words coming through her headset. She split her attention farther, dividing herself into four pieces. One part strained to listen to Harper. The second part tapped over her workstation controls, retracting the battle plates that had sheltered and hidden the hundreds of small but now electrically fed and bright-glowing crysium nodes that dotted the entire hull. The move forced a shutdown of the all the insystem thruster panels, an unfortunate side effect, but it was alright; the hull was tough enough to take the few wisps of interstellar gas that lay between them and their target . . . and she knew she had aimed the ship true.

The third corner of her mind listened to her own broadcast . . . and the last piece of her attention span listened to her bridge crew, making sure Fonnyadtz ordered the port gunnery teams to fire on their own lesser countdown, thrust-bearing missiles soaring out from the *Damnation*'s P-pods. Right on time and on target, they immediately struck the hull of the Grey ship that popped into place beside them—they did no damage, of course, but not even the Greys could avoid the effects of physics; archaic chemical thrusters burning in full, they pushed the other ship just enough that, at half-Cee speeds, it veered wildly off course and well out of entropy gun range within a fraction of a blink.

". . . I do it because I am willing, and ready, to pay the exact same price."

"It didn't work." Harper sighed in her ear. *"I couldn't get any to come."* He sounded regretful, frustrated, and defeated. *"So, before we die for sure, I just wanted you to know that I tried to help. And that I will always love you."*

Youngest Ia lifted her chin proudly. "I go into the Space Force already knowing that today, *your* day, I go to my death. I myself shall willingly pay the price that I am going to have asked of many of you."

"I love you, too," Ia murmured, and cut off the comm link. She didn't have any time or attention left for anything more. They were within moments of ground zero; her main screen was now showing a near-real-time view of the swooping, sphere-clutching Feyori pairs dodging and weaving through twenty enemy ships. The countdown timer occupying a corner of every workstation, every screen, was now down to double digits at best, and not nearly enough of them anymore.

"But I give you this final warning," her young, fierce, determined self growled as the oldest and last version of Ia pushed down on the Godstrike button one last time, and held it down, "that I will take my enemies *with* me into the Room for the Dead. Whether it's in my time, or your time, or *ten thousand* years ahead!"

Something swirled into view right next to one of the Grey ships fighting several kilometers out from the *Osceola*. The explosion and its abrupt, extra-deep blackness startled two sphere-bearing Feyori—no doubt the ship's original target— into dodging erratically. The Grey ship abruptly vanished, startling them again; they dropped the sphere and sped off in opposite directions, one off to port, and the other swerving back toward the starboard, leaving their glowing cargo to roll on through the night until they could come back to fetch it.

Ia's last words were a whisper that came from the view-screen, her not-quite-eighteen-year-old body tight with fear, her teeth bared in determination, her amber eyes stark with a mixture of despair, determination, and love. *"For I am a soldier . . ."*

The Godstrike fired, spearing that poor, rattled Meddler in bright-hot red as it crossed between the *Damnation* and the broken rift. The sensors shut off protectively, blanking out their forward view at the last second, but it did not matter. It was the last second, and only one thing mattered to Ia: checking the timestreams one last time.

It should have been hard to see with the light almost gone from the timeplains' sky, but she could see it. In that last, slowed-down fraction of Time deep in the back of her mind . . . the Future was firmly on course. Every canal, every levee, every ridge and ditch had been dug as deep and as strong as she could make them. Every trick, every death, every sacrifice, every lie, all of it was finally, firmly in place.

Night fell on the battlefield of her efforts. As the last of the light vanished from the timeplains in her mind, as that blacker-than-black hole in space swallowed everything . . . *everything* . . . Ia knew she had *won*.

I stay sane *because I* am *sane! I am* sane *because I am willing to* stand up and fight, *when others would lie down and die. I will stand before you right now, and* swear *by my Prophetic Stamp:* No More!

No more violence, no more bloodshed, no more ceaseless, needless death—*not* one *pico more! By God, I will* not *stand still for rampant death, nor let it pass me by! Not at* my *post. Not on* my watch*! I will throw my* own *life into the danger zone and stand between our beloved homes and the war's worst desolation—and no* other *life shall pay!*

For I *am a* soldier . . . *and* that place is **mine!**

Energy shimmered into view, at first forming a single rippling, wavering line, then splitting and curving into an arch. It was pointed at the top somewhat like the pupil of a cat's eye, though if the bottom was pointed as well, its point was lost under the uneven stone floor. It wasn't the only source of light. Within moments, scudding balls of shimmering opalescent magic, like overgrown dust bunnies, soared in through the cavern walls. The energy balls impacted on the edge of the arch, brightening and strengthening it with each impact. Two, five, fifteen, then a trickle of a few more stragglers soared in to join the arch. A few seconds later, it stabilized.

A dark-clad body dashed through that shimmering portal into the dark cavern. The man spun, skidding a little as his boot soles slipped on the gritty, uneven surface. One of the marks tattooed on his tanned face shimmered briefly with an odd, faint, brownish glow. He turned in a circle, sword in one hand, crystal-tipped shaft in the other, ready to stab or smash anything that threatened the glimmering archway.

Nothing attacked. The iridescent lights played over the mottled, spotted granite of the cavern walls, and gleamed off the black hair of the only man in the chamber. The sueded silk and black leather of his clothes absorbed most of the light rather than reflected it, leaving him looking like nothing more than a head and a pair of weapon-wielding hands attached to a humanoid shadow.

"Ban?" a feminine voice asked. It was projected through the crystalline hoop piercing the middle shell of his ear.

Something about the chamber, with its uneven folds and ragged exit, made him twist and peer all around for several extra seconds. The only sounds he could hear were his own heartbeat and breathing, the soft scrape of his feet on the stone floor, and a faint hiss from the Veil. Scents were simple and plain: warm sandstone, dust, his own body, and a hint of moisture in the mostly still air.

Unable to spot what it was, he waited . . . waited . . . then shook his head slightly and spoke. "It appears to be clear. You may come through now."

The rippling, opalescent veil brightened, scintillating in streaks of light that pulled back to reveal a heavily wooded meadow, and a cluster of men and women moving toward the doorway in the Veil between worlds. Unlike Ban, all of them were golden-haired and golden-eyed, more lithe and lean than muscular, with ears that swept up to modest points rather than bearing the smooth curve of his own.

One of the three men stepped through and lifted a crystal in his hand. Energy flared outward, bathing the chamber in an iridescent mist before sucking itself back inside. He frowned a little, tilted the faceted oval and studied the shifting colors captured within, then shrugged. "It seems to be safe to use Fae magic, though I'll need to study this realm in depth. There are some oddities . . ."

"When are there not? Can you be specific, Éfan?" The voice came from the tallest and stateliest of the three women remaining on the other side. No sound escaped the portal archway; her voice was heard solely through their communication earrings.

"The portal stabilized much faster than anticipated, my lady," Éfan stated, still pacing slowly about the cavern. "A positive sign, but still something to be cautious about."

"It is not enough to turn us back," Jintaya decided. *"We will continue establishing the* pantean.*"*

Two of the four women on the other side stepped through; with the two men, they formed a chain while the dark-haired Ban stood watch by the exit tunnel and the blond male with the crystal egg continued to frown softly at the device. It was not a chain of muscles and limbs, however; instead, each of the four merely lifted their hands and the various boxes, bags, chests, and crates started floating across the archway. Goods moved from one universe to the other silently, almost effortlessly, though of course using magic instead of muscle would still cost each of them in some way.

The cavern selected for this transfer was fairly large, if uneven. The Veil had been pierced at one end, the exit tunnel at the other, with a dip and three terraces between the two. Bags and boxes, chests and bundles were floated through and settled to either side, sorted by color-coded ribbons and tags to differentiate between personal belongings and shared materials. This cave was at the bottom of a long chain of caverns and tunnels leading up to the surface, around a dozen. It would make an excellent, defensible home base.

The last of the crates and barrels came through, and now furniture floated past. Everything they would need to set up an initial observation outpost would be sent through for their use, including stores of food to last them long enough to either find edible things to cultivate and domesticate here on this world, or long enough to realize nothing was edible by their kind, in which case other plans would be made. The upper caverns would be claimed and occupied as rough living, working, and storage quarters, and eventually they would reshape the very rock of this place into something much more civilized. But that would take time.

With the Veil portal opened and stabilized, the light pouring from its magics was now equally steady. However, a hint of light off to the left of the archway flickered faintly, erratically. Narrowing his eyes, Ban watched out of the corner of his eyes—and sprinted for the spot, sword stabbing into the narrow rift even as he reached it. A frantic yell from the other side of the crack stopped his thrust, but only so he could pull the blade out and peer inside. Flames flickered and wobbled, casting weird shadows, but it did allow him to see a man running away from the crack, up a twisting tunnel raggedly illuminated by the burning torch in his hand.

"Ban! What is it?" Efan called out. Parren and Fali looked up briefly from their levitation efforts, but had to keep working.

"A spy!" Unsure if that passage connected to the others or not, he wedged his hand into the narrow crack and flexed the muscles under one of the many tattoos painting his tanned hide. Between one breath and the next, he shrunk down, scrambled through, and re-enlarged himself as soon as he could. Ban flexed another tattoo to keep track of the twists and turns of the mazelike caves so he could find his way back, and gave chase.

The wand in Ban's hand was brighter than the torch in the native's, making his passage hard to see whenever the other man got around a curve or a bend up ahead. The smell and sight of its soot lingering in the air, and the thumping of his feet on the cavern stone, kept the black-clad warrior on the fleeing man's track. A spy who saw the Veilway was not allowed to speak of it to anyone else. That meant catch, or kill.

Jintaya will want him caught, so that we can attempt to erase his memories, Ban knew, long legs catching up on the fleeing native slowly at best, thanks to the smaller man's evident agility. *Now how did he get in so close, on a path we could not see . . . ? Ah.*

These caverns were indeed connected to the others, though the connecting point was so low, he had to drop onto his belly to slither through the low gap the other man used more readily in a rapid, scuttling crawl. Ban's glowing wand remained steady, but the native's crude pitch torch nearly guttered out from being scraped along the floor. It didn't stop his flight, though. By the time he got through, the native was halfway across the sun-lit cave. It was not a direct exit, but the next passage was broad and led out to a cave that was half crevasse.

Finally free to run unimpeded by twists and turns in the granite face, Ban let his longer legs close the distance between him and his fleet-footed quarry. In the bright sunlight angling down from overhead, he could see the young man was about as heavily tanned as he was, with matted dark hair, some sort of primitive leather kilt wrapped around his hips, and very worn leather sandals strapped to his feet. One of those straps broke as he darted out of the crack they were following. He tripped, stumbled, then started yelling and waving his free arm, torch still held aloft. Sour sweat trailed in his wake, the scent of fear and an unwashed body, along with hints of pungent greenery and a drier kind of air than the caverns had held.

Abruptly wary, Ban skidded to a stop at the edge of that opening. Beyond it lay the green-speckled, wind-and-water carved ravine that the scrying spells of the others had scouted and checked. There should have been—and were—a number of wild-growing bushes, trees, grasses, even a few flowers, and a half-dried, somewhat muddy pond suggesting that this area did flood from time to time, despite the palpable heat radiating off of the rocky walls of the canyon.

There should *not* have been a good two hundred and more men, women, and children, ranging from babes in arms to gray-beards. Most of whom looked thin, dusty, haggard from hard travel on little food, and whom had apparently pulled sledges of primitive belongings, of leather goods and grass-woven baskets. Though the wind was shifting the air only a little bit, he could smell how desperately everyone needed a bath. There was water nearby for bathing, and he could see dampness on clothes and skin where some had slaked their thirst, but they must have only just arrived within less than an hour.

Just over one hour ago, when Jintaya herself had checked through the initial hair-thin opening of the Veil, the cave system and its immediate surroundings had been native-free. Natives who were now grabbing for their spears, their slings and primitive bows, and who were pushing their children back out of harm's way as they faced the black-clad stranger who had chased one of their own out of the caves.

"Ban, what is happening?" he heard Jintaya demand, even as the man he had chased, a middle-aged fellow with a good amount of stamina, started pointing his way and babbling in the local tongue.

"Jintaya . . . we have a problem," he murmured, carefully

lowering his sword so that it was not quite so threatening. The subtle blue tattoo marked around his eye, his ear, and all the way down to his throat twitched and itched a little, struggling to comprehend and translate their language.

"Tell me you did not kill the spy, Ban," she stated reprovingly.

"No, but I should have," he replied quietly, counting numbers, gauging weapon skills, and debating just how much of a fight he might have on his hands. The pale blue tattoo marking him from right eye to ear to throat and linked permanently to his personal, alien magics, finished making sense of their language. Syllables, vowels and consonants became sounds imbued with meaning. Words such as *magic* and *great power* and *anima beings*, whatever *anima* was, made him flinch. "He's now telling about . . . two hundred twenty people more what he has seen. Male and female, young and old. A tribe of some sort. They look like they have traveled far to get here, and have only just arrived."

"Shae? Tash keleth!" she swore. He blinked a little, not used to hearing the great lady curse like that, but otherwise kept himself calm and ready . . . until he heard several more running up behind him. Twisting sideways so he could face both groups, he held out his curved blade in warning, the pale gold metal reflecting the light like a slice of the sun.

Five more men and two women for a total of seven humans appeared behind him. They carried torches and were wrapped in rough leather garments held on with crudely woven cords, stumbling to a stop in the ravine behind him. They eyed his weapon and unfamiliar, neatly tailored garments with wide, wary eyes. The crevasse was narrow enough, Ban could easily keep them blocked off from the rest of their tribe. He could hold off both groups, so long as he stayed in the narrow opening, unless the larger one decided to start slinging spears and shooting arrows at him all at once.

"I need guidance, my lady," he murmured, prodding the woman on the other end of the crystal earrings linking the expedition members together. "Do I kill them, or not?"

She sighed heavily. *"The damage is done. Do not harm them. Return to the* pantean.*"*

Seven versus one, fully blocking his path, with an order not to harm any of them? Sighing roughly, he shifted his weight, rolled an ankle to activate another tattoo, and leaped at the wall on his right. Foot clinging for a brief, magic-assisted moment, he whirled and leaped higher, bounding back and forth across the gap of the narrow chasm. Each step angled him back, up, and over the heads of the gaping men and women, until he was free to drop to the ground and sprint back the way he had come without fear of being in range of an attack.

Or rather, he ran back almost the same way. Taking the main passages their spells had scouted, he reached the mouth of the innermost cave in time to find all six of the others waiting for his return, and the Veil Arch sealed against normal eyesight. He could still feel the Veil, the traces of warm, sunlight-like Fae energies radiating from where it had stood, but the portal was now hidden behind an illusion of the cavern wall having been moved forward by a few feet.

Only Fae powers could shift that wall back. Of the eight members of the *pantean*, Ban had not the right kind of magic to move it and access the way back. Then again, of the eight of them, he had no reason to go back. As soon as he crossed into the cavern, Éfan passed his hand over the opening. More rock sprang up—an illusion of rock, sealing them inside for their protection. A glance to the left showed the crack in the wall had a similar faux-stone patch.

The other two men, Adan and Kaife, had finished passing through supplies and belongings, and had joined their wives, Fali and Parren. They were busy donning the flexible, overlapping scales of *faeshiin* armor in the same shade of gold as Ban's blade. If this moment came to a fight, Ban would not be the only one armed and ready. The third woman in their group, however, did not look ruffled by the thought of combat. Instead, she was studying the water inside a silver bowl balanced in her hands, clad in a flowing golden gown that shimmered in the light of the crystal torches rapped and set around the chamber for illumination.

"Ban," Jintaya said, glancing briefly at him. She was older than Fali and Parren, older even than Rua by many decades, though she only looked a handful of years older than Ban did, at most. Her hair, however, was the telling factor; where Fali's fell to her shoulders, and Rua's and Parren's locks fell to mid-back, hers reached all the way to her knees. Pale and golden, she looked like a statue made of sunlight and honey to him. "Have you learned their language, yet? It is eluding my scryings."

"Yes." He moved closer when she beckoned him to her side, and politely peered into the mirror-polished bowl. The sounds were faint, but the images clear; the seven with the torches, the eighth who had spied upon them, and a clutch of a good ten more bearing weapons were tracking their way through the caves in search of the strangers in their midst.

"Translate for me."

"They are . . . looking for us . . . the younger ones are boasting how they'll take whatever we have. The eldest has just shushed them and said that I did not attack." He listened a moment more, and added, "One of the women says she is tired of traveling, and is willing to fight for a place to stay. The other, the one with the longer spear, complains she wants a safe haven, not another battle with people who are potentially stronger—she mentions my clothes and gear as being beyond anything they know how to make."

Éfan joined them. He was shorter than Ban despite being the tallest of the others, but then the black-haired human towered over all of the golden-haired Fae in the cave by a good hand span. He had stood taller than most of the natives, too, if not all of them.

"It sounds as though they are refugees," their magic specialist stated. He eyed Jintaya, and lifted the crystal egg still in his hand. "The energies of this world are different from our universe in certain key ways. Situational magics are responding sluggishly. I would not be able to catch all of them in a memory-altering spell at once . . . and I would be hard-pressed to alter their memories one at a time fast enough to keep them from talking to each other, cross-contaminating my efforts."

Jintaya bowed her head. She pressed the sides of her index and middle finger against the midpoint of her furrowed brow, a gesture Ban had seen her use before when she was annoyed and needed to think. Respectfully, he waited in silence. If the decision were his, he would have considered the most expedient of solutions: killing the entire tribe to keep their presence quiet. He might not have actually done so, but Ban did not care about any others, one way or another. He had not cared about anyone for a very long time, until Jintaya had rescued and stood up for him.

She was not a human like him, nor like the natives of this world seemed to be, but she had helped restore some of his long-lost humanity. He waited, patient, for her to decide what should be done about them.

Sighing, she lowered her fingers with a dismissive little flick, as if shaking off whatever negativity had arisen for a few moments in her mind. "We cannot alter their memories quickly at this time, and there are too many who will remember you to just repack everything, find another spot, and begin anew. Anything they remember of this moment will be recanted in legends, distorting the facts.

"We are therefore obligated to make peaceful contact ahead of schedule. If they are refugees," she added, slanting her golden eyes at the master mage of their group, "then they may not know that we ourselves have only just arrived. This gives us a chance to claim ownership of this region . . . which means we shall behave as gracious hosts. Diplomacy," she added to Ban, "is always more effective than combat when wielded *before* the first blow, not after. Thank you for not harming anyone."

Ban dipped his head in acknowledgment.

"They may have what appear to be primitive weapons and virtually no armor, but they are many and we are few," Jintaya told the other four. "We shall therefore make a show of civilized strength. Éfan, clear the way to the next cavern. Push them back, then check it for any possible spying point, and seal it. I realize this will take you time, but it must be done so that they understand *these* caves are ours, not theirs. They may have any others, if there are others, should they need such for shelter."

Bowing, Éfan moved back to the sealed-over opening, and began concentrating on the crystalline egg in his hand. Ban still had little idea how the man's magic worked, despite having lived among the Fair Traders for a handful of years now. He turned his attention back to their leader, and his mind back to practical matters.

"If they have been fighting other tribes, and have been

forced out of their home territory," Ban offered, "then they will want stone walls to guard their flanks. They may not give up these caverns easily. There is enough room to house them all, and a little bit for ourselves."

"We could offer them something more important. They will want water for drinking," Parren stated. She lifted her chin at Jintaya's scrying bowl. "I saw that pond. It will not be enough to slake their thirst for long. If we have clean water to offer, it will be seen as hospitable."

The three senior members of the expedition glanced at her, though Éfan returned his attention to his task after a moment. Despite not even being Fae, Ban outranked her simply by pure longevity. Not even Jintaya had lived as long as he had, though normally a Fae outlived a human by at least ten times the normal span.

"These ravines and their caves are the only patch of greenery for days of travel in any direction," Adan told Parren. "If we have an abundance of water, they may think to steal it from us. We should instead give them a display of our strength. Magic and sunsteel will back them off," he added confidently, his hand going to the *faeshiin* gold hilt of the sword he had slung at his hip.

"If we have very little to give, they may seek to kill us, just to ration what there is," she countered.

Fali held up her hand between the two. "It does not hurt to be courteous. As the Great Guardians say, 'If you offer kindness, you are more likely to receive kindness. If you offer discourtesy, you are more likely to receive discourtesy. We shall therefore offer courtesy first, and only react in unkind ways when we are treated unkindly. These are the Way of the Fae Rii,'" she recited, attempting to sound as wise and mature as their leader Jintaya. "I should not need to remind you of this."

"I should not need to remind *you* that we botched our usual careful arrival," Adan retorted.

"Peace, cousin," the other man stated, clasping Adan's shoulders. As Fali was the cousin of Parren, Kaife was cousin to Adan. He smiled and nodded at his mate. "Parren's offer would be a strong display of power if we conjured that water in front of them."

"We do not know how these primitives view their local

magic, yet," Jintaya reminded the young man, her gaze still on the bowl for all her pointed ears were on their conversation. "Nor how well they themselves can wield it. That was why we were to observe from a distance before making any approaches. The last thing we need is to be viewed as some sort of demons or gods. Now, what else should we consider, regarding magic and water?"

Parren sighed. "If they already know how to draw water out of the aether of this world, then they may be able to do so far more efficiently than us."

"Precisely. Parren, Adan, Fali, Kaife, begin your scrying exercises and study these natives, while Éfan makes more room in these caves for us," Jintaya instructed. "I shall prepare the *myjii* to boost our ability to learn the local language."

"And what will Tall, Dark, and Uncaring be doing?" Adan asked. His cousin smacked the back of his head. Adan flinched and shot Kaife a dark look, but didn't protest the swat. Ban ignored his quip, choosing to drink from one of the water jugs brought across among their other supplies. Chasing someone was thirsty work.

"They have reached the midrange caverns," Éfan stated, his attention on his crystal. "Since he can speak their language, if he were to gently escort them elsewhere, I could expand our territory more quickly without frightening them by abruptly relocating all these walls."

"Ban?" Jintaya asked, turning to him.

Taking a last swallow, he set the jug down and bowed to her. "As you wish."

"Gently," she reminded him.

He lifted a hand in acknowledgment even as he turned toward the sealed cave exit. Éfan waved it open with a flick of his fingers, then sealed it shut behind the dark-haired man. Ban passed through two more such portals, before spotting the flickering, golden-orange dance of approaching torchlight. Striking his crystal rod against one of the irregular walls, he extinguished it. Jintaya preferred the sweetness of diplomacy, but he knew that sometimes one had to prime the pump, so to speak, with a taste of potential unpleasantness.

When Jintaya had rescued him during a previous trade mission, she had persisted with her calm pleasantness in the face of his raging suspicion, distrust, and hostility. Three times, he had nearly killed her . . . and three times she had forgiven and embraced him. It was the Great Guardian himself who had explained it to Ban, after assessing the man Jintaya had insisted on bringing back to Faelan with her expedition, when that particular world had proven too uncivilized for the Fair Traders to continue visiting.

Jintaya is exceptionally gentle. She can be firm, yes—as unyielding as ice—but she does not care to kill, and will not personally kill. She is water in that she wears away bit by bit at hostility, distrust, and anger . . . but water is no hammer and chisel, able to carve a path in a single day. There are times when an expedition must be . . . expedient. You, Puhan—the only time anyone of the Fae Rii had bothered to get his name right, which made it stand out in his mind—will stay with her. You are ruthless beyond words when needed, expedient beyond thought. You shall be permitted to live among us, but you will guard Jintaya, and be the sword she cannot wield; not and remain who she is, who she must be. You are her opposite, and you each need the other, must be with the other, for there to be balance in both of your lives. This is your geas, for all you are not bound by it magically.

The torch-wielding natives came around a twist in the tunnels, spotted his head and hands in the dancing shadows, and stumbled to a halt. Shaping his words carefully, mindful of his translation tattoo, Ban stated bluntly, "These caves are forbidden to your people. You will remove yourselves immediately . . . and look for others to occupy."

There, Jintaya, he thought. *My own attempt at your preferred diplomacy.*

"All these caves are ours!" one of the younger men boasted. One of the older women tried to hush him, but he demanded, "We are many, and you are just one. Who are *you* to tell us where we can or cannot go?"

"Ban." He would have said more, but his name caused all eighteen natives to twitch and shift back. Some by only a finger-length, some by a full step. *Why would they . . . ?*

"He is named Death?" one of the older men whispered, eyes wide with fear. "This is an ill omen!"

Others whispered as well, a susurration of fear and

wonder. It seemed the corrupted, Fae version of his name had a distinct meaning in the local tongue. Ban had accepted the new name because it was what Jintaya herself had named him, and he had felt as if she had given him a second life when he had finally accepted her help and her caring. A new name for his new life. But it was ironic that on this world, in this tongue, the name that had given him a second life actually translated as *death*.

The woman with the longest spear, the one Ban had seen speaking earlier, stepped forward bravely, if warily. "There is only one of you, and we are many. Your name will not scare us away. There is water in this place, and food. Plenty for our tribe to take. You are only one man."

"I am not alone," Ban told her. "Jintaya, our leader, has claimed these caves. You will remove yourselves immediately. Go seek others."

"Djin . . . taje?" She frowned at him in confusion. "You mean, Taje Djin?"

"Jintaya," Ban asserted, wondering why the woman would get a simple name backwards like that. Then the translated meaning caught up with him.

Taya was similar to their word *Taje*, though the Fae used a softer "yuh" sound than these locals did. *Taje* in turn meant *Leader*. The rules of their grammar came to him with the realization that they always put the Taje before a name, not after. To do so after was . . . odd. Except there was a case where an emphasis could be made, he also realized.

"We are led by Taje Jintaya . . . ul," he added onto the end. It meant *Leader Djin, Leader of All*. The men and women, some young, some middle-aged, none old, eyed him warily. Repeating himself, Ban asserted one more time, "By her command, these caves are forbidden to all of you. Leave."

"No!" one of the younger males asserted. Bouncing a little, he lunged forward, stabbing at Ban with his spear. "These are *our* caves!"

Sunsteel flashed between them as Ban reacted. Metal hit wood when the sword in his hand connected with the hardwood shaft. The uneven cavern echoed with a ringing *tang* and a dull metallic clatter of the bronze point hitting the stone floor. The youth gaped at his weapon—then yelled and attacked, swinging the now bladeless shaft. Ban ducked and swung the crystal rod in his left hand. It connected with the other man's skull in a burst of steady, clean, golden-white light. Whipped around by the strength of Ban's blow, the youth crumpled with a sigh, slumping across the floor.

Ban eyed him, listening to the youth's breathing. Unconscious, and struck hard enough to awaken with a headache no doubt, but probably not suffering from a serious concussion. He hadn't activated any of his strength-based tattoos, so it wasn't as if the would-be warrior's brains had been splattered across the cave. Ban had far too many years of gauging his strength in more battles than this entire group would see in their combined lifetimes; he would not be so careless. Deliberate, but not careless. Holding the glowing rod off to the side, Ban pointed at the fallen youth with his sword, while the others stared wide-eyed at the crumpled figure, silent with fear.

"He still lives. You will take him, and yourselves, out of these caves. I might not spare the next to attack me. Your entire tribe is not great enough in numbers to stop me. I am Ban. I serve Taje Jintaya-ul. Be grateful she is willing to share these canyons with your people. She will not share these particular caves. *If* you behave and are polite, you may be invited to stay, rather than be told to leave this area. If you are rude and attack . . . you will be lucky if there are enough of you left to leave."

There was no inflection in his tone, aside from a point of emphasis on their choices in this matter. He did not stress their impending deaths if they chose unwisely. Ban didn't bother because he did not care. It had hurt him more than enough to learn after all these years that he could still care for someone. For Jintaya.

"Pulek. Eruk," the woman with the long spear ordered. "Grab Lutun. We will leave these caves alone. For now," she added firmly, holding Ban's gaze as if he were some sort of predator she had met. "Taje Halek will decide whether or not we will come back to them."

Two of the men moved forward at her command. Ban recognized one of them, the older of the two, as the man who had first spied upon the Fae. He had a few scars here and there, and was missing the tip of his third finger. He also eyed Ban warily, gaze flicking repeatedly to the blade that had nearly punctured him. The other fellow stooped and thriftily claimed the bronze spearhead.

Waiting until the group had dragged the unconscious would-be warrior off, Ban paced slowly in their wake, making sure none were lingering to try to ambush him. Every so often, he glanced behind, and saw the work of Éfan, sealing up cave after cave in his wake with what looked like blank walls sculpted and colored to match the rest of the wind-and-water worn rock.

I will have to remind Éfan to make the walls malleable enough that I can get through them at a touch, he thought, sighing with a touch of impatience. *Otherwise there will come a day I will have to bash my way in, and ruin whatever sculpting work they will be trying to do, reshaping these caves into a proper Fae home.*

———

Deep in the sand dunes to the south, Kuruk scowled at the coarse grains around them. They bore no traces of footsteps save the ones the five of them had made: Kuruk as leader, Charag and Tureg as fighters, Koro and his acolyte Pak. There should have been signs of the passage of over two hundred tribe members . . . but the winds of the desert, slow and sparse save at dawn and dusk, had erased all marks. "Are you *sure* the anima can track them? We haven't seen signs of their passage in three days, now."

Koro, their middle-aged *animadj*, made a *tsk* noise. "You know as well as I that the anima can do many things if the will is strong and sharp. My will is trained by twice as many years as you have been alive, hunt-leader. *And* . . . what do I have in my hand?"

"A torch," Kuruk grunted, lifting his eyes to the sky. He did not care for the teacher-prompting-the-student tone of the older man, but let it pass.

"A torch," Koro agreed, his tone bordering somewhere between chiding and pompous. The animadj had earned the right to be proud, however. "I draw my will from the fire that named our tribe. I draw my power from the encircling energies of the flame as it consumes all that it can eat. The torch flames point firmly north, while the wind, when it stirs, travels to the southeast. The fire I have bound with my will and the anima knows where they have gone. We will find them."

The scouting leader eyed the torch in question. "Well, it looks like it needs more dromid dung."

"We still have another finger or two before Pak will need to make another torch," Koro reassured him. "When we stop for that, I will use a bit of anima to pull up a little more water for us to drink."

"Good," Charag grunted. "Marching in sand with my battle-axe is thirsty work." Unlike the long bladed pole Kuruk used as a walking staff, and the lightweight bow and quiver of arrows Tureg wielded, he carried a heavy axe crafted of stout hardwood for the shaft and the wealth of two thick blades made of sharpened bronze.

"Try marching with enough firewood for fifteen days," Pak grunted. Charag gave him a disdainful look. Pak stuck out his tongue, then started to purse his lips.

"Enough, Pak. No conjuring sand devils," Koro added. "We don't need them to be seen."

"Heed your master," Kuruk agreed, chiding the young male with a jerk of his chin. "We are here to track those White Sands fools. Their animadj seemed to know of a place to settle to the north. For that many people, it would have to be a large and lush oasis. If they find such a place within half a moon's travel . . ."

"Then we will attack and take them over as war-slaves, claim their land for our own, and crush the Water Spears from each side," Pak recited, lifting his own eyes to the sky.

It was said that sky-anima was the rarest of all kinds that could be conjured, and thus the most powerful, for it made the lightning strike and the air boom and tremble. It caused the rains that made the landscape flood, which could kill people even on a cloudless day. Everyone implored the anima in the sky for kindness, patience, and mercy. Or mostly just for patience with others.

He eyed the torch in his teacher's hand. "Koro . . . Kuruk is right; the wind is picking up, and devouring the torch faster than I estimated. We should stop now, or as soon as we reach the next flat stretch. Those low rocks we saw from the last dune are near; it may be over the next rise, or the next two or three."

Grunting, Koro eyed the pitch-and-dung wrapped torch tip for a long moment, turning it a little to check how short the flames had become in the last *selijm* of travel, and nodded. The wind could and did disperse the smoke it gave off, but it was starting to smolder a bit more and burn a bit lower than it should. It would be better to prepare a fresh one. Fresh burned clean; the thin smoke from a mere torch would be lost in the wind, up until it started to gutter. Conjuring a sand devil, however, was something that could be seen for upwards of a full *selijm*, the distance a healthy person could walk in an hour.

However, when they crested the next dune . . . they found the sand rippling down into hard-packed earth, and a slight rise of rugged rocks. Hard desert, as opposed to the soft stuff they had slogged through. Squinting, all five men stared at the new terrain. Finally, Tureg spat dryly, far more sound than spittle—no need to waste saliva, even if Koro could conjure water wherever they went—and lifted his chin.

"I see cracks in the terrain ahead. Canyons," he stated, shading his eyes from the sun's glare. "There may be water in there, or there may be game. But mostly, there will be a lot of back-tracking as we try to follow the flames, which point straight and true regardless of what the actual trail chooses to do. This is where the anima-flame can do less for us than clear tracks would."

Kuruk grimaced. "That may be true, but we still have a job to do. If there *is* water for two hundred or more, and game and places to grow things, it is our job to scout it and decide if it's worth claiming, as well as continuing to pursue. Pak, start your torch-making in the valley behind us. Koro, draw upon the anima for water. We will take a dune-break behind this crest. Bury your waste, and keep an eye on all directions, just in case."

Scattering to their tasks, the other four followed his orders in willing silence.

From national bestselling author

JEAN JOHNSON

HELLFIRE

THEIRS NOT TO REASON WHY

As captain and commander at the helm of *Hellfire*, Ia must now assemble a crew that can rise to the challenge of saving the galaxy…a crew that will trust her prophecies. The Salik are breaking through the Blockade, plunging the known galaxy into war. Now only time itself can prove whether each member of her crew is merely a soldier or truly one of Ia's Damned.

PRAISE FOR
THE THEIRS NOT TO REASON WHY NOVELS

"Highly entertaining and extremely involving."
—*The Founding Fields*

"An engrossing military SF series."
—*SF Signal*

jeanjohnson.net
facebook.com/AceRocBooks
penguin.com

M1459T0314